Chasing Destiny

Chasing Destiny

ERIC JEROME
DICKEY

DUTTON

DUTTON
Published by Penguin Group (USA) Inc.
375 Hudson Street, New York, New York 10014, U.S.A.
Penguin Group (Canada), 90 Eglinton Avenue East, Suite 700, Toronto Ontario M4P 2Y3, Canada (a division of Pearson Penguin Canada Inc.); Penguin Books Ltd, 80 Strand, London WC2R 0RL, England; Penguin Ireland, 25 St Stephen's Green, Dublin 2, Ireland (a division of Penguin Books Ltd); Penguin Group (Australia), 250 Camberwell Road, Camberwell, Victoria 3124, Australia (a division of Pearson Australia Group Pty Ltd); Penguin Books India Pvt Ltd, 11 Community Centre, Panchsheel Park, New Delhi - 110 017, India; Penguin Group (NZ), cnr Airborne and Rosedale Roads, Albany, Auckland 1310, New Zealand (a division of Pearson New Zealand Ltd); Penguin Books (South Africa) (Pty) Ltd, 24 Sturdee Avenue, Rosebank, Johannesburg 2196, South Africa

Penguin Books Ltd, Registered Offices: 80 Strand, London WC2R 0RL, England

Published by Dutton, a member of Penguin Group (USA) Inc.

First printing, April 2006
10 9 8 7 6 5 4 3 2 1

Copyright © 2006 by Eric Jerome Dickey
All rights reserved

REGISTERED TRADEMARK—MARCA REGISTRADA

LIBRARY OF CONGRESS CATALOGING-IN-PUBLICATION DATA

Dickey, Eric Jerome.
  Chasing destiny / Eric Jerome Dickey.
    p. cm.
  ISBN 0-525-94950-X (hardcover)
  1. Missing persons—Fiction. 2. Teenage girls—Fiction. 3. Triangles (Interpersonal relations)—Fiction. I. Title.
  PS3554.I319C465 2006
  813'.54—dc22   2006001803

Printed in the United States of America
Set in Janson Text with display set in Laser & Trade Gothic Bold Condensed
Designed by Leonard Telesca

for
Dominique
☺

Enemies are so stimulating.

> —Katharine Hepburn

Destiny is not a matter of chance,
it is a matter of choice;
it is not a thing to be waited for,
it is a thing to be achieved.

> —William Jennings Bryan

It is hard to believe that a man is
telling the truth when you know that
you would lie if you were in his place.

> —H.L. Mencken

So far as the above quote,
Same goes for a woman.

> —Eric Jerome Dickey

Chasing Destiny

one

BILLIE

KEITH SNAPPED, "I THOUGHT YOU WERE ON THE PILL."

"Lower your voice."

"Billie . . . you sure you're pregnant?"

"People can hear."

We were outside in the night air, chilling at Starbucks in Ladera Heights, an area some people called the Black Beverly Hills. But it wasn't. If Beverly Hills looked like this, if Rodeo Drive was lined with strip malls, a bazillion fast food places, had horrible parking, and the best place to eat on that strip was a friggin' TGIF, white people would start howling while they slit their own wrists. All around me were murals of Magic Johnson, his larger-than-life grin on every pastel wall. The lot was filled with cars, but all the attention was on the late-evening crew who had pulled up on chromed-out crotch rockets.

Keith asked, "Well, were you taking the pill?"

"No. I just stared at it and used it by osmosis."

"Oh, you got jokes."

"No, Keith. I got pregnant."

We found a reason to stop talking when the lead rider of the biker girls rolled by doing a wheelie.

The girl wasn't doing a regular catwalk. She had another one of her crew members sitting high up on the handlebars. Her bike was pimped out like she was a chrome slut. While the sisters up front were showboating, the last rider in the group was on her crotch rocket doing a stoppie—riding on just the front tire with her rear end high in the air. All of them held up traffic, spliced between cars. It was dark and their headlights lit up the night.

Keith said, "No respect for the safety of others."

Oversized butts stuffed in tight low-rise jeans were cruising the strip mall on flashy Japanese sport bikes, showing off their chrome and thong. Young, arrogant riders. Ten years ago I used to be one of them. They parked, took their helmets off, and one of the girls came my way. Marcel. She was the shortest of the group, about five-six, three inches shorter than me. Beautiful, with an ugly attitude. Very feminine and loved attention the way fish love water. Light-skinned. No hips. All ass. Reddish blond hair. D-cups inside a tight top. She stopped in front of me, jacket wide open, pimping her hardbelly.

She showed me a smile. "Whassup, Ducati?"

"I'm busy."

She laughed, then turned to Keith. "Keith."

"Marcel."

"Think I just saw your wife at Fox Hills Mall."

"Marcel, didn't Billie tell you we were busy?"

Marcel laughed and headed over to her crew, overdoing the side-to-side switching thing she did when she walked. She rocked an indigo-colored Honda Super Hawk. Custom paint job on both her bike and helmet. Chromed to the bone. The bling bling of the motorcycle world. She wanted attention, and attention she got. Her body was devastating. All the men paused, watched Marcel and her posse as they strutted inside the Wherehouse music store at the west end of the plaza.

Keith said, "How far along?"

My heart rose up to my throat. I said, "About six weeks."

"Still early."

"What does that mean?"

"Means it's still early."

"You want me to send it down the toilet?"

"Don't tell me you want to have a baby." He rubbed his temples. "Do you?"

I opened and closed my hands. Fingers hurt from studying guitar tablature on my Takamine most of the afternoon. Had been feeling good, had been in a songwriting mood. All of that good feeling gone.

Keith asked me, "Who knows you're pregnant?"

"Right now, nobody but us."

"Your roommate? Viviane knows already?"

"She'll know eventually."

"What are you saying?"

"I'm saying what I'm saying, that's what I'm saying."

My lover's mouth was open, his eyebrows so close together that they had become a sideways exclamation point. I rubbed my hands over my jeans, adjusted my leather jacket, DUCATI labels on the sleeves and the same Italian name across the back. Keith was dressed hip, had on baggy jeans and a cream sweater, low-top Skechers, and a brown leather jacket.

He asked, "What are you going to do?"

You're pregnant. What are *you* going to do?

My throat tightened.

His cellular chimed. I tried to see whose name or picture popped up, but he covered his phone with his hand, slid it across the table, hid it, picked it up like he was picking up cards in a poker game.

I cleared my throat.

He made an exhausted face, sighed, answered his cellular with attitude.

"What? . . . With Billie . . . Starbucks . . . talking . . . yes . . . came here to talk . . . *no* . . . I'll call you . . . 'bye."

He snapped his phone closed.

And fell silent. Lines grew in his forehead. He was disturbed about something else now.

I asked, "Who was that?"

He rubbed his hands together, made an impatient face that told me to back off.

I hated it when he did that mess, tried to control me. Hated when any man tried to control me.

A couple of brothers were at the table next to us. I recognized one of them. Raheem. He was the exotic one who was a cocoa-brown mixture of Latin and African-American, the slender man with the short curly hair. Like most of us, he was part of what people called America's mixed-race future.

We made eye contact. I acknowledged Raheem with a short smile. I actually smiled. Felt warm. In that split second I wished there were no Keith in my life and no baby growing inside my body.

Keith motioned toward Raheem. "Why is he staring at you?"

"You gonna tell me who that was on the phone?"

"He better learn how to respect me."

Keith did a *Whassup, nigga?* head move at Raheem. Raheem was unfazed. A stubborn man.

I said, "That really wasn't necessary."

"What's up with you and that guy?"

"Nothing. I don't know him."

The conversation moved back to our situation.

He shook his head and said, "Pregnant."

"What are we going to do, Keith?"

Keith was an electrical engineer. A forty-year-old almost-divorced electrical engineer at an aerospace company. Handsome man with gray eyes and an easygoing way about him. His voice usually smooth and hypnotic.

But tonight he spoke in a stiff tone. "Billie, I already have a daughter."

A chill ran over me. I knew what he was doing. Building his argument. Establishing a firm foundation. Trying to turn an emotional moment into one of pure logic.

My troubled sperm donor ran his tongue over his teeth before he softened his tone and preached his woes. "My hands are tied. As soon as I walked out the house and initiated the divorce decree, she filed for child support. Now Carmen gets an outrageous chunk of my income. But it's really revenge money. She has the house and when we were in court she wouldn't come down forty dollars on child support. Forty damn dollars."

"Tell me something I don't know."

"I have two degrees and I'm barely pulling down fifty thousand a year—"

I sighed, hoped he wouldn't remind me of the whole story. "I know that too."

"She has the house that I bought with my money, the same money that helped get her evil ass through law school, and I'm trapped in a damn one-bedroom cave that I can't even afford. I can't afford to stay there, and I can't afford to move anywhere else."

I ran my fingers through my hair, a wavy mane in colorful browns, chestnuts, hues of caramel, a few streaks of blond hair that flowed down to my tail bone. Scalp tingled a little. I reached up and scratched the crown of my head.

He went on, "And since I can't claim Destiny, my taxes are going up six thousand. That's going to leave me under twelve grand a year to live on. I can't live on that. Nobody can."

"Keith—"

"Not when eight thousand of that goes to rent."

"Keith—"

"You know my situation."

"I can afford to do this by myself."

"Billie . . . substitute teaching . . . bartending . . . you're barely working yourself."

"I can get a real job and do this."

"That's a joke. All of you fanatic women say that—"

"Fanatic?"

"—and as soon as you realize that you can't do it alone, you realize it ain't easy, you come running and crying about how rough being a single mom is—"

"Don't go there."

"—how you thought you could do it alone, and even though you made the unilateral decision to have it, no matter how the man is against it, you exercise your own agenda, something you usually have from day one, and you drag us into court, stand up in front of the judge, and—"

"You're pissing me off. Don't you dare. . . . If that's what Carmen did, don't take it out on me."

"You're not working and I'm broke. Billie, I'm just asking you to think."

"You think that I haven't been thinking since I found out?"

"I mean take a breath and think about the next eighteen to twenty-one years. Your mind's not on the cost of a baby-sitter, day care, insurance, medical bills, braces, summer camp, piano lessons—"

He stopped mid-rant and massaged his temples.

I said, "Chuck E. Cheese."

"What?"

"You left out Chuck E. Cheese. I hear that place can set you back a grip."

His expression requested seriousness and silence.

"Billie, it's not just the money. It's the time too. My hands are already full. I barely have time to see you now. I don't have time to see my daughter as it is. You have a kid . . . I don't have any more time."

"You're saying . . . what are you saying?"

"I'm saying I can't be everywhere for every-damn-body all the damn time."

"So you're not going to be there?"

"That's not what I said."

"Then what are you saying?"

"Billie, we're dating and I don't have time to date. We have to see each other late at night, and I only get to see you once or twice a week. You know that I don't have time as it is. Between work, looking for work, going back to school and trying to get retrained, and my daughter . . . I don't have any time."

Silence settled between us. My misty eyes in one direction, his angry ones in another.

I said, "I can go back to flying."

"Pregnant and dealing with terrorists?"

"Okay, maybe I could stop subbing and teach full-time in L.A. Unified."

"With all of that racial tension? You already complain about how bad those kids are. Those kids are in a war. Blacks don't like the Mexicans, kids damn near killing each other."

"And I'm about to start looping."

"Looping?"

"One of Sy's background singers, Chante Carmel, is hooking me up with Kimberly Bailey and the looping crew. Not a bad gig. Pays over seven hundred a day, overtime if it goes there. Plus residuals."

Keith shook his head. "Looping is inconsistent work."

"I know. But it's work."

"Looping . . . you could have money one day and not see another dime for months. Billie, with a child you need consistency, a guaranteed paycheck every week. It's one thing for you to scrape and not know where your next meal is coming from, but to not be able to feed a child is unacceptable."

"And I'm thinking about singing again. Some studio work."

"How does that work? Can you make enough money to cover all of your expenses?"

"When you do a union job you get a flat eight-hour rate. And overtime. It's very calculated."

"How much a day?"

"About four-fifty for eight hours."

"But it's not steady work."

"No, it isn't."

Keith sat there, shaking his head. "You need steady work to take care of a family."

I rocked. "I can do this."

"Having a kid ain't something that you can try, and then, if you don't like it a year or two down the road, can be undone. There's no reset button to get things back to their initial state."

I couldn't stand to look at him, so I looked around, struggling with my love for Keith, trying to balance it with my self-love, my dignity. With my fear. I was so damn afraid right now.

Marcel and her biker girls came out of Jamba Juice, smoothies and helmets in their hands.

Through my tight lips I told Keith, "Well, I'm almost thirty-four."

Keith groaned. "The biological clock thing."

"All I'm saying is that I'm heading into that high-risk age group, that's all. Maybe this is God's way of telling me that it's time to trade in my bike for an SUV and . . . and . . . and . . ."

"Get real, Billie. Being pregnant out of wedlock is not an act of God. It's a sin . . . an act of . . . you . . . us not taking care of business the right way. Amazing how you women get pregnant—"

"*You* women?"

"—out of wedlock and have a damn celebration. What? You don't like what I said?"

"So, it was business. And I'm a sinner who got pregnant out of wedlock. Anything else?"

"Right now . . . Billie, a lot is going on with me. I don't know what to think."

"You think I planned this? With your broke ass? With all of your drama?"

Keith dragged his hands down his cheeks, his short nails digging into his flesh, elongating his face, doing that over and over hard enough to leave light scratches.

He went on, "You're, as you put it, high-risk. Have you considered that you might have to take off work early? That's a lot of lost income. Are you saved up for that?"

"You know I'm not."

"And what about after the kid is born? What about all of that down time?"

"Don't make it about money."

"Get out of the fantasy and don't pretend money won't be an issue. You're broke. I'm broke. Kids get sick. You have to take off work when they get sick because day care doesn't want sick kids in the place infecting all the other kids. What you gonna do then? All I'm saying is be realistic about this shit. They need and they never stop needing. Everything they need costs one way or another."

"You done?"

"I'm just asking if you're prepared, because I know I'm not."

"Well, if two people love each other—"

"*Love don't pay the goddamn bills, Billie.* Love does not pay for private school and diapers."

"You should know."

"What does that mean?"

"You're the one with the failed marriage, you're the one heading for divorce court."

That low blow put some serious pain in his eyes. No man liked to be read his failures.

He sighed. "I've been going to therapy. Carmen, well, all of us have been going."

"All of you? Separately?"

"Together." He cleared his throat. "It was the court's suggestion."

"The court?"

"Things were ugly. Uglier than I've ever told you. It can be horrible, having a child with the wrong woman, having to deal with her anger, her issues, her selfishness, her using your child as a pawn in her game. Having her constantly taking you to court because she is . . . just plain vindictive."

"Why would she do all of that to you?"

"That's how she is. Shit, ever since she saw me with you at the movies—"

"Since she found out about me."

"It's been a living hell. She's been relentless. And it's not getting any better. We talked . . . we argued . . . and when the dust settled . . . we needed some professional counseling together. Especially for my daughter. Destiny . . . she's been taking this the hardest. Fights at school."

"Fights? As in plural?"

"As in plural. Grades dropping. You know those private school people don't play."

"She's acting out." I backed down, wanted to know more. "You hadn't said anything."

"I just stopped talking about it . . . with you."

"I see. None of my business, right?"

"Not that. It's just . . . with you . . . didn't want that negative shit polluting what we had."

"You could've talked to me, Keith. Could've told me something. But it's cool. I understand."

"And my daughter's attitude, it's stressing me out. Destiny cursed her mother. Carmen hit her. It got crazy. After that she ditched school. All kinds of shit has been going on. Carmen said Destiny smelled like weed. Thinks she was getting high. Looks like she's been with some boy."

"Destiny is having sex?"

He took a breath. "She's fifteen."

"About that age. When girls start trading sex for love."

"Don't say that shit."

"That's what we do. We look for love the only foolish way we know how."

Keith made a face that told me he didn't even want to think about his daughter in that way. He shook his head, rubbed the back of his neck, took a deep breath before he could talk again.

I said, "I know you have a lot going on. Didn't mean to drop this on you, not like this."

"Anyway . . . Carmen . . . well, she's in warrior mode . . . fighting the divorce tooth and nail."

"She's still fighting it? Your divorce is taking too long. You've been separated a year. I've been with you most of that time. Seems like it should've been finalized months ago."

"Had a setback."

"Setback?"

He took another hard breath. "She had the decree revoked."

The sensation of falling out of a plane toward jagged rocks.

I repeated, "Revoked?"

"Yeah. Revoked."

"If the divorce was in process . . . for this long . . . how did . . . how did she get it revoked?"

"On a technicality. She lied, claimed she wasn't given adequate time to answer the summons."

"That's bullshit."

"On top of that she protested a clerical error or something. Bottom line, she won that round."

I paused, tried to digest all of that. "So, what, you have to start over?"

He rubbed his hands. "This shit is costing me money that I don't have."

"Fire your attorney. Get a new one."

"Don't you get it? I talk to an attorney for an hour, that's my money to buy food with for two weeks. I don't have the money. This has sucked. . . . I'm broke. She's sucked the life out of me."

He paused. I felt bad for him. His expression shifted. Became anguish to the tenth degree.

"Billie . . . look . . . don't mean to sound insensitive . . . today has been a *motherfucker* for me . . . but I have to be real . . . we have to be real . . . two people in love, two broke people in love will eventually be two broke people in hate. One night you're fucking and the next night becomes a War of the Roses."

Fucking. He had said *fucking.* Didn't refer to what we had been doing as making love, nor having sex. *Fucking.* Reduced our intimacy to its lowest, most barbaric terms. Don't get me wrong, *fucking* was good, and being barbaric was the best thing since the Internet. But there were sensitive times when fucking shouldn't be referred to as . . . as *fucking.*

I asked, "What are you thinking?"

"Thinking how marrying Carmen . . . How many damn bad decisions can I make in one fucking lifetime, you know? Realizing how we create our own hell right here on earth. Thinking about how I'm in a corner. You're telling me you're pregnant. Shit. Didn't see that coming. No matter which way I turn, it ain't gonna be pretty. Have to choose between love and economics. Bad decision after bad decision."

"You know what?" I lost it. "I'm just tired of hearing you gripe about that bitch. I told you I'm pregnant and all you can fucking talk about is that bitch this, that bitch that. Fuck that bitch."

Hormones. My damn hormones were out of control. Left me feeling nuclear.

His eyes went dark, his muscles tightened, he gave me an alpha-man stare that would've scared me if we were alone. Keith was the strong silent type, but he had a lot of South Central in his blood. If I pushed him too far in the wrong direction, I had no idea what would happen. His expression went total East Side, straight boy from the hood. His strong look told me that, despite what was going on, he was a man, he was *the* man, that I'd best remember that or his darkness would cover me.

But I didn't slow my roll. "Since you're so concerned about your budget, well, from *housing* and an *economics* point of view, it sounds like it might be better for you to get back with your ex."

He swallowed, then frowned, had a different kind of pained expression, one that was foreign to me.

He took a deep breath. "First off, I didn't know that you were going to drop a bomb on me. There were things that I wanted to talk to you about tonight, face-to-face."

A fist closed around my heart. It was never good when a man said he needed to talk to you.

"Where I am right now, hate it. Hate waking up. Depressed. Dealing with it. It's boiled down to me trying to figure out how I'm going to survive. I've made some bad decisions, but I've had to make some hard decisions. Some damn hard decisions."

That fist tightened.

He whispered, "Billie, you know I love you, right?"

Those soft and tender words strangled my heart.

Words seeped from my face. "The divorce decree . . . you are refiling, right?"

"My daughter is caught in the crossfire. As long as the courts are involved, it's lose-lose. You won't be happy, not in the long run, and my daughter won't be happy, and I sure as hell won't be happy. There is no pretty way out of this, not for everybody."

The winds shifted, changed directions.

Keith kept his tone soft. "Look, you know where I am financially."

I whispered, "Are you refiling? Yes or no, Keith. Yes or no."

"First I was sleeping on the floor in my raggedy apartment, then I was sleeping on an air mattress, then my back was killing me and I had to borrow money from you to buy a real mattress."

My eyes closed. "Keith, just say it."

"And I'm doing it for my daughter."

"*Say it.*"

He took a breath, a real deep one, then let it out.

"Billie, I wanted to meet you and tell you face-to-face that I was going back to my wife."

two

BILLIE

"YOU'RE DUMPING ME AT STARBUCKS? AT STARBUCKS? YOU'RE JOKING, right?"

Pregnant, I sat there, cringing, stunned, heartbeat strong and fast.

"Look, Billie, if I got back with Carmen—for the sake of my daughter and for no other reason—the child support, court costs, the possibility of having to get my daughter every other weekend and every other holiday, having to call twenty-four hours in advance to see my daughter any other time, not being able to take her out of town on vacation without a damn court order, and not to mention that they're all sitting up in the house I bought eating steak while I'm practically eating dog food—"

He reached for my hand. I pulled my hand away.

"You still love Carmen, don't you?"

"This ain't about love."

"You love her. After all the negative shit you said about her—"

"She's the mother of my daughter. I love my daughter."

"You're dumping me at a fucking Starbucks in front of all of these . . . This is bullshit, Keith."

My anger, my hurt, all of that was on my face. I ran my tongue across my teeth.

He cleared his throat and struggled. "You should think about, you know."

My eyes stayed on his face, but he couldn't return the favor. He couldn't bring those peepers up above my neck, couldn't gaze into these eyes that he claimed were so erotic and hypnotic.

I said, "You didn't answer my question."

"What question?"

"Do you love her?"

"I have to love my kid more than I despise my wife."

"A simple yes or no."

He closed his eyes like I didn't get it, shook his head like he was trying to wish away all of his problems.

He finally opened his eyes, brought them up to mine, and was startled by what he saw.

"Billie."

"Fuck you."

I reached in my jacket pocket and took out enough money to pay him back for my coffee. "I don't want a damn thing from you."

I threw that chump change on the table as I stood, most of it rolling off the table.

He said my name again and I stopped moving. He stood up and came to me. He put his hand in my hair. The cold part of me heated up. Wanted him so bad I almost died.

He said, "Billie, don't do this. Sit down. We need to discuss—"

"Discuss what?"

"We need some . . . some sort of a compromise."

"How do you compromise something like this?"

I stepped away from his touch. He looked devastated, totally destroyed.

I pulled my trembling lips inward, my face warmer than the center of the sun, and told my bucket of tears to kick back and hold on awhile, at least until I made it across the parking lot to my bike.

I showed him my traffic finger and said, "Enjoy that mental workout with your therapist."

So many times he said, "Billie . . ."

I found enough strength in my reserve tank and moved away from the table, disoriented. I hurried in the wrong direction, then was too ashamed to turn around, too pissed off to face him again. I bumped around people, went inside Starbucks, tried to vanish in the crowd. Couldn't hop on my bike and ride, not when I was messed up like this. I'd probably high-side and kill myself before I made it to La Brea.

My vision, clouded. Judgment so damn impaired.

The men who had been staring at every woman's ass stopped their intellectual conversation about how sorry the Lakers had become and whispered lustful words about the nice shape of the ass of a sister who had just sashayed in. The rude boys were whispering about me. Once again I had been seen as a collection of desirable body parts: ass they wanted to hold, thighs they wanted to drip honey over and lick away, breasts to massage, pussy that was ripe and waiting to be explored with fingers and tongue, nothing cerebral, nothing substantial, always reduced to my lowest terms.

The world remained a blur.

All I made out was the dark blue in his jacket before I ran into him, causing him to drop his book, his newspaper, and juggle with his cup of coffee.

Raheem. I'd embarrassed myself even more.

I said, "Did I mess up your suit?"

I expected him to look at me like I was the Klutz of the Week.

He said, "Hold on, Billie . . . think before you . . . look . . . okay . . . slow down."

He had a cellular phone on his hip, an earplug in, and was talking into that doohickey thingamajig. He'd bent down to pick up the papers before they got wet. Legal papers. Real estate listings. Then he dropped the book. We had a real Three Stooges act going on here.

I quickly said, "Let me get your book for you."

While he got off the phone and wrestled with his coffee and papers, I pulled a strand of hair away from my face and squatted, picked up the book. We made eye contact.

I wasn't here. Not even close to being here. I stared at him, thoughts jumbled.

My cell phone rang. I looked at the caller ID. It was Keith. He was right outside the door to the place he had picked to ridicule me, calling me like we were long-distance.

Keith asked, "What's up with you all over him like that?"

I didn't answer.

Raheem glanced toward Keith, saw him staring, then he asked me, "Everything okay?"

"Look, sorry about the . . . sorry I bumped into you."

"Listen, when you have a minute I want to talk with you about something. It's business."

"Not interested."

I stormed away, bumped past all the latte lovers, and went inside the ladies' room.

Billie, I wanted to meet you and tell you face-to-face that I was going back to my wife.

Those words echoed, each one like a punch in my bladder.

With a wad of toilet paper in my hand and three potty liners separating the germs from my butt, I sat and waited for my bladder to do its thing.

My throat tightened.

Tears fell like an anvil.

A raspy female voice that owned an uppity Brenda Vaccaro flair, an inflection that was almost as scratchy as my own voice, came up outside the bathroom door, getting louder. Closer. She told somebody to go keep Daddy company, that she'd be right back as soon as she went to the bathroom.

The door. I hadn't locked the door.

I hopped up, my sweats huddled at my ankles, and tried to duckwalk as fast as I could, but I tripped, had to push the wall to keep from going head first into the porcelain sink.

The door flew open. She stormed in like she was a bona fide superhero.

The art of speech abandoned me.

I tried to plop my butt back down so I wouldn't be standing there with my private parts on display. She froze, holding the door open. Her eyes were focused, very direct and intense. Mouth wide with big, full lips. Her body well proportioned, neither top-heavy nor bottom-heavy. Not slim, but nowhere near fat. She was beautiful, with her thick hair in a head-turning cinnamon-brown chic 'fro, upgraded from the corny, old-maid-looking looping ponytail she normally wore. Had funked up her wardrobe too. Her midlength snakeskin jacket with cuffed, dark-hued denims and stacked heels, all of that looked new too. Flawless makeup in earth tones. A combination of African-American pride and cosmopolitan flair.

The first and last time I saw that bitch was when Keith and I were walking out of the movie theater inside Howard Hughes Center. Our little Shangri-la. We walked out of a movie holding hands and laughing like two teenagers and stumbled right into the stunned face of his soon-to-be ex and their daughter.

That day I found out I was his secret; they hadn't known I existed until then.

That day, when Carmen saw us holding hands and laughing, her eyes filled with jealous tears. Keith had to stop, had to acknowledge his child, had to give her love and hugs, while both of us, Carmen being his past and me his present, silently evaluated each other and wondered about the future.

I snapped, "Close the door."

"He told you?" Her raspy voice was so powerful, like she was the attorney for the state and I was the perpetrator on the witness stand. "I just need to verify that what he told me is accurate and that you are aware that his fling with you is officially over."

"Close the fucking door, bitch."

"Good. He told you." She smirked. "So you understand your business with him is—"

"Close the goddamn door."

"—over and there will be no need for you to call him or e-mail him. No need to send him text messages. And oh, I went through his cellular phone, saw the topless pictures you—"

"Bitch. The door."

She straightened her clothing, let her eyes cut me up and down.

"Sorry, sweetie." She let her crooked smile roam all over my face, the tears, my angst. "But that's what happens when you play with fire. It's over. Remember that. Respect that."

"You're about to get your ass kicked."

"Touch me. Just one finger. Touch me and I'll have you locked up so fast it'll make your head spin. Please. After you've wiped your ass, come out here in front of the crowd and touch me."

She walked away without closing the damn door. I duckwalked over and slammed it behind her. I fumbled for my backpack, pulled out my cellular, and jabbed in Keith's number. Phone between my ear and my neck, the moment he answered I flushed the toilet, struggled with my clothes, and asked, "You knew that bitch was coming up here? You had me up here with you and you knew that bitch was—"

He hung up.

I tried to freshen up, made myself presentable, and headed for the door, punching in the number to Keith's cell phone again. He answered and I snapped, "Don't hang up on me."

"Where are you?"

I was standing near the condiment station, across the latte-scented room from him. His daughter was near him, a cute fifteen-year-old girl with Bambi eyes, a face too small for her big teeth.

She looked so innocent. Couldn't imagine her being any kind of problem for anybody.

I answered, "Your daughter is pretty. Looks like you."

I said that so he would know I was in the room.

He paused and looked around with jittery motions, then found me. Carmen was in the thick of the crowd, near the rack of CDs for sale, at the pick-up stand. The server called out a steaming venti apple cider and a tall mocha something-or-another with whipped cream. She picked up both cups. Keith's daughter was clinging to his side. A daddy's girl dressed in wide-leg jeans, clogs, bright yellow jacket.

She saw me, looked at her daddy, toward her mother, then back at me. Somewhere along the line she lost her happy face. I wondered if her mother had poisoned her with negative words about me.

I asked, "What, is this one of your court-recommended mental camping trips?"

He moved away from his child, repositioned himself in the crowd, and lowered his voice so his daughter couldn't hear. She followed him, complaining about not wanting to spend the night at her grandmother's house. He told her not to argue with her mother's decision, said that as if no one in that family were to challenge Carmen. When the kid wouldn't back away, Keith reached into his pocket, pulled out some money, told her to go to Wherehouse and buy a CD she wanted. She took the money, but before she left the building, she glanced back at me. Her young face was so vibrant, overflowing with innocence. Keith's daughter waved at me, soft and friendly. I waved back, wishing she was mine.

"Keith, this is fucked up. This is really fucked up."

"Don't do this, Billie. Got my daughter with me."

"And I have your son . . . or daughter *inside* me."

"Look . . . dammit . . . think about it. Having a baby . . . Billie, just be realistic. You should do it the right way. Be married first. Have a partner. Finances right. Have a plan. That's all I'm saying."

"Respect me, Keith."

"I respect you, Billie."

"I tell you I'm pregnant and the first thing you do is tell me to kill it? That's respect?"

"Billie . . . please . . . don't do this."

"You're dumping me at Starbucks . . . over a venti mocha what-chamacallit . . . this is respect? Why didn't you just send me an IM or a text message or an e-mail instead of meeting me up here?"

Carmen was sashaying through the crowd, pissed off, trying to maintain her image, but in the corners of her eyes, even with her overdone makeup, those crow's-feet broadcasted that she was stressed, that being here, with her child, was done to prove a point. Her message was loud and clear.

We are family.

Carmen saw me on my cell phone, saw Keith on his cellular. Her bogus smile dissipated.

Keith said, "I love you, Billie. No matter what, I love you."

"If you love me, don't let that bitch bully you. Be a man and walk across the room—"

Click. That came from his end.

With a smile, Carmen handed my agitated sperm donor a cup of brew, then glowered back at me as she rubbed his shoulder. Danced her long fingers all over his leather jacket.

She touched him. He didn't cringe or shrug her away. So many years of familiarity.

This was some bullshit. This shit hurt. I'd given him Iyanla Vanzant spirituality and loving that would make Vanessa Del Rio blush, whatever he needed, whenever, and now this was my gift in return.

Carmen glanced my way again. I didn't back down. We gave each other eyes for a while. Keith saw it all. So much tension and fear was in his face. Raging hormones sent me toward them.

Touch me. That daring look was on her face. *Just one finger.*

She was trying to set me up. Wanted me to bring it so she could put me on lockdown.

I wondered if I could do ninety days' hard time. Or half a year. Even a year. She just didn't know how close I was to grabbing a sharp object and bum-rushing her trifling ass. I was two seconds from an orange jumpsuit, a pair of silver handcuffs, and finding out how well the judicial system really worked.

But I was pregnant. I supposed that being in jail, pregnant, was not a great idea.

People were frowning. The room had picked up on the drama, and they were glaring, whispering.

Even that larger-than-life mural of Magic Johnson put down his cup of coffee and stopped smiling.

I shied away from those people, backed away. Had almost become a raging fool.

What I wanted was simple. All I wanted right now was to go home. Wanted to get out of this wretched place without passing by that bastard and that evil bitch. Couldn't bear to pass by them without opening a can of Whup Ass. Couldn't stand to look at them any longer without howling like a banshee.

I did an about face and mumbled to myself while I paced out in the hallway, kept away from all the eyes, remained sequestered away from a crowd of flirty and happy people who were living for the weekend, turned my eyes away from them as they celebrated love and lust and righteousness through lattes and the spoken word. Stayed in the hallway like I was a POW in my own little Hanoi Hilton.

When I finally came back out, they were gone, had vanished like a UFO.

three

❦

BILLIE

I YANKED ON MY LEATHER JACKET, TUGGED ON MY LEATHER GLOVES, LEFT my helmet locked to my seat. I got on my bike, took up the kickstand, started my baby, gave up some throttle. My bike revved hard and strong, I made her yell loud, give up sounds that echoed the same way I felt, like screaming full-throttle.

Heads turned and I attracted attention that I didn't want. My Ducati was the sexiest thing on the road, bodacious yellow with power and sleek curves, carbon fiber, Termi exhaust that made her sound great when she revved up. *Smooth*-sounding, a singer in a class of her own. She sang her seductive song and men stared at my baby with their mouths wide open, like they were seeing Halle Berry strut her Catwoman body across the lot buttnaked. Men headed my way, anxious swaggers, holding their crotches as if they were trying to hold down their erections, all wanting to look at and touch my baby, but I put on my backpack and pulled away from the lustmongers without putting on my lid.

Felt like I didn't fit in this world.

I was born in Japan. Was there until I was almost five. My father was in the military, stationed there at the time. He was black, and Blackfoot and Cherokee Indian. My parents settled in California after my daddy retired from the United States Air Force. He loved to ride his Harley. Loved to ride me on his Harley. I called it his *Hardly Rideable*. Always teased him about having his handlebars so high they looked like ape hangers, arms up so high he looked like Clyde from *Every Which Way but Loose*. He huffed and called my motorcycle a Jap-scrap. An all-American military man who insulted anybody who didn't buy American. Buying non-American was my rebellious act. He taught me all I know, everything from doing catwalks to Mad Maxing to how to goggle the horizon. I was almost a teenager when we landed out here. He had since passed away. First he beat prostate cancer, survived lung cancer, then had a heart attack a few years after he and my mother had divorced. I think all the fresh meat he met riding that bike wore him down. Always had a new fender bunny. That made it rough on us. And now my mother was gone too. She was a bona fide Iron Butt, became a serious rider after dad died, did it because of her love for him. Once a year she would take a vacation with her club and ride her Harley a thousand miles a day for ten days. We were close, rode together a lot, did that after Daddy died, I think Daddy's death made us closer, and her illness took us both by surprise. Diagnosed with liver cancer ten Aprils ago, died that June. Guess that made me an orphan.

I took it one day at a time, some better than others.

This wasn't a good day for me.

They were gone. But they were still here.

I had my father's height and my mother's body, but not her gracefulness. She was a dancer in her youth. Was dancing in Japan when my father met her in a club. Stole her away from that world. I had my mother's small eyes and my father's full lips. I had my mother's fine hair and my father's thick eyebrows. I had my mother's complexion, lots of browns and reds and oranges in my tone.

I had my father's hazel eyes. His dimples. His sense of travel. His restlessness.

In his lifetime he loved—and I do mean loved—in Germany, Okinawa, Japan, Russia, Korea, Holland, Mexico, Ireland, Saudi Arabia, and Norway. He used to tell me about those places.

But Hawaii. He loved Hawaii.

I had my mother's heart, one that lived for love and nurturing. Same went for her mother. And the women who came before her. I came from a family comprised of women whose beliefs were to cater to a man. Not bow down or become his servant, but be his fantasy, naughty girl, lady, and companion all in one. My mother was all of that for my daddy. No matter how bad things got, she was there at his side.

This was one of the days when I wanted to talk to them.

Sometimes I could close my eyes and hear their voices in the wind.

They were gone.

A car came up behind me, startled me away from my thoughts, moved like it was trying to catch up, first its lights were flashing from high to low, then the horn was blowing.

I would've sped away, but I needed to stop because the private lot ended right after its strip of shops, flowed into the bumper-to-bumper traffic out on La Cienega. And since Cali had helmet laws, I had to pull over and put my helmet on before my tires touched the public streets. And even if Cali didn't have a helmet law, I'd never ride these mean streets without my lid. Too much road rage out there.

I pulled over in front of Mail Connexion.

The car that was following me did the same.

I cursed and let out an irritated breath. It was Raheem.

He left his engine running, got out of his car, hurried toward me.

I was off my bike, unlocking my helmet from my seat.

He motioned toward a billboard. WHO MURDERED ME? A picture of Lisa Wolf looked down on the city. They found her dead in Playa del Rey. Gunned down. Her father used to be mayor of Compton. Her grieving mother was offering a serious reward and had billboards posted all over the city. Sixty-foot symbols. A reminder that the world was an evil place. That horrific things happened to good people.

Raheem said, "Her husband owns a limo company over at LAX. White boy from New York."

"So I heard."

"Yeah, they think the rich white boy did it and got away with it. OJ in reverse."

Raheem was rolling in a two-seater Porsche, jet-black with black interior, the top down.

I asked, "What's up?"

"What you mean?"

"You're following me. I mess your suit up and you're gonna stalk me?"

"Might have to take you on Judge Joe Brown and get compensated."

"I wish you would try to sue me. All you would get is practice."

He laughed. "Wanted to know if I could get you to teach me how to ride."

"I don't teach anymore."

"I mean, I want to hire you."

"Are you deaf or just plain stupid?"

"Private lessons."

"Don't go there."

"Serious. Straight business. I'll pay whatever you ask."

I turned my back on him, put my lid on, flipped up the visor, put on my chin strap. I had hoped that Raheem would've taken a hint and walked away by then, got in his four-wheel chick magnet and been gone with the wind, but he was still there. Should be a law against a man looking that fine. His car was a chick magnet and he was most def a clit magnet. Good thing mine had been demagnetized.

I repeated, "Cerritos College. Call 'em up. Take the MSF Rider class."

"That class is over two weekends."

"Not my problem."

"And two of the sessions are weeknights, and that doesn't fit my schedule right now."

"Not my problem."

"Look, help me out. Begging over here. I already bought a bike."

"Checkbook biker."

"What?"

"You're a checkbook biker. Buying a bike before you can ride. Make sure you have your estate in order. On a motorcycle a fool with too much money ends up being a dead fool."

"Thought I could get somebody to teach me."

He gave me eye contact.

I sighed, watched traffic pass by. The Ladera strip mall was a tight space with four horrible entrances and exits, was always clogged up, an ingress and egress nightmare, everybody being rude and impatient. The parking lot had jumped busy. Car after car passed by, most with music bumping.

I knew Keith was gone, but my heart was still searching for him.

I was shifting, had taken off a glove and was slapping it against my leg, ready for this interaction to end, wanted to be by myself right now, so I did the club routine, did what we did to end an unwanted conversation, told Raheem, "Tell you what, give me your number."

He took out a card, handed it to me. "My cell phone is on the back. Home number too."

I stared at him. Three numbers were on the back of his card, the ink still wet.

He asked, "You have a card?"

"Not for you."

He nodded, but didn't move on.

I asked, "Why are you staring at me?"

"The only way you know I'm looking at you is if you're looking at me."

He chuckled. My face was stone.

I tore his business card in half. His laughter ended. We stared at each other for a moment.

He said, "I saw Keith's wife. She was walking in when I was walking out. I went to the ATM. Wells Fargo."

I bit my bottom lip. "You saw."

"Maybe we should talk."

"I don't want to talk to you, Raheem."

"Billie . . ."

"Are you deaf or just plain stupid?"

With that, Raheem headed toward his car. I wasn't in a man-friendly mood. Denzel could walk up to me wearing a tuxedo and holding a bottle of champagne and the best he'd get would be a sneer.

I got on my bike, revved my engine, but didn't go anywhere. Traffic went by while I sat on my thoughts. My face turned warm. Throat was tight. Breathing thickened. I looked down at my cell phone. Keith hadn't called. Wouldn't call ever again. And I wasn't going to call his ass, never again. But thoughts about Keith and Carmen rampaged through my mind. A horn blew and I snapped back to here and now. Raheem tooted his horn again, waved at me as he drove by with the rest of the traffic.

I didn't wave, not even a slight head nod.

Then it got worse. Marcel and her girls rolled toward me before I could get out of the parking lot, came in from the busy La Cienega entrance, I heard their engines. I groaned, still had stubborn tears and regret and rejection living in my eyes. I pulled my visor most of the way down, hid my tears.

Most of them did The Wave, the cool move bikers did when they raised their hands to greet bikers going in the opposite direction. The Wave was becoming a lost art; I gestured to all bikers, regardless of what they were rocking, whether I liked them or not.

Marcel hit her horn, then motioned for me to stop, pulled up the face guard on her helmet, her indigo-colored bike looking spectacular underneath the street lights.

She said, "Kinda messed up, the way Pretty Boy left with his wife and kid, ain't it?"

I stared her down.

She said, "Number two always wants to be number one."

"You should know."

She said, "Anytime you want to change teams and roll with me, holla."

"I don't swing that way."

"Be dual-purpose. Let me take you off-road. I won't tell anybody you left the main highway."

"You're sick."

"Or if you ever want to race, we can make it worth both our whiles."

"Is that right?"

"Race me. If I lose, you get my bike and my lid."

I manufactured a laugh. "You watch too many movies."

"I won two thousand last weekend. I raced this cat out at the track in Lafland. He topped out at one-thirty-five. Pulled up next to him, downshifted, and left his ass in the wind."

"That was him. A straightaway ain't nothing. Doing one-thirty-five is a joke."

"Let's take it to the track."

"You think you're a bona fide knee-slider now?"

"Meet me at the track."

Part of me wanted to take that challenge. Needed a kick-ass victory right now.

I said, "Hypothetically. If I lose?"

"If you lose, I get you for a weekend."

I showed her my middle finger.

She laughed. "Don't offer me that finger if you ain't serious."

She revved her engine, sent me that challenge. She popped a wheelie and her crew did the same. I rolled on, left her young ass living in challenge mode. Like a fool who had been threatened one time too many tonight, like an idiot who needed at least one victory, I popped a wheelie and showed her who the better rider was. I could ride her into the ground, even in angst.

I was a loner. Not one for joining. Didn't like a lot of people in my space. Didn't like people knowing my business. I did individual sports, never was a team player.

I took to the madness on La Cienega, sped south like I was on the world-renowned Ricardo Tormo Circuit in Valencia, Italy. Had to clear my mind, had to evaluate my life.

I took my pisstivity to the 405 South. Took to the carpool lane, rested on my gas tank, got down low, allowed my engine to smooth out, downshifted, and picked up my speed, moved so fast it felt like the wind was trying to tear my head off, zoomed toward the 605 at about a hundred miles per hour, felt the vibrations coming both through my seat and through the pegs as I headed for that freeway transition hard and fast.

I blew by eighteen-wheelers, SUVs, felt like I was going so fast I could change the rotation of the world, make it go backward, make time reverse itself, and undo all that was wrong.

One-ten. One-fifteen.

I wanted to hit two hundred, spread my arms like wings, and fly like Superman, move against the world's rotation like he did when he made time go backward so he could save Lois Lane. Only I would go back in time and save myself. I increased my speed. Wanted to go back in time to the day I was shopping at Trader Joe's, the day I met Keith. This time I'd ignore his smile. Wouldn't smile and blush and make sure I passed by him on every aisle. Wouldn't laugh and make small talk, wouldn't take his card or give him my cellular number. Wouldn't invite him to come to the Temple Bar that night.

One-twenty-five on the speedometer, down on my bike, aerodynamic.

Any other day CHP would've been all over my ass. My thoughts sent me into the zone. I passed cars like they were children on skateboards.

When I came up on some slowpokes clogging up the carpool lane, I whipped lanes right to left to right. Transition curve to the 605 North was coming at me fast.

Thought about not braking at all, about rolling my clutch down and taking it to the max, seeing if I could get up to one-forty and wipe out, thought about dying and feeling no pain.

But I'd be killing more than just me.

But I think that was what I wanted. If I lost my baby in an accident, it would be different, I wouldn't have the same kind of guilt, I wouldn't think of myself as a murderer.

I got scared, went into the curve too fast, came off the throttle, downshifted to kill some speed, gave some hand and foot brake, felt my front tire lock up, released that front brake so my tire could roll, then reapplied, pressed, and rolled with the curve, and it seemed like I was so low my left knee should've been sliding, scraping the freeway, and screaming out my pain.

I straightened up, heartbeat so strong it made my leather jacket pulsate.

Time hadn't changed. It was still now. I was still here.

I swallowed and looked down at my jeans. A hole was in the left knee. But there was no pain. Another eighth of an inch or so, I'd've been hobbled and eligible for handicapped parking.

That was stupid. Reckless. Next I'd be doing a hundred in a school zone.

Traffic on the 605 was crawling, an accident up ahead. I zigzagged through traffic, then white-lined it awhile. Some jerk saw me—I know Asshole did because I saw those eyes glaring at me in the rearview—and tried to swerve his four-wheel cage and cut me off. So many motorcycle haters on the road. Always trying to run us down. The hater was in a Mercedes, a car just like Keith's wife's. I kicked that damn Mercedes' door hard as I could, left a generous dent, and rode off, that horn blasting behind me.

My middle finger shot up. Jerk. You just don't know. Don't fuck with me and my hormones.

Screw you and every arrogant bitch that drives a damn cage with a Mercedes-Benz emblem.

I kicked up the rpm's and sped north, sliced through night air until I made it to the 10 West.

My angst propelled me in one direction.

I rolled on my throttle and zoomed toward Keith's apartment.

four

BILLIE

MIDNIGHT.

I was parked behind a U-Haul truck, half a block down from Keith's apartment building, a mauve two-story structure on the corner of Stocker and Edgehill.

It looked like the bedroom light in his ground-level dwelling was turned down low, just enough to create a lover's glow. That was the only light on.

Carmen's Mercedes was behind Keith's Explorer, bumpers touching, kissing like old lovers reunited. Even in jeans and my leather jacket, I was cold. Riding that fast had me living in the land of hypothermia. Nose running, I shivered in the darkness, while sirens blared and cars zoomed by and helicopters flew overhead. Shivered until the lights inside his apartment went completely off.

An hour went by.

Carmen didn't come out. She wasn't leaving. Lights were off and she wasn't leaving.

All that time a baby was crying in the distance. Crying and crying and wouldn't stop. A young mother's frustrated voice shrieked out, cursed both God and Jesus, begging for peace.

That was when I laid both hands on my belly. Imagined myself months from now, tired and evil because of lack of sleep. I closed my eyes for a while, squeezed them so tight my head hurt, tried to fight off my rising *Play Misty for Me* mood. I thought about praying, but with all the drive-by shootings and holy wars and kidnappings and beheadings and homeless people and crack babies and women being killed by husbands in the world, why should He take the time from ignoring all of the real needy people to listen to a pregnant woman? Especially when I knew better. Besides, hadn't been to church in a hot minute. My hands had turned cold, my whole body on the road to becoming numb. I opened my eyes.

Keith's lights were still off. That Benz still kissing his SUV.

Cars were stopped at the red light, the one up front blasting out lights, camera, action, his music thumping and screaming loud enough to wake up the dead. I took off my helmet, pulled off my gloves, left my gear on the seat of my ride, and let that ghetto noise cover my footsteps, tipped toward Keith's bedroom window. When the light changed and that music faded, I heard him moaning. He was a serious moaner. That made me shiver and burn all at once. A night-light was right outside his bedroom in the hallway. I had put it there because I kept stumbling into things when I went to go to the bathroom in the middle of the night. That subtle light was enough for me to make out shadows in his love nest. Keith was in bed, on his back. Carmen's silhouette was in his lap, her shadow bobbing up and down in smooth rhythms, like she was so familiar with that part of him, knew how to please him back into her world.

I covered my mouth, stumbled out of the shrubbery, and picked up a baseball-sized rock. First I wiped my eyes and frowned toward Keith's bedroom window, then at his wife's Benz. I wanted to break her window, but a rock through Keith's bedroom window would give me the best results. I held it, pulled my arm back, but couldn't bring myself to throw the damn thing.

Had to be smarter than that. Had to play it the way Carmen played it.

I ran up the three stairs, past the small courtyard, stormed to the front door, and rang the doorbell. Then I knocked. Then I rang the doorbell. Then I knocked. Then I rang.

Lights came on inside. The floor creaked as heavy feet tipped toward the door. I stepped back so he could see who it was. Then the peephole went dark, then light again.

Keith said, "Billie?"

"Open the door. Need to see your wife for a second."

"What? Are you crazy?"

"Tell the bitch to wipe the come off her face and come here."

It got quiet. Then a raspy voice came from behind him. Then there were mumbles behind the door. I looked across the courtyard. Neighbors—both upstairs and facing this unit—peeped out of their windows. I don't know if they were scowling at the helicopter that was hovering in search of criminals, or waiting to see if a crime of passion was about to be committed down here.

"I'm not leaving, Keith."

Silence. So silent I could hear my hormones catching fire, smoke rising from my flesh.

I said, "I can either ring and knock and wake up the rest of your neighbors and act a fool until the police come, or you can open the door and we can handle this like . . . like . . . *Nigga, open the damn door.*"

I knocked. I knocked. I knocked.

Behind me the neighbors' lights came on one by one.

Keith opened the door.

I didn't know what to expect, thought that they might drag me in and start kicking my ass.

Keith had on jeans, no underwear, his thick imprint told me that.

He opened the door. "Let's do this."

"Yeah. Let's do this."

Carmen came up behind him, her chic 'fro muddled as she stood in the shadows with Keith's black housecoat on. Same housecoat I wore last week. She left it wide open, letting me see her breasts, her vagina, her thighs, modeling all of what she was giving him as a consolation prize.

She was beautiful, she knew that. And she was determined, I knew that.

Sweat stained my clothes and the moisture that had been on my skin had dried, left patches of salt on my face. Lips were dry and my nose was running and I was breathing hard, stress coming out my nostrils in flames, and my hair looked wild, disorganized, hanging any way it wanted to hang.

I smelled them, inhaled the scent of interrupted passion.

She smirked, shook her head like she wondered what Keith could possibly see in me.

We both stood there, indecisive, my anger rising because of the way she had disrespected me at Starbucks. She looked like she wanted to challenge me, battle me.

Her eyes cut me up and down. She said, "Pitiful."

The fist of jealousy clutched my heart again.

My voice was low and intense. I said, "I'm pregnant."

Carmen's face crashed to the floor.

She struggled, finally found her voice, winced. "Keith?"

He groaned and closed his eyes.

With more force she repeated, "Keith?"

Keith snapped at me. "Billie, it's fucked up the way you're handling this."

"Fucked up?" I went off. "You're going on and on about how you hate your ex and how you're being raped in family court and you can't make ends meet and then you never once talked about what I want to do and the first thing you do when I tell you I'm pregnant is just throw up abortion in my face, then blow me off like I'm some bitch on Figueroa, and what I'm doing is fucked up? If you had handled your shit the right way, then I wouldn't be out here in the fucking cold tipping around like a damn lunatic and watching your ex that you hate so much wipe your damn come off her lips, that's what's fucked up, Keith."

Then I was crying. I wasn't hysterical, but angry tears started flowing. Carmen's expression became volatile. She hated me. I hated her. She wanted to kill me. I wished the bitch would try.

I said, "Yeah, I'm pitiful. And a dollar for a doughnut, your conniving ass is pitiful too."

Keith lowered his head, banged it against the door. He stood there, between two women, one inside his apartment, one standing out in the cold, banging his head against the door.

Carmen asked, "Did you know this . . . ?"

Keith kept banging his head. "She. Told. Me. This. Evening."

My name was unimportant. I was *She*. A pronoun. Not Billie. Just *She*.

Carmen talked around me like I wasn't important at all. "After you told her that we—"

"Before. She. Told. Me. Before."

"Is there . . . are you sure . . . could . . . is it yours?"

He snapped, "Back off, Carmen."

"Dammit, I want to know if your little whore . . . if you think—"

Before she could finish, Keith had stormed to her, grabbed her arm so hard it scared me.

Again he barked, "Back off, Carmen."

He snapped out his words like he was tired of her shit. No, not tired. Exhausted with her shit.

Carmen yanked free, rubbed her arm, looked embarrassed for a moment, eyes down as she struggled to close her housecoat. She couldn't get the housecoat to stay closed and she gave up, frustrated that she couldn't control that either, ran both hands through her messed up 'fro and tugged like she was ready to explode, took a hard breath, lowered her head, shaking it the whole while, headed down the narrow hallway toward Keith's small bedroom, back to lounge in all the love stains I had left behind.

Checkmate, bitch. Check-fucking-mate.

The bedroom door slammed. But the door was cheap, wouldn't close that easily. She had to slam it six or seven more times to get it to lock, each slam sounding like the echo of a gunshot.

She had put herself on the other side of a door. I was still out in the cold.

Keith was frozen, head against the wall, a statue in mourning position.

Keith barked, "Don't corner me, Billie."

I snapped, "Don't disrespect me. I tell you I'm pregnant and you run off with that . . . that?"

"The shit you're doing now, if I didn't feel what I feel for you, they'd be pulling your fucking head out of that goddamn wall. Don't you ever bring your ass over here acting like a goddamn fool again."

"You have her in there on the damn mattress I paid for."

"I'll get you your motherfucking mattress."

"Don't talk to me like that, Keith."

"I'll get you whatever I owe you. Now get out. *Get the fuck out.*"

He came toward me, his hands in fists. I wanted to run, but stood my ground.

I said, "Tell her she can go back to sucking your dick now."

He looked at me; that frown told me that the rage he felt for Carmen, he felt the same for me.

I turned around, running away from the madness. Neighbors were in most of the windows, a couple holding phones in hands, like they were reporting the drama to people all over the world. I kept my head up high, went down the stairs toward the nonstop noise and traffic on Stocker

Street, faced the rows of shopworn apartment buildings that led into a mixture of streetlights and darkness.

Keith's truck was still kissing Carmen's car.

I headed toward Carmen's sweet ride. Stood at the passenger-side door. Foot tense. I was about to kick a few dents in her ride. Kick it like I was kicking her in her butt.

But that never-ending wail went up an octave, snagged my attention.

That baby was still crying in the distance, driving its momma crazy.

I stuck my riding gloves in my back pocket, zipped my jacket up as fast as I could, got my helmet on, started up my bike. Saw Carmen in that window staring at me. Flipped her ass off. Felt like going Mad Max, so I did. Got in the middle of the street and did a circular burnout, rocked my bike 360 degrees with the front wheel locked, then crossed the circle with a straight rubber mark when I was done. Put the hammer down and zoomed out of my smoke, rode my bike hard, roared up Stocker at a grueling pace.

That was my message to Carmen.

five

BILLIE

ALMOST ONE IN THE MORNING.

A naked man was in the kitchen.

I rented part of a three-level home in View Park.

It was an area that had been developed for the '32 Los Angeles Olympics, back in the Mary Pickford and Charlie Chaplin days, during the Great Depression, four years before Jesse "The Tan Cyclone" Owens killed Hitler's supremacy theory. Baldwin Hills was on the other side of Stocker, less than a mile away. Three hundred and twenty-one acres of this area was the very first Olympic Village for the Games. Portable bungalows, a hospital, post office, library, and a large number of eating joints were over here.

A naked black man who was well endowed was in the kitchen.

The crib was at the bottom of the hill facing a small park. I always came down the hill and shut off my engine before I made it to the house, always shifted to neutral and coasted by the queen and king palm trees and into the garage, parked next to a red F650, my roommate's BMW motorcycle. She had a car, needed that in case we had to make food runs or take clothes to the dry cleaner's, couldn't run real errands on a bike, but she left her four-wheel cage out on the streets, only garaged her F650.

The basement was a game room, still the same way her ex-husband had left it. Big pool table and a Ms. Pac-Man machine met you as soon as the garage door opened, one of the other rooms had a home gym and free weights, another was a media room with a gigantic plasma television anchored on the back wall. And she had a laundry room the size of a friggin'

Laundromat. I always dumped my backpack, helmet, gloves, and leather jacket on the pool table, kicked my shoes off, and headed up the stairs.

I climbed the stairs in a darkness that couldn't touch my mood. As soon as I made it to the main level, he was standing there in the kitchen, wearing nothing but dark skin and a goatee.

The naked black man jumped when he saw me. His super-sized penis did the same.

My body was frozen, ready to run or fight, but my eyes were between his legs, watching his penis bob and weave, staring at it the way a victim watches a robber's gun.

I said, "Uh. Hello."

He said, "Hey."

He didn't cover himself. My eyes eased up, moved across his firm stomach, finally made it to his face. Handsome. Brown skin. Built like a professional running back. Strong legs. Hairy chest.

I closed my mouth, swallowed, and said, "You are . . ."

"Cottrell."

"No, naked. You're . . ."

"Oh. Came to get some water."

"You are . . . ?"

"Friend of Thelma Mae. She said it was okay—"

"Who is Thelma Mae?"

"Nice . . . chest . . . Chinese . . . Thelma Mae."

"She's Korean, not Chinese."

"You sure?"

He didn't notice the magazines that were on the island. *KoreAm Journal. The Korean American Experience* in bold letters across the top of each one. Comic book guy Jim Lee on the cover of one; fine-ass Toby Dawson and his Rossignol skis on the cover of another one.

"Korean. And her name is Viviane."

"Damn. I've been calling her Thelma Mae all evening."

"Viviane is . . . where?"

"In her bed."

"Where did you meet her?"

"Barnes & Noble."

"Sci-fi section?"

"Yeah."

"You must read Isaac Asimov."

"Some."

"Philip K. Dick?"

"Yeah. How did you . . . ?"

"Cool. Asimov is tight. But she loves her some Dick."

"Yeah. He—"

"Which one of the Big Five you ride?"

"Huh?"

"Harley, Honda, Saki, Zook, Yam . . . what kinda bike you got?"

"Yamaha."

"Yam."

"Yeah. Got a Yam. How did you know I had a—"

"Displacement?"

"Huh?"

"Damn. What size is your friggin' engine?"

"Six hundred."

"Geesh. You must be another checkbook rider."

"Huh?"

"You ain't been riding long, have you?"

"About a month. Still have my learner's permit. No freeway."

"Be careful. I had to kick another door, this one on the freeway."

"Huh?"

"Lot of haters on the road."

"You kicked somebody's door?"

"Every chance I get."

"Why would you do that?"

"Because I get tired of people fucking with me, that's why."

My sudden rage jarred him. It was my hormones. Felt that change, that fire inside me.

He backed away. "Nice to meet you . . . uh . . . uh . . ."

"Billie."

"Nice to meet you, Billie."

Cottrell hurried down the hallway, his big feet sticking to the marble floor, then went up the stairs, rushing back to the master bedroom, his weight making the hardwood floor creak. That meant he weighed at least one-ninety. Took that much weight to make the floor sing. I hardly ever went upstairs. There were two bedrooms and two more bathrooms up there. My bedroom was on this level, right off the living room. I had my private little world down here and Viviane had hers up there in the heavens.

I grabbed bottled water from the pantry, opened the French doors, went out on the patio.

"Billie."

"Whassup, Viviane?"

She was halfway down the stairs when she called my name. The stairs didn't give her away. Never did. My scandalous and hedonistic roommate only weighed about a buck ten, if that.

She yawned. "Thought you were spending the night with Keith."

I said, "Thought you were with Jacob."

"Could you talk a little bit louder? People in New York couldn't hear you."

Viviane was coming out behind me, walking like she'd had a pretty barbaric horizontal workout. She came over and leaned on the rail. Her golden skin had a decent glow, made her look sweet sixteen.

Viviane was almost twenty-seven, all of five-six, long black hair in braids, arched eyebrows over tight eyes, thick eyelashes, full lips, skin so tanned she looked like her last name should be Brown. Perfect D-cups with a twenty-four-inch waist. Her toned body, plus her attitude, all of that made her seem more J Lo than Margaret Cho. She had a high waistline, narrow hips, breasts to die for, and thanks to playing semi-pro beach volleyball she had killer legs. Her mother married a black man when she was six; Viviane had a teenage sister from that union, so they'd been integrated into a brand-new Nubian world.

I said, "You smell like sex."

"No. I smell like great sex."

"Don't ask me why I look like crap."

"What did Keith do?"

Viviane had on a short housecoat, no shoes. Her nails were red with green designs. Her toenails and fingernails were attention-getting, always works of art. She smelled erotic, like sweat and lavender mixed with a man's cologne, those scents and hints of drying semen.

I said, "Dude upstairs, he thought your name was Thelma Mae."

She laughed. "That's because I told him my name was Thelma Mae."

"And he thought you were Chinese."

"Why is Korean so hard to remember? They remember all the *ese*. Chi*nese*. Vietnam*ese*."

I laughed. That was the one thing that pissed her off.

I said, "When you have breasts like that, I don't think they care what you are."

"Don't hate."

I lowered my voice. "Is your patio door open?"

She leaned, craned her head so she could look up toward her suite, then shrugged and whispered back, "Don't think so. If it is, so what? I'm Korean, dammit. I don't look Chinese."

"You don't look engaged either, but you are."

"Shhh." She bumped me. "I'm not engaged, dammit."

"Not yet. But the way Jacob acts, you will be soon."

"Could you say that a little bit louder?"

"Jacob is crazy about you."

"So is Kevin."

I whispered again. "His name is Cottrell."

"Cottrell? You sure?"

"Hell if I know. All I know is he told me his name was Cottrell."

"Oh, boy. I've been calling him Kevin."

"Match made in heaven."

She yawned. "I gave him my club name."

"Sounds like he gave you his too."

She bumped me and snapped, "Asshole."

"Don't asshole me."

"Shit, Daddy Long Stroke tried to asshole me."

"You let him go Greek?"

"He's too . . . gifted. Told him I only speak one language. No Greek, no French."

"I saw what you were working with. Thought he was about to go pole-vaulting."

She asked, "What's up with Keith?"

I pursed my lips. "He's a bastard and his wife is a bitch."

"What happened?"

Thought about venting to her about my jacked-up evening, but I wasn't looking for company or long conversations. Didn't know which way this would go, so I wasn't ready to talk about my mistakes.

I asked, "What happened to Jacob? Thought you two were getting serious."

"Still seeing him. He wants to take me to New York to see *The Color Purple*. As a matter of fact, he was with me at Barnes & Noble, took me to dinner before, then he had to leave. All of a sudden he had to go get his son."

"Baby momma drama?"

"She was blowing his phone up. God, why do I date men with children? *Why? Why? Why?*"

I laughed. "Another research night?"

"Yeah. Still trying to write this damn novel. Think I'm gonna call it *Comfort Women*."

"You start so many novels. Which one is that?"

"Korean women . . . forced to be sex slaves for the Japanese military during World War II."

"You've been working on that as long as I've known you, for at least five years."

"More like six. If only I could get past chapter three."

"Uh-huh."

"I was at the bookstore, took a break, was sitting on the floor reading *I, Robot* for the umpteenth time, looked up and saw this Adonis walking down the aisle. I'm talking two seconds after Jacob walked out, and this brother who looked like Will Smith walked in, in leather, biker helmet in hand."

"You should get that Lasik surgery. If you think he looks like Will Smith, you're damn near blind."

She shrugged. "Whatever."

I said, "So, Jacob walks out of the bookstore and . . ."

"And Daddy Long Stroke walks in." She smiled. "There is a God and She *loves* me."

"Playa play on. Somebody playing the field big-time."

"Nice guy, Jacob is real nice, but he can't satisfy me."

"Uh-huh. Took you two years to come to that conclusion?"

"I had hopes."

"Don't we all."

"He has the smallest penis that I've ever seen, and that ain't no joke."

"Smallest?"

"Maybe not the *smallest*. But damn."

"What's your definition of small?"

"Under six. Six to seven is average. Seven to eight, large. Over eight, huge."

"Damn. Jacob is what, six-two, about two-hundred pounds."

"Six-four. About two-twenty."

"You're killing the myth. Don't make me cry."

"Jacob has huge hands. He makes me come like crazy with his hands. I love his hands. If he didn't have hands, I'd leave him. If we were married, I'd divorce him and take one of his hands."

I chuckled. "His hands have you sprung."

"But I need more than a hand." She motioned upstairs. "This guy, Kevin—"

"Cottrell."

"I was moaning out *Kevin* the whole damn time."

"Doubt if he cared, *Thelma Mae*."

"Cottrell is good. He inspired me. One minute we were talking Asimov. Then we were talking about a short story by Walter S. Tevis called 'The Ifth of Oofth.' You know that one?"

"Read it when I was around fifteen."

"One of my favorites. How often do you meet someone who reads Tevis? If he reads Tevis, well, then he's well read. What are the odds of two strangers standing around talking about Tevis's works?"

"Long story short. So you were talking Tevis."

"Next thing I knew, I was . . . was wet. Was in that mood. It was strange. One minute Asimov, the next Tevis, then Heinlein . . . we started kissing . . . and kissing . . . and kissing . . . the guy can kiss like . . . like . . . then . . . he had me on the pool table and was eating me out. Intense like a Klingon."

"Wait. On the pool table eating you out? I think you left out a few steps."

"You said long story short."

"Not that short."

"Okay, we were talking about Heinlein's 'I am God, you are God' theme, how it's essentially Heinlein's means of emphasizing the personal responsibility of each individual for his own life. I told Cottrell that, for the sixties, Heinlein was controversial, very antireligious. Cottrell was saying that it's not strictly antireligious, and I told him—"

"Viviane."

She moved her braids from her face. "You just want to hear the freaky parts, huh?"

"Pretty much."

"Well, we went from talking about 'I am God' to me screaming 'Oh God Oh God Oh God.'" She chuckled at her own joke. "I was planning on just being his Pillow Queen, lick me to heaven, then send him home. But it got out of control. He put it down like crazy. And next thing I knew, I was giving Cottrell the best head he's ever had."

"How do you know it was the best head he's ever had?"

"Hmm. I don't know. Maybe it was just the best head I ever gave. He drinks plenty of liquids and lays off the sodas. He drinks a lot of fruit juices, I can tell. Fruit juices are best. Turned him out."

"Yeah, it's the best if they don't drink sodas. Fruit juices are the best."

"My gag reflex has gotten so much better."

"TMI."

"Probably almost as good as you claim yours is."

"*Viviane.*"

"Hand sex." She chuckled. "Russian. They love Russian."

"Don't forget Greek. They all want to go Greek."

"Why do straight men love Greek? Then there was the guy who wanted to use his nose."

That got a raised eyebrow from me. "His nose?"

"His nose was huge. Like a penis with nostrils. Strangest orgasm I ever had." She laughed and shook her head. "After that he wanted to give me a facial. God, I'm always in weird relationships."

"You're always having weird sex."

"I'm always having great sex. If I die, remember to burn my journals before my mother gets here. She'd have a stroke before she made it to page two. Hell, a pearl necklace is on page one."

"That's the mess you should put in a book. You could become the Asian Zane."

"Asian Zane. I like the way that sounds. A wonderful alliteration."

"Actually, it's more consonance than alliteration. Repetition of the 'z' sound in both words, that makes it consonant. Both words would have to begin with an 'a' or a 'z' for it to be alliteration."

"Bitch. Always correcting me."

"Your tight-eyed cousins mess up the curve all across the nation and I'm a bitch?"

She mocked me. "Here we go with that stereotypical racist shit again."

"Learn to take a joke the way you take a dick."

She laughed. "You need to quit. Your Japanese ass."

"I'm not Japanese."

"Where were you born?" She laughed. "You were made in Japan. That makes you Japanese."

"Whatever."

Viviane said, "My problem is this . . ."

"Uh-huh."

"Jacob . . . take away the kid, lose the baby momma, and he's perfect. Fine as hell. Wants to commit. We have a great relationship. A great communicator; open; very loving. He's intelligent and has great presence. We both talked about how we loved the fact that we can take each other anyplace."

"I'm listening."

"And my being Korean . . ."

"Uh-huh."

"Well . . . more like my *not* being African-American."

"Uh-huh."

"At some point that always becomes an issue. *Always*. Like I become some sort of exotic toy."

I asked, "If Jacob's such a great package . . . if he ain't making you a trophy . . . what's the problem?"

"I'd rather be single and lonely than married and miserable."

"Why you so hard on marriage, *Viviane*?"

"Because I've been married, *Billie*. I'm not obligated to be that stupid ever again."

I laughed at her crazy ass.

She sighed. "Hell, I slept with my ex more after we divorced than I did when we were married. We had sex more in a month than we did in two years of marriage."

"Damn. You made love much?"

"Oh, please. We didn't make love. We fucked."

"I stand corrected."

"Hotels. Parks. Malls. Did it damn near everywhere. Best breakup sex I ever had."

"Only divorce you've ever had."

"Only takes one to change your view of the world."

"Again I stand corrected."

"If he'd hooked me up like that when we were married, we might've still been married."

"How did he treat you after the divorce?"

"Same way I treated him." She smiled. "Like a damn whore."

"Nice."

"Very nice. He tried to fuck me senseless, thinking I would come back to his ass."

"Didn't work."

"Oh, please. He loved me in private, but in public my being Korean, it became a problem."

"Why did you keep sleeping with him?"

"Loved 'im."

"Uh-huh. Love. That sweet addiction."

"Outside of the emotional and legal drama, we got off easy. Glad we didn't have kids."

I asked, "Think divorcing would've been harder if you had kids?"

"Don't know. And don't wanna know. All I know is my little sister, as smart and beautiful as she is, she has identity issues that run so deep. I don't see how she will ever reconcile."

"She's so pretty."

"But she's trying to fit into a world that loves and hates her. She over-compensates trying to be black, think being black is about spitting out the

N-word as much as she can and being all hard and shit, always trying to be down, trying to be what people want her to be."

"Your parents still having a hard time with her?"

"She breaks my momma's heart. Refuses to speak Korean in public, will even act like Momma isn't her momma. She'll walk ahead of our mother, or linger far behind her in the mall, but she will cling to her daddy. And her trying harder to identify with that half of her family, it shuts the other half out, so that makes our mother sad. Momma calls me complaining all the time. It kills me. I look at my mother and my sister, see all the emotions, live in the middle of this never-ending struggle between them, and I wonder how I would handle that, couldn't imagine what it would do to me, how it would make me feel as a mother, if my child did that to me. I couldn't imagine giving birth to my greatest source of grief."

"Damn."

"Yeah, damn. She embarrasses our mother. She embarrasses me."

"You and your little sister ever . . . you ever talk to her about it?"

"She told me that I don't know what it's like for her being who she is all day, the way people treat her every day, how people always ask her what she is, not who, always *what*, as if she were from another planet, how she hates living in a world that owns so much hate. That Korean people reject her, look at her like she's a war baby. When she speaks Korean to them, the looks they give her, she can't handle it. Well, Q's Korean sucks, that's part of the reason they look at her like that. And our mother's English, well, it sucks, so black people mock her, imitate her, so that hurts like hell. But if my sister says something, if she stands up for our mother, it only makes it worse. She told me that she was from two cultures that hate each other and it was hard to fit in both at the same time. Yada, yada. That with her looks it was easier to be black than Korean, and being black wasn't easy, not at all. She went on and on and on."

"She's young, Viviane."

"Maybe she was right. What do I know, right? She told me that she was a strong black woman who loved her African-American brothers and that I was just a Korean woman who dated black men."

"Damn."

"Man, I cried. That hit me hard."

"She went off on you?"

"Went straight off. Told me that I was pretending to be what she was. That I had no damn idea of what she was going through. Basically told me to mind my own business. Told me I had a perfect world. That black men loved me more than they would ever love her. That our parents loved me more."

"Wow."

"It got ugly between us. Wanted to grab her hair and whoop her ass. I was the one who raised her butt, not my mother. My mother didn't have a clue what to do with Q. My sister . . . Billie, I went off on her. Made her sit in a chair, look me in my eyes, and I went off on her. Told her that life ain't been a cakewalk for me. My father was gone for good, I grew up with a black stepfather, her mean-ass father, in goddamn South Central, so what were my options? Ain't like no Korean boy would come to my house. Or if I went to his, no way his Korean parents would be happy about me. All the jokes, all the mean-spirited, prejudiced people, I had to put up with that shit. Q's daddy made the same damn jokes. Thought that shit was funny. Thought it was supposed to make me hard or something. Hated him for a long time. Didn't have nobody to turn to. Used to sit in class, all nervous, afraid to answer questions with the right answer, afraid to pass with an A because of all the Korean jokes. After school, every day I ran home, ran all the way to my front porch, scared that somebody was going to jump me. Daddy, he always said that I was his stepdaughter, never his daughter. I wasn't his daughter. Just the baby my momma already had when he met her. I cried so damn hard. Cried in a room by myself, or in the bathroom with the water running, just wanting high school to be over."

"Damn. That's sad. Your ass about to make me cry."

"Not in the mood for being depressed. Suck it up."

"Okay. Sucking, sucking, sucking it up."

"When I was done going off, she apologized, cried like a baby. She's a good kid, love my sister, but she ain't got what I had when I was growing up, that hardness. I forgave her, but that still hurts."

"I had no idea, Viviane."

"Fooled you with the happy Korean act too, huh?"

"What changed everything?"

"Sports. Nobody liked me being too smart, but when they saw I was good at sports, that I didn't back down no matter how hard they played, kids respected me. Even the black girls wanted me on their basketball team. Boys paid attention to me and talked to me, but I still didn't get asked to the prom. Then when I started riding a motorcycle to college, which I had to learn to ride because it was cheaper than a car and I couldn't afford a car and even if I could afford a car I couldn't afford gas, seemed like every man noticed me, respected me, wanted to get to know me. Something about a woman on a motorcycle."

"Maybe you need to teach Q to ride. She could ride with us, make some new friends."

"When she's ready. If she wants to. Can't force it. Riding ain't for everybody."

"This is unreal. You and Q, always laughing, y'all seem so cool. So tight."

"Like it or love it, we're sisters until we die. We have the same momma, a common ancestry. But that doesn't modify our separate realities. Her experiences are one thing, mine will always be something else. But where we intersect, at the family level, that's what we have to hang on to. We can't lose that, because if we do, we lose each other. I love her to death. She's my little sister."

"She's my sister too, dammit. You're my sister, so that makes her my sister."

She smiled, then frowned. "So for more reasons than one, I'm glad me and my ex didn't have kids. As a matter of fact, let me amend my earlier statement. Yeah, I'd rather be single and lonely than *either* married and miserable *or* divorced with a friggin' snotty-nosed kid and both of us miserable."

I said, "So, I take that to mean you're passing on Jacob too."

"Damn. Forgot I had somebody upstairs."

"Cottrell, in case the name slips your mind."

"Cottrell. Kevin. Whatever."

"Condoms?"

"Never ride bareback. Keith coming over? You need some?"

"I'm cool." I almost told her. Couldn't. I asked, "Why do you mess around on Jacob?"

"Something is wrong with me. Sometimes I feel like I need to have sex with a good-looking, intelligent man who won't tell me his problems or ask me to cook friggin' breakfast."

"What's wrong with cooking breakfast?"

"Quit playing."

"Okay, okay."

"Sometimes it's too much. Stay involved too long . . . people want so much from each other. Sometimes it's nice to be with somebody who can't want anything more than you're willing to give."

"Is that what Jacob's doing? Getting too deep? Becoming a bugaboo?"

She growled, touched her braids, shook her head. "What's your take on the love thing?"

"It is what it is and that's all it is."

"Just another friggin' addiction." She tapped her veins. "You just have to get rid of the addiction."

I sighed. "Falling in love is like falling off a building—it doesn't hurt till the end."

"You finally said something that made sense."

"Oh, kiss my ass, Thelma Mae."

She said, "Love is magic. Magic is an illusion. Therefore love is an illusion."

"Bitter, bitter, bitter."

"Not bitter. Marriage and divorce were my red pills. My eyes are wide open now."

"Are they? Hard to tell."

"Forget you. Don't start with those tight-eyed jokes."

"Bitter and paranoid, Thelma Mae. You are bitter and paranoid."

"And you're Japanese."

"Keep it up. Get slapped."

She rocked, stared at her beautiful fingernails, did all she could to delay going back to the man lounging in her den of pleasure. Guilty. She was feeling guilty. It showed in her terse smile. I understood her. I owned the same type of smile, only for a different reason.

She asked, "So, whassup? You skipped working at the Temple Bar to be with Keith."

"Don't you have a butt-naked stranger waiting on you upstairs?"

"You can smile, Billie, but your eyes don't lie. It's bad. What happened with Keith?"

I did want to vent, started to tell her then, that I was pregnant, that Keith's words were rattling around in my head, that I was trying to think of what to do, how I could make it through this all by myself. But I didn't. She was my friend, I loved her scandalous butt, but she wasn't the one to talk to about this.

I shrugged and avoided the subject. "I'll screen your calls."

"If you need to talk, I'm only fourteen stairs and a short hallway away."

"Thanks."

"But don't knock too soon."

She headed back into the house.

I was alone.

I fell into a trance, gazed down at the backyard, at the gazebo, the Jacuzzi, the palm trees, at the marigolds in bonsai orange and Antigua yellows, at the red and sun-colored celosias, at all the dianthus.

The flowers, the moon, the stars, no matter what I looked at I saw Keith.

I saw us swimming in the pool. I saw us naked, in that darkness, making love in the backyard, and the moon over our heads like a big flashlight. I heard us laughing and talking when we were done.

I heard him telling me he couldn't do this.

I closed my eyes to make him go away, but he wouldn't. They wouldn't.

I saw Carmen on her knees, her face in Keith's lap, bobbing up and down, same thing I was doing this time last week. I saw them. Only this time I was in the room with them. Keith had his hands on the back of her head, stabbing her throat with his hardness. He looked at me, said, *Billie, just think about it. Be married first. Have a partner. Finances right. Have a plan. That's all I'm saying.*

Carmen stopped savoring his jism long enough to wipe her mouth, masturbated him as she frowned at me. She snapped, *Close the fucking door, bitch.*

I jerked out of that self-imposed nightmare, shivered, felt so damn cold.

A few minutes later sweet moans were floating over my head, seeping through the bedroom window and the French doors. His baritone moans were abrupt and strong, tangled up with her keen howls and cat-like wails. I listened. She moaned for Kevin. I listened. He moaned for Thelma Mae.

He had put it on her good. She'd already given up being a Pillow Queen.

I shook my head in disgust and amazement. But I listened to them, both chanting like Tibetan Buddhists, imagined them savoring each other, creating their own hydrogen fusion.

She barely knew his name and he couldn't care less about hers, yet they were comfortable enough to hump each other and she felt safe enough to let him wander naked through her home.

Couldn't judge her on that one. I'd done that so many times in my lifetime.

Live like a woman and date like a man. The only way to stay sane.

God bless equal rights. We truly were living in fucked-up times.

I went to my bedroom. Locked my door.

Stared at the picture of me and Keith that sat on my dresser, positioned in the center of my other pictures, photos of me and my parents, as if Keith were the sun that my fractured world rotated around.

I wanted to meet you and tell you face-to-face that I was going back to my wife.

Wanted to rip my ears off. Dig inside my brain and remove some of my memory.

Right now I needed a cool bottle or a warm shoulder, some sort of comfort. Wanted to sleep in my makeup and skip brushing my teeth, do all the wretched things lovers do when it's over.

I wanted to get on my bike and ride away from the sunrise, live in the dark as long as I could.

I stripped down. Showered. Put my head under the water, wet my hair, and cried.

They all added up. For one it was six months. For another it might be three years. For another a weekend or two. But they all added up.

They all added up to time spent on relationships that didn't work. Time I wished I owned again. But time wasn't ownable. And days spent on useless relationships were irreversible.

Age crept in and the slim pickings became even slimmer.

Without drying off, soap trailing down my skin, water running from my hair and making a river across my face and back, I stared at myself in the full-length mirror on my closet door.

Rubbed my hands over my stomach.

Imagined being nine months pregnant and alone.

In the middle of the night my phone rang.

It didn't wake me because I was still pacing. Hating. Up thinking about the simple art of murder.

Keith's number on my caller ID. His name lit up my phone and it felt like I was parasailing.

I answered. "Keith?"

"This is his wife."

The world stopped rotating. Felt like a knife had been jabbed in my throat.

I lost it, went ballistic. "How did you get my number?"

She didn't have to answer. I knew. She was on Keith's phone.

She asked, "Are you with child?"

I growled, stared at my phone like I just knew she didn't have the nerve to call me.

Then she said, "Pregnant. That's the oldest trick in the book."

I cursed her out, told her, "Don't ever dial this number again."

I hung up. Sat on the bed staring at the wall. Then I turned on the light, went to the bathroom.

As soon as I sat on the toilet, there was a crash, followed by loud music.

Then the sound of a racing engine, a vehicle burning rubber on the pavement.

I jumped up and ran back into my bedroom. The window facing the streets was shattered. Broken glass was everywhere. A red brick was on my bed, the same spot I should've been sleeping on.

Someone had thrown a fucking brick through my bedroom window.

Taillights were speeding away, saw that through the shattered window.

That bitch did this.

I ran to the front door, yanked it open, and cursed out at the vanishing SUV.

six

DESTINY

"HOW OLD ARE YOU?"

"Eighteen."

"You're lying."

"I am."

"Mo, Baby Phat says she's eighteen."

"She lying, D'Andre. Shawty ain't no eighteen."

"Ain't she though."

"I'm fifteen."

"You ain't but fifteen with a badonkadunk like that?"

The Black Eyed Peas were fading away, their music on the store's sound system. *"My Humps."* Before there was any dead air Kanye West and Jay-Z picked up the slack. *"Diamonds Are Forever."*

Destiny said, "I'm almost sixteen."

"When your birthday?"

She told them.

"You a Sagittarius like me. No wonder."

"You a Sagittarius too?"

"Thought you was at least eighteen."

"Did you? Cool."

"Ain't but sixteen? Damn, Baby Phat got it going on."

Destiny blushed. "You just saying that."

"Those real Baby Phat jeans you got on, or knockoff?"

"They real. I don't wear knockoff."

"Damn. You must be rich."

"Oh, please." She shook her head. "I'm not rich."

"You get an allowance?"

"Uh. Yeah."

"Then your ass is rich."

"Well, my momma has money. Daddy is broke as a joke."

"So you staying with your rich momma?"

"Most of the time. Sometimes I stay at my daddy's apartment."

"Two cribs. Ain't that some shit."

Destiny. Keith's fifteen-year-old daughter.

Earlier that night, minutes after she had seen her daddy's friend, the girl on the motorcycle.

She had left her angry parents at Starbucks and was inside Wherehouse music, browsing CDs, holding Kanye West's new joint, when two brothers came over and started talking to her. One did most of the talking, the tall dark one who had a short nappy Afro. He looked damn good. He wore baggy sweats and Timberlands. He had a worn-out black backpack. Full of bootleg CDs and DVDs.

The other boy was light-skinned, more yellow to his hue than brown, with freckles that started on his broad nose and cascaded back toward his ears, a mane filled with sandy brown curly hair, a thin mustache, armed with a Jamie Foxx smile that made Destiny want to . . . to be his girlfriend.

Two good-looking soldiers were coming at her. Eyes on her lovely lady lumps. She liked that.

The one with the Jamie Foxx smile asked, "You wanna be in a video?"

She asked, "You do videos?"

"Yeah. Saw you over there getting your groove on."

She blushed. "Was I?"

"You rocking those humps, was backing dat ass up big time."

"They was playing my jam."

They *was*, not they *were*, intentional on her part.

One of the boys said, "I see you getting your groove on, but can you do the Mo?"

"What's that?"

The light-skinned boy with the Jamie Foxx smile started doing a jerky dance, arms bent in circles moving back and forth like a choo-choo train, legs firmly planted, and at the same time his upper body moving in a rhythmic motion. His homeboy joined in, did that same crazy-looking dance, and chanted.

"Do the Mo, do the Mo, do the Mo . . ."

Destiny joined in with them, danced and danced and danced.

"Do the Mo, do the Mo, do the Mo . . ."

"You got it, Baby Phat. You doing the Mo like a mofo."

They laughed.

The dark-skinned one. "Bet you have a tight body."

His toned, light-skinned friend. "Her body does look tight."

"Take your coat off. Show me what you working with."

The one she liked. "Yeah, take your coat off, Baby Phat."

She smiled when he asked, eased her coat off, playfully modeled. They peacocked around her, doing the Mo, staring at her ass, smiling. She danced the Mo with them. Like they were in a video.

"Pa-dow. Baby Phat is phat."

"All that and you ain't but fifteen?"

"Almost sixteen."

"You wanna hang with us?"

"When?"

"Tonight. We working on a documentary."

"Documentary? Thought you did videos."

"That too."

"Sounds tight."

"Gonna hit the strip, then might stop in at the studio up in Hollywood and watch our homey work on a cut. They doing a video shoot pretty soon. Then we got a little get-together going on."

"Can't. With my parents."

"Where they at?"

She motioned. "Starbucks. Getting on each other's nerves."

"Whassup with that?"

"My daddy's girlfriend down there too."

"Oh, shit."

"Your daddy got your momma and a girlfriend?"

"My parents are getting divorced. Daddy's girlfriend is one of the girls on the motorcycles."

"Damn. He hooked up with one of them bitches?"

Destiny said, "They ran into each other. Sort of. Momma was on the phone with Daddy and Daddy said he was over here with his girlfriend and Momma left the mall and sped over here."

"Sounds like some Jerry Springer shit."

"So, I'm with the donors."

"Donors."

"My sperm donor and my egg donor."

They laughed.

Dark-skinned one. "You need to get one of our CDs. We got Lil Jon, the new 50, er'body."

"How much?"

"One for five. Three for ten. Got that new Mary J. Blige too."

He moved to the side and opened his backpack. Destiny looked at the CDs. *Spit or Swallow. Buckwild. Latinas Fuck Better. Bad Girl Booty. Cock Craving Chicas. 'Shaw Hos. Slamhogs.*

Not CDs. Triple-X DVDs.

She said, "These are Roman numeral thirties."

"What that?"

"Three X's look like Roman numeral thirty. Movies for perverts. Daddy has a lot of these."

"My bad." He laughed. Jamie Foxx smile with R. Kelly eyes. "Turn the page."

Destiny read the cover on *'Shaw Hos.* "Deep cock sucking, cum swallowing, hard booty fucking."

"Turn the page."

"Black Orgies Volume Eleven. Mad Michelle and Friends."

"I give you the right book?"

"How much are these nasty DVDs?"

"Three for twenty."

Destiny shook her head. "Y'all going to hell."

"I grew up in Compton. And Compton to hell is a local call."

They laughed. Destiny didn't understand the joke, but she laughed anyway.

"C'mon, nigh. Support a brother."

She turned the page. More movies. *King Kong. Crash. The Island. Four Brothers. Hostel. Ray. Are We There Yet? Diary of a Mad Black Woman.*

Turned the page again. Saw Lil Jon. Mike Jones. New Tweet. New 50 Cent. Mario. Omarion. Bootlegged on Maxell discs. Names written in with a black Magic Marker, handwriting as legible as hers was when she was in the third grade. He handed her a computer-generated list of all of their bootlegged products. Ghetto entrepreneurs.

He said, "I got some Disney movies too, in case you got a little brother or something like that."

"I don't have a little brother or nothing like that."

"Shit, security walking up in here."

He closed his backpack real fast, pretended to be browsing CDs.

Destiny said, "Y'all better raise up before y'all get busted."

He asked, "Can I holla at you?"

"Go on and holla."

"On the grind now. Got a number or something, Baby Phat?"

"Give me yours."

She was proud of the way she said that. Like in the movies. Like she was in charge.

He told his dark-skinned friend, "She'd be tight in a video."

"Drop Baby Phat one of your cards so we can biz-ounce."

"Here's my card, Baby Phat."

She looked at it. Thin printer paper. Homemade on a computer that used an ink-jet printer. Cut with scissors. Just a phone number. That was all it had.

"Make sure you call a nigga up."

"I will. Fo' sheezy."

"Fo' sheezy?"

She tensed. Wrong slang. Outdated. Had been hanging with too many Bel Air children.

She played it off with a laugh, simplified her words. "Just messing with ya, bruh. Fo' sho."

"Too bad you're gonna miss tonight."

"What else is cracking tonight?"

"Working on this phat documentary and getting crunk and shit."

"That right?"

He laughed. "You get blown?"

"Hell, yeah."

"Like Alize?"

"Hell, yeah."

He smiled. "You ain't got no number so I can holla?"

His dark-skinned friend. Now looking nervous. "She ain't but fifteen."

"She got mad body, dawg."

"Let the girl call you, man."

"What school you go to?" the one with the Jamie Foxx smile asked. "Your smart ass. Be articulating your words and shit. Know all about Roman numerals and shit."

And shit. They ended sentences with *and shit*, what her mother called ghetto punctuation.

She told him. Wanted to lie and say she went to Crenshaw, Inglewood, one of the *and shit* schools, but the truth came faster than she could think of a lie.

He said, "Never heard of that school."

"Private school. Up in Bel Air *and shit*."

"Oh, shit. The Fresh Princess."

"I wish."

"Smart girl, huh?"

They laughed.

That made her uncomfortable. She wanted to be normal. Not a private school freak living in the hood. She wanted to be from Crenshaw High. Dorsey. Anywhere but a private school in Bel Air.

She asked them, "Y'all got names?"

The light-skinned one said his name was Mo.

The dark-skinned soldier said his name was D'Andre.

Mo and D'Andre headed out of the store.

Mo, the cute one who put butterflies in her belly, looked back.

R. Kelly smile.

She grinned.

Age ain't nothing but a number.

D'Andre had lost interest when she told him she was fifteen. She didn't care. Mo was cuter, had a better smile. But D'Andre was so damn fine.

Destiny danced the Mo dance, chanted "Do the Mo" as she browsed CDs. Hoped the boys were still watching her. T. I. Mario. Saw the John Legend CD that her mother played all the damn time.

The roar of motorcycles came in as somebody else walked in the door. The motorcycle girls. Dykes on bikes, what her mother called them. They all looked so cool. Tight jeans. Sweet leather jackets. Popping wheelies. Actually they were cooler than cool. They all looked so free. So uninhibited. Like Billie. The long-haired, leather-wearing woman her daddy loved. The woman her mother hated.

The door to the music store opened again and her mother rushed inside, her daddy in tow.

Her mother looked pissed.

Her mother always looked pissed.

Her father looked unhappy.

He always looked unhappy.

Unless he was away from them.

Unless he was with Billie.

The day she saw her daddy and the motorcycle girl coming out of the movies she almost didn't recognize him. She had never seen him smiling and laughing like that. Holding hands with the motorcycle girl. Holding her so close. As if she were his world. She had never seen him happy. And that brand-new tattoo. That cool tattoo her mother hated so much.

Then when her daddy saw them, she had never seen him look so surprised . . . so bummed out.

Her mother said, "We're leaving."

"Daddy said I could buy a CD."

"We're leaving *now*."

Her mother grabbed her arm. Squeezed her until it hurt. Destiny tried to get free, dropped the CD where she stood, let it crash to the floor, jerked away from her mother, and hurried away.

She went outside the door, pain in her arm, tears in her eyes.

She told her father what her mother had done. "She won't let me buy my CD."

He cringed. "Destiny, I have a headache."

"Whatever."

Her father snapped, "Hey. What was that?"

"Daddy, do something."

"Go to the car."

"Daddy . . . why do you let her treat me—"

"Now. Go to the car now."

"Daddy, I want to ride with you."

"Ride with your mother."

"Please?"

"I don't need this right now, Destiny. Go to your mother's car."

She walked away, head hurting, crying.

She hated her mother. She hated her father. She hated her world.

The guys she had met were talking to some other girls now. One of the girls, black-mixed-with-Mexican. Destiny lived in a melting pot, she could tell. The girl looked at her and smiled, checked Destiny out head to toe, winked, then turned away. Strange. Destiny ignored that girl, sent her attention back to the boys. They no longer noticed her. She was no longer special. They had their backpacks open, pushing bootleg CDs. She was glad they didn't notice her. They were laughing and dancing.

Destiny watched Mo, wanted to go back over there and tell him 'bye, but saw him stop a girl who was walking up toward the Wherehouse, a girl in tight jeans, a tight top, long black hair, a face that reminded her of the singer Amerie, black-mixed-with-Asian. Real tall girl. In two seconds Mo had her laughing, doing that rotating jerky dance, her breasts bouncing as her long arms bent in circles, as her elbows moved back and forth like a choo-choo train, her upper body moving in a herky-jerky motion.

"Do the Mo, do the Mo, do the Mo."

Heat rose, spread across Destiny's chest. That should've been her over there doing the Mo.

Inside her mother's car, jealousy and silence.

Her mother dug inside her purse, took out her inhaler. Asthma. Her mother had been having anxiety attacks that triggered her ailment, a weakness that had been dormant for fifteen years or better. Arms folded, body turned away, Destiny didn't care. A paperback was on the floor. She picked it up. *The Alchemist*. She tossed the book to the side, stared out the window, arms folded, lips pulled in tight.

As they drove by the boys she'd been with, her mother glanced over, shaking her head.

The speech. A closing argument. Her mother. Always the attorney.

"Destiny, when I was growing up, we were encouraged to be doctors.

Lawyers. Engineers. Times have changed. And not for the better. The music you listen to, it's offensive. It offends me. I raised you better. That music . . . now swinging from a pole is the occupation of both choice and praise. Being shot nine times and rapping about it is cool. Dressing the same way people do in jail is the fashion of choice. Being ghetto is acceptable, embraced as if being ignorant were cool. That's not how I want you to be. That's why I try so hard. I need you to have a sense of rootedness and spirituality, a positive identity, and adult involvement in your life. I need you to be physical and popular in a nonsexual and nonmaterialistic way. And most of all, I need you to have family. A mother and a father at home."

"Daddy said I could buy a CD."

"I listen to the news and it scares me. Never used to scare me, not until I had you. You changed my world, made me aware. An eleven-year-old girl was killed when bullets tore through her apartment last night. Her fourteen-year-old sister was wounded too. Another girl was killed in a hit-and-run in Hawthorne. A newborn was found dead in an alley behind USC on Hoover. It's a horrible world, Destiny."

"Why didn't you let me buy my CD?"

"I hear those things and I cry."

Destiny took a hard breath, stopped listening, her mother's voice becoming white noise. Her mind drifting away. Remembering her mother's hypocrisy.

Destiny eavesdropped on her mother's conversations. Whenever her mother used the phone, she would pretend there was an emergency so she could interrupt her mother's tête-à-tête, then act as if she were hanging up and hold the mute button. Finger on the mute button, she would listen:

"What do I have to do to get you off my back, Carmen?"

"Who was the bitch I saw you with at the movies?"

"I introduced you. You know who she is."

"Your girlfriend."

"That's what I said. You got a problem with that?"

"You have no idea how that made me feel, walking across the lot, with your daughter, and to have her running into you all hugged up with some tramp. You tell me that you're sick, that you're staying home and can't spend time with your daughter, and I run into you, all shits and giggles, with some tramp."

Her mother's voice owned a lot of anger and some slur. Destiny knew her mother was on her second bottle of Pinot Noir. Wine imported from Burgundy, not grown in California. She drank often and she drank the best. Destiny knew that her mother drank wine most nights. That was her sleeping pill.

Her father snapped, "How's the guy you're sleeping with?"

"You have no idea how embarrassing that was, running into you and that tramp."

"If I had the money, I'd pay your ass off."

"Is that what you left me for, Keith? Is that why you abandoned this marriage?"

Her father and mother. Gemini and Aries. Destiny had read how Aries always needed to dominate. But her father wasn't intimidated by her mother. Never backed down.

"Carmen, if I won the lottery I'd give you every dime just so you would leave me the hell alone."

"Would you?"

"Fuck yes."

Weeks before, Destiny had eavesdropped on her mother inviting her lover over. Heard her mother talking nasty to him over the phone. Had never heard her mother talk like that. Heard her mother ask him if he wanted to fuck her from behind. Heard him ask her mother to touch herself. Heard him telling her mother that he wanted her to come for him. Heard the strange man tell her mother to get her vibrator and fuck herself while he touched himself. Listened as her mother did what he asked.

She listened then.

She listened every chance she could get.

That was the only way she would ever learn the truth.

"You hate me that much, Keith?"

"Don't ask me no shit like that."

"You'd leave me for that tramp?"

"If our marriage was a horse, I would've shot it five years ago."

"You'd give up my daughter, our daughter, for a dyke on a bike?"

"Call me when you're not drunk, Carmen."

"I'll call you when I damn well please."

"What do you want, Carmen?" her daddy snapped. "What the fuck do you want from me?"

She heard her mother sipping her wine. In control. "Don't you ever miss me, Keith?"

"Don't ask me that."

"Don't you miss the way I fucked you, Keith?"

"You're still fucking me, Carmen."

"The way I made love to you, all the things I did, don't you miss that?"

"Carmen, don't."

"Don't you miss the way I sucked your dick?"

"Don't go there, Carmen."

"How many years did I suck our dick?"

"Our dick?"

"Damn near twenty years. That's our dick, Keith. Ours."

"You're drunk, Carmen."

"Fine. Then it's my dick."

"Is it?"

"That's my dick and you know that's my dick."

"Don't start with that shit, Carmen."

"I miss sucking my dick, Keith."

"Don't do this, Carmen."

"I miss fucking you. I can still feel the imprint of your dick inside me. Can still feel your hands grabbing me around my waist, pulling me into you. Can still feel your tongue on my breast. Wish you were here pulling my hair, smacking my ass, shit. You are so amazing. Want you back inside me."

Silence.

Destiny imagined her father, head down, so frustrated.

"You ever miss us, the way it used to be, Keith?"

"Don't ask me that, Carmen."

"Do you?"

"Don't yell."

"Do you?"

"Sometimes. The way it used to be. It used to be nice."

"When we first married?"

"Before we got married."

"Before I was pregnant, huh?"

"When you were a waitress. Before law school."

"When we were renting that crappy overpriced one-bedroom apartment in Fox Hills."

"Yeah. When I was busting my butt to pay for a place you just had to have."

"Before we . . . when it was just us?"

"It was different then." Her daddy took a hard breath. "When it was just us."

"Seems like we had sex five or six times a day."

"Yeah. Seems like."

"You gave me twelve orgasms one day. Remember what day that was?"

Her daddy said, "On Valentine's Day."

"Our first Valentine's Day."

"We didn't leave the apartment."

Her mother chuckled. "Neighbors were banging on the walls."

"I remember."

"That was when we could come and go . . . movies . . . working out . . . do as we pleased."

"It was . . . it was nice when . . . back then it was nice."

Her mother took a hard breath. "Children change the dynamics of a relationship."

"Yeah. Yeah, children do change the dynamics of a marriage."

"If we never had a child, do you think it would've been different?"

"If I never met you it would've been different."

"Fuck you." Just like that her mother exploded. "Fucking fuck you, Keith."

"That's all you've done since I met you. Fucked me. Fucked me to get what you wanted. You have a house. You have a law degree. You've come up at my expense. You got what you wanted, now you're still fucking me. Get your dick out of my ass, Carmen. Get your motherfucking dick out of my ass."

"Sounds like you're hitting the dark liquor again."

"If I am, it's one thing I have left that makes me feel good. The only thing you can't take away."

"Bastard."

"I never wanted any children. Wait, let me modify that statement. Not with you. Never wanted children with you. I told you that. That was your agenda."

"You don't love your daughter?"

"Of course I love my daughter. I just hate . . . this . . . this situation. This is a horrible existence."

"Then come back home, Keith. Come back and end all this madness."

"I don't love you, Carmen."

"You love her? You're in love with that tramp?"

"What about the nigga you fucking, Carmen? Have you forgotten about him?"

"What makes you think I'm involved with someone?"

"Destiny told me."

"Well, she is mistaken."

"She told me she walked in on you and him."

"She said what?"

"He was in the kitchen I paid for, cooking you dinner."

"She's lying. You know how she lies."

"I know how you lie, Carmen."

"And if I am seeing someone, I'm not parading him in the places we used to go."

"Don't lie on your daughter, Carmen."

"I ain't got nothing to lie about."

"Who is he?"

"He's nobody important."

Silence.

Her father asked, "Is it serious? If it is, why are you sweating me?"

"He . . . he's not you, Keith. I find it very wonderful that he's given a lot of thought to what a relationship between us would mean. He knows what he would need to do to step up to the plate and is interested in doing that. Including going to church."

"Hallelujah. Then take him to church and move on."

"I can't. I am just not thrilled by the sex at all. I guess I'm being picky.

But when you have had the best there is, it's so hard. You want the truth? Okay, here's the truth. I was with him last night."

"You took him to my house?"

"It's not your house anymore."

Silence.

"Of course I didn't taint our home." Her mother went on, voice strained, tears falling. "I was at his house. I can't bring another man in here, Keith. I wouldn't disrespect our memories like that."

"But he cooked for you at my house."

"We didn't have sex in this house, Keith. I'd never do that."

Destiny shook her head. Her mother, the expert liar, now caught in a trap.

Her father's breathing became so thick. Destiny felt his heat coming though the phone.

Her mother said, "When I got up this morning, I sat on the edge of the bed and told him that I wouldn't be back. He knew I regretted what we had done. Had to gather myself and realize that I might be throwing away something good just based on the physical. But I couldn't love him. I also felt that I didn't want to be sneaking out or feeling pissed off because I wasn't getting it the way I want it."

Then Destiny heard her mother's bedroom door open. Her lights off, Destiny peeped out her door, saw her mother walking with the phone in her hand, heading downstairs toward the kitchen.

"Son-of-a-bitch." Her mother's voice cracked. "You've ruined me, Keith. Damn you. Eighteen years have gone by and I still get the shakes when I think about you. I don't want nobody else."

"Where is Destiny?"

"You want to know where your daughter is?" That bitter tone again. "I'll tell you where the fuck she is. Destiny is in pain. Divorce shapes the emotional tenor of childhood. Our daughter is acting out because she has to reconcile two worlds. Inner conflict. That's what the counselor called it. Children of divorce inhabit a difficult emotional landscape. Live between two worlds. She's being restructured emotionally. The only way the world will make sense is if she grows up in a home that makes sense."

Her father remained unmoved by the dramatics, repeated the question: "Where is Destiny?"

"Don't worry. She's sleeping." Her mother made a wounded, pre-crying sound. "This last year has been so damn hard. Hard on me. Hard on our child. I told myself that I need to let you go and move on. I tried for a year. Destiny can't do this. I can't do this. I can't, not when I love you like this."

Destiny sat on her bed. Heard her mother pouring herself another drink.

Destiny waited, listened to their uneven, harsh breathing. Her father angry. Her mother in pain.

She wished they made some sort of echinacea for wounded hearts.

Her mother said, "Keith, are you still there?"

Her father sounded fatigued. "I'm here."

"Say something."

"Were you seeing him while we were together?"

"Of course not."

"You still fucking him?"

"Is that all you heard? Is that all you care about?"

Her father's voice turned to stone. "Are you?"

Her mother's tone became a feather. "Of course not."

Her daddy let out a curt and harsh laugh. "You're so full of shit."

"How long will it take before I don't feel you? How long before I don't want you anymore? I'm trying to move forward. I'm still your wife. Still wearing our wedding ring and trying to date."

"So you're dating."

"I'm tired of waiting for you to come to your senses."

"You slept with him . . . you're dating . . . why are you sweating me?"

"Took four lemon-drop martinis to get me feeling good enough, to get me relaxed enough to throw caution to the wind and . . . and . . . seeing you with that bitch at the movies . . . all up under you like she was your wife . . . no ring on your finger . . . yeah . . . I got drunk . . . went for it. We never had sex before last night."

"Last night."

"Fuck you. I needed to be held, I needed some attention, I needed some intimacy and I wasn't calling your ass . . . well . . . I did call you . . . you didn't answer . . . I know you were with that bitch . . . pissed me off . . . so I did it . . . had sex . . . and it just did nothing for me. All I could think about was that, damn, he doesn't feel like Keith. Damn, he doesn't do this like my husband. Closed my eyes and pretended he was you. But he wasn't you. It wasn't right. It wasn't . . . it wasn't us. The size, the stroke, the feel was just all wrong. Woke up this morning, put on my clothes, and could not wait to get home to self-serve."

"So, you spent the night with him, the brother you claimed Destiny didn't see you with."

"Is that all you heard? Don't you hear what I'm going through over here?"

"You suck his dick?"

"Don't ask me that."

"He make you come?"

"Don't ask me that."

"Let's keep it honest. Billie is my girlfriend. I have sex with Billie. It's the best sex I've ever had."

"Son-of-a-bitch."

"I eat her pussy and it tastes like sweet peaches."

"Don't do this Keith. Don't be mean to me."

"I make her come like a river."

"Yes, I sucked his dick, and yes, I had a goddamn orgasm. You're over there fucking that . . . that tramp . . . you have your whore . . . you're taking her out in public . . . my mother and father saw you with her . . . and I'm supposed to sit over here, night after night, waiting for you to come to your senses?"

"You know what, it's high time the image of the good mother you pretend to be is shown for what it is. Manipulative, greedy, materialistic, and a cheap facade of sensitivity when it suits you."

In that black and bitter tone her mother said, "I fucked him and came hard."

Destiny didn't know these people. This wasn't her mother, not her father.

These were children trying to hurt each other. She wondered if adults ever grew up.

"I fucked him and pretended he was you, Keith. He didn't make me come. I made myself come. I allowed myself to come. I came and I had to go to the bathroom and cry because I felt so damn guilty."

Mariah Carey came on her mother's CD player: "We Belong Together."

Her father released an exasperated sigh. "Where was Destiny last night?"

Then her mother was crying. "I don't give a damn about any man but you."

"How many times did you sleep with him?"

"Keith . . . why? Don't tell me you're jealous."

Her father groaned. "I'm about to hang up."

"Do you love me, Keith?"

"You fucked somebody last night and you're asking me if I love you today?"

"Just answer the goddamn question."

"No. Carmen, I do not love you. Not the way a husband should love a wife."

Silence. So silent Destiny wondered if they had hung up.

Finally her mother asked, "You love her? We're being honest, so be honest, Keith."

Her mother sounded so old when she asked that, like she was struggling with her own youth, with her mortality, losing a battle but still refusing to be overcome by senescence.

"When I'm with Billie, I don't need anything. She's sweet, not needy. She doesn't suck the life out of me. She says my name and it gives me life. She makes me laugh. And she thinks I'm funny."

"Don't make me vomit, Keith. Is that what you're trying to do, make me vomit?"

"You're a taker, Carmen. All you do is take."

"Do you love her?"

"She knows how to love."

"Answer me, dammit."

"Here's the truth. Our time has come and gone, Carmen."

"Do you love her?"

"Yes, Carmen. I love Billie."

Then there was this horrible sound.

The abrupt wail of her mother crying.

Her mother was crying hard. Whining like a two-year-old.

That shattered Destiny even more.

"You don't have to love me, Keith."

"This is too much for me, Carmen. Look, let's talk tomorrow or the next day."

"No, no, no. Come see me, Keith."

"I'll see you when we get to counseling."

"I'm hurting, Keith. You're hurting me. Don't reject me, Keith. I need you."

"Carmen, please."

"I crave you still. . . . I love you, Keith. You don't have to love me, not like I love you. Marriage isn't about being in love. Marriage is bigger than love. Just come back home. We'll pray. We'll work it out."

"Carmen, sweetheart—"

"If not for me, then think about our daughter."

"Carmen, the only reason you got pregnant was because of endometriosis."

"True. I didn't think I would ever have a child."

"Maybe we shouldn't have."

"Maybe. Then I wouldn't be . . . this isn't how I pictured my life, Keith."

"You think this is how I pictured mine?"

"I didn't picture myself being a divorced single mother."

"Well, when it came down to the baby, that was what you wanted."

"I hate you, Keith. I fucking hate you. Nigga, I hate I ever met your sorry ass."

"This sorry-ass nigga got your broke ass through law school. I paid to get your ass where you are now. Paid for that house you're in. For that damn phone you're calling me from. I made you what the fuck you are now. Haven't I paid enough? Why don't you end the fucking child support order, Carmen?"

She chuckled. The laugh of a winner. "Am I doing anything illegal?"

"You're calling the courts every other week. You call so much the people down there are getting tired of your vindictive ass. I gave you the house. I mean, fuck, haven't you done enough?"

"Well, the locks haven't been changed over here."

Her daddy lost it. "Why in the fuck do you keep doing this to me?"

"Stop acting like you're a pathetic martyr. Be a man, for Christ's sake."

"Be a man."

"That's what I said."

"I am a man. The problem is that you're still a child. A spoiled brat in expensive clothes."

"Well, this spoiled brat has outgrown you. Look at your check stub, then look at mine."

"You know what? You can wipe your ass with that law degree, for all I care."

"Broke-ass nigga. Ain't nothing worse than a broke-ass nigga."

"This nigga broke because of your trifling, temperamental, psychotic ass."

"Fuck you. Son-of-a-bitch."

"You know what . . ." Her father took a hard breath. " 'Bye, Carmen."

"We're not done talking."

"I've had enough disrespect for today. 'Bye, Carmen."

"What, is your tramp coming over? Or are you driving up to View Park to that bitch's house?"

"What was that?"

"That tramp, that bartender you're seeing, she's renting a room from a Korean woman, right?"

"You've been following me?"

"Maybe I'm following her."

"Don't play with me, Carmen."

"I know people at LAPD, down at the DMV, even the IRS; not much I can't find out."

Her daddy exploded. "The only thing we have to talk about is Destiny, understand? And she's old enough to call me and talk about whatever needs to be talked about. Don't fucking call me again. Ever."

"Wait, don't hang up on me, Keith."

"Next time my phone rings and your number is on caller ID, it better be my daughter calling."

"Talk to me. Please? Five minutes. Just five more minutes."

"What do you want from me, Carmen?"

"Come back home. If not for me, for your daughter."

"Don't you ever use my daughter like that."

Her mother snapped. "A daughter you didn't want to have."

"Don't ever let me hear you say that bullshit again, Carmen."

"Keith, you'll never be happy outside this house."

"Why are you doing this, Carmen?"

Destiny sat in her room and listened.

"Because I love you, Keith." All the harshness was gone from her mother's voice. She sounded so soft, so sincere, so wounded. "Because we are a family. Because we stood before God."

Destiny's eyes filled with tears.

Now she knew.

Her mother was a whore.

Her father was in love with someone else.

If she had not been born, her hypocritical parents would still be child-less and happy. Or they could've left each other, been free of parental obligations, instead of her being the tether for their misery.

She'd never stop thinking about that phone call. Never. She didn't feel bad about invading her parents' privacy. The only way she got the truth in her house was by stealing it.

"Destiny?"

Her mother's sweet and raspy voice brought her back to the here and now, stole her away from that memory. Her mother owned a subtle, victorious smile. They were speeding down Stocker, doing at least eighty down the four-lane corridor that separated View Park from Baldwin Hills, kicking up trash that lined the residential area, coming up on Crenshaw Boulevard, not far from her grandparents'. That damn John Legend CD was playing. It was always playing. Destiny wanted to scream. Her daddy's apartment was right up the street from where they were, walking distance from her grandparents' house.

She looked up and saw her daddy's beat-up SUV was right behind them.

They turned left, headed toward King. Her daddy went straight into the heart of Leimert Park.

Destiny sighed, didn't look at her mother. Her mind was already some-where else. Her eyes were on the cruisers, people who hit the strip every weekend. Crenshaw Strip. Not too far from where Merlin Santana was gunned down, set up by a fifteen-year-old sister. Barbershops. Tattoo parlors. Second-rate businesses on six lanes of pothole-filled madness. All over the strip were signs that said no left turns down side streets from early evening to late night. And more signs were posted that said NO CRUISING. At the bottom of each sign was writing that defined cruising as passing the same point twice within six hours. So to beat the system people parked at damn near every parking lot from Century to the 10 Freeway, at least ten miles of loitering. Honda car club was in front of Wings and Things. Volkswagens club in front of Chris Burgers. Low Riders representing in front of the car wash, some next door at Jack in the Box. Girls in short shorts. The brothers too scared to get their Mack on. Everybody chilling. Music bumping three-sixty. Car clubs were out in full force.

Destiny asked, "Mommy, when are you going to let me get my driver's permit?"

"Ask your father."

"He let me drive a little bit."

"He did what?"

"Relax. I drove around the parking lot at the forum, not on the streets."

"Well, me and your father will have to have a little talk."

"Why is teaching me how to drive a problem?"

"Because he does things to turn you against me."

Destiny sighed. "When can I get a tattoo?"

"Never. Don't even think about it."

"Daddy has one."

"Change the subject."

"You're mad because daddy got a tattoo?"

"Shut up, Destiny."

"Yup. You real mad."

"Shut up or change the subject."

"Whatever."

Her mother frowned. "That's your last *whatever*."

A car pulled up next to them, music blasting, thumping so hard she felt the vibrations.

We fucked on the bed, fucked on the floor, fucked so long I grew a fuckin' Afro.

"Horrible. Destiny, that music is horrible. Where are these children's parents? What kind of parents do they have?"

Her mother turned up the volume on her CD, John Legend yelling that they were ordinary people.

Destiny turned the volume back down.

"Mommy, you used to cruise the strip?"

"Years ago. Used to walk these streets. Shopped at the swap meet like everybody else."

"Daddy too?"

"Before I knew your daddy. Ask him. He grew up in the hood. Bad area, but he got out. Unlike his big brother. Your uncle Jody was killed robbing a liquor store, that was years before you were born. Your daddy ran with the crazy crowd on that side. He'll tell you he used to cruise Crenshaw too."

"How long ago was that?"

"Before rap came out. When singers could sing. And dancers didn't dance like strippers. Hip-hop killed R & B. Put a bullet in its heart."

Destiny laughed as if she couldn't imagine a world without hip-hop. That would be like trying to live in a world that had no air. "That's so unreal, Momma. There was a time when there wasn't any rap?"

"And no HBO. And no MTV. Only had three channels. *Soul Train* was all we had."

"That was it? *Soul Train*? That show sucks. And just three channels to look at?"

"Four if you count PBS. And television went off not too long after midnight."

"That's whack."

"And 7-Eleven opened at seven a.m. and closed at eleven p.m."

"Is that why they call it 7-Eleven?"

"Crips and Bloods were having a gang war. Crack houses. LAPD had battering rams. They were banging hard back then. I've worked hard. Momma has come a long way from where she started."

"I'm still stuck on you not having HBO. Network television sucks."

"So you were listening." Her mother smiled. "No cable. No music videos. No Internet. No Michael Jackson singing 'Thriller' and no Downtown Julie Brown. Now, she wore some cool hats."

"Who is she?"

"She was the Dick Clark of the video age."

"Who is Dick Clark?"

"God, I'm getting old." Her mother laughed a laugh that owned no joy. "And nobody had cellular phones. Had to use those same nasty pay phones that the homeless people use."

"Nasty."

"God, seems like yesterday, but that was so long ago."

Destiny tried to lighten her mother's mood, joked, "They actually had cars when you were my age?"

Her mother smiled. "Yeah. But we had to stop them with our feet."

An Escalade whipped in front of them. Destiny saw at least six DVD screens. All playing porn. Another SUV next to them was playing *Baby Boy*. Tyrese's character having an all-out argument with his baby momma in one breath, then in the next they were having mad sex. Hard and relentless sex, getting her ass slapped by a warrior in the hood. Destiny knew all the dialogue to the movie. Even now her lips were moving. *I love daddy-dick he feel big I love daddy-dick I'mma cook I'mma clean.*

Destiny thought about last year, the first time she had sex. It wasn't like that.

She didn't scream *I love you, I love you* like Tyrese's baby momma. She didn't yell that she was about to come, about to come, about to come. She didn't lie on the bed smiling at him. There was ass-slapping, but no cuddling. The expression on the actress's face, she wanted to feel that kind of love.

Destiny remembered. That was the look she had seen on her mother's face when she was six, almost ten years ago. She had woken up in the middle of the night, heard noises, scary noises, and walked into the living room. Her parents had their clothes half on, half off. Her mother was bent over their ottoman. Her daddy was behind her mother, what she knows now was doggie style. She had never seen that barbaric look on her daddy's face before. He was in control. He was king. His skin was slapping against her mother's skin so hard it sounded like he was beating her over and over. She had never seen that yielding and vulnerable look on her mother's face before. The ottoman scooted across the wooden floor every time her daddy thrust, didn't stop scooting until the ottoman touched the Oriental rug.

Destiny was horrified.

About to scream.

Then . . .

Her mother howled and moaned for her daddy to fuck her pussy, pushed her ass backward over and over, growled for him to fuck her fucking pussy because it was his pussy to fuck the way he was fucking that fucking pussy. Told him how good he was making her feel, moaned out how much she liked what he was doing. Her daddy's hand was on her mother's waist, yanking her back into him as he thrust forward, her mother begging her father to go inside her as deep as he could. Those noises, that symphony of lust and fornication, her daddy's grunts, that skin-slapping adding to their rhapsody—

And when they were done with that violence, there were smiles and laughter.

Her mother laughed. Like it had been a game. Like it had been fun.

Her father did the same. Laid on top of her mother, kissing her, touching her hair.

She remembered that more than the sex. Seeing their smiles and hearing their laughter.

How they held each other.

The love.

She wanted that. To be loved. Like the girl in *Baby Boy*.

Her mother said, "You hear me?"

Destiny snapped out of her trance. "What?"

"Taking you up to Starbucks, that was wrong. Mommy shouldn't have done that. I did the same thing that my momma used to do. Same thing I swore I'd never do to my child."

"You're becoming your mother. Nobody wants to become their mother."

"I'll choose to ignore that."

"Like you choose to ignore everything else I say."

Her mother took a hard breath, the sound of her patience being tried. "But . . . but . . . Mommy didn't have time to drop you off. Mommy should've have dropped you off first, then went up there."

"What happened at Starbucks?"

"Your father has made some selfish choices. It's hurting us all." Carmen smiled an uneasy smile, rubbed her temples with one hand. "I'm sorry that you keep getting thrown in the middle of this."

"What happened at Starbucks, Momma?"

"Nothing."

"Daddy's girlfriend was up there."

Her mother snapped. "That bitch is not his girlfriend."

"He said she was."

"Well, she's not."

"I saw her staring at you. Something jump off?"

Her mother frowned like she wanted to grind somebody's jaw in the mud. "Nothing jumped off."

"Something happened. What happened? What did the girl on the motorcycle do?"

"Nothing. Little Miss Swap Meet was there. But that's over." Carmen made a rugged sound, took a sharp breath. "Mommy's sorry. Mommy has been stressed. So damn stressed it ain't funny."

Destiny took a breath and looked away. It was dry today. Last year L.A. had been filled with perpetual rain and mudslides. Parts of L.A. County, Orange County, Kern County, pretty much most of the West Coast were considered disaster areas. State of emergency. A category five named Katrina had devastated New Orleans. Another state of emergency. That's what her life felt like. A disaster area. The governor or the president needed to intervene and declare her existence a state of emergency. And it was getting worse. Ever since the earthquake that caused the tsunami and killed over three hundred thousand people, the world had changed. She had read on the Internet that the earthquake was so powerful that it had altered the earth's rotation. Made the world spin faster. Since then it had been raining so hard and long in L.A. that flowers were blooming in the desert. Global warming had melted Kilimanjaro's snowcapped top. Everything was out of balance. Nobody noticed. Her conclusion was that since people were mostly sacks of water, the new rotation had changed everybody. And global warming helped in that change. Everything was connected. And maybe that was why her parents kept acting like they were both auditioning for the lead in *Flowers for Algernon*.

"Destiny?"

"What?"

"You hear me?"

"No."

"I said that after I drop you off, I'm going around the corner to your father's apartment."

"For what?"

"To help him pack." Her mother hesitated. "He's coming home."

"Home?"

"With us."

"When?"

"Tomorrow."

"Tomorrow?"

"Yes. Tomorrow. Your father's little divorce decree has been revoked."

"Why was it revoked?"

"Because I'm smarter than he is." Her mother smiled. "We're going to be a family again."

"When was this decided?"

"Aren't you happy?"

"Momma, when?"

"You may not appreciate what I'm saying now, but you'll appreciate it later."

"Which means you don't have time to explain. Or want to explain."

"Everything I do is for you, do you not know that?"

Destiny grunted. "Why is it so hard to get a straight answer from you?"

"Now you and your dad can play chess, maybe watch *Battlestar Galactica* every Friday."

"And when I fall asleep, you and Daddy can work out the new ottoman."

"What was that?"

"Could you please stop iggn' me and answer at least one of my questions?"

Her mother pulled up in her grandparents' narrow driveway. Single-family home. Green stucco.

Destiny repeated, "When was this decided?"

"Aren't you happy?"

"Does it look like I'm clapping my hands?"

"For better or for worse, Destiny. Marriages are for better or for worse."

"Well, hurry up and get to the 'for better' part."

"Relationships are so hard. Don't rush to be hurt. Stay young as long as you can."

"See how you don't answer my questions, Momma?"

"I'm almost thirty-seven. Seems like I was your age only yesterday. Time goes by so fast when you're having fun. Then moves treacherously slow when we are experiencing pain. Time. It's our greatest enemy. Be careful with your choices, Destiny. No way to undo whatever we have done."

"Act like you don't hear me." Destiny had raised her voice, shook her head, her mother's voice like broken glass against her ears. "I know you heard me. Nothing I say is important."

Carmen sighed. "So, you stay with Big Momma tonight."

"I'm old enough to stay at home by myself."

"Not on my watch."

"Whatever."

"I'll be back to get you after breakfast."

"Since you're going to be with Daddy, can I just kick it over here all day tomorrow?"

"You should be with me and Daddy. We need to spend time together. Family time."

"Could you please kill the Disneyland speech?"

"That's what the counselor said we needed. Family time. Thought maybe we could go bowling."

"Please?"

"If not bowling, then a movie. Tell you what, I'll call you in the morning."

"I don't want to go bowling. I don't want to see a movie. I want to stay over here."

"Why?"

"Because it's . . . quiet over here. I have some serious homework I need to do anyway."

"What *serious* homework?"

"Ogden Nash."

"Who is Ogden Nash?"

"Writer. Have to do a critical analysis of his poem 'Fleas' and write a paper. That will take all day."

Carmen sighed, rubbed her temples. "We'll talk in the morning."

"Why do we have to talk about if I can stay over here?"

"Because we have to."

"Because you say we have to, that's why we have to."

"Don't argue with me."

"I'm tired of the eristic arguments."

"The what?"

"Eristic."

"And that means?"

"You're the lawyer."

"What does that word mean?"

"Look it up. You're the *smart* one."

"Get smacked with a dictionary. Don't let that mouth get you in trouble."

"Whatever."

Her mother snapped, "What was that, Destiny?"

"Nothing. Absolutely nothing."

Carmen sighed, rubbed her temples. "Too bad parents don't get to pick their children."

Destiny retorted, "As if children can pick their parents."

"Last time, Destiny. Last time."

"You and Daddy can have your drama. I want to stay over here tomorrow."

"We'll talk in the morning, see how it goes, take it from there."

Destiny grunted. "Despot."

"What did you call me?"

"You heard me."

Destiny felt her mother's hand, her sudden rage, slap the back of her head.

Carmen snapped, "I've had about enough of your shit."

"I've had enough of your shit too. Everybody's had enough of your shit."

"Curse me again."

"Stop hitting me."

"Go ahead curse me again."

"Stop hitting me."

"Or what? Or what?"

Destiny watched her mother raise her hand for the final blow.

Her mother howled, *"An ungrateful child is an abomination in the eyes of God."*

Her mother hesitated, so much hurt and frustration in her eyes.

Destiny snapped, "I don't want to live with you *and* Daddy."

Carmen, in shock. "What?"

"I want to protect you and I want to protect Daddy."

"Protect us from what?"

"From each other."

Just like that tears rolled down her mother's cheeks.

"I'll live with you *or* him, but not both of you. And if both of you want to be together and drive each other crazy, go ahead. Kill each other if that will make you feel better. Let me stay with my grandparents. Why? Because you are a despot. Despot means tyrannical ruler. You are a fucking despot."

Destiny watched her mother back away, watched her lower her hand, wipe her eyes.

"And Daddy is always grumpy, always stressed out. He's happy when he's not with you."

Destiny got out of the car, slammed the door. No kisses. No goodbye.

"Destiny." Her mother called out her name. "Destiny, I know you hear me."

Destiny turned around, ready to sigh, wanting to scream.

Then she saw the wealth of tears in her mother's eyes.

Her mother, so offended. Trying so hard to create an ideal world, failing miserably.

Carmen's voice cracked. "I love you, baby."

Just like that Destiny wanted to cry. But not for sentimental reasons. Her mother. Always impatient. Always swift to judge. The consummate actress, changeable, charming, contradictory, and cruel. And temperamental. Could shift gears so fast she could leave Destiny's father in a swirl of dust.

Destiny said, "Love you too."

Destiny stared at her mother. Her tears. The softness in her beautiful face. Her new hairstyle. Her new clothes. Her total makeover. The day after she and her mother had found out there was a Billie in her daddy's life, her mother came home with a new hairstyle, with new clothes. A makeover and two days of mall therapy. Destiny loved her mother, but wanted to be anybody but her when she grew up.

Carmen struggled, asked, "Want to see *The Vagina Monologues* with me next week? VIP seats. We can take Momma. Get our hair done. Manicures. Pedicures. Have a girls' day out."

Destiny almost snapped that maybe her mother should go see *Menopause: The Musical.*

Almost.

Carmen wiped her eyes and smiled.

Destiny wiped her eyes, smiled back.

She almost said it right then. Almost reminded her mother that her name was Destiny. *Destiny.* And destiny was something you couldn't control. Something you couldn't change.

Destiny almost told her that she wasn't her daddy. That she couldn't threaten her with child support and revoke her divorce papers to try and scare her. Almost snapped, went into a rage, and screamed out all the things she'd wanted to say for years.

But she didn't. Not because she was afraid to say what was in her heart.

Her mother had her inhaler up to her mouth again. Anxiety had closed her lungs. It started up again last year when her father left. When things got really horrific between her parents. One started drinking like a fish. The other was about to suffocate from loneliness. Asthma. But her father had stopped drinking. She watched her mother take a deep breath as she inhaled her steroid-ridden medication. Destiny waited to make sure her mother was okay. Now wasn't the time.

She had better insults. Other ways to express how she felt about her mother.

Destiny told her mother, "See you next Tuesday."

Destiny blew her mother a kiss.

"What does that mean, Destiny?"

"Means what it means." Destiny held on to her smile. "Love you like you love me."

"So scary." Her mother stared at her, shaking her head. "You're me looking back."

"What does that mean?"

Her mother took a breath. "Means what it means."

"Whatever."

She used her key to get in, head aching from where her mother had struck her.

She heard noises coming from the back.

"Destiny?"

"It's me, Big Momma."

"We up waiting for ya." Her grandfather. "Carmen here too?"

"Just me, Paw Paw."

Her grandparents. Both in bed already. Their shredder at the foot of the bed. Her grandparents always shredded their junk mail. Owned a heavy-duty monster shredder that ate up credit cards, junk mail that was still in the envelope, ate up anything. Always worried about identity theft. Her grandparents' eyes never came to her. Both were watching television. Oprah on TiVo. Terry McMillan and her ex-husband. Her grandparents, been in the States forever, still Jamaican to the bone. Destiny couldn't imagine a world that had no TiVo and only had three television channels. Four if you counted PBS.

Her grandmother. Outraged. "Dey dem kind a man dey Rent-A-Dread inna Negril."

Her grandfather, even-toned, "Nuff a dem dey pon di beach."

"The boy did well and now sey she have money and ting. And a dat him did want. Gay or not. But fi all a dat. Enough pure one hundred non-gay man we have a Jamaica. Dem idiot ya."

"Something wrong wid him. Da bredda dey need to good lick."

Their words were coming so fast. Destiny didn't understand anything they said.

Destiny hugged her grandmother, said, "Momma said Daddy moving back home."

"He supposed to." Her grandmother. "He your father. He married to your mother."

Destiny went around the bed, hugged her grandfather, sighed. "Going to bed."

Her grandmother. "Take the shredder back into mi office, will you, child?"

Her grandfather. "I can do it."

"Let her do it, William. Your back."

By then Destiny had already picked up the shredder. "I got it."

Then her grandparents, in harmony, in clear English, "Goodnight."

Shredder in hand, she walked away, left them watching Oprah.

Behind her the television went off. Early risers. They would be asleep soon.

Inside the bedroom, door closed, television on, bootleg version of *Baby Boy* playing, muted, with her saying all the dialogue, Tyrese's character now lying and telling his irate baby momma that sleeping with her coworker would be breaking the code and he would never break the code, CD player jamming a bootleg CD, Usher and Luda, the explicit version of "Lovers and Friends." Destiny had the phone up to her ear, calling the cellular number on the homemade business card the ghetto-entrepreneur had given her at Wherehouse.

Destiny said, "Whassup?"

"Who dis?"

"Destiny."

"Who Destiny?"

"Baby Phat. You met me at the Wherehouse."

"Which one you?"

"Baby Phat, remember? Uh, hello. We were inside doing the Mo?"

"Oh, right. 'Sup, Baby Phat?"

"Dag, you doing the Mo with somebody else already?"

"Didn't think you'd give a nigga a holla."

"What y'all doing now?"

"Watching movies on the DVD player. Getting blown."

"Sounds loud. Ya'll crunk over there."

"Like a motherfucka. Buncha us over here. You missing out. About to tape some shit."

Sagittarius child. December-born. She wondered why her Sagittarian curiosity never ended.

"I wanna hang for a minute."

"Shit, Baby Phat, c'mon through."

"Don't have a ride. Fifteen, remember?"

"Where you at?"

"Off Crenshaw and King. Almost across the street from Krispy Kreme."

On her bootleg DVD, Tyrese's face was between his baby momma's legs, eating her out.

"By Baldwin Hills mall?"

"Yeah. By the hoodrat mall."

"We ain't far from there. 'Bout five minutes. Stopped by this little get-together off Slauson."

"Cool. Then come swoop me up."

"We about to roll. Nigga hungry. Meet us up at Krispy Kreme."

"Nah. Pick me up at the bus stop over on Stocker and Crenshaw. Across from the Liquor Bank."

"No problem. On the way."

"Give me about thirty minutes."

Destiny eased down the hallway and peeped into her grandparents' bedroom, the home decorated in both the bright colors of Jamaica and relics from Barbados. It was close to midnight. Both were asleep. Destiny knew that as long as she was back before sunrise they'd never know she was gone. She could do this and get away with it, no problem. She'd done this many nights before.

Destiny went back into her bedroom. The same bedroom that was her mother's bedroom. It still had the same pink motif. Queen-sized bed with plenty of stuffed animals. Still had pictures of Michael Jackson and Prince on the wall. One feminine man with eyeliner and a Jheri curl and another man in high heels and a perm. Not soldiers. Go figure. Destiny locked the door. Hurried and changed clothes. Same Baby Phat jeans, this time with her boots, the ones with the three-inch heels. Boots she had stolen from her mother's closet. Jimmy Choo. Stretch suede. Three-inch heels. Boots that—in her mother's sea of unworn shoes—would never be missed. The same for the diamond earrings.

She put on lipstick, light makeup, then, like in the magazines, let her hair down.

She laughed. Laughed because of the lie she had told her mother. That she had to do an analysis of an Ogden Nash poem. "Fleas." The shortest poem ever written. Only three words long:

> *Adam*
> *Had 'em.*

Adults were so stupid.

She lied to her mother the same way her mother lied to her father, without evincing the slightest sign of fear or nervousness.

She put on a short leather jacket, one that stopped above her waist, showed off her butt, like it was the pot of gold at the end of a rainbow. She stood in the mirror, modeled, proud that she didn't look fifteen anymore.

Now she owned the face of a college girl.

The body of a woman.

She double-checked the bedroom door, made sure it was locked from the inside.

Then she opened the bedroom window, eased out like a cat, crept across the neighbor's yard, singing like Beyoncé, then looked up at the police helicopter flying overhead not too far away. Looking up at the ghetto bird was why she stumbled. A brick was in the grass. She looked around to see if anybody saw her lose her cute sway and almost fall. She frowned down at the brick. Then picked it up and put it in her designer purse, one she had stolen from her mother's many unused high-end purses. Shoes. Purses. Clothes. Dejection had changed her mother into a bona fide shopaholic. Destiny gave the purse the weight of the brick. Just in case she needed to hit somebody. Rehab centers were all up and down the boulevard, a reminder that this was the land of oppression and depression, the land of beggars and crackheads. Sometimes begging crackheads. She walked like Beyoncé, if only in her mind, never looking back as she headed up King Boulevard, moved into the sounds of sirens and loud music, stepped deeper into the bright lights and din of Crenshaw Boulevard, the devil waiting for her with open arms.

Destiny was just getting to the corner of Crenshaw and Stocker when a black SUV pulled up.

"Baby Phat, that your ass?"

"No, Mo, it's the tooth fairy."

"Damn, what your ass do?"

"Hair hooked up. That's all."

"I'm talking about your tight-ass frame." Those freckles and that Jamie Foxx smile. "You was looking good, but you wasn't looking that damn good a little while ago."

She laughed. "I was looking tore up, huh?"

"You like . . . like . . . like Ciara and J Lo and Christina Milian rolled into one."

She laughed again, false modesty. "You need to quit."

"Shit, might have to make you my girlfriend."

"Whatever."

A girl snapped, "Leave that young bitch alone and change the music, D'Andre."

Several girls and more guys were stuffed inside the truck. Two of the girls stared at Destiny. One girl was light-skinned, black-mixed-with-Asian. The other, black-mixed-with-Mexican. Same girls she had seen with them earlier. The kind of girl she wanted to be. The kind of girls in hip-hop videos. The girls wore tight clothes and brummagem costume jewelry, not the real deal like Destiny had on.

Destiny said, "You disrespecting me?"

The girls laughed and gave each other high fives.

The black-mixed-with-Mexican girl said, "She all over Mo; bitch stepping to your man."

"She ain't crazy." The black-mixed-with-Asian girl snapped her fingers, did the neck. "I will *beat a bitch's ass* if she even looks at my man, let alone trying to step to him. I don't play that shit."

Destiny snapped, "Your half-breed-looking ass got a problem with me?"

The girls looked at each other again, then four arrogant eyes cut Destiny up and down.

Destiny said, "I'm talking to you, bitch."

"Who you calling a bitch?"

"Come closer and I'll show both of you mutts who I'm calling a bitch, bitch."

"No, she didn't." The black-mixed-with-Mexican girl. "No, she didn't just call out your name."

The black-mixed-with-Asian girl. "Let's kick her ass, Lupe."

"I got your back, LaQuiesha."

The brothers laughed.

The black-mixed-with-Asian girl threw her purse down, was getting out of the SUV. She was at least four years older, at least five inches taller, at least twenty pounds heavier. Next to Destiny's frame, a Goliath in three-inch heels. Destiny stepped back, in a way that made it look like she was about to run, then moved back so she'd have enough room to grab the girl's hair, enough room to yank her off balance, enough room to sock her in the eye five or six times and send the girl straight to the pavement.

That was her plan.

That was what she did. Hit the girl more times than she could count. After the first blow the girl had grabbed her face. A shit-talker, not a fighter. One blow and she wanted to suck her momma's titty.

"Damn, Baby Phat. Lighten up on her ass."

The girl scrambled on the ground, kicked at Destiny, kept making threats.

Her purse.

Destiny thought about her purse.

Its weight. Its mass.

She swung her purse, the brick inside giving it power and momentum. Acceleration.

It hit the girl in the center of her face. With force.

Sounded like her face cracked.

"My face . . . you messed up my . . . I'm a model . . . an actress . . . not my face . . . not my face. . . ."

All around them, in SUVs and cars, brothers howled, laughed, gave each other dap.

The black-mixed-with-Asian girl was on the streets, disoriented, six feet of attitude now crawling between cars, crying, coughing, wiping away her own blood.

Destiny growled, "See you next Tuesday."

Purse in her right hand, Destiny looked at the girl's friend, a woman who was at least six feet tall, raven-haired, almond-eyed. Destiny held her arms out at her side, said, "What? What? What you gon' do, bitch? What? Talking all that bullshit. Now what? What? If you gonna bring it, bring it."

The camera was on her, she saw that red dot blinking in her face.

She was important. She had attention. She was the star.

The men looked at Destiny. Not in disgust, in awe.

They cheered, screamed for more.

She saw that men loved this kind of shit. Girl fights. Breasts flying. Asses bouncing as girls tore each other to shreds. She knew that men were aroused by the sight of women destroying each other.

Girl fights. The ultimate hand job. No better stroking for the male ego.

Cars passed by. Nobody stopped. Nobody intervened. Nobody cared.

This was Crenshaw Boulevard. This was Los Angeles. This was Southern California.

Destiny frowned at the black-mixed-with-Mexican girl in the truck, stared at another Goliath.

Eyes wide, mouth open, outside of trembling, the other girl didn't move.

The men were still cracking up, still laughing, music still bumping.

My pussy and my crack . . .

The black-mixed-with-Mexican girl screamed, "That's my jam, my jam, crunk it up, that's my jam!"

She moved over, made room for Destiny. Offered her plenty of space, the best seat. The throne.

Destiny didn't move, stared the girl down, said, "So we cool now or what?"

"*Girrrrrrrrrrrrrrrrrrl*, you my nigga! Come on and get in."

My pussy and my crack . . .

The girls in the SUV bounced and sang the song like it was their national anthem.

The roar of motorcycles came from the north. Around ten bikers rolled up, got caught at the light. The beautiful motorcycle the color of indigo was in the front, leading the way. That rider was popping a wheelie.

Same girls that she had seen earlier, when she was at Ladera Center with her parents.

Destiny got in, sat next to Lupe. D'Andre was passing a joint to another girl.

They drove away. Left the loser girl limping through traffic, doing her best to get out of the streets.

Destiny asked, "That chronic or stress?"

The hip language of the urban weedheads. The language of acceptance. D'Andre. "Stress."

"Stress? Awww, man, y'all whacked." Destiny shook her head. "Thought y'all were official. I was ready to blaze some chronic."

They laughed.

Mo asked, "What you know about chronic, Baby Phat?"

"It's harsher and the high is more . . . more . . . it's different, gets you right, know what I mean?"

"Baby Phat, you tight."

Destiny took a hit of the stress. "Peep this, I need to make a quick stop."

"Where?"

"Around the corner."

She told them to cut up Victoria, slip into View Park from the back way. Her mother had made that drive a thousand times. Always drove into View Park to see if her daddy was at Billie's house.

Since the day they saw her father and Billie on a date, she couldn't count the number of times her mother had driven by here in the middle of the night, couldn't count the number of times her mother had driven by her father's apartment with her lights off, angry when she saw that yellow motorcycle outside.

Was always stalking in the name of love.

Destiny knew the difference between stalking and true love.

That Me'shell N'degeocello song, the one her mother always listened to, the one about sitting outside somebody's door, begging her lover to come talk to her, the music made it seem like a love song, but the words weren't love. If they didn't want you, didn't want to talk to you, left you sitting outside in the rain, it was stalking.

Love greeted you with open arms. Stalking with a restraining order.

A light was on in Billie's bedroom window.

The woman her daddy looked so damn happy with.

The woman her mother hated.

Destiny got out of the SUV. Took the brick out of her purse.

"What your crazy ass about to do now, Baby Phat?"

"Be ready to roll when I come back."

They all laughed.

A moment later that brick crashed through the bedroom window.

She walked back to the SUV, her pace so casual.

That red light blinking in her face.

Still the star.

Then.

She felt something, as if someone were watching.

Across the street, parked diagonally from Billie's house, there was a white SUV.

The vehicle looked familiar. She tried, but couldn't make out the license plate.

Its windows not fogged over like the rest of the cars that had been on the streets most of the night. Couldn't be. She thought someone was inside that SUV, thought she saw someone move. Somebody ducked like they didn't want to be seen. Destiny's heartbeat sped up. She lowered her head. Destiny hurried back to her new friends.

Everyone laughed as the truck burned rubber getting away.

My pussy and my crack . . .

Destiny looked back. Saw the lights come on inside Billie's bedroom, thought she saw Billie run out onto the porch, but she was more concerned with the SUV. Saw that vehicle still sitting there. No lights. Not following them. Maybe no one was inside that white SUV. Maybe it was her imagination.

Lupe said, "Baby Phat, you one crazy bitch, you know that?"

"Got it from my momma."

"That right?"

"She owns the proclivity toward a negative and vindictive disposition."

Mo asked, "What that mean, Baby Phat?"

"She's the bitch to end all bitches."

Laughter.

Her mind was on the girl fight, glad she had won, but hoping that girl was okay. She wondered why that girl couldn't have been nice to her. Wondered why she had to be so mean. She hated that girl, hated herself. She felt like she was doing what her mother was doing with Billie. She had just fought for her right to hang with these guys, had fought for the right to be with Mo, same way her mother was willing to fight to be with her daddy.

As if it were coded in her DNA.

She wondered if she would have horrible periods like her mother used to have. Wondered if once a month the curse would really become a curse. If she would double over like she had been stabbed with a knife, heating pad on her stomach for days at a time, if she would need a man's hand to touch her belly, to massage the pain away, if she would have to have a baby to make the pain stop.

Then she knew why she threw the brick.

Not because of her mother. Not for her mother.

But because of the way her father had looked when he saw them, her and her mother, that day they ran into him and he was laughing, smiling, holding hands with Billie. When his cheerful face dissipated. For a moment he had looked at them with regretful eyes, as if he wished they didn't exist.

Right now Destiny wished she didn't exist.

Western Boulevard.

Motel row.

About twenty people were in the cramped motel room when they walked inside.

Dancing wherever. Kissing wherever. Half naked. Blown to the bone.

A couple of the guys and one of the girls were freestyling.

Misogynistic music blended with a steady stream of billingsgate.

Destiny's musical tastes ran the gamut from Bach to Janis Joplin to Usher.

Living in the hood and being shipped off to white-bred private schools made her versatile.

Most of the men were out of shape, not that attractive. Jay-Z without the money.

All the women were either light-skinned or exotic or had huge asses, some all three.

Just like in the videos.

Some were touching each other.

Just like in the videos.

"That's my jam! That's my motherfucking jam!"

The room was straight crunkdified.

All the women were up, dancing the 1, 2 step and chanting, *"This beat is automatic, supersonic, hypnotic, funky fresh."*

One of the brothers kept that video camera turned on, recording all the madness.

Songs and dancing came and went.

"I ain't sayin' she a goldgigga, but she ain't messin' wit no broke . . ."

One of the guys popped in a DVD. Part of the documentary filmed on the 'Shaw, what they recorded last week. The cars. Destiny saw girls younger than her giving college-age brothers blow jobs as they drove, high school sisters doing the same in between cars, grown women having sex in the back of SUVs as the drivers rolled on, all that action with LAPD cruising and flashing lights in the background.

Destiny said, "Look at those hos."

The black-and-Mexican girl smiled at Destiny, walked away.

Destiny turned away from that video, danced her way to the other side of the room.

A girl was on the bed counting a lot of colorful pills. Counting pills like she was a bank teller counting money.

Destiny asked her, "What are those?"

Brown eyes looked her up and down as the neck snaked. "Who you?"

"Baby Phat."

Neck kept on snaking. "Who you wit?"

"Mo' 'nem."

"Dem my niggas." Neck stopped snaking. "Then you cool."

"What you got?"

"Depends on what you need. Antihistamines. Cold meds. Ecstasy. The blue pills are Viagra. Those are the most popular right now. I've got some RU-486. That's off the charts too."

"What is RU-486?"

"Kill pill." Matter-of-factly. "If you think you're pregnant, pop one of these, gets rid of the baby."

"Just like that?"

"These are sweet. Problem solved just like that. No doctor, no nothing."

"You slangin' those?"

"Yeah. I have a mad hookup on this shit. It's a nice little gig." She hit a joint and laughed. "Sell niggas the blue pill to keep their shit hard, then sell the bitches the Kill Pill to make the problem go away."

"Vicious cycle."

"Shit. Profitable cycle. You know how it jumps off at Crenshaw High. And at Audubon Middle School. Those young, dumb-ass, hot-to-trot girls lettin' high school niggas get all up in the cut."

"In the cut?"

"Pussy. In the cut."

"Right, right. In the cut."

Destiny thought about the high school boy she had given herself to. She used to sneak out the window to be with him. Now he was gone to college. Now she was alone.

"Shit, between Audubon Middle School and Crenshaw High, I sell so many of these fucking pills it's a damn shame. And don't get me to talking about all the other schools in L.A. Unified." The girl hit her joint, hit it hard. A pro in her own arena. Destiny thought the girl looked her age, but acted so much older. Like she had aged in dog years because of living the street life. "I'm slangin' tough, but I'm helping out the community. Keeping these young-ass girls from being young-ass mommas."

"You could make a grip in Bel Air."

"Baby, that's way on the other side of the 405."

"You could charge more than you do to the peeps at L.A. Unified."

The hard-faced girl raised a brow, smiled a smile that asked Destiny if she had lost her mind. Bel Air was a world away, her eyes said that. The girl's *tsk* and twisted lips said that she was more comfortable hustling in the areas that had low graduation rates and standardized test scores that never rise.

Destiny watched the girl put pills in plastic bottles. Some went in Tylenol bottles. Others went in Midol bottles. Others in Anacin. The RU-486's were gathered last, counted, and put in an Aleve bottle.

Destiny said, "You keep them in regular medicine bottles?"

"Slick, huh?"

"They don't get mixed up?"

"They all get they own bottle. That way I don't get 'em mixed up. Not only that, if I get pulled over and somebody look in my purse, they won't know. That way they don't look suspicious."

The girl laughed the laugh of a street-made genius. Destiny joined in out of kindness.

She asked, "What's your name?"

"Goldie."

Goldie. The complexion of her skin. The color of her weave. Thin girl, huge breasts.

Goldie said, "Them some bad-ass boots you got on."

"Thanks."

"You look kinda familiar."

Destiny asked, "Where you go to school?"

"Crenshaw. You?"

"Other side of town. That's why I was saying you could make a grip up in Bel Air."

"Bel Air? You stay way up there?"

"Hell, no. I'm from the hood. I stay in Leimert Park, that's my spot."

"Leimert Park ain't no hood."

"It's where niggas from South Central move to. Off MLK. MLK is as hood as hood can get." She tried to sound down, tough. "Chillin' wit my grandparents. Live right off the 'Shaw. Where you stay?"

Stay. Not live. Stay.

She had heard her daddy say that white people lived in America. Black people *stayed* here.

"East side most of the time. Palmdale when I can get a ride up there. Wherever in between." Goldie hit the joint. "Don't really have no family, so I ain't got no real address or nothing."

"You holding it down."

"For real. I'm cool. Gettin' my hustle on. See something you might like?"

Destiny smiled, her world now light and serene.

A song came on she loved and she went to the middle of the room and danced with the strangers. Shook her ass, dropped it like it was hot, snaked. Laughed with them. She felt good.

She got into a conversation with her new friends.

She told them her problems. The weed made her talk from her heart.

The dark-skinned guy. Jay-Z with no money. "Hey, check this shit out."

" 'Sup."

"Baby Phat's parents getting a *deeeeeee-vorce*."

"No shit?"

"Damn. First it was white boy Nick what's-his-face and Jessica whatchamacallit."

"Babyface and Tracey, don't forget them."

"Now Baby Phat's parents?"

Laughter. The kind that said no one was impressed with pedestrian people's problems.

Destiny nodded. The world had become surreal. "The donors *were* getting a fucking divorce. I have no idea what they're trying to prove now. The way they act, I'd rather live with Shaq and Kobe."

"Donors?"

"Sperm donor. Egg donor."

"Donors. That's tight. Need to use that. Need to put that donor shit on a track."

Destiny said, "Rhymes with loner."

"And boner."

"Peep this," Destiny said, then broke freestyle, postulating and throwing her hands, pointing fingers, looking hard, fitting in. "Put a jimmy on that boner, ain't looking for no donor."

One of the guys jumped in: "Your ass gets pregnant, you'll be all a-loner."

Laughter.

"That why you threw that brick through that window?"

Destiny hit the stress again. Third time getting high, already a pro. "Guess so."

"You sixteen and your parents are still together?"

"Yeah." She choked a little. "I mean, no. They getting back together. But it's all fucked up."

"Damn."

"You sixteen and your folks still fucking?"

Laughter.

She didn't correct them that time. In her mind she was sixteen.

"Somebody better call them world records people."

"Your parents actually got married?"

"Strange shit. I have no idea what it's like to have a damn daddy."

"Yeah, that is some strange shit right there."

"Better to not have two parents." Destiny shrugged it off. "They fight all the time."

"At least they fight. My folks ain't said shit to each other for the last ten years."

"Why not?"

" 'Cause my daddy on lockdown for three strikes. Momma ain't accepting his calls."

Laughter.

Someone asked Destiny, "If all they do is fight, why they still together?"

Destiny took a breath. "They been together since . . . shit, before I was born."

"Been together since *before* you were born?"

"I know. A trip, ain't it?"

"That some white people shit."

Laughter.

Music blasted. Ying Yang Twins. Bumping "Halftime."

Room a haze of smoke.

In between watching the women drop it like it was hot, GED conversations filled the air.

Almost two in the morning. Three hours before she had to be back in her bed. Already planning to pretend she was sick so she could sleep all day. Knowing she could get away with it with ease.

Her world was crunk. Mo smiled at her. So damn sexy.

The black-mixed-with-Mexican girl came over with two drinks, handed her one.

"Had to hook my homegirl up. Get my Baby Phat something to drink."

"Fo' sho."

The girl handed Destiny a glass, then went away, dancing up a storm.

Destiny sipped. Didn't care what she was drinking. Just sipped.

They passed her the blunt. She took a hit.

Puff the magic dragon, puff it again, then pass it along.

She sipped.

After that her world became peaceful, so very placid.

Then her world went black.

"Fick mich in meinen arsch! Ja! Aah! Fick mech!"

Destiny was naked.

For the most part.

Pants pulled down, hanging from one leg.

Blouse open.

Bra loosened.

Breasts exposed.

She was naked.

A groan escaped her as she rolled over on her side. The bed she was on squeaked. It was cheap. So unlike the furniture her mother owned. Furniture her father had bought. Furniture they fought over at the dimming of their relationship. Furniture her mother won the rights to in court.

"Oh! Fick mich! Fick mich!"

Destiny ached.

Between her legs she ached.

Stickiness.

She knew it was blood.

Had to be.

Not period blood.

The other kind of blood.

She pulled herself upright.

Coughed.

Pulled herself out of a world of limitless time and space.

Fought her way out of the darkness.

She opened her eyes.

They watered.

She coughed again.

Her eyes narrowed as the light invaded her senses.

"Fick mich in meinen arsch! Ja! Aah! Fick mech!"

The voices came from the television. A black man and a German woman having sex.

Destiny pulled herself around to the side of the bed.

Her foot touched the carpet.

Squish.

Rubbery. Wet.

Squish.

"Oh! Fick mich! Fick mich! Ja!"

She looked down.

The squish was the sound of her bare foot on top of a condom.

Eyes went to the floor.

Six.

Seven.

She stopped counting condoms when she got to eight.

"Oh! Fick mich! Fick mich! Aah! Fick mech!"

The scent of blunts.

Empty bottle of hard liquor.

Fifteen years old.

Going on sixteen.

Already a woman.

Still a child.

Naked. For the most part.

In an empty motel room.

Empty Pizza Hut cartons. Doritos bags. Subway sandwich wrappers.

Nine.

Ten.

Eleven.

Close to a dozen used condoms on the floor.

She wanted to scream.

But she didn't.

Her mother always screamed.

She didn't want to be like her mother, not now, not ever.

She hurt.

She hurt bad.

"Fick mich in meinen arsch! Ja!"

She opened the door praying for darkness, but the sunlight slapped her face.

Sunlight.

The heat of a new day.

The rays blinded her, slapped her over and over again.

"Oh shit, oh shit, oh shit, oh shit, shit, shit, shit, shit."

Her heart beat so fast. She couldn't think. Her IQ hovering at 130 and she couldn't think.

The chipped, weathered sign standing high on Western Boulevard said CASURA BAY MOTOR INN.

Casura Bay. On the same strip as Snooty Foxx and Mustang Motel.

Hookers' haven.

Even the palm trees looked like whores.

She closed the door, staggered back into the room, walked circles, one hand grabbing at her hair.

Couldn't think.

"Oh shit, oh shit, oh shit, oh shit, shit, shit, shit, shit."

She looked down at her feet.

Saw pink toenails on bare feet.

No socks.

No boots.

She panicked, searched the room, threw back the covers on the bed, searched the floor.

Her mother's Jimmy Choo boots were gone.

"Oh shit, oh shit, oh shit, oh shit, shit, shit, shit, shit."

Not too far from her grandparents', but too far at the same time.

Destiny found her way into the bathroom, found towels, cleaned herself the best she could.

Her face, the skin on her neck felt sticky.

She pulled her hair back into a ponytail, took to the stairs, stairs that shook under her weight.

Concrete stairs that were coarse on her bare feet.

Light-headed.

Last few hours blurry.

Remembered taking a drink.

Feeling so crunk after that.

So carefree.

So uninhibited.

So adult.

But still. Unable. To. Remember.

Her soreness slowed her down, but not much.

Fear gave her pace.

So much traffic on Western Boulevard.

The din of Martin Luther King, Jr., Boulevard was a block away. Her grandparents' house no more than two miles west, straight up the urban strip toward Leimert Park, straight toward the hoodrat mall.

Barefoot, she hurried toward King Boulevard, had to get to the bus stop.

So much traffic, but not many people were walking. It was Saturday morning. Not many people walked in L.A. Unless they were on the beach, or Third Street Promenade, or up at Universal City Walk. Outside of strolling in places that attracted tourists, wearing out the soles of shoes was a sign of being destitute. Public transportation was seen as a lower-class necessity, not a way to save the environment.

The bus stop was filled with Mexicans and blue-collar workers with darker skin. One young black girl had her three children with her. Same for another young Spanish girl who had a baby on her hip.

The bus was heading their way, everybody moving in closer to get on the already-crowded bus.

Destiny reached for her purse.

Then she realized her purse was gone.

"Oh shit, oh shit, oh shit, oh shit, shit, shit, shit, shit."

Her money was gone.

"Oh shit, oh shit, oh shit, oh shit, shit, shit, shit, shit."

Just like her boots.

"Oh shit, oh shit, oh shit, oh shit, shit, shit, shit, shit."

She looked at the man. Short, brown-skinned with silver capped teeth.

He smiled at her.

She asked, "Can you give me enough money to catch the bus? I have to get back home."

A blank look washed over the man's face. His eyes saying, *No hablo inglés.*

With desperation she said, "*Dinero.* Can you loan me bus fare? I need to get to . . . *mi casa.*"

She grinned the way disadvantaged brown-skinned people had grinned at her when she and her mother had traveled into Tijuana, held her hands out like cups, the universal language of the beggar.

The short man lost his thin smile and shook his head emphatically, moved away from Destiny.

She cursed because the poor avoided, maybe even despised, the ones they thought were poorer.

Poverty, that disease no one wanted to catch.

She had no Chiclets to offer, no oranges, no flowers, nothing to barter with.

These people worked too hard to give money away to a barefoot stranger in designer jeans.

Destiny hurried up King Boulevard, arms folded across her breasts, the bus zooming past her.

She put her thumb out, but nobody stopped. Nobody would. Not in L.A.

Wal-Mart.

An anchor store at Baldwin Hills Crenshaw Plaza.

Used to be Macy's when Destiny was growing up, she remembered that.

Then Macy's wanted no part of this community.

Too much employee theft, Destiny remembered hearing her mother say that.

In a land of melanin-filled consumers, no money was being made by Mr. Macy on this corner, his old-school economic pimping wasn't thriving, not like on the other side of town.

Macy's closed overnight, gave employees no notice—no notice meant no time for the leaders in the community to organize a protest. Just met the employees one Friday morning, greeted them with no smile, didn't let the blue-collar workers inside in the building, and sent a black representative to shower the frustrated with an Uncle Tom smile and let them know that they didn't work at Macy's anymore.

Now three floors of Wal-Mart.

The superstore that would run every black mom-and-pop store in the community out of business.

The ones that were left. The ones who refused to give in.

She remembered hearing her daddy say that.

Fuck that.

Destiny knew that Wal-Mart had everything she needed.

She walked into Wal-Mart barefoot and unnoticed, blended in with the crowd.

She shopped.

Picked up hand towels. Soap. Tennis shoes.

God bless Wal-Mart and its one-stop shopping.

Found the bathroom.

Took off her smoke-smelling blouse, washed her skin, and put on a T-shirt.

Put on new underwear.

New bra.

Then.

The tennis shoes.

She left Wal-Mart, mixed with a crowd of Hispanic girls, and walked out into the mall.

Destiny went across the parking lot, stopped in front of Magic Johnson's movie theater.

Hungry.

Aching between her legs.

Looking up at the sunlight.

Such a beautiful day.

Too scared to go home.

Or even call.

She decided that she was going to run away.

Far away.

As soon as she found some food.

Got some money.

She closed her eyes.

Saw them again.

Six. Seven. Eight condoms.

Saw more.

A wave of nausea swept over her body.

But she didn't vomit.

She opened her eyes, was up on her feet, dizzy, about to leave.

But then the men came.

The men in matching jackets.

One black. One Mexican.

One thin. One buffed.

They came in a hurry.

They stopped her.

Actually they had caught up with her.

Security from Wal-Mart.

"Oh shit, oh shit, oh shit, oh shit, shit, shit, shit, shit."

Destiny ran.

seven

BILLIE

"YOUR LUNATIC WIFE JUST THREW A BRICK THROUGH MY BEDROOM WIN-
dow, Keith."

Keith took a hard breath. "Impossible."

"Impossible? I'm looking at the damn brick, Keith."

"And I'm looking at Carmen."

Seconds after the brick flew through my window, Viviane ran downstairs, stumbled in the darkness, naked, pulling her housecoat around her
body. She was screaming out my name, asking what the hell that noise was.
I heard her lover's heavy footsteps coming right behind her.

I was on the phone screaming at Keith.

I snapped, "She just tried to kill me, Keith. I saw her driving away. I was
just on my porch and saw the bitch driving away."

He stressed, "Carmen did not throw a brick through your window,
Billie."

"Well, the bitch had somebody do it."

Then I heard that bitch. Carmen was behind him, going off, swearing
that I was the one flying over the cuckoo's nest. She was calling me all
kinds of names, most of the insults I didn't understand because they were
Jamaican.

I cursed her a thousand ways, dared him to put her on the phone.

Keith hung up on me.

While her still-naked midnight lover backed away and headed back upstairs, those stairs creaking under his weight, Viviane had gone over to the
window, her mouth wide open like she was in shock, had stepped around

the broken glass, was looking at the damage, shaking her head, cursing in a combination of English, Ebonics, and Korean.

She asked, "What the hell is going on, Billie?"

I swallowed, my saliva feeling so thick. I summed it up in two words. "I'm pregnant."

West Los Angeles. Almost a year ago. Trader Joe's. A hybrid of gourmet grocery store and international supermarket. The epitome of L.A. eating culture. Pushing carts through the aisles. Saw him looking at me when I was picking fruit. Those eyes. He smiled. I did too. Again in the frozen food section. He smiled. Again I reciprocated.

I broke the silent flirtation and rolled my basket over to Keith.

My first words to him were, "Look, if you're going to keep passing by me and staring at me, and I'm going to keep passing by and staring back, we might as well introduce ourselves."

He was surprised, stood there holding frozen salmon in his hand. A hand that wore no ring.

"I'm Billie. What's your name?"

He smiled. "I'm . . . damn . . . I can't remember my own name right now."

We laughed.

I said, "Why don't you put down the frozen fish and check your license?"

"Keith. I'm Keith."

It cracked me up that he couldn't remember his own name. It was quite a first impression, a powerful one. Nothing that would make U.S. history, but would definitely make it into my journal.

After he recovered, the next thing he said was, "You know who you look like?"

"You tell me."

"Like Beyoncé and Tyra Banks put together."

"You trying to say I have a big ass and a Klingon-sized forehead?"

He laughed. I mean he laughed hard.

I did too. That was our first laugh. Our laughter became a song of happiness.

My hair was down, had just got it hooked up, looking fresh, hanging to my tailbone. Had on my wide-frame leopard-print glasses, yellow tint on the lenses. Leather, low-rise hip huggers. Black tank top, no bra. Full lips dressed up in Mac Lipglass. No designer clothes. Never wore any. Didn't have a designer budget. The only thing name brand I owned was the Mickey Mouse watch I was wearing, a watch I've worn for twenty years, present from my parents. Keith's eyes had been on me since I walked in Trader Joe's.

He recovered, said, "You got the best of each one of them."

"Good answer."

Keith and I were still strangers. No emotional attachment, only mutual interest. Minutes later we were in the parking lot, Mervyns to our left, Sav-On to our right, still getting our flirt on.

I asked, "You ride?"

"Used to. Long time ago. Had a 750 when I was in college."

"Really?"

"That was how I got around."

I asked, "Ever think about riding again?"

"Doubt if I'll ever become a born-again biker."

"That's too bad. I need somebody to ride with on weekends."

That was a lie. A flirtatious lie. I kept touching my hair, touching my face. My mother used to do that when she stared at my father. I softened and my eyes lit up, just like Momma. I put on a gentle smile that could charm the feathers off a bird. Keith flattered me with his words and savored me with his eyes. The wide grin that was posted up on his handsome face, all of that told me that I was looking damn good. Loved my hair long because it looked awesome when I was rocking my bike. It flew like it was my cape. My low-cut leather pants, they were deadly. Whenever I put on my leather and hopped on my bike, all I have to say is that I could cause some serious traffic jams. And an accident or two.

He said, "Wish I could get a bike and ride. Have my daughter most weekends."

I said, "You said you have a daughter?"

He smiled. "Yep."

"Oh. How many?"

"One."

That caught me off guard. You could tell a lot about a man—or a woman, for that matter—by what they bought when they shopped. The contents of the basket were a tell. Keith didn't buy much, a lot of single-serving-sized foods, nothing that screamed that he had a family at home. Juices. Turkey sausage. Egg whites. Fruit. Wheat bread. Frozen pancakes. Not a single feminine product was in his basket.

I asked, "How . . . uh . . . how old is your daughter?"

"Fifteen. Has a vocabulary out of this world. Half the time I have no idea what she's talking about. She's doing a paper on global warming. She's using a photo of Mount Kilimanjaro stripped of its snowcap as dramatic testimony for action against global warming."

I repeated, "Dramatic testimony for action against global warming?"

"Her words, not mine."

He'd become the proud father. I loved that and hated that all at once.

I could've turned and walked away. By sunset I would've forgotten about him and that charming smile. Would've forgotten about his beige skin and freckled nose. Would've forgotten about his eyes.

Could've. Should've. But I didn't.

I asked, "How old are you, if you don't mind my asking?"

"Forty in June."

"Cancer?"

"Gemini. You?"

"Leo. Fire sign. Thirty-four on my next birthday."

"Pegged you for being mid-twenties."

For a moment insecurity crawled over my skin, tried to settle into my smile. Nobody liked feeling old. Nobody liked looking in the mirror and see their youth fading with each blink.

I played it off, joked, "Well, not being married and having no kids will keep you looking younger."

I smiled. It wasn't the ideal situation, but that wasn't bad. As you get older the reality of dating changes. That fantasy of meeting a man who had no children or no ex-wives went out the window. You expected men over thirty to have a child, if not children. If he said he didn't have children you either thought he was gay or lying. That's part of getting older, of being older. Part of growing up and interfacing with the real world. But the kid thing could be a deal-breaker, a nonnegotiable. If his daughter was a newborn, maybe even less than five years old, hell no, not good. A teenager was better. If you fell into a relationship and the kid was older, you didn't have to play surrogate baby momma. No trips to Disneyland with a screaming rug rat. All you had to do was be cool and be a friend, if that much.

"How long have you been divorced?"

"Almost divorced."

"What is *almost* divorced?"

"Just waiting on the paperwork to go through so I can rent the forum and throw a big-ass party."

Divorced people were a different breed.

My roommate and her ex-husband had had a horrible divorce, lots of cussing and screaming, but had booty calls up until the decree was approved. They fucked through their divorce and fucked after.

Men would always be men. Same went for women.

So, right off the bat I knew Keith was a candidate for baby momma drama.

That left me concerned. Tentative. Wanting to break away from those hypnotic gray eyes.

Still, Keith strolled with me, helped me load my groceries inside Viviane's Mustang. The Mustang that used to belong to her ex-husband. The one he adored and she won in court and neglected out of spite. He put my empty basket to the side, then I followed him to his dirty SUV.

Keith. Born in June. When Geminis fell in love, they put all their energy in that direction. When Geminis stopped loving, that was all she wrote. Knowing that made me feel a lot better about his situation.

He asked me, "You live around here?"

I leaned against his SUV, and he stood in front of me, that smile so infectious. So positive. It was hard not to reciprocate. Couldn't just walk away from him. My brain had taken a wonderful first-impression Polaroid— created a composite of all the signals given off by a new experience. Direct eye contact. Shy, but not afraid. Firm handshake. Square shoulders. Pretty face with some roughness, very Rick Fox, in my mind. His smooth voice. Wasn't wearing name-brand clothes. No mack daddy conversation. That emotional punch hit me all at once, formed an impression larger than I had realized.

I said, "I've been living with a friend, Viviane, for the last couple of years. Only planned on staying with her a couple of months, but it's been working out for both of us. Big house. Plenty of space."

"Well, I've tumbled from Baldwin Hills down to Leimert Park now. Renting. One-bedroom spot."

That was good. A local call. With rising gas prices, geographically desirable was always good.

He asked, "What do you do?"

I told him I sang a little. Not as much as I used to. I could sing second soprano, but I was an alto. With a decent vibrato. Picked that up from imitating Whitney Houston. The Leo in me loved the attention, but for some reason I was always a background singer, not for lack of skills. Always ended up being the girl in the tight jeans and sexy tops that stood to the side, away from the spotlight.

Keith said, "So you sing."

I didn't really have the discipline to be a real singer. Didn't like all the politics and bullshit and being in a studio with asshole producers who wanted to have sex with you to help you with your career. Never understood the correlation between fucking me and helping me. I wasn't interested in blow-jobbing my way up the *Billboard* charts. And right now, no matter how good I sounded when I stepped up to the microphone, I was a little too old for the game.

I told him, "Stopped singing. Then I was a flight attendant for about two years."

I told Keith that I flew for the benefits and buddy passes. Was tired of being stationary, thought flying would help ease that anxiety. Got to go to Amsterdam, Brazil, Paris, the islands. And at the same time, if I wasn't flying, I taught a motorcycle training course at Cerritos College.

I said, "And a substitute teacher."

"What else you do?"

I laughed. Told him that at night I headed to the Temple Bar in Santa Monica. Where the girls were hot and the vibe was straight wicked. Underrated and well-received artists like Sy Smith, the Justice Leeg, and Geno Young brought the neo-soul that rocked the house. The duo Best Kept Secret put on a damn good show, and then my other favorites were Erin Anova and Rahsaan Patterson. Told him he had to hear Hope sing "The Rain Don't Last."

Keith said, "I've never heard of those singers."

"Then you really need to check out the spot."

Keith said he was free the next night, so he said he might meet me at the Temple Bar.

I said, "When you get to the door, ask for Ducati."

"Who is that?"

"Kind of bike I rock. My alter ego. My club name."

I told Keith that one night I was riding my bike to work and this guy damn near ran me down trying to catch up with me. Yellow leather jacket on a yellow bike always turned heads. He did photos for a motorcycle magazine that had a section dedicated to Ducati girls. Liked the way I rode. Loved my bike and my gear. Wanted me to pose for some shots riding my bike in full gear. He took a look at me in my tight jeans and low-cut top, my makeup in full effect, and asked if I would pose in a swimsuit as well.

Keith asked, "Did you?"

"I said yes to both."

"Was he just trying to hit on you?"

"He's so gay. So he was legit. Needed the cash. Signed a contract. Did the photo shoot. Got paid. The whole nine. I mean, he had the hookup. The pictures he used were the ones he took with me on the 749 and the 999."

"Damn. You know about motorcycles." Keith laughed. "So you're a model too."

"Wouldn't say all that. It was one-shot. I didn't get my own billboard on Sunset Boulevard, but I did make cover and centerfold in a hip-hop magazine. It's a small publication, but the photo was tight. Had a makeup artist come in, one of the Hollywood sisters who works on movies. Had a hairstylist come in and do my hair up real nice. Surprised me. It was the first issue for urban bikers. Tight. Surprised that I let them talk me into posing on my bike in a thong. This body is over thirty, but thank God for being a gym rat all these years. All the bikers were ragging me about it, asking me to sign it."

"In a thong?"

"You okay?"

"Just stuck on the part where you said you were in a thong."

I laughed.

He asked, "What color?"

"Bright yellow. Like my bike."

"Matching bra?"

"No bra. Had a jacket on, but no bra."

"Where can I pick the magazine up?"

"I'm not telling."

We laughed.

He asked, "What time is a good time to stop by and check out the music?"

"Anytime after ten-thirty. Place will be in fifth gear by then."

"That's pretty late for a workingman."

"Not for the nocturnal. Sy should be on by then. If you haven't seen her show you'll be in for a treat. If you like rap, then come earlier and check out the Justice Leeg. Or just hang out at the bar."

"I'll see if I can."

"You don't have to stay long. Have a drink and you can be back home before Leno goes off."

"Why don't you give me your number?"

"I'll give it to you. At the Temple Bar."

"You playing a game?"

"Nope. Just have to be sure you're not."

"What does that mean?"

"Means I can understand if you can't get away from the wife."

"No wife to get away from."

"Then pop a No Doz and come through after ten-thirty."

He smiled. "Will you be wearing a yellow thong tomorrow night?"

"Guess you'll have to come to Santa Monica to find out."

I was anxious, couldn't wait to get to work the next night. Wore my sexiest leather pants, had my face done up like I was auditioning for the lead in an independent film. Three-inch biker heels, sexy boots made by Harley. Ass was looking super-tight. Had on a brown sleeveless T-shirt. Funky and mod. Had Michael Jackson's face and round Afro on the front, a throwback to his J-5 days when he was brown-skinned and qualified to be a member of the NAACP, framed by the words FREE MICHAEL.

One of the waitresses had on a T-shirt that had Robert Blake's face on it. Framed by the words NOT GUILTY. But on the back it had a picture of Robert Blake from his TV series. The image of a bullet hole in the material over the words FUCK WITH BARETTA, YOU GET A BARETTA. The DJ had on a T-shirt that had a picture of Scott Peterson, handcuffed, wearing his San Quentin orange jumpsuit. Instead of getting a lethal injection, it showed him sitting in an electric chair. The word GUILTY over his head.

This was my crew. Our political statements and funky little T-shirt competition in full effect.

Next thing I knew, some stranger at the bar called out to me, "Ducati, can I get a mimosa?"

I loved that. I'd been called a lot of names but never had a nickname before I bought my bike.

Everybody wanted to feel special in some way. Everybody needed some kind of love.

I don't think I have ever felt as special as the night I was at the bar, in my zone, singing and dancing and being the queen of mixology, making mimosas, sloe comfortable screws, and gorilla farts for faceless patrons, and saw Keith walk in. He was dressed in all black. Looked damn good.

Electricity ran through my body.

Not because Sy was onstage singing and the crowd was bumping.

His smile did that to me. And that same electricity settled between my legs.

I didn't expect him to come hang out with the dreamers and slackers. He might've been on the road to divorce, but he had married, had a kid. Had made decisions. Had tried things. Had his degree.

I was an overachieving underachiever. A professional dilettante renting a room in View Park.

I'd started a lot of things, but in reality had finished nothing.

Sy was singing her ass off.

And Keith was here looking so damn good it was straight-up ridiculous.

I looked up at the clock. Ten-thirty on the dot.

He was punctual and didn't have a wife, at least not that night.

Just like that I was infatuated.

I didn't care if he had a kid. He seemed like a nice guy. A responsible man.

I didn't care if he had an almost-ex-wife. Right then she was faceless and it wasn't that serious.

He said that the relationship with his estranged wife was over. I believed him.

I could make this work for me, could see him without interacting with his kid. Or his ex-wife.

That meant no baby momma drama would be heading my way.

And even if none of what he said was true, something inside me shifted into the Don't Care zone.

I knew I wanted to be with him.

Not in a forever kind of way; in a right now, *carpe diem* kind of way.

He was twelve seconds away.

My breathing caught in my chest.

Then four seconds away.

Made myself breathe, made myself smile.

Then he was so close to me I could smell his freshness.

He stood at the bar and smiled at me.

Just like that, I was wet.

Couldn't play it off, couldn't shake it off, not like I wanted to.

His Gemini to my Leo. Air and fire. That fire inside of me wanted him to see the yellow thong I had on underneath my leather pants. Wanted to pretend I was onstage, wanted to be the center of his attention. Wanted to set free my sexual libido and see if the Gemini in him could keep up.

I played it cool, real cool, hoped thought bubbles weren't floating over my head.

He said, "Saw your Ducati. Sweet. Sleek. Fashionable. Aerodynamic. Like you."

I blushed. "Let me guess. Greyhound or cognac?"

"Easy Jesus."

"E & J? Had you pegged for a Greyhound man, maybe cognac."

"You're trying to be a psychic too?"

"And a surgeon at Daniel Freeman on Wednesdays."

"That explains all the malpractice."

"And a lawyer on Fridays."

"Would rather French-kiss a rattlesnake than accept a drink from a lawyer."

"Why the long face?"

"Soon-to-be ex is a lawyer."

"What's her sign?"

"Aries."

"The first sun sign in the zodiac. Selfish and quick-tempered. Impulsive and impatient."

"Not into that zodiac crap." He shrugged. "But that sounds about right."

Now I knew. His soon-to-be ex was an attorney. That was the part that got to me.

I turned away from him so I could make his drink, hiding my intimidation behind a smile.

A friggin' lawyer. Hearing that made me feel as if I didn't have a purpose-driven life.

Just like that I was through with Keith. I was done with him before we ever got started.

But when I handed him his drink, our hands touched. Skin grazed skin. That gap between us closed.

Again, electricity settled in sensual places where electricity shouldn't settle.

Music faded away, couldn't hear Sy and her band rocking the house anymore. The horns and drum kicks, all the sweet lyrics, the cocky and funny lyrics, faded. My world went quiet. Didn't see anybody else in the room. Like when I rode, I had tunnel vision, only saw what was in front of me.

He had told me that he had been the one to break it off.

I was thirty-three. Seasoned. Not a neophyte who needed to be indoctrinated into the world of dating; didn't need to have a two-day orientation and get schooled on the philosophy of this game.

I knew that even if Keith had broken it off, that was better, but wasn't much better. It usually meant there was a bitter, clinging, determined harpy somewhere in the background.

But I didn't care. Had a deepening itch for him already.

Keith saw my nipples were hard, poking out on both sides of Michael Jackson's pale face like devil's horns. He grinned at my dual erections. Knew I wanted to give him a coochie coupon. Hell, fuck a coochie coupon. I wanted to give him a season pass on this ass.

Wanted to dust this pussy off and wrap it around him so bad.

He asked, "What's up after this?"

I asked, "What do you want to be up after this?"

The fireplace was on. Candles lit. Two shot glasses and an unfinished game of chess were on the coffee table. A bottle of dark liquor and most of our inhibitions almost gone.

Keith and I were in my living room—well, the living room of the house where I was renting a room—on the oversized love seat, fondling each other like two high school kids. My roommate wasn't home and that bodacious fireplace made us glow. My CD was on and Badu was bringing up the background.

We kissed until it was too late to turn back.

He touched my breasts. I cooed, purred like a cat, wiggled with that sensation. He had my T-shirt pulled up, right breast in his warm hand. Then his tongue was on my nipple, making circles, then sucking me, taking as much as he could in his mouth. My hand was between his legs, rubbing.

I needed this itch scratched. My body needed this so damn bad. Needed to feel a man's touch.

I struggled with his pants, told him, "Take it out. I want to see it."

I was so damn tipsy.

He unzipped his pants. Fished out his penis, held it. It was long, but not hard, semi-erect.

I licked my lips, swallowed, caught my breath, squeezed my legs together.

I whispered, "Stroke it for me."

"Sing."

"Mama's Gun" was playing on the sound system. First I hummed, then I sang along with Erykah, sang low and easy, motioned at Keith in a way that told him to hold up his end of the bargain.

I stared at him, watched him stroke himself erect. Watched him grow, my tongue at the tip of my lips. My eyes went from his eyes to the colors on his penis, all the browns and pinks.

Erykah sang.

I sang.

Keith closed his eyes, stroked himself.

I sang stronger, stole the show, made Erykah my background singer.

"Your voice is so damn beautiful, Billie."

I smiled. Smiled and wondered what his ex was like. If she had a mommy body. I could hit the gym when I wanted, nap when I was tired, make love when I wanted, eat when I felt like it. Kids ended all that. I wasn't ready to get the mommy body and live the rest of my days as an indentured servant.

"Billie, I don't believe you have me doing this."

"Baby, you are blessed."

"Don't stop singing."

Mesmerized by his sensual movements, I sang some more.

He did his thing, his pace the same as my mine, matching the music.

It was erotic. It was lovely.

He moaned. Erykah sang. I hummed.

I said, "Beautiful."

He moaned again, smiled like he was a shy schoolboy. I liked that.

He said, "Kiss me."

I did. We kissed until the song went off. I picked up the remote, made "Mama's Gun" play again.

He moaned again, then slowed it down, got it under control.

I sang like a woman on fire.

He asked, "Do you help? Or just watch?"

"Depends. Both."

"Which will it be tonight?"

"Not sure."

I sang until the song ended, keeping my eyes on his penis until Badu's voice faded; then ran my hand over his forehead, wiped the sweat away from his brow. I moved his hand away and took his tool in one hand, then held it with both hands, not hiding how anxious I was to touch him, started stroking it up and down in a kind and gentle and respectable way, did that while he sucked my tongue, while he touched my breast, while he put his hand between my legs, while he sucked my lips, while his breath thickened, while my breathing did the same. I was giving him a tender hand job while he massaged my clit through my pants, which seemed strange. Petting like this seemed outdated. We were in our thirties. Too old to be giving and getting hand jobs. But I have to admit, I did dig it. Wasn't really sure how far it would go. Thought I had gotten too used to men who went for the jugular right off.

I said, "Keith?"

"Yeah?"

"Hate to slow your roll, but I don't have any condoms."

"Me neither."

"Ain't you supposed to have one in your wallet? Or in your glove compartment?"

He laughed a little. "Haven't had to use one in years."

"You don't use condoms?"

"Well, I've been married for half my life."

"What about when you messed around on her?"

"What makes you think I messed around?"

"Be real."

"Haven't been with anybody but my ex."

"How long were you married?"

"Eighteen years."

"For eighteen years? And she's the only woman you slept with?"

"For the last ten."

"See what I mean?" I laughed. "Still, that's remarkable."

"Like I said, I haven't used a condom in years."

"You're not missing anything. They pretty much steal the sensitivity and fuck up the party."

I held his penis, stared at it, used my thumb and finger to measure the circumference.

I asked, "Ever measured it?"

"Not since I was a kid."

"Can I?"

"Sure."

"Let me get my measuring tape."

"And get your vibrator."

"What makes you think I have a vibrator?"

"Get your vibrator."

I laughed.

I left the room, went into my bedroom, pretended I was having a hard time finding my midnight substitute, and finally came back with one of my toys, taking slow steps, singing and grinning like a shy girl.

I measured Keith's penis. Wondered if his wife handled all he had to offer.

The fireplace continued lighting up the room, Erykah Badu continued singing, and all was wonderful in the Land of Oz while I took Keith in my mouth. Licked the sides, sucked the head.

Had been too long since I had done this. Much too long. Missed doing this too much.

He moaned and moved. I backed away, stroked him, and teased him with my tongue.

He tasted too good to be true. Had a good diet. Lots of sugars. Smoothies. Maybe wheatgrass. The idea of using my vibrator went away. As wet as I was, I had to have the real deal inside me.

I said, "Want you inside me."

"Okay."

"Would have to get on top so I could control the depth."

"Okay."

"But . . ."

"But what?"

"Sorry, boo." I bit my bottom lip, gave him the face of regret. "No condom, no sex."

He shook his head. "You don't have anything?"

"Nothing."

"No Saran wrap?"

"Okay, MacGyver. We need to make some decisions here."

We sat there stirring in our own heat. Breathing ragged. Frustration rising.

We went back to kissing and touching each other. Keith took my vibrator, turned it on, put that perpetual hum between my legs, sent vibrations through my leather pants. I made him stop, put it down, couldn't take the teasing. I was sweating. So horny that it felt like I had become another person.

I growled. "No condoms."

"I can try to find a store open."

"After three in the morning."

"I know."

I made a frustrated sound. "How long will that take?"

"Where is a 7-Eleven?"

"Damn . . . uh . . . La Cienega and Rodeo . . . no . . . Slauson and Angeles Vista is closer."

"Twenty minutes."

I held his penis. "Think you can drive like this?"

"Give me a minute."

"You can't walk in 7-Eleven like that. Habib would think you were carrying a shotgun."

We laughed a little, kissed some more. Had gone too far, couldn't turn the passion off.

I groaned, didn't want the moment to dissipate. "I want you so bad I can taste you."

"Taste me."

"You want me in your mouth?"

"Yeah."

"Say it."

"Take me in your mouth, Billie."

"Like this?"

"Shit. Like that, Billie."

"You want to be inside my mouth? Like this?"

"Oh, God."

"Do you?"

"Yes. Fuck."

"Like this?"

"Like that."

On the Oriental rug, in front of the fireplace, Badu still singing.

Working him slowly, letting my throat muscles relax. He stretched me open with his fingers.

He moaned, "Take your clothes off. . . ."

"No. Can't. No condoms, no sex."

"I want to eat your pussy."

I shivered. "Shit."

"Would you like that, Billie?"

"That's my red kryptonite, baby."

"Let me eat your pussy."

"Brings out this other side of me."

"Wanna make you come with my tongue."

"Can you handle that?"

He started undressing me. Tossed my leather pants and T-shirt asking the world to FREE MICHAEL to the side. I took off my bra and yellow thong. He was up on his feet, taking his shirt off. I watched him get naked. Nice body. It was awkward watching him struggle to get his pants off, tug them over his award-winning hugeness. It jutted out, bobbed up and down, pointed at me like I was the one.

Beautiful. Simply beautiful.

Keith put his hand back between my legs, that middle finger massaging my spot. Made me moan, sing. Butterfly-soft lips against mine. My insides dripped like honey. Wanted him inside me filling me up.

"Kiss my body, Keith. Want to feel your mouth on my skin. My neck, kiss my neck. Bite it. Let me feel your teeth. Let your teeth pull my skin. Graze my skin. Like that. Hold me tight."

He did what I asked him, did all of that with his hardness grinding against me, driving me crazy.

I said, "Feel how wet I am for you?"

"I'm yours, Billie. Whatever you like, I'll do it."

He took one breast in his mouth, then the other, ran his tongue across my nipples. So hard, they felt so hard. He praised them, squeezed them, licked them, made sucking noises that set me on fire.

I said, "Get ready."

"For what?"

"Lick your lips and get ready."

I shifted around, positioned myself over his face.

In a sweet voice, almost begging, I said, "Eat this pussy for me, baby."

He held my ass and sang, "Like this?"

That tongue. Oh, God. That tongue. My moans were so loud. Tingles turning into liquid fire. Hovering dangerously close to the edge. I was grabbing at his head, rocking my hips into his face, rocking steady, rocking slowly.

I couldn't stay focused. He was working me too damn good.

"Coming . . . keep it right there . . . I'm coming . . ." I was masturbating him again, stroking him with the rhythm and intensity I was feeling. "Ooo, baby . . . right there right there right there . . . oh, God . . . oh, my God . . . Oooo . . . keep licking . . . lick me . . . just like that . . . want you to come with me . . . come with me . . ."

I stroked him faster.

Then stopped when my orgasm consumed me.

There I was, shaking uncontrollably, coming.

Should not have let him do that to me. Should not have let him start that fire.

Wanted us to move from being contiguous to being connected.

Wanted penetration so bad.

Needed penetration so bad.

But didn't want to go there at the same time.

Would let him do anything but come in my mouth.

Couldn't wait anymore. Was crazy. Didn't care anymore. I sat up, rubbed his dick against my pussy, let the head open me up. The sensation made his eyes roll, made him as insane as I was crazy. I moved him back and forth, made him sing for me, that sweet baritone voice hitting so many notes.

In that same sweet, begging voice, I told him, "Get on top of me."

"You sure?"

"Don't put it inside me. Need to feel your body on mine."

He did, moved up and down, rubbed his penis against my wetness.

That kind of teasing made me want to howl and rip his skin off.

My hands held his ass like that ass was mine to hold.

His hands gripped my ass like this ass belonged to him.

We grabbed asses and kissed and kissed and ground against each other.

Heavy breathing, squirming, unable to stop, the inferno between us was devastating.

So wet I could hear the sounds.

The inviting sounds.

Then I put my legs down, kept them together around his penis, tight, his erection rubbing my clit.

His hips rose and fell, moved like he was stroking me to paradise, like he was inside me.

It felt like he was making love to me, nice and slow.

This was insane.

Feeling this horny, being set on fire like this, was madness.

Electricity shot through my body, made me jerk over and over.

I moaned, "You're on my spot."

"You like this?"

"Right there. Like that. Yes, baby. Damn. I'm getting close again."

"You're amazing."

"Keep moving like that."

"Damn, you're amazing."

That inferno, that sweet inferno.

Los Angeles was burning down and I was the epicenter.

My legs floated apart, opened on their own, moved like I was surrendering, inviting into paradise.

He adjusted himself, kept the length of his erection on my vagina, moved against me.

The length of his stiffness glided up and down my wetness.

We kissed.

He sucked my breasts.

I sucked his fingers.

Then he slid down until I felt what my body wanted so bad.

The head of his penis moved against my opening.

Moved up and down in shorter motions.

I shifted with the feeling.

Shifted away when it felt too damn good, then shifted back into him because I couldn't stop.

I felt him slipping inside me.

Accidentally.

Or not.

Not sure.

But I was so wet.

So open.

He glided inside me.

Not much.

But too much at the same time.

I felt him stretching, peeping inside my walls.

I jerked.

Wanted to push him away.

Wanted him to pull away.

Lust glued us together.

I moaned.

He moaned.

Couldn't push him away.

He couldn't stop, his choppy breathing told me that.

The head was inside me, moving in and out, back and forth over my spot.

My fingernails went into his back, dug into his ass.

He didn't complain about my scratching his butt. He didn't care about the marking.

He was single. Didn't care about the woman he was divorcing.

Those wet sounds were like sweet, sweet music.

Caution left the building, walked out holding hands with common sense.

I pulled him toward me.

Pulled pleasure my way.

Three inches of sweet amalgamation slid inside me.

He backed away, tried to pull out.

I said, "It's okay."

"Sure?"

"If you're cool with that, then we're cool."

He eased back inside me, but not too far.

Not too deep.

Played it safe.

Just a little deeper.

Told myself that I just wanted to feel him a little deeper.

Not for long.

Just for a moment.

Convinced myself that I'd stop as soon as he scratched this itch.

That he'd stop.

We'd only do this for a hot minute.

Just until sanity returned.

Keith was teasing me, sliding in and out just beyond my fleshy folds, but not deep enough.

I grabbed his ass, dug in deep, held him like I was trying to keep from floating away.

Wanted to feel what I was feeling forever.

He groaned, slid deeper inside me.

Three.

Four.

Five inches.

Slid back out.

Three.

Two.

One inch deep.

Held it there.

Stirred me like coffee.

Then back inside me.

He called God. Prayed like he needed help right now.

He surrendered, went deep.

Lost control and went inside me.

Six.

Seven.

Eight.

Nine.

Keith opened me up like I'd never been opened up before.

He asked, "More?"

"Not so deep, baby, not so deep right now."

"Sure?"

"Let me get used to this."

I was dying a wonderful death.

So was Keith.

He was moving inside me, but I was controlling the depth. Controlling the depth wasn't just about the penis; I wanted to control the depth of this moment. I wanted to decide how deep I would let him go.

In the far corner of my mind I wondered how my vagina felt compared to his wife's.

I wondered how deep he had been inside her.

She had the advantage. I hadn't had a child. Hadn't had my vaginal walls stretched giving birth.

Then again.

Maybe I had the advantage.

Maybe I felt tighter, moved better, gave him a better song than the music he'd left behind.

She was in my mind, in my moment, and I hated that.

That kind of misplaced thinking was instinctive. It has been ingrained so much that we do it by nature. Would only go away after years of deprogramming.

Keith stroked me and all of those thoughts went away.

His penis scared me.

Not because of the size.

Because it fit and felt so damn good, because it made me sing a song from deep within.

I hated the way it felt.

Hated feeling that damn good.

Hated it because it felt like home.

"I'm going to come, Billie."

"It's okay, baby. I'm on the pill."

I blurted that out and relief washed over his face. In his eyes I saw what he didn't want. He saw the same thing in mine. A new level of comfort blanketed us. Trust had moved into the room.

"Wanted to fuck you the moment I met you."

"Then fuck me, Keith. Fuck me."

After that it was on.

He slowed down, controlled his need to come, had my ankles on his shoulders, was on his knees, moving in and out of me, staring down on all the ugly faces I was making, his face so intense, like a king.

He commanded, "Get on the ottoman."

He turned me over, had me face down on the ottoman, took me from the back. Didn't think I'd ever been fucked like that, not the way he stroked me, spanked me, made me curse and lose control. I put my fingers inside my mouth, moistened them so I could touch myself. Touching myself intensified every sensation going through my body. I was sweating, panting, weak. But still wanted more.

He was about to come. Felt him swelling.

Keith growled like he was releasing all of his pent-up rage.

Seven.

Eight.

Nine.

Ten.

I called God and Jesus.

My hands reached out, tried to hold on to anything I could find to hold.

Moaned like I was falling.

Falling.

Falling.

We got towels and cleaned ourselves, turned off the fireplace, grabbed our clothes, and moved the party to my bedroom after that. Two good orgasms left me hyped with a brand-new song in my heart. I took out my Takamine. My guitar was sweet. Naked, Keith rested on his side and smiled at me.

I said, "Tell me about yourself."

"Thought I did."

"Tell me something you didn't tell me."

He winked. "Why don't you do the same?"

I told him about my parents. About growing up and living pretty much everywhere.

He put his head between my legs, licked me soft and easy, like I was a delicacy.

I said, "Don't think . . . don't think that's going to keep you from telling me about yourself."

"What do you want to know?"

"Every . . . shit, that tongue of yours . . . damn . . . feels so good . . . tell me everything."

I could come again.

He came up to me, kissed me, his tongue tasting so damn good.

He told me that he was an L.A. boy, born and raised. High school had been Washington Prep. Junior High, Foshe. His elementary days spent at

Menlo. Rolled with the Van Ness Gangsters. A franchise of the Bloods. Drinking malt liquor, getting high, having feuds. Shooting. Getting shot at. Walked the same mean streets as the other gangs in the area. Knew them all like they were members of same church, just went to different services. Eight Trays. Piru Bloods. Hoover Crips. He had a older brother, Jody. Killed robbing a bank. Keith's wake-up call.

"Your brother robbed banks?"

"I did too. Once. When I was seventeen."

"Didn't get caught?"

"Nah. We rode out to Riverside."

That badness in his blood excited me.

I held his dick while he talked, stroked it up and down. He touched my breasts.

He said, "My ex-wife doesn't know that."

"She doesn't?"

"Nah. Told her my brother was killed robbing a liquor store. Never told her we robbed banks."

"We?"

"I was a teenager."

"How many banks?"

"I was in on two."

"You quit, right?"

"I outgrew that mentality. Outgrew a lot of my family. Would've been dead or in jail, like most of my relatives." He paused. "You can't pick your family, but you can choose your destiny."

He didn't like the world that he was born into, so he left. Left the drugs. The feuds. Vanished from that world. First he enrolled in a J.C. Got his A.A. and moved on to a four-year. Couldn't pick his family, but he could pick his destiny. Destiny. He used that word a lot. His daughter's name. Destiny. He had no support. Grants. Loans. Worked three jobs at one point. Whatever he could find. No help at all. Other relatives were on lockdown, drugged out, or just plain old missing from life as we knew it.

He told me that his daughter was what changed his life the most.

She was the reason he didn't go back to his old stomping grounds. She was the reason he gave her mother the house. Everything done to benefit his daughter. If he'd had a son, he'd fight for the house, do what he had to do to get his wife to leave, let the king and his prince rule his own Wakanda.

But he'd had a girl. That changed the rules of war.

Still that didn't change the fact that he couldn't take his wife's arrogance anymore. That he couldn't take her parents anymore. That he had to leave before it got any uglier. Or physical.

Once again he was choosing his own destiny. Had to try and figure out the rest of his life.

I stroked him good. Tried to make him forget. Tried to make him shut up.

Sometimes we don't like the answer to the questions we ask.

He was getting hard again. I held on to that sweet miracle.

But curiosity had the best of me.

I asked, "Where did you meet your . . . your daughter's mother?"

Almost twenty years ago he had walked into a restaurant, saw the broad smile on a brown-skinned girl that represented the kind of life he wished he had. At some point we all stare into the eyes of someone who represents what or who we want to be in life. We all have that kind of love. His had been with a girl who had gone to Westchester High, the better side of town. A former cheerleader who grew up right off Crenshaw. Her mother had uprooted her family, brought that Jamaican money to the states. Money made in real estate. Keith fell in lust, then fell in love with the beautiful island girl who worked in Beverly Hills.

He said, "That was a dark time for me. Needed some light. Back then, Jody . . . my brother hadn't been dead too long. Think I needed something to help me out of that hole. Something. Or someone."

"Sorry about your brother."

"Kept wishing I had helped him. But he stayed in that life. I got married, left it all behind."

He switched up, asked about me, about my riding, if I was in a group. Was so glad he didn't go on about his ex or his daughter any longer. I was two paragraphs from getting turned off and turning on my damn vibrator. Save that hate-the-ex-wife conversation for the daylight hours at Starbucks.

"Did a Fresno run with some bikers last weekend."

He pulled me over, had me sit on top of him. I kissed him, moved against him.

He said, "L.A. to Fresno? That's about three hours. Long ride on a crotch rocket."

"Little over two hundred miles. It was fun. And fast. Didn't take three hours. Not me, anyway."

"How fast you ride?"

"On the way up I stopped out at about one-thirty and the guys hit one-sixty, easy. On the way back, I hit one-eighty. That was better than para-sailing. I tucked in and rocked my baby. She did me good."

He kissed me. Held my ass. I felt him rising again.

He whispered, "Can you do that now? Can you ride this crotch rocket and hit one-sixty?"

I raised my hips. Felt that hardness being rubbed back and forth against my warm vagina.

"Depends." I was wet. That itch becoming a fire again. "Let's see how many gears you got."

I eased down on him, moaned as he opened me up.

He held my waist, eased me down, filled me up.

Keith moved my hair from my face, put his fingers inside my mouth, made me suck them.

He whispered, "Baby, I ain't made it to second gear yet."

"A sister can . . . can . . . can only ride . . . ride . . . as fast and hard as the bike will allow."

I rode. He slapped my ass. I rode faster. He slapped my ass again. I rode harder.

I held my headboard and rode him from L.A. to Fresno and back. Popped wheelies, did handstands, showed him I had mastered all the stunts. Had him moaning and the headboard banging.

I tensed up, that feeling overwhelming me, fought it until I had to give in, and I came.

He strained, held my waist, bounced me up and down so damn fast, and he came.

Before that ride ended, I came again.

"*Damn, Keith.* Are you trying to own this pussy?"

"Me? Damn. You move like . . . damn."

"You fuck like a damn porn star." I wanted to sing again. "Ain't been sexed like this since . . . never."

"Me, either. Needed that. Damn, I needed that."

"Me, too," I sang. "Needed to get fucked. Just. Like. That."

The vulgar and crazy things people said when they were high and on fire, we said them all.

We caught our breaths, sweat all over our skin, then we cleaned ourselves again.

Not long after that I heard the sound of a BMW coming down the street, a motorcycle, not a car. The sweet hum of a red F650. Music to my sweat-filled ears.

Minutes after that the garage door went up. The sensor beeped, then announced that the basement door was open. Viviane was home. Heard her coming up from the garage, and then heard her heading up the stairs. The stairs creaked. And I heard her giggling. Her sneaky butt wasn't alone.

Keith looked worn out and uncomfortable.

I said, "My roommate. The owner of this castle."

He made a bitter face. Playful, but bitter, and yawned. "The castle she won in her divorce."

I started back playing my guitar, played and hummed while Keith struggled to stay awake.

Our carnal ride to Fresno and back had worn his ass out. That made me feel like a goddess.

I became Sy Smith. I became Simfani Blue. I became a superstar like Chante Carmel.

I played my acoustic guitar and I sang.

I told him, "Had been working on my tablature before I went to work."

"What's tablature?"

I showed him the six-line staff that graphically represented the guitar fingerboard.

I said, "The top line indicates the highest-sounding string, high E."

I told him a little more, fell into teacher mode, and gave him a two-minute lesson while I played "Arms of a Woman," a poignant song by Amos Lee, only I changed the lyrics to say arms of a man.

"Tremolo. Fret. Muffle." He smiled, yawned. "All of that is over my head."

"Sleepy?"

"Lot on my mind."

"Like?"

"The real reason I don't have to work tomorrow." He paused. "Got laid off today."

"Awww. Sorry to hear that."

"It's cool. Been up and down like this for a minute. Getting used to it."

"Anything I can do? Breakfast? Maybe another blow job to ease that stress?"

He smiled. "Billie . . . damn, baby . . . where did you come from?"

I smiled.

We kissed. Tongue-praised each other for a moment.

He asked, "Water?"

"Sorry." I put my Takamine to the side. "I'll get you some."

"I'll get it. Keep working on your tablature."

He said that like life was troubling him and he needed to get away for a moment.

I told him where the kitchen was and he got up, stretched. Damn. I looked at his tall and lean frame, hoping he could take me to heaven at least one more time before the sun crept through my bedroom window, my clit throbbing for more of him as I worked on my bend and release, pick slides and rhythm slashes, and smiled, watched his naked frame move around my bed and down the hallway.

Then that thing happened that made me feel like a damned fool.

His cellular went off. On his caller ID, saw his wife's face light up my room.

Hair in a bun. Mid-thirties. Light brown skin. From what I could see, she was a pretty woman.

And she was here. Her face on his phone, her smile in my bedroom glowing like radiation.

I stopped singing, an abrupt ending to Amos Lee's masterpiece.

That cellular jingling in the thick of the night made me lose my rhythm.

It resounded like a fire alarm going off. That was the warning I ignored.

Before discomfort could overwhelm me, before common sense could pull me away from my desires and shake me back to my senses, I saw Viviane hurrying down the stairs.

I smiled. She had on her white housecoat, two empty wine glasses in her hand.

She walked into the kitchen and saw a tall and lean, butt-naked Adonis getting water.

"Good Lord. Look at the *size* of your . . . do you have a brother who likes Korean women?"

I thought that was funny as hell. Two women, living and loving *Sex and the City* style.

I yelled out, "Viviane, that's Keith. Keith, my roommate Viviane."

Viviane yelled back, "I'm not your roommate. You're *my* roommate."

"I stand corrected."

"Don't perpetrate." Then she told Keith. "You know she's Japanese, right?"

I called, "Don't start with that mess."

"Don't let the black skin fool you. She's Jap-ah-kneees."

"For the last time. My parents were black. Military. I was born in Japan."

"And that makes you Japanese."

"Viviane, slap yourself three times and take a Tylenol."

"Nice meeting you, Keith."

Keith hurried back, embarrassed.

That wasn't the first time that had happened. It cracked me up. That moment was funny enough for me to ignore the storm warning that had come on his cellular phone.

But that was almost a year ago.

When it was all about fun and pleasure. When it didn't matter if he was laid off. When it didn't matter if his soon-to-be ex might be pissed off because she knew he was somewhere getting laid.

Before the bed we were loving on would end up covered in shattered glass.

Before Carmen invaded my world, her jealousy a brick crashing through my bedroom window.

Hadn't been warned that I'd be staring at that gaping hole, cold air rushing in as my heated anger made me curse a thousand curses, my roommate at my side, lights flashing as the sheriffs came.

eight

BILLIE

THE FEMALE SHERIFF ASKED, "SO, YOU'RE INVOLVED WITH A MARRIED woman's husband?"

"It's wasn't like that. Look, they separated last year—"

One difference between the monied residents in View Park and the people on the other side of Crenshaw was as simple at the sheriff's department and LAPD. On the LAPD side of town crime was higher and the response time was slower. Especially since they put that new Krispy Kreme down on Crenshaw and The Street Formerly Known as Santa Barbara Boulevard. There were no doughnut shops in the hills. No doughnut shops meant no distractions. No distractions meant better response time.

"And you said that you saw them together this evening, before the incident, and she called you before the window was shattered, from her husband's phone number, which is at least a mile away, and that immediately after that phone call the incident occurred, and when the incident occurred you pushed redial on your phone, and her husband answered, telling you that she was still with him, is this correct?"

"I'm not crazy."

"Did you say their divorce had been revoked? So then they are still legally married."

"What does that have to do with a damn brick being thrown through my window?"

Five minutes after the brick sprouted wings and came though my window, three sheriff's cars were out front. All the ghetto bourgeois neighbors knew something was going on. I told the lead sheriff that Carmen threw the brick, but since I didn't see her throw the brick, since the SUV I saw speeding away wasn't her Mercedes, since they contacted Keith and he said that his wife had been with him all evening, there was nothing they could do. And even if she wasn't with him and he was lying, they couldn't make a husband testify against his wife.

"Just trying to keep it straight." She showed me her report. "Now, is this report accurate?"

I went off. "A brick almost killed me and, what, there is nothing you can do?"

"Nobody saw anything."

"So, what does that mean?"

"At the moment, outside of filing a report, not much we can do."

"Aren't you going to take pictures? This is a crime scene."

The sheriffs looked at each other. Then they looked at me, faces made of stone.

They gave me a copy of the hard-to-read report and headed for the door. That was it. Just scribble-scrabbled down some bullshit that made me sound crazy. They barely looked at the shattered window. Didn't bother to photograph the broken glass that was all over the room and across my bed.

They left like Krispy Kreme was having a sale on doughnuts.

All I had was anger and a police report in my hand. I tore that crap into a dozen pieces.

Viviane frowned at the broken glass, arms folded, shaking her head.

Her friend, Daddy Long Stroke, had gone back upstairs like he was allergic to the police.

Viviane adjusted her housecoat and repeated, "Pregnant?"

My voice cracked. "Pregnant."

Viviane pressed on. "You're pregnant and Keith is moving in with his wife?"

"Don't start sounding like a broken record, Viv."

"When did all this happen?"

I gave her some backstory, told her about my adventure at Starbucks, how Carmen had tried to bum-rush me in the bathroom. Should've beaten her ass then. Then told her about peeping through Keith's bedroom window and seeing that act of congress. Really should've stomped her ass then.

I ranted, "I don't care what they said, Carmen threw that brick."

"Hold on. Let me . . . gotta take care of something."

She ran out and I closed the bedroom door. Picked up the phone to call Keith, dialed six of the seven digits, was about to scream that he and that bitch better come over here and clean this shit up, that they'd better write a check for this damage, then put the phone back up. I snatched on a pair of jeans, tugged on a T-shirt, house shoes, stormed into the kitchen and grabbed the small trash can, stopped in the hallway, and yanked up a broom and dustpan, cursing and thinking evil thoughts the whole time.

In my mind I was outside Keith's bedroom window, flaming Molotov cocktail in hand.

A car went by. I jumped. Ran to the window. Saw nobody. Nothing.

Then my phone rang. I jumped. Keith's number.

I answered, "What?"

"You sent the police over here?"

"Where is she?"

"What is your problem, Billie?"

I hung up.

I jumped when I heard footsteps in the hallway. Despite the anger and humiliation, a brick flying through the bedroom window in the middle of the night had left me scared. Felt like I was living in a Dean Koontz novel. My heart sped up when I heard voices, heard a male voice I didn't recognize.

Viviane was escorting her lover to the front door, her hand on his elbow, house shoes slapping the floor at an intense and rapid pace, rushing him out of the house.

He asked, "When can we hook up again?"

"I'll call you."

"Maybe we can meet at the bookstore."

"I'll call you."

"Had a great time."

"I'll call you."

Heard her kissing him. Heard her telling him that she needed to be with me right now.

As soon as the front door slammed I thought she'd be at my door, pissed off and screaming for me to call the police, but she ran down the hallway, her small feet slapping the marble floor, then headed back upstairs, her pace swift and urgent. Sounded like she fell down.

I opened my bedroom door and yelled, "You okay?"

She cursed. "Think I broke my toe on the stairs."

"Can you wiggle it?"

"Yeah."

"It's not broken."

She limped up the stairs.

I closed my bedroom door, looked out the window, wondering if Carmen was gone, if she was out there lurking in the bushes, or hiding in a tree, waiting to throw another brick through my bedroom window.

Minutes later I had thrown the big pieces of glass in the garbage, was sweeping the rest of the mess. Viviane rushed down to the basement. I knew her routine. Understood her panic. That meant Little Miss Playa had taken her soiled sheets off her bed and tossed them in the washing machine. Had put Tide and hot water on the evidence of her indiscretion. She ran back up the stairs, saw her zipping by, limping, hair in a ponytail, now wearing Old Navy pajamas and a wrinkled Anne Rice T-shirt. She stayed up there long enough to put fresh linen on her bed. Came back down again. Heard her in the hallway on her cordless phone, talking, leaving her boyfriend a message.

Viviane came and tapped on my door, then came inside before I could answer.

I said, "Kicked Cottrell out, huh?"

"Sorry I had to bail on you like that in the middle of . . . you know. Had some other issues."

I said, "You treat them all like they're whores."

"Because they are."

We stared at that hole where a window used to be.

I asked, "Any cardboard in the basement?"

"Not sure."

"Duct tape?"

"Look in the kitchen." She took a sharp breath. "My cellular phone's been blowing up all night."

"Somebody is trying to track your butt down."

Once again she said, "Pregnant?"

"Took an EPT yesterday morning."

I tried to laugh. Tried, but couldn't. Was too hard to pretend right now. One of those stubborn tears crept out of my right eye. Before it rolled past my lips, its fraternal twin crept out of my left eye too.

Viviane's voice softened. "You okay?"

I don't know how long I sat there, lips pulled in, shaking my head, a child in confessional. Felt like I was fourteen with ashy knees, faced covered in pimples, betrayed by my own skin, wearing braces, thinking about some stupid boy I knew I couldn't live without, wanting to hold my breath until I died.

Viviane sat on my bed, put her arms around me, then held my hand.

I wished I hadn't told her. Wished I hadn't told Keith, wished he had told me his part first.

I stared at that gaping hole. "That bitch tried to kill me."

"She's crazy. Keep away from her, Billie."

"What do you think I should do?"

"If you get an abortion, I'll go with you."

I said, "I meant about the window."

"Oh. Not much you can do. It's after midnight."

Viviane held me. Her hair was wet. She smelled like jasmine and Herbal Essence shampoo.

She said, "How you feel?"

"Feel so stupid." I remembered what I wanted to forget. "I've been down this road before."

"It's okay; it's okay. I've been there. I feel you. Go ahead and cry."

"I'd kill myself if I did that again."

We heard the engine of a bike humming out in front of the house.

Viviane cursed and shook her head, looked damn nervous.

I let out a weary chuckle, wiped my eyes, said, "Sounds like your favorite CBR."

"What happened to calling before a brother came over?"

"You got homeboy out of here just in time."

"Kinda figured Jacob would drive his ass out here when I didn't answer."

The doorbell rang. Viviane didn't move. She pulled her braids back into a ponytail, said, "I think I got spoiled."

"How?"

"Guy before Jacob, he had a twelve-inch dick."

"Why'd you break up with him?"

"Because he had a twelve-inch dick."

"Gotcha."

The doorbell rang again. She grunted, groaned, went to the door, slow steps, mumbling, turning lights on along the way. She put on her little-girl voice, sounded so sweet and demure that it was sickening, pretended that she was surprised and elated to see Jacob. The man with the big hands. The brother who wanted to take his Asian princess on exotic trips, give her the world, make her his erotic queen.

He asked, "What happened to the window?"

"Shhh. Kiss me."

My door wasn't closed all the way. My bedroom was right next to the front door, faced the streets. I heard them kissing, that wetness that comes from integrating sweet tongues.

Jacob said, "Your skin is glowing."

"Your kisses make me glow. Kiss me."

"You smell fresh."

"Just showered. Was stressed after I left Barnes & Noble. Needed to calm down."

"Want a massage? Brought some oils."

"Not right now. Bad timing."

"You up writing?"

"Was. Then Billie needed me. Kiss me again."

"What's up?"

"Keith's wife went off the deep end and threw a brick through her damn window."

"You serious?"

"Long story. She got into it with Billie. Had to call the sheriff. Like ten police cars were up here."

"Damn."

"I know. So discomforting. Thought I heard the phone, but it was crazy up here a minute ago."

"I was wondering what was going on. Was worried about you."

"Yeah. We were caught up with that drama. That's why I didn't get to the phone."

More kisses, and lies spoken too soft for me to hear.

Viviane stuck her head back in my door. "I'll be back down in a sec."

"Check your bathroom garbage can."

"Already emptied it."

"Condom wrappers?"

"In the outside trash."

"Toilet seat down?"

"I made sure I put it back down."

"Check for pee on the rim before you let it down?"

"Wiped it down."

"You check your neck?"

"No marks."

"Daddy Long Stroke hit it from the back?"

"Of course. Whassup?"

"Leave your hair down just in case you got a monkey bite where you can't see."

"Good looking out."

I shrugged. "You should be cool."

She undid her ponytail, let her braids hang free. "Am I forgetting anything?"

"Sounds like you're covered. No evidence, no crime."

"Damn good looking out."

"Holla."

"I'll come back to check on you."

"I'm cool. And I promise to not load up my gun and do anything stupid."

There was a pause between us, a moment of us speaking in silence.

"Don't worry, Viviane. If I keep this baby, I'll move."

Frustration covered her face. "Billie."

"Some big hands are waiting on you. Go handle your biz."

"Jacob had to show up." She ran her hands over her braids. "Sorry that I . . . you know."

She motioned toward her lover, apologizing for putting my personal life on blast, letting me know she had to pretend, that she wasn't in an amorous mood, but had to fake the funk, and there was no telling how many tongue and hand-induced orgasms she'd endure in the name of duplicity.

She didn't have to explain. I understood the game. Understood the rules.

She backed out the door. Before the door closed I peeped Jacob waiting for her at the foot of the staircase, black motorcycle jacket on, large red helmet in one huge hand, backpack in the other. Big guy with a gentle demeanor.

His baritone voice called out, "Whassup, Billie?"

"Jacob. 'Sup?"

"You okay?"

"I'm great. Just great."

"Raheem said he saw you at Starbucks. You knocked over his coffee."

I groaned. "That irritating guy's a friend of yours?"

Jacob said, "I just saw him at the Unocal on Slauson and Fairfax. Happens we were gassing up at the same time. Said he ran into you up at Starbucks. More like you ran into him."

Jacob chuckled at his little joke. My sense of humor was off-line.

I put my eyes on the floor. "What's your point? Where you going with this conversation?"

"Cool guy. Single. Professional. He told me he bought a bike."

"I heard."

"Check it out." He laughed. "Want you to read my script. It's called *Lost Housewives*. A plane filled with horny housewives crashes and they end up on a deserted island. With one man. And he's gay."

"Look, it's been a long night."

"A'ight, a'ight."

"Goodnight, Jacob. And tell your boy to stop sweating me."

"Just want to put a word in for him. You wouldn't get no bricks though your window."

"You think that's funny, huh? Get your laugh on, Jacob. Get your laugh on."

"Lighten up."

"Goodnight, Jacob."

They headed upstairs, Jacob mumbling about my attitude, the stairs creaking under his weight. Fifteen minutes from now, maybe ten, if I stood out on the balcony in the cold air, I'd hear Viviane moaning, hear her praising his wonderful hands, telling him how much she loved him, lying to his soul.

So easy to lie. So damn easy.

I found a roll of plastic in the basement, cut it, found duct tape, covered the large hole, sat in my cold bedroom, shivered, and cried. Hormones. Had to be hormones. I never cried. Never felt like this.

Couldn't get Keith off my fucking mind. Couldn't get Carmen out of my goddamn head.

Somebody slowed down in front of the house. Stopped. Backed up. Turned around like they were lost. Bright lights hit my bedroom window, lit up my walls for a few seconds. As if they wanted their lights on this house. I trembled. Listened. Heard the rumble of an older SUV. A slow-moving SUV.

I thought it was Keith coming to check on me. Half a smile rose on my face, then turned into a deeper frown when I realized it wasn't him. Keith's four-wheel cage was a red Explorer.

The light-colored SUV pulled away, came back, and stopped in front of the house.

Sat there for few minutes, engine humming.

The SUV was white. Maybe tan.

After the brick had smashed my window, I'd seen a dark SUV speed away.

I thought it was dark. Right now the world was suspicious and I wasn't sure about shit.

Carmen couldn't be that stupid.

But maybe it wasn't about being stupid. It was about being bold.

I turned off the light on my nightstand, peeped around the plastic in the window.

The SUV pulled away, didn't take off fast, but it didn't slow in front of anyone else's home.

This was the house they were looking for.

Heart in my throat, I hurried to the front door, ran out on the porch, then went to the curb.

The truck had vanished.

Carmen was taunting me.

I ran back inside and picked up the phone.

Was about to dial Keith's number.

But it was staring at me.

The damn brick was on the floor gawking at me and my paranoia.

I hurried and got dressed. Thick jeans. Biker's jacket. No high heels, flat and durable biker boots this time. Just in case I had to take to the battle-field and engage in hand-to-hand combat.

I picked up that brick and dropped it in my backpack.

Then I fired up my Duke and rolled out.

Riding a motorcycle and being in love have this in common: tunnel vision.

You focus on what is ahead of you, not really seeing what is behind you, in some ways ignoring the past. And my swelling anger, well, that beast stole my focus too, took away my periphery.

I had severe tunnel vision.

Which was why I didn't see I was being followed, at least not at first. Their headlights weren't on and they were trailing me down Presidio toward Angeles Vista, following me like it was my infuriated history. I was riding around the block, taking the long way to Keith's funky little apart-ment. Wanted to ride my anger, surf every wave of hostility. Wanted to think a few extra minutes. Presidio was two lanes with parking on both sides, not enough room for two cars to pass side by side, not a lot of room to maneuver. But I glanced at my sideview mirror and saw that white SUV barreling up behind me. I sped up. They sped up. Came at me fast. Even with my anger I knew a motorcycle wasn't able to go up against four wheels. I slowed down, hoping they would too. They sped up. The SUV was right up on me. They hit their bright lights, did that like they wanted to surprise me, leave me disoriented. I downshifted, kicked up my speed, and shot through the stop sign at Angeles Vista, prayed nobody was com-ing this way, and made a hard left, leaned low, damn near hit the curb. Ex-pected the SUV to rampage into my back tire, sending me flying toward the pavement. When I straightened up, fear kept me riding hard, kept me speeding, my heart thumping, my eyes on the side mirror. I sped down the hill, was almost at Stocker before I hit my brakes and downshifted. Cruis-ers were clogging up Crenshaw Boulevard. No one was behind me. When

I swooped left they must've gone the other way. Or maybe they went down West Boulevard. I made a U-turn and sped back that way, saw a lot of drivers now, but not the SUV I was looking for. I hit the side streets, went all over the neighborhood looking for that bitch, but didn't find her.

I gave up some throttle, cut through the night air, and sped back to the crib.

Rushed to my closet. Reached up on the top shelf.

Opened my leather bag.

Got my gun out.

Took out a handful of bullets.

Started loading the gun.

Carmen had fronted me at Starbucks, had punked me in the bathroom. I thought about how Keith had treated me tonight. Then my eyes went to that broken window. That brick wasn't just a brick, it had been a weapon. It had been death. Sweat was on my lips, the back of my shirt damp with my own fear, heart still beating hard, the image of that maniacal SUV trying to run me down fresh in my mind.

First I dropped my piece in my backpack, was going to let it keep the brick company.

Thought about that SUV rampaging down on me.

Changed my mind.

I stuffed my snub-nosed .38 inside my jacket, had to have it in reach.

I bolted out of the house again, alert, hunting for trouble, hoping for trouble, ready for anything.

"Looks like you're ready to kill somebody."

"Where is she?"

I cut though the darkness and ran up to Keith's porch, breathing hard, backpack on, gun in one hand, helmet in the other. He was outside, in his jeans and wife-beater, sitting on the steps in the dark. He was rubbing the tattoo on his arm. That same symbol was on my arm. Our wedding ring made of indelible ink. We had bonded beyond our loins.

Keith said, "You're strapped."

"And the brick she threw through my window in is my backpack."

Keith smelled like dark liquor, the tall and empty glass he held in his hand telling me that he'd been drinking for a while. Thinking for a while. He had a cigarette at the tip of his lips, unlit, just dangling there as if he were contemplating picking up a habit he had dropped twenty years ago.

I asked, "She finish milking the cow?"

"Billie, don't come over starting no shit. The neighbors are all over my ass as it is."

"I'm surprised your landlord isn't coming down and cuss me out."

"That bitch is out of town."

I'd never heard Keith call a woman a bitch before. Had never heard such venom.

He said, "She left yesterday, had to go take care of some relatives down in New Orleans. Hurricane displaced half her family. But she'll hear about last night before the sun comes up."

I looked out to the streets. Keith's SUV was there. I thought that maybe he could've been trying to kill me because I told him I was pregnant, but he was three sheets to the wind, no way could he have driven in his condition without tearing up half the neighborhood. He wasn't that kind of man. As far as I knew. But Lacy probably thought that about Scott. Carmen could've run me down in Keith's ride, but the hood was cold, had checked it as soon as I parked. The hood was cold, meaning the engine was cold, and the windows were frosted, meaning his truck hadn't been moved all night. Besides, his truck was red. The wrong color.

Carmen's Mercedes was gone, no longer touching bumpers, no longer kissing Keith's ride, no longer sucking his dick. The space where her car had been parked was empty when I pulled up, meaning she hadn't been gone long enough for any of the apartment dwellers to snatch up that prime parking.

Now my motorcycle rested where her car had been, my front tire kissing Keith's bumper.

I asked, "Why didn't you park in your garage?"

"Don't like being in that alley. Niggas be back there dealing. Bullets don't have no zip code."

Nothing made sense. My heart told me the truth, even if my mind disagreed.

"Where is she?"

"Why are you carrying a gun, Billie?"

"When did she leave here?"

"Well, the police were here not too long ago. We argued after that. She left."

I stared at him. Hated him so much right now.

I sat down next to him, left my helmet and backpack between us.

"Your wife threw a brick through my window. Don't cover for her."

"Carmen throwing a brick? Be real. She wouldn't do anything that might break a nail."

He reached over, took the gun out of my hand, put it down.

Then I took the empty glass out of his hand, put it down.

I pulled the cigarette from his lip, tossed it in the grass.

He put his hand on mine, rubbed my skin.

I said, "Stop."

He didn't.

I didn't push his hand away.

Love rose as anger melted, if only for the moment.

He said, "Look, I have to apologize for the way I acted earlier."

"Bastard."

"It scared me. Was already frustrated. I was a straight-up asshole."

"You were. Said a lot of mean things to me."

"This shit with me and Carmen . . . the shit that just went down between us . . . you know I love you?"

"You're drunk."

"Tipsy, not drunk. I'm aware, functional."

I huffed. "If that's how you treat somebody you love, feel free to hate me."

"You have to see it my way, Billie. Letting you go, I was doing it for you, not me."

"Don't start lying. Last thing I need to hear is some self-righteous bullshit."

"I'm just scared, you know. Seems like I've done a good job of messing up my life. Just wanted to push you away, wanted to do that for you, didn't want you to have to be with me and all of my bullshit."

Silence.

"It happened again. Just when I thought everything was on track."

"Just when everything got better for you, I got pregnant."

"No." He sighed. "I lost my job."

"What?"

"Cutbacks. Last hired, first fired. Yep, got laid off again."

"When?"

"Three weeks ago."

"Three weeks ago? You've been going to work every day."

"Pretending I've been going to work."

"I spent the night. You got up to go to work."

"Got up and went looking for work. Got up and did what I had to do. Kept on fighting. Looking for a job every-damn-day. Behind on my rent. Didn't tell you that I was getting evicted."

"Evicted?"

"Got a three-day notice yesterday morning. Juanita grinned and slapped me with that notice as she was on the way to the airport."

"That bitch."

"Think she wants me evicted so she can put some of her Hurricane Katrina relatives up in here."

"A three-day notice?"

"Juanita has wanted me out for the longest time anyway."

"You're not going to fight it?"

"It costs money to fight anything. What's the point? I've already received a notice to quit. I could look into a process called REO, they file a motion to extend a notice to quit, then I'd get an unlawful detainer two months later. And when that was done, I'd still have to move, still have nowhere to go. My options are pushing a grocery basket and collecting cans in the day, then at night getting cardboard and sleeping on concrete down on Skid Row or . . . underneath a freeway overpass . . . or . . ."

"Or moving in with Carmen."

"More like going back to the house I bought. My blood, sweat, and tears bought that house."

"I could help you get another place. Consider it a loan."

"I thought about asking you, I did."

"Male ego?"

He rubbed his eyes. "But it's bigger than that."

"How much bigger?"

"And, since I'm baring my soul and telling you all this, I'm a little behind on my child support. Carmen had been all over it. She has connections and she is wearing them out. One hundred in arrears and they're about to pull my driver's license. Because of a hundred damn dollars. They do that, can't get around even if I get a job. And if I do luck up and get a job that requires me to drive . . . like the one I'm looking at right now . . . or if I need any kind of clearance . . . with my finances . . . catch-22."

I didn't like it, but I nodded. At least I understood what was going on. Didn't make me feel any better, but what had been opaque was a lot clearer. Said, "Carmen has you up against a wall."

"With a knife to my throat."

He laughed a laugh that sounded like misery personified, shook his head, and frowned.

He said, "If I go back to that house . . . no child support . . . a place to stay."

"It all goes away."

"I trade problems for problems. Not a lot of choices at this point, you know?"

He took a deep breath, let his frustration seep out nice and slow.

Sirens punctuated the air, coming from down on Crenshaw. In the distance, helicopters were circling another area. Cars passed by, a few with music so loud vibrations ran through my body.

I asked, "Why didn't you tell me you got laid off?"

"And you would do what?"

"I could've tried to help."

He chuckled. "How?"

"Like I said, I could've loaned you some money."

"I'm not good at asking for help, not from a woman."

"That male ego will have you sleeping on the streets."

"And how was I supposed to pay you back?"

"Could've asked Viviane if you could crash there awhile."

"I can't bring my daughter over there, you know that. Carmen would have an aneurysm."

"You could've worked something out."

"You barely have a roof over your head. Besides, this ain't your problem. I didn't want it to be. Whatever drama that went on between me and Carmen would've ended up in your home."

"Well, part of it has already come through my window."

"She didn't do that. Serious."

"So, you were gonna kick me to the curb for my own good."

"You know how I feel? I try and I try and . . . I'm a loser, Billie."

"Having hard times don't make a man a loser."

"Either way, you deserve better. My drama has become your drama. I don't want you inheriting my bullshit. I love you enough to let you go so you can be happy. Love you enough to want you to have better than what I have to offer, which ain't much." He took a hard breath. "I need another fucking drink."

"No, you don't." I pulled his arm, kept him from getting up. "How is the job search going?"

"It's going. I have another bullshit job interview on Monday. Labor. Two degrees and I'm down to looking at labor jobs. Too old for that shit. Can't compete with boys half my age. Yep, have to put on that slave suit and look for another job on another plantation. It's such a mind thing, you know? Being forty, unemployed, with a kid. Last three interviews told me that I was overqualified. The last three people who interviewed me were at least ten years younger and not as educated. Never thought I'd hear that I was too smart to get a damn job. Overqualified. You can't be both unemployed and overqualified. Now, that's some fucked-up shit. I'm trying to work. Maybe I should've skipped college, should've been a barber. Done landscaping. Should've had some skill I could pack up and take on the road. Could've cut hair in Brazil or Amsterdam. Overqualified. The system has me by the balls. Looking and interviewing for jobs you need instead of being able to do what you really want to, that's depressing. That's what I admire about you, Billie. Your freedom. You are able to do what you want to do. I ever tell you that?"

"You're drunk. And it's freezing. Let's get you inside."

"When is our baby due?"

That halted me, sent a different kind of chill down my spine. All of the mean things he said at Starbucks, all of that came back, every single word. "Don't play with my emotions, Keith."

"You know if it's a boy or a girl?"

"Would it matter?"

"Told you it caught me off guard. Thought about it since then. Would be great if I had a son. Not a daughter. Don't need another woman in my life. Women suck the energy out of you. Need me a son."

"Where did all of this come from?"

"Whatever you want to do, I'm here for you. It won't be much, but I'll do what I can."

"But you're moving back in with Carmen."

"I'm broke. I have to live somewhere. And if I go back over there, like I told you before, the child support, the court orders . . . I get some breathing room. I get a place to rest my head. Things are bad for me. I need to regroup." He rocked, took a deep breath. "We could still see each other, if that's okay."

"You're going to fuck her and sleep with me."

"I'd find a way to make love to you every day. Don't ever want to stop making love to you."

I paused. "How long would this go on?"

"When Destiny turns eighteen, I'll be free from the court, on that level anyway."

"What am I supposed to do for the next two years? Be pregnant by myself while you play the court game? Have this baby and be home while you're snuggled up to Carmen? Be celibate while she sucks your dick to put you to sleep? See you on the down low? How do you see this working out?"

"Tell me my options, Billie."

I shook my head. "I don't know what to tell you, Keith."

"I don't know what to do."

He put his hand on mine.

I didn't move it away.

I didn't embrace it.

But I didn't move it away.

Like Keith, I wondered how I ended up here. A part-time substitute teacher and part-time bartender, sitting out in the cold on a Saturday morning, a brick on one side of me and a loaded gun on the other, hormones raging, pregnant by an unemployed married man who was damn near homeless.

All I wanted was somebody fun and smart. And cute. Eyes that smiled when they saw me. And soft lips to greet me. Somebody who gave great hugs. Honey-flavored kisses. Somebody down-to-earth.

I don't think what I wanted was superficial. I knew that happiness wasn't always happy. It just wasn't that easy. But if you could find somebody you could be open with, it was worth it. Not easy to find somebody who accepted me for who I was with all of my shortcomings and insecurities. Someone who wasn't afraid for me to know he had some shortcomings and insecurities too.

Keith had been all of that to me.

I held his hand.

Then I heard a baby crying in the distance.

That baby cried and cried and cried.

Heard that sleep-deprived woman screaming for that baby to please shut up.

She was going insane.

Shrieking to God and Jesus for peace.

Just her and the baby.

The baby kept on crying and crying and crying.

The colicky cry of reality turned my heart into stone.

I let Keith's hand go.

I said, "Don't believe you just offered to make me your whore on the side."

"I'm not trying to make you a whore."

"So, does Carmen get to be the whore? Which one of us will get that title?"

Keith said, "You have to understand that this isn't easy for me."

"I never said it was easy."

"My daughter is getting older. I'm not there for her every night. I should be there with her when she goes to bed and when she wakes up in the morning. Every night I don't see her, part of me dies."

"Why were you with me?"

"What do you mean by that?"

"It's always been like this with you and Carmen. Why did you involve me in your mess?"

"I told you my situation when we met."

"Did you? I mean, did you really?"

"You had a choice."

"If you had said, hey I'm getting back with my wife after I get some new pussy for a few months, then yeah, I would've had a choice. But you gave me a million and one I-Can't-Stand-Carmen speeches. A million I-Hate-Carmen speeches. A million and one How-Much-I-Love-Me-Some-Billie speeches."

"I do love you, Billie. It's just that life isn't that simple. Since I met you, I've always wanted you. You never realize how far you are from something you love than when you're standing right beside it."

"Stop, Keith. I don't want to hear any of that mumbo jumbo."

He took another hard breath. "I need another drink."

"I don't understand. Help me understand."

He paused, nodded.

I said, "I'm listening."

"Billie, I'm not going to lie, being with you was selfish, helped ease that pain, that depression, but you, no matter how wonderful you are, you can't fix what's broken inside me. I have to be there with Destiny. And to be with her means I have to deal with my ex for at least the next two years."

"Cheaper to keep her, right?"

In the background, that baby was still crying.

The mother was still shrieking. So much hatred in her voice.

Keith heard her. His eyes followed the sound. He shook his head over and over.

Keith said, "You're going to hate me."

"Why do you say that?"

"Because of your expectations. Your expectations will lead to your disappointments."

"My expectations?"

"Disappointments are the results of expectations. No expectations, no disappointments."

"Is that how you see it?"

"You're gonna wake up one morning, depressed, angry, see how you're all wrapped up in my shit, plus all the additional shit we manage to create together in the aftermath of this shit, and you're going to think back to this moment, then you're gonna remember that I told you that the value on my life was upside down, and you're going to realize that you should have run like the fucking wind."

"Don't say that. Stop saying that. Having a bad time in life does not make you a loser. If that's the case, then ninety percent of the country is filled with losers."

"You're gonna be kicking yourself, nauseous, and hating me. Your feet are going to be swollen, then you're going to look at your belly, at a life we're creating, feel that kick of reality coming from inside you, and all of the romantic notions you feel right now will be gone and you will feel like you're stuck."

"Damn, Keith. Should I have popped a few Prozac before I came over here?"

"That's the way it goes."

We listened to the crying, to the shrieking.

Whoever that mother was, she was alone. By choice or abandoned, she was alone.

Alone.

I said, "Maybe you'll hate me, Keith. Maybe you'll be kicking yourself for ever meeting me. Maybe you'll see me all swollen up and resent me. Face it; you're almost done raising Destiny. Maybe you'll look at me with a brand-new baby and feel nothing but hate. Keith, I'm not trying to trap you."

He chuckled. "Can't trap somebody who's already in a cage."

"Don't start with that woe-is-me noise, Keith."

He raised his palms in mock surrender. "Once again, I digress."

I felt like a girl for saying it, but the words floated out of me. "I hate that I love you, Keith."

"Love me enough to stay in this one-bedroom with me? Me, you, and the baby right here sleeping in a regular-sized bed, same neighborhood as Section 8 apartments, can you handle that?"

"Don't talk like that, Keith. Not if you don't mean it."

"I need another drink."

"No more alcohol."

Then the crying stopped. Didn't fade. The wailing ceased like the voice on a television when it gets unplugged. The screeching halted too.

We had silence.

Keith said, "I have so much stress right now. Too much stress. Some days I hate the fact that I woke up, you know that? This . . . this . . . this . . . is so overwhelming. So not the way I wanted my life to be."

"Yeah. Sure. And this is the life I wrote down in my high school memory book."

"Look, I love my daughter. I will do whatever it takes to make sure she's okay."

"You're her father. You're supposed to."

"My not being there for her, I can't handle the guilt. I can't handle that kind of guilt every day."

"So you'll sleep with Carmen to make it better for your daughter."

"The sofa. I'll sleep on the sofa."

"Bullshit."

"You're a good catch."

"What makes me a good catch?"

He rocked, rubbed his hands together. "You don't take forever to get dressed. You don't talk forever about nothing. Not once have you given me one-hour conversations about how bad your day was. Always positive. Always smiling. You're not on antidepressants. You don't have deep daddy issues. You're already happy. You're not an emotional vampire. And you're not in therapy."

"And?"

"You know how to get a man from L.A. to Fresno."

I laughed. "Sex, sex, sex."

"It's more than sex. But the sex is good because of what I feel for you. Because I love you."

His words melted most of my hate. Most, not all. Never was good at hating, not for long.

I came over here ready to kill somebody and Keith's drunk butt made me laugh.

I took my jacket off, exposed my tat, the chill of the night making my nipples rise.

I said, "I don't have a big house. I don't even have a real job. All I have is a motorcycle."

"Billie, you're a little black dress worn with a strand of pearls."

"What does that mean?"

"You're timeless, Billie. I've been in awe of you since I met you. I envy you."

His sincerity was my green kryptonite, weakened me to my knees.

Right then if he had tried to kiss me, right or wrong, I would have let him. The mind part of me wanted me to leave, to go back home and regroup, but the heart part of me was in control, was beating hard and strong, wanted him to take me inside his apartment, put me on that mattress, undress me, kiss my skin, make me sweet promises, do things to me or just cuddle with me. Couldn't shake that feeling off. Strange needing to feel somebody, horrible needing that kind of affirmation when it was all wrong.

He said, "The gun. You were coming here to kill me?"

"Her."

"Would love for you to bring me her head on a stick."

"You want me to?"

"But I can't let you kill her." He sucked his teeth, thinking. "Two reasons I can't let you do that."

"Destiny."

"Right."

"And?"

"Premeditated. You left and came back with a gun."

"Now you're sounding like a lawyer."

"Never. I watch *CSI*. They'd give you a lethal injection. Just like they did Tookie. They would kill you because of Carmen."

I blew air. "That sucks."

"Anything bad happened to you . . . that would destroy me."

I paused. "Would it?"

He paused too, still thinking. "But I can't let you kill my daughter's mom."

"I know."

"Just like I can't kill her. If Destiny was a lot younger, too young to remember . . . Too late for that."

"You've thought about it?"

"Every married man thinks about killing his wife at least once."

I asked, "What about unhappily married men?"

"A thousand times a day, a thousand different ways, sometimes in alphabetical order." He yawned. "I've dreamed of everything from arsenic to strangulation. I'm only up to the *S*'s right now."

I yawned too. "Why don't you?"

"Takes a lot of money to get away with murder. I'm a broke-ass nigga."

We actually laughed.

He put his hand on mine. I held his hand this time.

A moment later he touched my tattoo. I touched his.

Keith scooted closer to me. Too tired to move, I put my head on his shoulder. He put his arm around me. Warmth covered me. I closed my eyes. I imagined I was riding through the darkness, going up that stretch of road where Highway 1 broke away from the 101 up by San Luis Obispo. A soft breeze came and I imagined the wind was in my face, coastal plains and cliff scenes at my side.

A car screeched around the corner, came to a dramatic stop in front of the building.

Our moment of peace died an abrupt death.

The car was a Mercedes. It was Carmen.

She left the car double-parked and ran up the stairs.

Keith groaned, shook his head, tugged at his hair.

Carmen ran hard, her mules slapping her feet with her frantic pace.

I heard a mumble, a geriatric curse raining down, and looked up.

They were there. In practically every window.

Saw old-as-dirt neighbors peeping down on us.

Spies in the house of love.

Didn't know how long they had been there.

One of them must've shuffled to their Princess phone and called Carmen.

Carmen must've heard I was back over here.

Now she had screeched back over here to create another shitstorm.

Anger rose in flames, melted any love I felt.

I stood up as fast as I could.

She stopped running when she saw me.

Surprised her before she could surprise me.

Her frown was so deep, a thousand crevices carved in a wooden face.

Almost as deep as mine.

I'd been humiliated at Starbucks. My window had been smashed. I'd almost been run down.

I wanted to throw the brick at her and grab my gun.

She rushed into the light and I saw a million tears sparkling in her eyes. Keith stood up.

Carmen hurried by me as if I were insignificant, as if she were in a zone, possessed single-minded concentration, as if she were focused on one objective, that objective more important than me.

She moved by me like I was a piece of trash fluttering in the wind.

She went right up to Keith, took his hand.

She told Keith, "Destiny's missing."

Two words from Carmen and parental fear covered Keith's face.

Two words from Carmen and Keith was sober.

Two words from Carmen and Keith was suffocating.

"What do you mean, she's missing?"

"She's not at my parents' house."

"Then where is she, Carmen?"

"She ran away."

Their words were so fast, so in sync, almost another language.

Sirens blared in the background, the echoes from a dangerous world.

Keith stood like a bear; his voice boomed, "Ran away?"

"I don't know. All I know is she's gone, Keith."

"Carmen, why would she run away? What did you do?"

"What makes you think I—"

"What did you do to Destiny, Carmen?"

She took a hard breath. "We had an argument—you know how she gets."

"I know how *you* get." He got in her face. "Did you hit her?"

"She cursed me again, Keith. She cursed her own mother."

"One thing after the other." Keith cursed. "How long has she been gone?"

"Nobody knows."

"How can nobody know? What the hell are they doing over there?"

Carmen snapped, "My parents thought she was asleep; her door was locked from the inside."

"Locked from the inside?"

"Yeah. And the deadbolts are still on all the doors."

Keith ran his hand over his head. "Did somebody come in through the window?"

Carmen gasped. "Shit. I don't . . . the window . . ."

Keith raised his voice. "Did you think about that? That maybe somebody came in the window?"

"Don't yell at me, Keith."

"Did you think that maybe somebody came in the goddamn window and . . . and . . . and . . ."

"Oh, God. Oh, God. Oh, God."

I swallowed. We were in Los Angeles. The land of child killings, pedophiles, and Amber Alerts.

I put my hand on my stomach. Did that like I was protecting what was inside me.

Keith hurried to get a shirt. I put my jacket back on, grabbed my backpack and headed for my Ducati. I looked back and saw Carmen wiping her eyes, mumbling, looking at me, shaking her head. She gave me her back.

Carmen called out, "What should we do, Keith?"

"Call the police. *Now.*"

Carmen took out her cell phone. "Okay, okay."

"And start calling her friends."

"Okay, okay."

"Wake them up and see if anybody knows anything."

"Okay, okay."

"Hit redial on the phone in the bedroom. Find out if she's tried to call anybody."

"Okay, okay."

Eighteen years of history, I heard in his voice, saw it in her reactions.

"You're wheezing, Carmen."

"I know, I know."

"Take your medicine."

"Okay, okay."

Carmen was not as strong as she pretended to be.

He had been the leader of that household.

I left, almost running.

By the time I made it to my bike, Keith was rushing down the walkway with Carmen. Like husband and wife, running down the aisle after the nuptials had been rendered, their faces in the reverse of happiness. He took the keys from her, opened the door for her, then bolted to the driver's side. He opened the door for her. Don't think he'd ever done that for me. I stared at her four-door Mercedes as they sped away, as Keith made a hard right onto Degnan and raced toward King Boulevard.

Keith drove while Carmen made the calls.

Their child had vanished.

They had a crisis.

They were a family.

I was invisible.

I sat on my bike, wide awake, cold air chilling my thoughts.

One by one, the lights in the neighbors' windows turned off.

The building went black.

The streets were silent.

No sirens.

No baby crying.

No shrieking mother.

The absence of noise was eerie.

The absence of noise was deafening.

The absence of noise meant everything was wrong.

Ten minutes later.

The roar of iron horses greeted me as I turned off the 90 into the parking lot at Jerry's Deli. The sound of midengine bikes took my mind away from Keith and his wife, away from their family drama, took my mind off my own fermentation, if only for a moment. I wanted to call Keith, wanted to be there for him.

But I couldn't. They were family. I was his mistress, if that.

Mistress.

If that.

That was unsettling.

Mistress.

Just thinking that word made me feel like speeding into a brick wall.

A hornet's nest. I'd messed around and fallen into a hornet's nest.

It was late and early at the same time, the in-between hours.

I had driven around awhile before I came here. Had seen three police cars stopped in front of one of the single-level, single-family homes on King Boulevard, their lights flashing. Had seen Carmen's four-door Mercedes in front of the house. Didn't know she had grown up that close to where Keith lived. Had no idea she was a Crenshaw girl too. Had imagined her bourgeois attitude was from the West Side.

Anyway.

Parking lot at Jerry's Deli.

Platinum Ryders. Ruff Ryders. Steel Horses. Infinite Ryders.

The place was packed with bikers. Marcel's crew was here too. Saw her bodacious Super Hawk up front. That indigo paint job rocked, had to admit that. Anyway. Figured it would be crowded. Outside of Denny's, most of the eating places in L.A. shut down before midnight, and since last call was at one-thirty, as soon as all the clubs started to play the last song the nocturnal congregated in Marina del Rey for the after-party.

I rolled into the lot behind a black Escalade, its music bumping so hard the vibrations ran through my body like a defibrillator, chrome rims shining underneath the streetlights, those rims spinning like the teacup ride at Disneyland, the whole ride pimped out like it was the after-shot from an episode of *Pimp My Ride*, videos blazing on four monitors. Young girls wearing too much makeup and hard-core gangsta brothers wearing too much gold getting blazed and getting their freak on on Crenshaw Boulevard. Knew it was the 'Shaw. Knew all of its barbershops and second-rate stores like the back of my hand.

The Escalade was packed. Young brothers and an army of girls in tight clothes crawled out.

"That's my, jam! Crunk it up!"

"*It's about to be a* what *girlfight*—"

Everybody was singing, laughing, and loud-talking, the Escalade rocking with their groove until the song ended. As soon as the door opened, the scent of alcohol and ganja mixed with the ocean breeze. One of the girls staggered out, moved away from the truck, and threw up. Her girls moved away from her and made nasty faces, made comments about that girl not ever being able to hold her liquor. One of the guys had a video camera on, had the camera all up in the girl's face, recording everything in sight.

One of the girls looked at me. A thin young girl with golden skin and huge breasts. Her feet caught my attention. She had on some killer boots, matching purse, all of her gear expensive, the kind you'd see on *Sex and the City*. It was odd. Her clothes weren't on the same level as her boots and purse.

She saw me staring at her boots and she smiled.

She said, "Jimmy Choo."

Then she came over to me.

She asked, "Need anything?"

"Anything like what?"

"Anything like anything."

"I'm cool."

One of the guys called out, "Goldie."

She turned around, her stroll awkward, like she was wearing brand-new boots.

The girl with the golden skin and her girlfriends walked away, two of them still singing and dancing, one of them singing and holding the drunken girl's hand as they headed toward Jerry's.

The girl in the boots had a strange walk, like her boots didn't fit, maybe a size too small.

The guys stayed behind, laughing, calling the women disrespectful names.

"Her ass better be glad she didn't throw up inside my ride."

"These girls a trip."

"Ain't they, though? This DVD gonna be hot. Better than the last one."

"Yo, Mo, I don't think you shoulda left Baby Phat up in the motel room like that."

"*Oooo wee.* Her little ass could milk a cow. A bona fide cum dumpster."

They laughed.

"Mo, Baby Phat, she went buck-wild. What did she take to make her wild out like that?"

"Her ass was already crazy and that Ecstasy is a motherfucker."

The brothers saw me sitting on my bike. I had taken my helmet off and was resting on my Duke, still trying to decide if I was going to go inside JD's, minding my own business, when I saw the cameraman had turned my way. That red dot was blinking in my face.

I raised my helmet to hide my face and snapped, "Get that camera away from me."

"Yo, check it out. We're shooting a docu—"

"Get that damn camera out of my face."

He lowered the camera, no apology, then yanked up his baggy pants and swaggered across the lot and toward the restaurant, camera up and taping whatever and whoever. One of the brothers he left behind grabbed his backpack and came over toward me. I tensed up at the sight of his Mack stroll.

"Phat bike. Damn, that's a sweet Ducati."

"Tell your boy to keep that camera away from me."

"No problem. I'm Mo."

"Was your boy Larry or Curly?"

"Larry or Curly? You mad funny."

I motioned at his Escalade. "Interesting video you were playing."

"We make like these docu-porns."

"Docu-porn?"

"Documentary and porn. Kinda like *Girls Gone Wild*, but we use Crenshaw Boulevard."

I shook my head. "Crenshaw Boulevard?"

"Local talent."

"Those girls look pretty young."

"They grown women. Like you, baby."

I looked at him, saw nothing attractive, zero charisma. "Where you get these *grown women*?"

"What, you wanna be in one?"

"Just asking where you get the girls from."

"Girls we meet up in clubs, on the street, at music stores, whatever."

"Regular girls from the around here?"

"They hot. Yeah. We gonna flip it and have that on DVD by tomorrow night."

"By tomorrow night?"

"Gonna have at least two hundred units. Maybe more. Better reserve your copy."

"Quick turnaround."

"Might have sample DVDs in the morning if you wanna check 'em out. Here my business card."

"I don't need your card."

"So it's like that? Why don't you gimme some digits so I can holla?"

"How old are you?"

He said, "Twenty-one. How old you?"

"A lot older than twenty-one."

"What, you twenty-five or something?"

"Add almost ten to that."

"Damn. No shit? Don't matter. Age ain't nothing but a number."

"Look, brother, while you're still young, do something productive with your talents."

He motioned toward his Escalade. "I am being productive."

"Selling bootleg music and making porn?"

"Like Jay-Z said, I'm not a bidnessman. I am a bidness, man."

"Whatever. Look, brother, stealing music and exploiting women ain't productive."

He walked away shaking his head, the scent of ganja and alcohol fading with his every step.

I heard him grumble something, ending his paragraph of vulgarity with one single word: "Bitch."

Helmet in my lap, I leaned against my bike. Had a headache so severe, thought my cranium was about to pop. My hypocritical butt. A thirty-four-year-old slacker trying to give somebody else advice.

Somebody who was rocking an Escalade while I sat on a bike I could barely afford.

Yeah, that was hilarious.

I rested my helmet on my mirror before I let my backpack slide off my shoulders; that extra weight taking my mind back to all the bad things that had happened since the sun went down.

A little while ago I was ready to kill somebody. Right now I could've been in the backseat of a police car, angry tears in my eyes, taking my last look at freedom, and I knew it. I reached inside, wanted to check the gun, at least take the bullets out and throw them away, do that so I wouldn't make any stupid mistakes. Well, so I wouldn't make another stupid mistake, one that was unforgivable.

I reached inside and felt the brick.

There was nothing else in my backpack.

The gun wasn't there. My heartbeat sped up.

I jumped off my bike, went through my backpack again and again.

Nothing.

I freaked, hoping it hadn't fallen out while I was riding. But the backpack was zipped tight.

Had to think.

Keith had taken it.

I don't remember putting it back.

Couldn't remember if Keith had taken it inside his apartment or if I'd left it on his front porch.

Tried to remember if it was on the porch when I left.

Or if Keith had taken it inside.

It was the last thing I wanted to do right now, but I pulled out my cellular phone and called Keith. He didn't answer. I left him a message, first hoping all was okay with his daughter, if he needed anything to let me know, then asked him to let me know if he took the gun inside his apartment.

My cellular rang. Not Keith. Viviane. Imagined she'd still be spread-eagled, moaning to the breeze about now. I answered. Asked what was up. She was at Daniel Freeman Hospital.

That surprised me. My first thought was another brick had flown through the window and hit her.

Somebody was hurt, but it wasn't her.

She said, "It's LaQuiesha. Somebody beat up Q."

Q was what she called LaQuiesha, her younger half-sister. Same mom. Q's father was African-American. Lived with her parents down by Crenshaw and Century, about fifteen minutes from the house.

Viviane told me that some girl jumped on Q, jacked her up down on Crenshaw.

She said, "Broke her nose."

"*What?* Broke her nose?"

"Yes. Her face is messed up. Both eyes swollen. At least three teeth chipped or broken."

"Good Lord."

"She got it real bad."

"How is she? I mean . . . you know what I mean."

"She's crying, distraught because her nose is messed up and she won't be able to be in some video, scared she's going to lose her chance to be on *America's Next Top Model*. And she had auditions for two movies on Monday, which is definitely not going to happen now."

"What happened?"

"She's going to need reconstructive surgery."

"Are you serious?"

"All that blood and swelling. I didn't recognize her."

"What the hell happened?"

"She said she was down by Crenshaw and Stocker and—"

"What was she doing down there?"

"Who knows? Said she was at the bank and some crazy girl just jumped on her for no reason."

"She was robbed?"

"By a black girl. Said the girl was younger than her. Hit her with something."

"*What?* These young girls are getting to be as violent as the boys out there."

"She's going on and on about how black girls hate her. You know how she always complains. Her self-esteem is so low it kills me. She's down here crying about how *they* hate her. Some of her hair was yanked out. Crying how they're jealous of her hair. How she hates being black and Asian because she always has to prove herself over and over. She is working my nerves like you would not believe."

"Look, I'm in Marina del Rey. Outside Jerry's Deli. Need me to come down there?"

"I'm cool. My mother is going off—in Korean—and embarrassing the hell out of me. Not by her talking Korean but because of the way she's acting. And Q's dad, he ain't no better. His ghetto ass is acting as ghetto as ghetto can be. Just wanted you to know what was up."

We said a few more things.

I told her Keith's daughter was missing. That I'd seen Carmen again.

Viviane said, "Damn. Keith's daughter ran away?"

"I have no idea. All I know is Carmen burned rubber getting over there and he left with her."

"Damn."

"One more thing. Somebody in a white or tan SUV tried to run me down."

"What?"

I told her what had happened. That I had come back home and gotten my gun.

She said, "Somebody in a light-colored SUV was parked out in front of the house."

That halted me. Scared me. "When?"

"About an hour ago. I turned on the porch light and whoever it was pulled away in a hurry."

I looked up at the sky, searched for the moon, said, "This has been one crazy night."

"Be careful, Billie. Confrontation at Starbucks. A brick through the window. Carrying a gun."

"I know."

"Pointing a gun at somebody gets you ten. Shooting somebody will get you twenty."

Silence.

She had called to tell me about Q, but she'd also called for another reason.

I knew her. I sensed her uneasiness.

She said, "You know I love you, right? You're my best friend."

"I know."

"Even if you're Japanese."

"Quit it."

"Joking. But on the real, you're the only real friend I have."

"I know."

"The only one who understands me. The only black woman who actually likes me."

"Stop being paranoid. Has to be at least one more who likes you."

She laughed a little. "My feelings are hurt. I'm trying to not start crying over here, Billie."

"I don't want to cry either. Get to what you want to say, Viviane."

"Your Made in Japan ass."

"That joke is getting old, Viviane. Time to drop that one and make up a new one."

"Billie . . . didn't mean to react like that when you told me you were pregnant."

"It's cool."

"The window being broken . . . then you told me . . . the sheriff . . . all of that caught me off guard. I mean, you let me stand out on the patio and ramble to you . . . why didn't you tell me? Don't you trust me?"

"I trust you, Viviane."

"Why didn't you tell me? I mean, that's why I reacted the way I did."

I managed an easy chuckle. "You should've seen the way Keith reacted."

"Serious. That hurt. I tell you all of my problems."

"Sorry. Just wasn't ready to talk about it. Not until I figured out what I was going to do."

"I mean, you don't have to move, you know."

"Viviane—"

"I'm serious. Don't . . . don't . . . just don't make your decision based on that, okay?"

She gave me guilt. I gave her silence.

I said, "I'll decide what I'm going to do."

"Billie—"

"Then we'll talk."

Before this conversation could get too deep I let her go, told her to keep me posted.

After talking to Viviane, couldn't decide which way to go. Wanted to be alone but didn't want to be by myself at the same time. My mind was spinning. Then the roar of another iron horse caught my attention, yet another biker pulling up in the lot. It caught my eye because the rider was rocking a red Ducati 749 Testastretta. Had on matching Ducati jacket, helmet, and gloves. Expensive gear. Ducati was the Gucci of bike gear. So he had on a couple of thousand in leather. The rider was moving slow, like he was scared to get out of second gear, like he was scared to turn too fast. He went a little wide, didn't give up enough throttle, his ride jerky, engine about to shut down, damn near dropped his bike coming into the lot. He recovered. Still, I gave the neophyte the thumbs-up. He fumbled around, hit the passing lights then his high beams before he managed to sound his horn in reply. He circled the lot pretty much riding in first gear before he pulled up next to me. He killed his engine and pulled his helmet off.

We stared at each other.

He smiled.

I frowned.

He said, "Billie."

He was exotic. Cocoa-brown skin, a sweet mixture of Latin and African-American. Slender man with short, curly hair. A prototype for America's mixed-race future. No way could he make an ugly baby.

I whispered his name: "Raheem."

He nodded. "Everything okay?"

"Why?"

We stared at each other, the night air fogging away from our faces.

I said, "You're trying to learn how to ride on a fourteen-thousand-dollar bike?"

He shrugged. "Not like I have anybody volunteering to teach me, you know?"

"This is pissing me off."

"What I do?"

"Guys like you end up dead within six months, then the lawmakers come down hard on the real riders." I was livid. "Take the damn MSF class before you end up being an organ donor."

"Told you the class doesn't fit my schedule. Thought I'd come down here. Heard a few bikers hung out here after hours. Decided to come and network, find somebody to give me a few lessons."

I pulled my lips in, shook my head.

I asked Raheem, "*Catwoman* or *Matrix Revolutions*?"

"Huh?"

"Which movie made you run out and shoot your wad on a Duke and leather?"

He laughed.

I laughed too, at him, not with him. Learning to ride on a Ducati 749 would be like taking driver's education in a friggin' Lamborghini. Boys and their toys. Men and their midlife crises.

I asked, "How many times you been down?"

"Down?"

"Dropped it. You've got road rash all over the side of your bike."

"Road rash?"

"Where did you drop your bike?"

"Dropped it in the driveway. Did that a couple of times."

"When?"

"About an hour after I bought it. Broke the mirror the first day; got it replaced twice."

"You've got road rash all over your fairing. Get engine guards."

"Road rash? Fairing? Engine guards? What are those?"

"You'll be sleeping under a tombstone in a week. Keep the lid on so you can look good in your coffin."

"Lid? Where is the lid on the motorcycle?"

I laughed some more.

He said, "Bike is hot as hell. Think something's wrong with it?"

"It's fine. You're on a race bike. Made to move, not meant to stop-and-go or sit idle in traffic."

He made a face that said he wished somebody had told him that before he wrote the check.

He asked, "Hungry?"

I looked up at the sky, at the darkness that would lose the battle with light pretty soon, looked up and felt like I had nowhere to go, no one to talk to, then I looked at his pretty face and nodded.

This was as peaceful as my life had been in the last few hours.

I didn't want this calm to abandon me.

Didn't feel like company. But didn't want to be alone.

I said, "Yeah, I'm hungry."

Inobe's soothing and soul-shifting voice greeted us at the door. Over the house speakers her CD was on, blending with all the chatter and conversations, singing "Love for All Seasons." Before I knew it I was humming, then singing along, her music, her hellacious beats pulling me in, intoxicating me, taking the chill away from my soul. Standing by the front door waiting to be called to a booth, Inobe's voice raining down on me, I became her backup singer like it was second nature. She was doing the damn thing, younger than me, on her second CD, taking the same risks I should've taken ten years ago.

Raheem said, "Your voice . . . wow."

I stopped singing when I saw a sister walk in, pregnant and about to pop, hand in hand with her boyfriend.

I turned my back on that happy couple, stood by Raheem, him in bold red and me in yellow, looking like the sequel to *Biker Boyz*, both of us in black biker boots, both of us with our helmets in our hands. People looked at us like they thought we were a couple of bohemian rebels. We were a good-looking couple, an older lady and her husband made a point to tell us that on their way out.

Then the girl we had just seen outside walked up to us.

She asked me, "Need anything?"

I said, "You just asked me that."

"I did? When?"

"Sister, whatever you're selling, I don't need it. And you need to get off it."

She walked away, ganja perfuming the air, still having a hard time in those boots. She headed to a table in the back. Her crew had taken up the back wall. Could hear them talking and laughing all the way up here. The brother with the backpack was trying to tip around and sell his bootlegged goods.

Raheem said, "Different crowd tonight."

"I guess hoodrats and pimps gotta eat too."

The place had been redone. They used to have pictures of dead celebrities and ancient movie paraphernalia all over the place. Now the walls were red, looked very modern. But they still had the largest menu in the world, what looked like at least two thousand items listed.

That was why half of L.A. ended up here after hours.

We were taken to a booth. Before we sat down, we took our jackets off. Raheem had tats on his forearm. He didn't look like the type. I put my backpack on top of my jacket.

I said, "Guess I looked pretty bad at Starbucks."

"Seemed like you and your boyfriend were having some issues."

"Sorry about the suit. I'll pay for the dry-cleaning."

"It's cool. Just hoped you were okay."

"Thanks."

His speaking voice was soothing, like jazz at midnight, like listening to Joe sing.

I hated that. I really did.

Keith was with his wife. And I felt guilty. I had no idea why.

I excused myself and went to the ladies' room, started typing Keith a text message, asking him to keep me posted on the state of his daughter. Let him know that if there was anything I could do, call. The inebriated girl I'd seen in the parking lot was in a stall with her girls, moaning and trying to get it together. Think she had tossed her cookies some more. They left by the time I was finishing up my message. The bathroom door opened again just as I hit send. It was Marcel, following me, stalking me, harassing me.

She asked, "Ready for that race?"

"Don't sweat me."

"No traffic right now. My crew can block cars and we can rock the 90 from Culver Boulevard to Slauson. Wide-open freeway. About six miles. Let's see who tops out."

"Marcel, it's late, I'm tired, not in the mood for your nonsense."

"Chicken?"

I paused and looked at her. She was Carmen. She was every woman who had ever confronted me, every woman who had backstabbed and stepped to my face over some bullshit.

I thought about it. Honestly, I was two seconds from telling her to hop on her damn bike.

Something kicked inside me.

I heard that haunting sound, that baby crying, its colicky howl stuck in my head.

I said, "You're really trying to lose that iron horse."

"You win, you get the bike. Pink slip is yours. I win, you follow me home."

I ran my hand over my hair.

I told her, "You need to quit."

"I'm putting up over ten large and what you have will cost you nothing."

"Sorry you feel that way."

"And you need to trade teams. At least check it out. Homeboy's wife was all up in your shit tonight. Heard she hemmed you up in the bathroom and was about to open a can of whoop ass."

"Well, if you heard that she was about to whoop me, you heard wrong."

I stood in the mirror, doing my face and hair. She stood next to me, redoing her lipstick.

She asked, "Who's the brother you're with now?"

"Why?"

"Saw that cutie up at Starbucks too. Seems like you're getting more than lattes from Starbucks."

"Your point?"

"Didn't know you were rolling like that."

"Rolling like what?"

"Billie, Billie, Billie. You have some playa in your blood."

"Why you so interested in every man I'm with? Don't tell me you trying to bring it back home."

"I am home, baby. I am home. Trying to get you to visit. It's comfortable over here."

"I've got my own address. I'm having fun at Sixty-nine Heterosexual Lane."

"I used to live there. Nothing over there but heartache and diseases. Can't count the number of times I had a yeast infection. Got cheated on. Can't think of all the men I gave my heart to, ended up used and none of them gave me anything back. Unless you count chlamydia a gift. It's safe over here. You risk heartbreak, but it's safe. You should trust me, Billie. You really should. No one understands a woman the way a woman understands a woman."

"Stop offering me the other side of the coin, Marcel."

She shook her head and chuckled. "Sixty-nine Heterosexual Lane."

"That's right. Sixty-nine Heterosexual Lane. My *permanent* address. So stop the hard sale. Not interested in real estate on your side of town."

"Can I come by?"

"Sure. Soon as you lose the boobs and grow a penis."

She ran her hand over her neck, a very sensual move that made me uneasy, moved her hand back and forth over her light skin. Moved her hand down over her ass. Moved her reddish blond hair from her face, let part of her mane fall down her back, the rest down over her tight top and D-cups.

I thought I had rattled her, thought that Little Miss Carpet Muncher was about to leave me alone.

She smiled. "I have what you need in my backpack. It straps on. Never goes down."

"You're sick."

"Well, baby, so far as that street you claim you're living on, the word at Starbucks is that the original owner of that little piece of property you were sleeping with on Heterosexual Lane showed up and you got evicted. Baby, you were living on Dead End Road. And baby, I don't want you to be homeless."

She stood there staring at me, moving her tongue over her full lips, smiling like she wanted some of this so damn bad. Couldn't lie, Marcel was a beautiful woman. She had confidence and style. And beauty. And the perfect booty to match. The kind of woman that made a lot of heterosexual women want to cross the street and investigate. Tight eyes. Despite her hard talk, her words were very soft, filled with saccharine, very womanly. She had a bold, hypnotic stare.

She asked, "Ever been kissed by a girl?"

"Get out of my way."

"Don't tell me those soft and sexy lips have never had a girl kiss before."

"Out of my way."

"One kiss, Billie. Nobody is in here but us. Nobody has to know."

I ignored her, hand-combed my hair. She didn't vacate. I didn't budge an inch. I was here first and refused to let her run me out of here, wasn't leaving until I was done doing what I came in here to do, whatever that was. This bathroom had become the victim of some sort of territorial battle. I took a long breath, calmed myself just so she wouldn't see how much she rattled my cage, stared at her, dared her.

She whispered, "You really should let me take you out."

"Take me out? Is that right? And do what?"

"We can get dressed up, roll up to Peanuts on Tuesday. Dance. Drink. Have some fun."

She was so serious. I had to laugh.

I told her to get out of my way.

She didn't move. It was like being in a club with an asshole who didn't know when to quit.

I moved around her, then stopped when I felt her hand grazing my ass.

Hands doubled up, I faced her, snapped, "Don't you *ever* do that shit again."

"Do what?"

"Get stupid and I'll slap some sense into your perverted ass."

She laughed, turned around, posed. "Baby, you can slap this ass anytime you feel like it."

I left the bathroom wishing I had my gun, thinking about going to get that brick.

On the way back to the booth, the golden girl in the expensive boots stopped me.

She asked me, "You need anything?"

I damn near exploded, but I just shook my head and kept going.

The brother with the black backpack was at our table, hustling Raheem. I got back just as Raheem slid him some money, the brother moving by me fast. Two bootleg DVDs were on the table.

I asked, "What you buy from that jerk?"

"Just supporting a young brother who trying to do his thing."

"It's porn. Girls he picked up off the street. Disgusting."

Raheem laughed. "Well, he's been my bootleg DVD supplier for a while."

"You're joking? You rocking a Porsche and a Ducati and buying bootleg? C'mon, man."

"That's Moses Jones. Used to run track at Long Beach Poly."

"Now he's running women."

"All I know is that he ran track at Poly. He ran the one hundred, the two, and the four."

"Guess either he didn't run fast enough or have the GPA for a scholarship to a four-year."

"One year at USC."

"Dropped out or kicked out?"

"He jailed out. Selling drugs." Raheem shook his head like losing another black athlete was a major loss to the free world. "Anyway, he's the one who told me a lot of bikers hang out down here."

"And you're supporting his exploitation of black women?"

"He's got the hookup. Bought the porno DVD with Eve on it from him. Got Janet Jackson sunbathing. Why you giving me that face? It's Janet Jackson. And she's naked. Be real. If Beyoncé ever slips up, believe me, I have my copy reserved."

Men.

Maybe Marcel had a point.

Maybe.

Over salads, Raheem sat across from me in our booth and told me he bought a bike because he wanted to ride with the wind in his face. All bikers said that. I said it a lot. Cliché to the bone. Said that he wanted to ride the coast and stop at the Lucia Lodge, maybe spend the night in the honeymoon suite, even if he was alone. Move on from there and eat in Carmel and Monterey and Davenport.

He said, "By summer I'll have it down."

"If you don't kill yourself first."

A Joss Stone song came on, soft and easy, blended into all the chatter in the busy restaurant. Joss was singing how she thought she wanted to be over her love in a week or two, but she was spoiled, couldn't let go. Damn near every song that came on was going to take me to a place I didn't want to go. If they played Hope's "The Rain Don't Last," I'd break out crying.

I looked around.

Marcel was with her crew, licking her lips, still staring me down. Men were all over her, all over her crew. At least three basketball players were jocking them hard. One of the guys in the room had taken them roses, no doubt had bought them their meals in hopes of a sexual encounter. The girls were getting their gear, putting on their jackets, grabbing backpacks, getting their helmets and gloves, a couple putting lipstick on, a few doing hair. When they walked by me, most of them spoke.

After they passed by, Raheem got up, said he was going to the men's room.

Marcel spoke to Raheem as he went by her, actually flirted with him, then gave me eye contact. She had picked up one of the flowers that someone had given her. Was sniffing it as she walked my way.

She asked, "See that? You're right here and your boy was all up in my grill."

"Goodbye, Marcel."

"Should I wait for you in the parking lot?"

"Why don't you get your strap on and go play hide the vibrator with your *Got Milk?* convention?"

"God, you turn me on when you talk to me like that."

She dropped the rose on my side of the table and moved on, her ass swaying left and right, advertising and teasing the room. I slapped the flower to the floor, hit it so hard it flew to the other side of the room. I shook my head. No matter how bad things got, two tits and a clit would never make me want to give up the dick. I've had curious moments, but I wasn't interested in switching teams.

Raheem came back, sat down, asked, "Heard you work at the Temple Bar."

"Who told you that?"

"Jacob."

"What else did big-mouth Jacob tell you?"

"That you're Japanese."

"I am black. I was born in Japan. I'm not Japanese."

"Does that make you black Japanese, or African Japanese or something?"

"You know what?" I bit my tongue. "You almost got cursed out."

"Didn't mean to piss you off."

"What else he tell you?"

"That you were involved with a dude you shouldn't be involved with."

"So, rich boy, you're judging me?"

"Well, I used to be involved with a woman I shouldn't have been involved with. Same as you. She was married, going through a divorce, had a kid. That was months ago. So I understand what you're going through."

"You know what . . . time to change the subject."

"Sure." He nodded. "I'll change the subject."

"Yeah, do that. And I'll be cursing Jacob out as soon as I see him."

He took a breath, shifted. "Motorcycles? Safe subject?"

"Whatever. Doubt if you know much about riding."

"What trail do you like to ride?"

Raheem didn't matter to me. Keith was kudzu, spreading all over my mind right now.

I sipped my soda, washed down my food, said, "Dragon Trail."

"Dragon Trail. Where is that?"

I rubbed my temples. "Foothills of the Smoky Mountains. Highway 129, south of the Tennessee and North Carolina state line. Three hundred and eighteen corners in eleven miles."

That was the kind of thing I had been able to save my money to do. Take time off work whenever I wanted to. Ship my bike across the country, hop on a plane, then ride trails out in no-man's-land.

Those days might be over. My eyes went to the clock, my mind still on someone else.

Inside me, every second, a new life was getting bigger.

I asked him, "What's the best place you've been?"

"In or out of country?"

"Out."

He sipped his soda. "Amsterdam."

"I went there a few years ago."

"You did?"

I smiled. "Those coffee shops . . . ?"

"I know. I asked for the menu and saw . . . Afghan . . . Indian . . . names on it. . . . I was trying hard to remember if those countries were famous for their coffee. . . . I knew Brazilian . . . Vietnamese . . . but Afghan?"

"Herbs, baby. Not coffee."

"Then I understand why everyone in there had those dreamy smiles on their faces."

"Of course. What they have on their menu puts Starbucks to shame."

He chuckled. "And they have those other shops in Amsterdam."

I asked, "What other shops?"

"Places like Casa Rosso and the Banana Bar. Beautiful women from all around the world."

"Ahhh. The red-light district. I'm not even going to ask how much of Amsterdam you sampled."

He laughed and winked at me.

He said, "Jacob told me that you used to be a flight attendant."

"Why am I not surprised?"

"Said you flew all over the world."

"Pay sucked, but I miss those benefits. It was a lot of fun."

"Why did you stop flying?"

"You sure Jacob didn't already tell you?"

"Why? Seems like you have a spirit made for traveling."

"Nine-Eleven. That's why I quit. When they started training us to fight terrorists at thirty thousand feet with no increase in pay, was time to move on. If I wanted to fight a war, I would've joined the military."

"Jacob told me your parents were military."

"Jacob will be getting his butt kicked real soon."

We ate for a moment. The silence between us started to get to me.

"Okay, Mr. Porn Buyer." I shook my head. "Where else have you been?"

"Istanbul was nice."

"Now, that's one place I've never thought about going. How was Turkey?"

"Wonderful people. Amazing places and music. Delicious food. Beautiful women."

I laughed. "It always comes back to the women."

"What's the point of traveling?" He laughed. "Want to hear more?"

"Let's take this in another direction. Worst place you've been?"

"Thailand."

"Thought men loved trips to Thailand. Heard the whole country was another gentleman's club."

"Heaven for some, hell for others." He took a breath. "Thailand. Bangkok. Saw a little boy holding his daddy's hand. Little boy was around four, maybe five years old. And very beautiful. I touched his hair and smiled at him. And guess what happened? His daddy told me his price."

"His daddy told you . . . his price?"

"Told me his price. In very broken English. Freaked me out."

"Good Lord. He was pimping his son?"

"He waited for a while, saw I wasn't buying, shrugged, and kept walking with the little boy. Don't know how long I stood there, tried hard to digest what I heard. Then I looked around. Little prostitutes. All around, every street. Big, red-nosed European guys walking hand in hand with those little girls."

"A daddy pimping his little boy." I shook my head. "This world is a very cruel place."

"And some places are even crueler for some people."

Raheem had an aware side to him. Eve and Janet on the table, but thin-skinned about children.

He said, "It wasn't *The Matrix* that inspired me to get a bike. Was something else."

"What was that something else?"

"Almost embarrassed to say."

"No need to be."

He took out his wallet. Inside was a page from a magazine, folded up. He opened it and slid it across the table. It was that erotic photo I had taken on a 749, in a yellow thong, low cut, sweet jacket on.

My mouth hit the floor. I felt naked. Uncomfortable that I had posed for that shot.

I asked, "Where did you get that?"

"Was in Atlanta. Some of my family lives down there. There's a Ducati shop on Piedmont, right below Buckhead. Next to a strip club and across from the Gold Spa."

"Strip Club. Gold Spa. You and your landmarks. Damn."

"Well, there aren't any churches on that street. Strip clubs and adult stores."

"So they had the magazine at the Ducati shop."

"Enough of that. They had your picture blown up, made a tight poster, so you're up on the wall."

"On the wall? Get out. I'm on the wall at a Ducati shop down in the ATL?"

"Over the cash register. Big poster of you on the wall. See it when you walk in the front door."

"You're joking. My butt . . . all of this . . ."

"All of that."

"My butt is . . ."

"Yeah."

"On a wall at a Ducati shop?"

"And you didn't know?"

"Next to a strip club and across from a freak spa?"

He laughed. "You didn't know?"

"Uh, no." I tugged at my hair. "Had no idea. Bad enough knowing that brothers and *others* in prison are probably using my image to . . . to help them relieve stress . . . but on a poster at a Ducati shop?"

"Brothers in prison."

"Sisters in prison too. Trust me on that. Half of that Peanuts crowd had been on lockdown."

He said, "Couldn't find the magazine, so the guy let me have the original. Told him I saw you driving your Ducati around L.A. all the time. That blew him away. His name was Ray. Yeah, Ray. Think he had a thing for you. This cat has ridden with Michael Jordan and he was more impressed that I knew you, would you believe that?"

"Well, maybe Jordan doesn't look that good in a yellow thong."

"I'm eating over here, Billie. Some things I don't need to imagine, know what I mean?"

I ate my salad, smiling a little, shaking my head a little.

Couldn't move my mind from the same thoughts. Keith. Carmen. This was torture.

I said, "You carry that poster around in your pocket? Why?"

"Was going to ask you to sign it for me."

"You want my autograph?"

"If that's appropriate. Kinda embarrassed to ask. Guess you can say I'm one of your fans."

"Got a pen?"

He dug inside his pocket, pulled out a ballpoint. I made a face, signed it, slid it back to him.

He said, "You're right."

"About what?"

"Jordan in a yellow thong. You think his playing baseball was a bad move. Yellow thong. Yuck."

I laughed.

He shook his head. "Don't think he could inspire me to buy a Ducati. Or a thong."

"Wait. You spent that much on a bike *that you can't ride* because of me?"

He nodded.

I swallowed. Raheem had asked Jacob all about me. Carried a poster of me in his pocket. I asked him about his tats. He told me he had been inked in different countries, the first time being in his homeland.

I asked, "Where are you from?"

"Was born in Tegucigalpa."

"South America."

"Yeah."

"Heard it's rough down there."

"Yeah. Got out of Honduras fifteen years ago. Away from all the prostitutes and drug trafficking."

"Guess in Honduras . . . exploitation must be legal down there."

"A lot of the women want to come to the States. I've done well for myself, considering where I came from. I grew up around prostitutes. The women in my family worked the streets. Those women would be lucky to get one hundred *lempiras* from a nasty *gringo* old enough to be their grandfather."

"What's one hundred *lempiras*?"

"About seven U.S. dollars."

"You don't get but seven dollars to sell your coochie to a man on Viagra and wearing Depends?"

He laughed a little. So did I.

I said, "You don't sound like you're from South America."

"*Eres muy bonita. Eres casi demasiado bonita.*"

"Damn. You switched up on a sister. Accent and all."

He laughed and took a deep breath. "*Huele deliciosa.*"

"That last word sounded like delicious."

"Want me to translate?"

"No. I'm not sure I need to know what you said."

"It was respectful. That you are . . . beautiful. And you smell nice."

I didn't blush, but that softened me. I asked, "What do you do?"

"I'm an actuary."

"Actuary . . . that's like a corporate psychic, right?"

"Never thought about it like that." He laughed. "More about evaluating risk and probability. Backbone of all business. I'm self-employed. Deal with several Fortune 500 companies."

"Family? You have family here in L.A.?"

"Six brothers still in Honduras. All married with a lot of children. Three brothers in different parts of this country. They are married too, lots of kids. My older brother has a daughter out here. So I have one niece here in Los Angeles. She's in film school. No kids. You?"

"Only child."

Outside, engines were finally firing up. Marcel and her crew were demanding attention.

"Billie, if I asked you out . . . ?"

"We are out."

"You know what I mean."

"Raheem, don't go there."

"You intrigue me. But I recognize and respect your involvement with Keith. It's doesn't have to be anytime soon. We could get together, just like this, talk, let me tell you a few things about me, all you have to do is listen, you don't have to tell me anything about you, just listen and see how you—"

"Raheem, I don't want to know you. I'm not interested."

He backed down. "Is that right?"

"And stop investigating me. I don't want to be known by you."

"Didn't know you found me so . . . offensive."

"It's not that." I shook my head. "You have bad timing. Very bad timing."

"Only as bad as you want it to be."

I sat back and smiled at him, that smile being my concrete wall, barbed-wired across the top.

He said, "I'd like to get to know you better."

"I'm seeing somebody. Why is it so hard for you to respect that?"

"Well, the way things looked at Starbucks, even if it's not with me, you can do better."

That hit me hard.

Seemed like the whole world had seen me at Starbucks.

I said, "I'm . . ."

"You're what?"

I almost said it, almost told him that I was pregnant. Then I had a flash, saw Keith and Carmen, her rushing up to Keith, her face a blanket of terror, estranged from her husband, wanting him back no matter what, and I saw that scene again, only I was Carmen, and this seed was the child we shared, and years had gone by, years had changed us, turned us into people we never thought we would become, and all of a sudden, just like that, everything that was clear became opaque and I didn't know what I was going to do. I knew what I didn't want to do, but I didn't know what I would do.

What halted me was the fact that a Maxwell song came on. "Lifetime." Raheem started tapping the table and humming, then his humming changed into soft singing. His voice was nice, edgy and raw, sort of reminded me of the rock and soul of Darius Rucker, lead singer from Hootie and the Blowfish.

The brother could sing.

Then he switched up and sang in Spanish.

The gods could be so cruel.

I said, "Raheem, look, man, getting late, time for me to raise up."

I put my money on the table. Dropped enough for my meal and a tip. Then I headed toward the door. Head down. Free hand combing through my hair. My mind and heart aching. I'd done the right thing. I'd kept this honest. Kept this from feeling like a date. I hadn't misled or betrayed anybody.

I kept going until I got to my bike. Checked my cellular, no calls, no text message from Keith.

Raheem had followed me. He asked, "You okay?"

I nodded. "I pay my debts. Let me work off that dry-cleaning bill."

"What do you mean?"

"It means I might not *want* to teach you how to ride, but I have a *respect* for the machine you're on. It's not a toy. You might have that kind of money to play with, but that's beside the point."

"Okay."

"It's about the bike, not you. Can't believe I let you sucker me."

"Look, I'm not trying to sucker you."

"Why do you have my picture in your wallet? You're telling me you bought a fourteen-thousand-dollar bike because of me. I mean, I don't know if I should get a restraining order or break out the violin."

"Look, I've had this picture for a while, just never got up the nerve to ask you to sign it. Was going to ask you earlier, but it looked like you and your friend . . . Just didn't seem like a good time."

"Whatever."

"And I bought the bike because . . . the way you ride . . . well . . . you make it look cool."

"Wrong reason. Lot of peeps who wanna be cool end up cooling in the morgue."

"And I'm not playing you. Told you, I'll pay you for one-on-one instruction."

"*Don't you get it?* I don't want your money, Raheem."

"Why can't I pay you?"

"Because you want more than I can give you, dammit. Have I not made that clear?"

"What am I asking for?"

"Don't play. Don't pretend."

He took a breath, backed away. "What do you . . . when do you want to show me how to ride?"

"*Now.*"

"Now?"

"*Now.* Look, I want you to learn to ride. I'll show you a few things, make sure you get home. Then I want you to park that bike in your garage, or on the streets, wherever, and stay off it until you take the damn class. I'll get you home, then leave me alone. I want you to stop staring at me the way you do. Don't ask Jacob another goddamn thing about me. Stop investigating me like you're with the FBI."

He bounced his helmet against his leg and shook his head.

He said, "You're kind of mean, you know that?"

"*And you're stupid*. Buying a damn 749 and you can't even make it around a parking lot."

"Damn, you're mean."

"You have no idea what I've been through tonight."

"What are you going through?" He said that like he thought I ruled the world. "Tell me, what?"

My lips trembled, but my voice remained even. "None of your . . . just mind your own business."

Stress, anger, humiliation, and damn hormones had me about to go nuclear.

The golden girl with the boots came up behind us, tapped my shoulder. She asked, "Need anything?"

My hand tightened around my helmet, wanted to smack her across her face.

I snapped, "If you don't get away from me . . ."

Raheem laughed. But I shook my head.

That girl walked away singing, *"Beee aye beee why, em aye em aye . . . dis goes out to all—"*

Her heel twisted as she walked away, she went down fast, sent her crashing to the asphalt.

She got right back up. *"Em aye em aye . . . dis go out to all my baby mommas—"*

Marcel and her crew were getting geared up, doing endos, popping wheelies, showboating like they always did. They owned the night. Overheard one of her crew say they were getting ready to race that strip of the 90 that led from the Marina into the mouth of Culver City. I started my bike, revved it hard. Marcel rode by me and gave me the thumbs-up. I flipped her off again.

She circled the lot, pulled up next to me doing an endo, put her back end down, clicked down neutral, then threw her hands out to her side. Still challenging me. I left Raheem, walked over to her.

I got in her face. "Here's the deal, Marcel. If we race, it's like this . . ."

"Like what?"

"You win, you get my bike. I win, you leave me the fuck alone."

"Baby, now, you know that won't do it for me."

"I just want you to stop harassing me and leave me the fuck alone."

"Okay. I'll bet you this Super Hawk *and* a thousand dollars."

"A thousand dollars."

"Trust me, Billie. With my bet, even if you lose, you still win."

"Next week," I said. "We can do this next week. My terms, not yours."

"Why not tonight? My terms."

"Because I said next week. My terms. I'm tired of a damn homosexual on a friggin' chromosexual bike coming at me. When I run you off the road, I want you to leave me the fuck alone."

"You're cute when you're angry, you know that?"

She laughed, revved up, and pulled away, popping a wheelie until she got to the end of the parking lot. I wanted to race her so bad. Wanted to peel out and humiliate her in front of her crew. If I didn't have to deal with Raheem, I would've shown her how a real rider rocks the pavement. They took to the streets, headed toward 90. I was going to have Raheem stick to the streets, away from those arrogant riders.

Raheem said, "Damn. They can ride."

"Put your lid on and shut up."

Raheem never made it out of second gear. Barely got the bike over thirty miles an hour. He held his clutch like he was in a death grip. Every time he turned left he went wide; when he turned right it looked like he was going to low-side. He didn't understand countersteering and didn't have a clue how to roll off the throttle. Every time he stopped, he choked and his engine died. Then he couldn't find neutral to restart the bike. Middle-of-the-night traffic kept zooming around us. Catwalks, endos, even rode on my handlebars for a hot minute. I was anxious. Did all kinds of tricks waiting for pretty boy to catch up.

I cursed. "The way you ride, I should peg you all the way home."

"Peg?"

"Just stay focused. Easy on the throttle. Goggle the horizon."

"Goggle the horizon?"

"Geesh. Just pay attention, okay?"

Took us over an hour to make a ride I could've done in under ten minutes.

When we got to his house, I was angry, freezing.

I got off my bike and told Raheem, "Let me see your helmet."

He handed it to me, then pulled a remote out of his pocket. The garage door went up. Next to his convertible Porsche was another Porsche, this one their latest overpriced offering in the world of gas-guzzling SUVs.

I said, "Looks like your roommate's home."

"Don't have a roommate."

"Two Porsches and a Ducati?"

"Yeah."

I locked his helmet on my bike, its chin strap on the helmet hook below my seat.

He asked, "What are you doing?"

"Keeping your lid. Saving your life."

"What?"

"Until you get some lessons, I want that bike parked."

"You're jacking me for my helmet?"

I ignored him, said, "Get in contact with me when you're ready to get this lid back."

"Had no idea you were this mean."

I snapped, *"Stop calling me mean."*

"How am I supposed to get in contact with you and get it back?"

"Tell big-mouth Jacob to tell my roommate to tell me. He seems to know everything else."

"Why can't Jacob just tell you?"

"After I curse Jacob out, I ain't talking to that jerk, never again."

I got back on my bike, gloves resting on my gas tank, my helmet in my hand.

Thinking.

We stared at each other.

Raheem asked, "Sure you don't want to come inside?"

Come inside.

Come.

Inside.

My mind was on Keith. I didn't answer Raheem. Just sat out there in the cold and stared.

I said, "Ever had one of those days where you assumed that things couldn't get worse and it did?"

"Of course."

"Well, that's what's going on with me right now. All in a few hours. I'm absolutely angry. This isn't an emotion that I'm completely familiar with, but it's much more empowering than self-pity, so I'll take it."

He asked, "Anything I can do to help?"

"For the last time, could you stop being so damn nice?"

I pulled my helmet on, strapped it, started my bike, then pulled on my gloves.

He said, "Hey, look, you shouldn't ride while you're upset."

"Is that right?"

"I don't have much furniture, but you're more than welcome to come inside for a few."

"Why are you trying to get me in your house?"

"Motorcycle handbook said people shouldn't ride when they were drunk or emotional. So I guess you can say that I'm trying to save your life. Just trying to return the favor. Trying to not be so . . . stupid."

I shot him a look. "Oh, now I'm stupid."

"Come inside. Until you calm down. Drink some coffee or some hot chocolate."

My eyes went to his home. Two levels of contemporary magnificence in Black Upper-classville.

I looked up at his big house, asked, "You have kids?"

"No. You?"

Yesterday that question would have been easy to answer. Today that question disarmed me. There was no yes-or-no answer. So I coughed, did things with my lock, shook it off, played it off.

Then I asked, "Married?"

"Divorced twice. Married when I was eighteen, married too young, divorced at twenty-one. Married again at twenty-five, divorced that same year. Either she was the wrong woman or I was the wrong man, not sure, either way it was over in three months. Been single for the last ten years."

His impeccable credentials. Twice divorced. Two-time loser. But no kids. That was a plus.

I asked, "You like science fiction? Asimov? Philip K. Dick?"

"Not really."

That was good. He wasn't perfect.

None of them were.

I asked, "Who is your favorite author?"

He answered, "Paulo Coelho."

"Never heard of him."

"Brazilian, born in Rio. Wrote *The Alchemist*. Brilliant writer from South America."

"That's in Spanish, right?"

"Brazil is Portuguese. But it's been translated into pretty much every language."

I shrugged. "Not much into literary mumbo jumbo."

My throat felt tight. Frustration was doing its best to leak from my eyes.

I said, "I'm pregnant."

Amazement covered his face.

I felt so small, diminished by my own honorable confession.

I said, "Guess Jacob didn't open his big mouth and tell you that, did he?"

Looked like Raheem's mind went back to the turmoil he'd seen at Starbucks, putting the dramatic pieces of that puzzle together, it all making sense. This house, those cars, he wasn't the kind of man who was interested in an RMF—Ready-Made Family—let alone a woman who was still baking one in the oven.

He had visited the red-light district in Amsterdam, probably did the same in Istanbul, without a doubt had sampled Thailand, probably had traveled to countless other places that had women who made love for fun or finance. He was enjoying life, wanted to have wild sex, new adventures, and fun.

Raheem stood there like he was knee-deep in mud.

So did I.

He managed to shake like he had the chills, make a sharp noise, and utter, "Pregnant. Wow."

He blinked a hundred times, stunned, fantasies and hopes dissipating.

If only he had met me a year ago. There could have been infinite possibilities.

I'd done the right thing. I'd shut this party down before it got started.

I revved my engine, shifted from neutral to first, gave up some throttle, and sped away.

Inglewood, California.

Not too long before the sun would rise over Daniel Freeman Hospital.

Q was messed up.

What Viviane described to me over the phone didn't come close to the damage that had been done to Q's beautiful face. The cartilage was shattered. Lots of blood. Lots of bruising. Lots of swelling around her eyes and cheeks. Two patches of hair had been yanked out of Q's head too. She was having a difficult time breathing through her nose, had to breathe through her mouth.

Without a thought, one glance at her and I shuddered, asked her what happened.

Q struggled to breathe, cried, and told me that some girl called her a mutt and jumped on her for no reason. Poor girl was in pain, crying nonstop, going on and on about how prejudiced black people were against mixed-race black people, about how she had been in so many fights because of the way she looked, which she couldn't help because nobody got to pick what they were going to look like.

Her whining, like Viviane had said earlier, it was getting to be a bit much.

Viviane asked Q, "The girl that did this to you, what did she look like?"

"I . . . I . . . I . . . long hair . . . about nineteen . . ." She got her breathing right. "I don't remember her face."

Viviane slapped her biker's gloves against her hands. "What do you remember?"

"Her boots were real nice."

Viviane groaned. So did I.

Viviane said, "So damn superficial."

Viviane and I left Q with her parents, went downstairs to the cafeteria, and got some coffee. We talked about Q. But we didn't mention my pregnancy. With their mother there talking nonstop in Korean and Q's father there, upset and angry, my issue had become a pink elephant. I welcomed that.

I dropped my backpack on the table. It landed with a clunk.

Viviane said, "Don't tell me that was the gun."

"It's the brick. Don't believe Carmen threw this through my window."

I took the brick out and we frowned at it, then I dropped it back in my backpack.

I told her about Raheem, that I wasn't happy that big-mouth Jacob had fed him my info.

She said, "I'll talk to him. He's knows better than doing that shit."

"I don't care what you say, I'm still cursing his ass out."

"Go for it."

"I told Raheem I'm pregnant."

"Why did you do that?"

"He was coming at me hard."

"Raheem, he's a good-looking brother. You see his house?"

"Have you seen his house?"

"Stopped by there with Jacob. Last week. Maybe the week before."

"Did you have anything to do with this little matchmaking thing?"

"I plead the Fifth."

"Bad enough Marcel keeps coming at me. She was at JD's too."

"What she do this time?"

"Stalking me. Followed me to the bathroom. Invited me to her place. Same old."

"Raheem wants you. Marcel wants you. Damn. Must be that pregnancy glow."

"Am I glowing?"

"You're radioactive."

Her mother got off the elevator. Came for coffee. Viviane went back upstairs with her, both of them holding hands and talking in Korean as they left.

I vanished for a while, had this irresistible impulse to creep up on the floor that housed the maternity ward. Saw brand-new babies in incubators, others being breast-fed. Smiled awhile.

Then.

Heard women moaning, at least three in the throes of a torturous labor. Saw nurses moving around at a casual pace, sipping coffee and laughing among themselves as if those screams were no big deal. Saw two women, one black and one Hispanic, both all alone, gripping the handles of their beds. I went inside the Hispanic woman's room, stood just beyond the doorway, and stared at her agony. Then I did the same with the black woman, stood and stared at her. No ring on her finger. No man at her side.

Her face became my face; her tears, my tears.

She reached out for me.

I backed away, terrified.

I hurried to the elevator, running, went back downstairs, back to Viviane and Q.

Viviane was in the hallway. We walked awhile. Rode the elevator to the basement again. We sipped more coffee while we watched the news. People were getting killed all over the city. Gang-related shootings. Road rage was on the rise. There had been eight freeway shootings in three months, three of those people had died.

Viviane shook her head and said, "What is wrong with these people? Has everybody lost their goddamn minds? So many random acts of violence in this part of the country."

"In the world."

I scratched my scalp, felt how dry my hair was, in need of serious moisturizing.

Viviane asked me, "Working tonight?"

"Yeah." I was still shaken, still disturbed. "I'll be rocking the bar until closing."

"Was thinking. If you got a band, some music, you could blow up, you know that, don't you?"

I patted my stomach. "I am about to blow up."

We gave each other tender smiles. That pink elephant was crunching our toes.

Neither of us wanted to talk or acknowledge the pain, so we didn't.

We headed for the elevator.

The doctor and nurse were with Q when we made it back to the room. The doctor was worried about the extent of the facial swelling, and how difficult her breathing was. Q had passed out from the pain right after we had left and that had created a dangerous situation. She could need air-passage assistance with a ventilator, or the blood could inadvertently be inhaled into the lung cavity.

The doctor said, "That could create pulmonary crisis, leading to pneumonia. Bacterial."

Viviane was crying. So was her mother. My eyes watered up as well.

I told Viviane that I wasn't going to stay, was going to let her go back to her family.

Her family.

I had none. Just the family that was growing inside me.

The elevator door opened on the main level; I hugged her and got ready to leave.

I said, "If you need me to do anything . . . I can stay . . . or come back first thing in the morning. Wait, it is morning. I could come back later."

"Get some sleep." Viviane wiped her eyes, yawned. "Should be a lot of brothers at the Temple Bar tonight."

"I know you're not thinking about getting out tonight?"

"After this shit I'll need to put on a tight top, short skirt, and high heels so I can decompress."

"I'll put you on the guest list."

"Thanks, Billie."

"Hope Q . . . I'll pray for her."

"You don't pray."

"Okay, then I'll send positive energy out into the universe on her behalf."

Sometimes imagining someone with problems greater than yours eased your pain.

It was after ten in the morning. Had to sleep. Needed to do my hair.

I left the hospital disturbed. Viviane's sylph half-sister wouldn't be pretty for a long time. Q could give up any lofty ideas she had of being an actress or a model and slipping into Tyra Banks's dream world, at least until she got some serious cheddar and hooked up with a damn good plastic surgeon.

I mean a *damn* good one.

Jacket wide open so the cool air could caress my body, face shield flipped up so that same chill would keep me alert, I headed for the Baldwin Hills Crenshaw Plaza, white-lining through early morning traffic like it was a simple obstacle course. Needed to get that conditioner before I closed my eyes. If I went home first, after being up all night, I knew that I wouldn't go back out anytime soon.

Busy morning. Saw Dwayne Orange and his running crew heading toward the mall. Tooted my horn. They waved. The bean-pie sellers were out. Sisters who couldn't make it to their nine-to-five on time had been up and gotten their nails and hair done. Brothers with the knockoff goods and the crews selling the *Praise Jesus* and *Praise Allah* were stationed up and down Crenshaw Boulevard.

I was in line at the beauty supply store when my cellular rang. Keith's face popped up.

I said, "Keith?"

"Could you please stop calling my husband's cell phone?"

It was Carmen, her voice a harsh whisper, as if she didn't want anyone to hear her rampage.

I sucked my teeth, made an uneven sound, asked, "Why are you calling me?"

"Stop fucking my husband."

"Excuse me?"

"Could you *please* stop fucking my husband? Could you do that one thing for me?"

"Look, I was just checking to see if you had found your daughter."

"Bullshit. I leave his apartment for fifteen minutes and you run right back over there."

"Excuse me?"

"What do you want?"

"What do I want?"

"Why won't you go away? Why are you calling him over and over? What do you want?"

"Look, I just called to see if he had heard from his daughter."

"Blood clot. Suck mi out nagah."

"What was that?"

"*Our* daughter. Whatever is going on in *this* family is none of *your* damned concern."

She was beyond upset. Heard the tears and anger and fear that splintered her timbre.

I heard Keith come up in the background; asked Carmen why she was on his cellular.

Sounded like she threw the phone at him. Other people were talking in the background. Maybe her parents. Maybe all of their family had come over there. Could only imagine what their night was like.

Keith fumbled with the phone, said, "Who is this?"

Mistress. That unpleasant word came up my throat, hovered at my lips, rested on my tongue.

I sighed, but pisstivity colored my tone. "Your wife just called me going off."

"Billie?"

"What does *suck mi out* mean?"

"We're in the middle of a crisis right now, Billie."

I almost went off. Now wasn't the time.

I moved away from people, asked, "What's going on, Keith?"

"Look . . . we're still at Carmen's parents'. We've been up all night. The police are still over here."

"Your daughter . . . ?"

"Still trying to find Destiny. Police are here asking questions. Looking at the computer for clues. Called all of her friends. We've walked around the neighborhood for the last few hours. Up through Leimert Park, down to the 10. No one has seen or heard from her. We got it on the news."

"On the news?"

"Carmen called the D.A.'s office, pulled a few strings. The media is still here. They just taped us in a prayer circle. You have to be the next Natalee Holloway to get ten seconds with the media. Carmen knows some pretty important people. She's calling in favors, making it happen."

"I got you in my prayers, Keith. If there is anything I can do . . ."

"Carmen's parents have already issued a five-thousand-dollar reward to anybody who finds her."

So much hurt and fear was in his voice too. Never heard him sound that bad.

He said, "My daughter is missing and I don't have a dime to offer to get her back. Not one dime."

Images of dead children found in the city, memories of models who had been reported missing, then found dismembered in the Los Angeles National Forest, all of that crossed my mind.

"Billie, this is so unreal. I'll give my life and everything I have . . . This can't be happening."

I put my hand on my stomach. He cared so much for one child. The other got no love.

I didn't know what to say. Didn't know what to feel.

Carmen was in the background, her voice intense and even, telling him to get off the phone.

He took a breath. "Billie . . . let me get back to you."

"Look, I apologize for the timing, but when we were on your porch I think I left my gun—"

The connection broke.

I paid for my hair conditioner, put it in my backpack next to the brick, headed for my bike.

I was caught at the light when a young girl wearing tight jeans, an oversized T-shirt, and brand-new white tennis shoes came hauling ass away from the parking lot by Magic Johnson's movie theater. Arms pumping, she sprinted around young girls and old people, dodged teenage girls pushing their babies in strollers. She ran hard, long hair flying in every direction, like she was fleeing for her life.

Two Wal-Mart security guards were in pursuit. One of the guards was a brother, the other one Hispanic. The terrified girl ran like all she saw was in front of her, bolted right toward the intersection.

That drama was racing my way. I'd witnessed this scene a thousand times.

I rooted for the girl like I was rooting for poverty to triumph over the system.

Her shoestrings had come loose, were flying around her ankle. Knew it was going to happen. The girl stepped on her laces, stumbled, recovered, then made a face like she was in severe pain.

The security guards were winded, sweating, yelling for her to come back.

"Stop that girl! That's her! The police are looking for her! Stop her!"

The young girl bolted around a car and then she was in front of me.

She looked at my motorcycle, at my helmet, my jacket, her body trembled with recognition.

She struggled to catch her breath, severe oxygen debt causing her to loose her stride.

My face protector was already flipped up, had it up so I could breathe, so I got a good look at her.

The moment became surreal, as if time slowed down, elongated when she got in front of me.

An innocent fifteen-year-old girl with the Bambi eyes, a cute face too small for her big teeth.

We were eye to eye. Just like we had been that day she and her mother ran into me and her father at Howard Hughes Center. Her mouth was wide open, her face gripped in shock, just like it was then.

She looked so much younger than fifteen. So much younger. Just an innocent child.

As soon as she caught her breath, she broke out running again, pain etched in her face.

Wal-Mart security ran by me, still chasing her, greed and determination in their eyes.

nine

DESTINY

THE GIRL ON THE YELLOW MOTORCYCLE APPEARED OUT OF NOWHERE.
Her daddy's girlfriend.

Her mother's enemy.

The girl on the motorcycle had appeared and stared at her as if she knew about the brick.

Destiny ran. She ached between her legs. And she ran.

Pain wouldn't let her forget that she'd woken up in a cheap motel.

Alone. Violated.

Nauseated, sunlight in her eyes, she ran hard.

Ran away from the men in blue jackets.

Ran away from Billie.

When she made it across the street she stumbled on the curb, but didn't fall. She saw that Billie was right behind her, had driven her motorcycle up on the sidewalk, was riding right next to her, calling her name over and over as she labored by the strip mall that was housed in a shopworn parking lot.

Billie shouted, "Stop running."

Tired and terrified, Destiny ran down MLK until she realized she couldn't outrun the motorcycle.

At Marlton she stopped, bent over, panting, hands on knees. She looked down at the ground. At the debris and filth. Saw condom wrappers smiling up at her. The aching between her legs increased.

Six. Seven. Eight condoms.

That vision came back with brilliance; attacked her like the morning light.

Nine. Ten.

Billie raised her voice. "What is wrong with you? Keith has been looking for you all night."

Eleven. Twelve. So many condoms.

Destiny tried to stand up, then doubled over again, out of breath.

She watched her daddy's girlfriend turn off her bike, put down the kickstand, take off her helmet, her hair long and unruly, saw her take out her cellular, saw her push the number one, hit speed dial.

Destiny groaned. "Who are you calling?"

"Your daddy. He's not answering. The police are at your house."

"The police are at my house?"

"Shit, don't know what to do." Her daddy's girlfriend, her mother's enemy, she was frustrated; Destiny could see Billie's eyes, saw her struggling with some sort of decision, frowned at Billie as she took a hard breath, then handed her the yellow helmet. "Put this lid on."

Destiny panted, held her side, asked, "Why?"

She snapped, *"Put it on."*

Destiny stared at Billie. Billie was busy taking another helmet from the side of her motorcycle.

Billie pulled her hair back, put the red helmet on, a helmet that was too big for her.

Destiny's lips barely moved, read the name RAHEEM that was etched across the back.

RAHEEM.

Destiny mimicked Billie, pulled her hair back, grabbed the chin straps like she did when she went snowmobiling, tugged the helmet on. The fit was loose, but she still felt claustrophobic.

She told Billie, "I can't breathe. It's pulling my hair out."

The winded security guards were almost beside them. Had taken them forever to run a half mile to catch up with them. Fear motivated Destiny to hop on the motorcycle and cling to Billie.

The Mexican struggled with his breathing, said, "We. Saw. Her. First."

"Five thousand dollars' reward if anybody found her," his friend said. "We should get the reward."

"That's right. Five thousand dollars. What they said on the news. Five thousand."

"We're gonna split that shit."

Billie shook her head. "Not today."

The black security guard. "We found her first."

"I have her. Possession is nine-tenths of the law."

"What dat mean?"

Destiny held on tight to Billie's waist, the wind raking across her body as Billie pulled away.

Billie said, "Hold on, but don't hold me so tight."

"O . . . O . . . Okay."

The woman her mother hated had rescued her from the men in the Wal-Mart jackets.

The woman her daddy loved was taking her home on a motorcycle.

The world was so out of sync.

Everything was wrong.

She didn't want the motorcycle to slow down, didn't want it to stop at her grandparents' home.

But no more than a mile later, it did.

People were on the lawn. Friends. Neighbors. Strangers who wanted to be on television.

Billie blew her horn, then killed the engine.

Destiny heard her grandmother's spiritual scream, "She's back! Praise the Lord! They found her! She's here! All glory to the king!"

Her grandmother appeared in the door, long hair in a ponytail, dressed in a white Nike running suit. She sprinted out onto the lawn like she was headed toward the finish line in the L.A. Marathon.

Her grandfather hurried out into the yard, he too in a Nike sweat suit, hair gray and short, mustache as slender as the edge of a credit card, anxious and calling Destiny's name, overcoming his stiff-legged limp, that injury a present from one of the wars, Destiny never could remember which one.

Destiny pulled the helmet off her head, felt pain as she eased off the motorcycle.

Once again terrified of what was yet to come.

Then her father came outside, hurrying, eyes red.

Destiny saw who she didn't want to see. Her mother ran outside, saw the motorcycle, stopped cold, stood on the porch, mouth open, tears in her eyes, arms folded. Destiny felt her mother's eyes going from her to Billie, who was now locking her extra helmet on some contraption on her motorcycle.

Slow steps. While everyone else ran toward them, her mother took slow steps.

Her father was talking to Billie, asking questions.

"Found her up by the mall, Keith. Tried to call you."

Destiny saw the anguish in her father's eyes. It made him look so old, so terrible.

Destiny saw Billie glance toward her mother.

Then Destiny looked back and saw her mother's bloodshot eyes, her glare living on Billie.

So many people hurried by her mother's slow walk.

Billie was back on her yellow motorcycle, red helmet on, the engine kicking to life.

Destiny's throat tightened. The tears came. She couldn't breathe.

Crying now would keep her from having to talk, would give her time to think, she knew that.

The art of manipulation. Something she had learned from watching her mother.

Lining MLK were so many police cars. So many news vans. A camera was already on her. In the blink of an eye she was becoming breaking news. So many people.

News camera on her, people asking questions, Billie waved them away, left without a word.

The cameraman was recording the whole thing.

Recording.

Flashbacks from last night. That blinking red dot.

Baby Phat . . . the way you shake it . . . ain't never seen an ass like that.

Baby Phat. That moniker echoed in her mind.

Then her mother was standing in front of her. Silent. Rage and shame in her eyes.

Destiny held her father, put her head in his chest.

Her mother extended her hand, said, "Come."

They moved away, moved through the crowd, went inside the house, her mother taking them away from the pandemonium into the bedroom she had escaped from, closing the door.

Her mother said, "Keith?"

"What?"

"Could you talk to the police, to the media, let everyone who has been up all night praying and helping us look for her, tell them we'll be out in a moment? I just want a few moments with my daughter."

"Daddy . . . don't leave me with her."

"Keith, please?"

Her father looked at her, then at her mother, then walked to the window and looked outside. A simple act of defiance that rang so loud.

Her mother said, "See what your leaving has cost? Keith, do you think any of this would have happened, do you think she would continue acting out if she had a solid family structure?"

"Shut up, Carmen."

"Do you?"

"Do you think she would've run away if you hadn't hit her? Do you, *Carmen*?"

Destiny looked at her feet. Again they talked as if she wasn't there.

"Don't touch her, Carmen. You touch her again and you'll have to deal with me."

"Are you threatening me, Keith?"

"Touch my daughter again and you'll see how much of a threat that really is."

"How did that bitch end up with my daughter on her motorcycle?"

He snapped, "Does it matter?"

"I don't want her around my child. I don't want her insinuating herself into my family."

"Goddammit, give it a rest."

"If that bitch has that baby, I don't want to know about it. Don't *ever* want her around us."

Destiny raised her head. "What baby?"

Abrupt silence. Now they noticed her.

She repeated, "What baby?"

Her mother looked away, rubbing her temples, bouncing her foot.

"Go talk to the police, Keith. Please."

The door closed hard behind her father. Frustration. Disgust.

Her mother touched her with love, hugged her, kissed the side of her face, put her mouth next to her ear and whispered, "What your father said about me hitting you, don't say that to the police."

"Why not? You scared you might go to jail for child abuse? Or get disbarred?"

"Are you challenging me?"

"I'll tell them how you hit me."

"Two things, my darling. Don't threaten me. And don't you dare play the martyr, Destiny. We have one pathetic, trifling martyr in this family. And so far as what you say, don't become a liar."

"I'm not lying."

"I'm your mother. I know my own child."

"Do you?"

"Now, my child." Her mother smiled. "Where were you all night?"

Her mother moved closer, lowered her voice even more.

"Where did you get that T-shirt? Those tennis shoes?"

"Fairy godmother."

Her mother grabbed her hair.

"Don't play with me, child." Her mother was whispering. "Where have you been all morning? How did you end up on a motorcycle with that bitch? Why did you let her bring you back?"

Destiny swallowed. "You're hurting me."

Her mother loosened her grip, put her nose close to her scalp, inhaled, then let her hair go.

"Your hair smells like weed. I bet if I asked them to take a urine sample it would be filled with drugs and alcohol. Is that what you want me to do? Tell them I touched you and you will be tested. Any little lie about me hitting you will be thrown out so fast it'll make your head spin. And then I'll have them take you away. I'll take you away from that nice school you're in and put you in one for incorrigible children. My child, if you threaten me, utter one thing to the police, you will suffer the consequences."

Destiny looked at her mother's gentle smile.

Her mother said, "And I will have them check you to see if you had sex last night."

"You can't do that."

"Try me. You're still a minor. *I own you*. I can do what I damn well please."

Destiny stared at her mother like she had never seen this woman before.

"Don't forget what I told you," her mother said. "You're me looking back."

"What does it mean?"

Her mother smiled. *"See you next Tuesday."*

Destiny swallowed.

"See as in the letter *C. You*, the letter *U*. First letter in *next*, *N*. First letter in *Tuesday*, *T*."

Again, Destiny swallowed.

"C. U. N. T.," her mother sang. "Did you call your mother a cunt, sweetheart?"

Destiny looked away. Her mother had deciphered the code.

Her mother gritted her teeth. "I'm not stupid, child. I practically invented that phrase. I let you get away with things because I love you. I gave you a hundred chances to stop it. But you didn't."

Destiny tried to look away, but her mother held her face, made her stare in her eyes.

Her mother said, "Call me a *cunt* again and this *despot* will beat the life out of your smart ass. Understand? *I am your mother*. Look at me. Look at me, dammit. You came from this vagina. These sagging breasts fed you. This wounded heart went through hell to make sure you made it into this world. I love you, gave you life, and if you continue to disrespect me I will take that life away, you ungrateful—"

Destiny wiped her eyes, nodded over and over, just wanted her to shut up.

"Do not shake your head at me, little girl. Answer me. Do you understand?"

"Yes. I understand you, Mother."

Then her mother hugged her, kissed her cheek again, lips warm and tender. Her mother went to the dresser, took out a comb and a brush, told her to sit between her legs. Her mother combed her long hair, put it in two innocent ponytails. Made her wash her face, brush her teeth. Found a colorful T-shirt that had a religious saying across the front, made her put that on.

Another tap on the door.

Her grandmother stepped inside, stiff anger all over her face.

She asked, "The girl on the motorcycle . . . ?"

"That was her."

"That blood clot, she has a lot of nerve, pulling up in front of mi damn house."

"A lot."

"Don't tolerate it."

"I won't. I'm not."

"Keith is your husband. You stood before God."

"Yes, ma'am."

"Remember your vows."

"I do, Momma."

"Until death do you part."

"Yes, ma'am."

"Don't let some whore . . . I didn't allow your daddy to . . . just ask him why he has that limp. He'll say it's from the war. From the war we had in this household. I've run women out of hotels, had to go to women's homes in the middle of the night—"

Carmen snapped, "Momma, I already know."

"Do what you have to do."

"Momma . . . please, not now."

"Protect what's yours. *Do what you have to do*, Carmen."

"Close the door on your way out, Momma."

"If God brings you to it, He will bring you through it."

"Momma, close the damn door."

They stared at each other, mother and daughter.

Her grandmother left, then her mother put her hands up over her eyes, rubbed her temples. Then she reached inside her purse, took out her inhaler. Destiny looked down as her mother took her medicine.

"Destiny, this is one of the most selfish and self-centered acts I've ever seen."

"Learned from the best."

"What does that mean?"

"Means what it means."

Destiny felt the heat from all of her mother's anger, all of it suppressed.

Destiny whispered, "Looks like you want to hit me. Do you want to hit me again, Mother?"

The stare went on forever.

"Go ahead. Hit me."

Her mother trembled. Then the storm passed. She dropped her inhaler back in her purse.

With the sweetest smile her mother told her, "See you next Tuesday."

Destiny returned the same smile. "And I'm you looking back."

"Keep challenging me, Destiny. That's right, keep challenging me."

"I just hope that you're not me looking forward."

Another blistering stare.

People were outside, so many voices. Her grandfather tapped on the door. Through the door he said that the television people were about to go live, told Carmen to turn the television on.

He said, "Right now they running a story about a young girl who was attacked in Inglewood, got beat up real bad last night, some sort of a racial thing, they're saying. Then . . . then they putting us on live."

Carmen said, "We'll be out in a moment, Daddy. I'm having a talk with your grandchild."

"Destiny?"

The door creaked open. Destiny looked up at her worried grandfather. He struggled with his leg and limped into the room.

Destiny said, "I'm okay, Paw Paw."

"Granddaddy doesn't like to see his grandbaby crying."

"Thanks, Paw Paw."

"Same goes for you, Carmen."

"Thanks, Daddy."

Destiny watched her mother get up off the bed, go to Paw Paw. Watched how her mother became a little girl in his arms.

Paw Paw said, "I don't like to see mi little girl cry, Carmen."

"I'm okay, Daddy."

"Ruth is upset. Mi grandchild is upset."

"Daddy, not now, okay?"

"You breathing okay, Carmen?"

"Yes. The anxiety . . . it's under control, Daddy."

"You're wheezing. How you getting on?"

"Don't worry about me, Daddy. I'm fine."

"Ruth . . . mi wife, she's not too happy with the way Destiny was returned to us. Not at all."

Destiny sighed. *Tsk*ed.

He said, "Give mi the full undred bout this situation."

Paw Paw's accent thickened, was sounding pure Jamaican. That meant he was upset.

"Daddy . . . the bitch on the motorcycle . . ."

He snapped, "I 'member her from dat time. She no worth it."

"And Keith . . ."

"He no worth it. Dey no worth it, all dis trouble to mi poor granddaughter."

Then her grandfather let Mother go, headed for the door. Her mother sat on the bed, same exact spot as before. Paw Paw looked at both of them, his lips pulled in, so upset, so helpless. He pulled the door up behind himself, left with his head down, that stiff-legged limp of his fading with his every step.

Destiny handed her mother the remote. Her mother turned on the television.

"What baby, Momma?"

"Hush."

They showed a scene from her being dropped off, then the camera focused on Billie as she sped away. They called her a saint. Her mother cursed. Destiny wondered how they did that, put that together so fast. Then her father was on television, telling the city that his daughter was back home, safe and sound. He looked good, that dimple in his cheek as he put on a relieved yet worried smile.

All of that was going on right outside the bedroom window.

Destiny asked her mother, "Is Daddy having a baby with the motorcycle girl?"

Her mother paused. Looked like she wanted to fall apart.

"The devil always tries to win. Always brings a new crown of thorns."

"What does that mean?"

"And the devil wins sometimes. But not on my watch. Not if I can help it."

"What are you talking about?"

"Come, child. That is no concern of yours."

"Why can't you ever answer anything I ask you?"

"Look, dammit, if he has a child with that bitch, he will forget about you. Especially if he has a son. He will be with her and we will become the second family, and he will forget about—" Her mother stopped, struggled to control herself again, voices still outside the door, people still out on the front lawn. "I'm trying to keep this family together, Destiny. We're at a crossroads. I need your support."

Another stare, this one short and intense.

"Decide, Destiny."

"Decide what?"

"Will you be my daughter and my friend, or will you become my enemy? Decide. Now."

Tears came. "Your daughter. Your friend."

"Wise choice. Now, this is what you're going to tell everybody."

"I don't want to talk to them."

"I didn't ask you if you wanted to. You caused this, now own up to your responsibilities."

Her mother told her what to say, word for word, made her repeat it like an Easter speech.

Destiny said, "You make it seem like I'm going to court."

"You are. When that camera comes on, you will be in court. This is your fifteen minutes."

She followed her mother, went back to the family, stood in front of the police, the media.

Tears in her eyes, Destiny did what she was asked, recited her mother's words, looked in the camera, told them that she had run away because her parents were getting a divorce. That she wanted her mother and father to stay together. That she didn't know that her parents had reconciled last night. And she was happy because family was important. She apologized for all the trouble she had caused.

Then she stepped to the side, head down, eyes filled with tears. Not crying because of what she had done but because she felt like she was on her mother's game board, part of a chess opening in which a player risked one or more pawns or a minor piece to gain an advantage in position.

Since her birth, she had been a pawn, that was how she felt.

With her ponytails falling across her chest, Destiny looked at her feet, stared at her stolen tennis shoes, tugged on the edges of her white T-shirt, JESUS WALKS across the front in golden letters, pulled and elongated the savior's name, said nothing as her mother did the rest of the talking.

Her mother took her father's hand and stood in front of the camera.

That was a message to Billie. Destiny knew that. To Billie and every other woman in L.A.

Her mother spoke highly of her marriage of eighteen years, did everything except break out the *Book of Common Prayer* and confess to her own manifold sins and wickedness. Maybe she was saving that for the day she flew the Archbishop Rowan Williams from across the pond to bless their reunion.

The perfect lawyer. Her father had sent her to the best law school in Los Angeles.

That was why she would get everything. She heard her mother on the phone telling her girlfriend that, laughing about how good she was, about how, in the end, Keith would lose the shirt on his back.

The reporters were filming her mother's speech and Destiny saw them zooming in on her. But she could see it in their faces, the media was losing interest now that the crisis had passed.

There had been no claims of finding treasure buried in her backyard, or alleging that she had found a finger in a bowl of chili, and she wasn't a runaway bride who claimed she had been kidnapped.

Destiny saw that she was not newsworthy almost as fast as she was late-breaking news.

Just a black kid who ran away from home. A little black girl who ran away from the ghetto.

Her father moved away from her. From them. The look in his red-rimmed eyes told her he was fed up.

Her mother came to her, told her she had done a good job. She was pleased.

"One more thing, Destiny."

"What?"

"You're grounded."

"For how long?"

"Until infinity becomes measurable."

By early afternoon the police were gone, the media had rushed away in search of better news, and her father had gone to the backyard. He stood alone. Thinking.

Destiny watched him for a while, wanting to talk to him, but walked away, left her daddy to his thoughts.

The motorcycle girl was pregnant.

Destiny kept thinking that she was going to have a little brother or a little sister.

That was their destiny.

You couldn't control destiny; you couldn't make it change to fit your needs.

At first Destiny was a little excited. Somebody to love was coming her way.

She wanted a little sister. Always did want a little sister.

Her mother did not want that to happen.

Destiny wondered if her father would be happy with a second family.

If he would love that child more than he loved her.

Wondered if her father would move on with his life and forget about her. The condoms. The hurting.

Destiny went to her grandparents' bathroom, searched for something to ease her soreness.

She looked through the medicine cabinet. Blue pills. Viagra. Her grandfather's. Propanol. Her grandmother's. A straight-edged razor was on the counter. The kind her grandfather used to shave.

If she had never been born, her parents . . . only God knows. She wanted to be unborn.

She picked up the razor, its blade so sharp, held it to her wrist.

Up and down for the people who were serious about bleeding out, that was how she read you cut yourself if you were ready. Slicing sideways was for the people who only wanted attention. Destiny held the blade up and down. Wondered how deep she would have to cut, how long it would take before—

There was a knock at the door.

She jumped, dropped the blade.

"Destiny?"

"I'll be out in a second, Big Momma."

"You okay?"

"Mi okay, Big Momma." She used a playful island accent. "Mi con-sti-pa-ted."

"Don't you go mocking your roots, child. I'll get you some fruit and water. Maybe make you a smoothie with a teaspoon of mineral oil."

Destiny turned the water on, then turned the radio on, noise to cover her indecision.

'Cause I ain't no holla-back girl, 'cause I ain't no holla-back—

Destiny stared at the blade, finally picking it up, folded it closed, then put the razor in her pocket.

She was thinking about how hard it had to be to make it through life without killing yourself.

Or killing somebody.

Her mother walked around, thanking God, praising him for delivering her daughter unharmed, wiping tears from her own eyes, hugging people, thanking everyone for their love and prayers.

Destiny watched her mother perform, an attorney in the courtroom, a drama queen onstage.

Outside, her grandfather was leaning against her grandmother's SUV, raising his voice at her father. Destiny stayed close to the side of the house, eased up. Eavesdropped. Wanted to hear what they were saying about her. Heard the anger that was being shared between the two men she loved.

"Look, bwoy, comes a time where a man deeply regrets some of the decisions and choices he done made. All men do. But you have to live with them. That's what a man does."

"Miss Ruth told you to corner me and have this talk with me? You're her mouthpiece now?"

"Mi wife. She is tired of hearing her daughter cry. She is tired of our daughter being miserable. Mi wife is concerned about the mental well-being and health of our only daughter. Dat girl just pulled her backside up on mi front lawn. She was practically in mi home. Mi wife no like that. Ain't dere some way you can unravel this mess, turn things back they way they were? Can't you turn this around, bwoy?"

"Don't come to me with your hypocrisy."

"You're suppose to forsake all others and cling to your wife."

"If you had remembered that and had been clinging to your wife instead of those other women, then maybe you wouldn't have that limp. Right, old man?"

"Watch what you say, *bwoy*."

Her father walked away, shaking his head.

Then her grandfather limped away, head down, looking so old and defeated.

Destiny slipped back inside the house. Hid from everyone. Aching. Throbbing between her legs.

The sun went down.

Traffic picked up outside. Crenshaw's Saturday night crowd coming to life.

Destiny went into the laundry room. Stared at the bottle of bleach. Read the warning label.

It urged people not to get it into their eyes. Destiny wondered if bleach caused blindness.

Then she saw another part of the warning label: DANGER: CORROSIVE.

Corrosive. She nodded. That was good.

She was planning a war.

She went in the garage, leaned against her grandparents' SUV.

In between thoughts of vengeance, in between wondering how she was going to get away and find the people she was with last night, in between thinking about hurting whoever had her boots and stole her money, in between wanting to find the boys who had raped her, Destiny cried her best cry.

ten

BILLIE

I PARKED MY BIKE IN FRONT OF THE HOUSE WHERE I RENTED A ROOM, SAT there for a minute, then went inside. I tried to sleep. Couldn't.

Keith remained on my mind. Always felt him inside me.

Hours later, Keith was at my front door.

My heart beat so fast. So damn fast.

After all that I had been through in the last twenty-four hours, as angry as I felt at myself for ever getting involved with him, I thought that if he ever stepped on my porch I would slam the door in his face.

I didn't.

Love was a tempest to be reckoned with, moving around inside me like a typhoon.

I opened the door, stood there, eyes dark, lips tight.

He said, "Thanks for bringing Destiny home."

"You're welcome."

"Had to go off on those motherfuckers."

"Don't bring me no drama, Keith. Please. No drama."

We stood there staring at each other. His gray eyes looking right at me.

I asked, "My gun?"

"Looked on the porch. I didn't see it."

"Well, it didn't just vanish into thin air."

I wanted him to say something stupid before I said something stupid.

I asked, "Why are you here?"

"You know I love you, don't you?"

"What's the bad news this time?"

"What do you mean?"

"Are you HIV-positive? You have cancer? Got drafted and you're going to Iraq? You always make that puppy-dog face and tell me you love me before you give me bad news."

"No bad news. That was it. I love you."

Then I moved away so he could come inside.

Come inside.

Coming inside me was the reason I was in the situation I was in now.

I thought about the day when we had left the movies, the first day I saw Carmen and his child, thought about one single moment where jealousy took root and changed everything. This was insane. Love was insane.

He asked, "What you doing?"

"About to get in the shower and wash my hair."

I turned around and headed toward the kitchen.

He closed the front door and followed.

Those eyes. His cool demeanor. He still made me as nervous as he did the day we met.

We posted up on barstools and sat at the island.

I said, "Your wife is a piece of work."

"Runs in her family."

"If looks could kill. Your baby momma looked at me like I had kidnapped your child."

We didn't say anything after that, not for a while.

I wanted to hate him. Couldn't.

I asked, "Why don't you man up against that bitch?"

"I've manned up for eighteen years. Right now, I'm just tired. Manning up is more than screaming and shouting and acting a fool. Sometimes a man needs to think. I've had more fights with Carmen than you'll ever know. A man screams so long, then he doesn't feel like screaming anymore. A man screams long enough and all he ends up doing is losing his voice. Lost my voice a long time back."

Silence.

I asked, "Hungry?"

"Not much of an appetite."

"Thirsty?"

"Easy Jesus?"

"Water. At least drink some water."

"Sure."

A moment later I was handing him a glass of water.

His fingers touched mine.

I didn't move away from his touch.

His hand covered mine.

I didn't move away from his touch.

He put the glass on the counter, pulled me closer to him.

I felt so weak.

His lips covered mine.

I died like I had never died before. His lips were soft, his tongue so smooth.

My eyes were open, breathing getting thick as I stared at him. His eyes were on mine.

His tongue moved over mine, around my lips, kissed me for so long.

His kisses were like pouring water on sugar.

He said, "You have any idea how much I love you, Billie?"

My fingers covered his lips.

My flesh on his flesh.

I said, "Let's not . . . don't say anything."

"Forget everything I said at Starbucks. Forget it all. I want you to keep our baby."

"Don't play with me like this, Keith."

"Billie . . . don't get an abortion. Forgive me for what I said. Let's do the right thing."

"Why the change of heart?"

"You're the best thing in my life, Billie. Don't want to lose you."

Again I put my fingers to his lips.

I said, "I am doing the right thing. It's the best thing to do. For everybody."

"I overreacted. Had just had a big fight with Carmen before I met you at Starbucks, knew my back was against the wall, felt trapped, my mood carried over from that, wasn't thinking right, you know?"

"No, you were right. I should be married first. At least have a life partner. Or be in the right kind of relationship. I mean, why would I bring an innocent child into the middle of all of this bullshit?"

"Billie . . ."

"Are you going to marry me, Keith?"

"If I could . . . but . . . Billie . . . you know I can't. Not right now."

"Then you can go back home to your wife, to your daughter, to your therapy sessions. No strings over here. You won't hear from me again, you can let your wife know that when you get home."

My back was turned to him, my voice so strong. I was crying. Didn't want to, but I was.

He took in a deep breath. Inhaled me. He pulled my hair back, put his warm mouth on my neck, sucked my flesh. I leaned my head back, kissed him with tears running down my face, kissed him with tears seeping into my mouth and spicing our tongues with salt. Kissed him and felt him getting hard against my ass, kissed him and put his hands on my breasts, then reached back and touched his hardness as his fingers began easing from my breasts and slid down toward my pants, then undid the top of my pants so he could put his hand inside, then moved and shifted so I could feel his fingers covering my vagina, kissed him harder when I felt his finger going inside me.

"Did you eat her pussy, Keith?"

"No."

"You fuck her?"

"No."

"Have you fucked her since we've been together?"

"No."

"You let her suck your dick. What was up with that shit?"

"That wasn't love, Billie."

"What was it?"

"It was hate. I was trying to push my anger down her throat. Wanted her to choke to death. Was trying to . . . to . . . Then you knocked on the door. My hate would have ended it all right then."

Inside me. In the shower, he took me from behind. My face against the tiled wall. Warm water raining over me. Keith held my waist. Kept telling me he loved me. Was so deep inside me. When he came he held me so tight, let out a primal wail, like all of his stress was oozing out of his body.

I came the same way, came harder, came louder than he did.

Inside the shower, sweat mixing with water, skin against skin, we remained in awkward silence. A scary silence. Keith caught his breath, then helped me wash my hair. His hands felt so good in my hair. He scratched my scalp with his fingertips. Rinsed my hair, then put conditioner in my mane, rinsed all of that out. I stood there, body temperature so high from having a serious orgasm.

I said, "You tried to choke her to death."

"Wanted to ram this . . . push it . . . down her throat. Wanted to choke her to death."

"Wouldn't have worked."

"Why not?"

"She would've bit down real hard."

"Nothing comes without sacrifice."

Towels around our bodies, we headed toward my bedroom.

We stood there for a moment, both of us staring at my broken window, a window now covered by cheap plastic. Everything about this relationship had been broken. Needed to be replaced.

Keith walked over to the window, looked at the damage.

I said, "Viviane's sister was attacked."

"Attacked?"

"Q was jumped on. We're having a bad weekend over here."

"Where did the assault happen?"

"Down on Crenshaw. Right down the hill from here." I wrapped another towel around my head. "They're still at Daniel Freeman. Q got messed up pretty bad. Some crazy people in L.A."

While we dried off, his cellular rang. Keith looked at the number, then put the phone down.

He said, "Since we were on the news, everybody's been calling."

I knew he'd be leaving. I told myself not to stop him from leaving. To let him go. To let go.

His eyes were on my stomach. He said, "Billie . . ."

"Don't say it, Keith. Whatever it is, don't say it."

Then.

His mouth was on my breasts again.

I turned around and he pulled my towel all the way off, and his mouth was between my legs. Was down there a long while, made me moan and writhe and call his name, took me close to orgasm before he came back up and entered me again. He kissed me and kissed me and kissed me.

Made me come again.

Then he rode me rough, strained, came again, stayed on top of me, breathing hard.

My hand moved back and forth, writing a love letter in his sweat.

He whispered, "Have our baby. We can make it work."

"With you living with Carmen and me over here by myself?"

I pushed him off me. Sat up, hands in my wet hair.

He rubbed my shoulders. Was so tense. That felt better than the sex we had just had.

He said, "Have the baby."

"We're broke, remember? Day care, private school, Chuck E. Cheese. All that costs a grip."

"Have the baby."

"And you're still married. Divorce decree revoked. Not any immediate plans to file those papers again. Not cool to be pregnant . . . having a baby for a full-fledged married man, you know?"

"Have the baby."

"What, be your mistress? And have to deal with Carmen the rest of my life? *Shit.* She is determined to mess up your life and the life of anyone who gets in the way of her messing up your life."

He stopped massaging me. Stood up, went back to that broken window.

I asked, "Why didn't she know about me?"

"What?"

"Before that day we ran into her. Why didn't she know?"

"You're losing me."

"Why didn't Carmen know about me? Why hadn't I met your daughter? It fucks with me that I've never had the courage to ask you that. What the fuck was I? Your secret? Your fun away from home?"

"We don't talk like that. I don't ask who she's seeing and vice versa."

"Then why hadn't I been introduced to your daughter?"

"You met Carmen. You tell me. Has meeting her made you feel any better about us?"

I shifted. Didn't like his answer, but accepted it.

He came back over, pushed me down, got on top of me, kissed me.

His cellular rang again.

He rolled off me, checked his caller ID.

He answered with a snap, "What now, Carmen?"

I rolled over, stared at that broken window.

My mind drifted back to the day I first met his wife. His child. His family.

Carmen. Hair in a bun. Wearing dark Donna Karan head to toe. Heifer had on some badass shoes that had to cost more than a year's rent in some cities. So classy in a place that was so casual. Outside of my yellow leather jacket in my hand, I had jeans, clunky biker boots, and was sporting double Old Navy wife-beaters, a white one over a green one, no bra, tattoo of a dragon on my left arm, same tat my mother had, a symbol that represented her fondness for Buddhism, my hair pulled back in a ponytail.

Her daughter was with her. Barely saw her. Too focused on Carmen.

And the way Keith reacted.

How he tensed, how his body language changed.

Keith had on jeans that day. Nikes. Was sporting a wife-beater too. Was looking damn good.

His wife said, "You have a . . . tattoo?"

He nodded. "Got a tat."

Lips pulled in, her hand on her daughter's shoulder, Carmen stared at Keith. We all shared a wordless moment. He had gotten inked, put a tribal band on his right bicep, when were hanging out in Venice about two months before. That let me know that she hadn't seen him naked.

At least not from his waist up.

Carmen stared at me as I kept my eyes on her.

Talk about feeling like crap. Wanted to run away. I wasn't dressed for this moment. Was dressed motorcycle chic, for riding, didn't have on the right meet-the-soon-to-be-ex-wife-and-meet-the-child clothing.

Compared to Carmen's gear, I needed a manicure and a serious fashion intervention.

Like it or not, the moment had come.

Part of me wanted to meet Carmen, wanted to see her. Wanted to see how he would introduce me. Wanted to see her reaction. Wanted to feel . . . special. I already knew she was an attorney. Well educated. Had a real job. A career woman. But I had to see her. Size her up. See how he behaved in her presence. Find out what she was to him. Wanted to see what kind of woman he had chosen to marry and procreate with and stay with for over a decade. Didn't want her to be butt-ugly, that'd mean that he had no taste, no standards, but didn't want her to be stunning, no way I could compete with a supermodel.

Couldn't help it, but she became too real. There was an undeniable familiarity between them. I felt like an outsider. I imagined them together. Couldn't help it. Imagined her taking all of what he had to offer inside every orifice. Imagined her making him come. Imagined her pregnant with his child.

Her complexion was smooth. Her body was nice. From what I could see. Clothes hid cellulite and flab. What she was rocking wasn't exactly aerodynamic, but it was nice. To be older. With a kid.

I self-evaluated. Spent more than enough time in Viviane's home gym and up and Magic's 24-Hour Fitness to keep it tight. Not one lover had complained about anything, but I wasn't too crazy about my body. This was L.A. Everybody was trained to have hang-ups about their bodies in La-La Land.

His child looked at my gear, said, "Cool jacket."

I nodded. "You must be Destiny."

Her hair was in a ponytail. Shades. Baby Phat jeans and matching top. Hip-hop generation.

Keith said, "That's my daughter. Destiny, this is Billie."

His daughter. Proof that Keith had ridden Carmen and come hard. He'd given her a child.

The young girl looked surprised. "He told you about me?"

Carmen interrupted, "Your daughter has been calling you all morning."

Keith took a breath, didn't smile, just shook it off and said, "Carmen, this is Billie."

She turned to Keith and talked like I wasn't important. "And Billie is your . . . ?"

The world quit spinning like it was Judgment Day. Six eyes stared at him.

Wrong answer and I would lower my head and walk away.

Keith firmed up his tone, gave Carmen no love, said, "We're dating."

The world remained still. Dating. That vague term. A safety net.

His daughter said, "So, in other words, Daddy, the motorcycle girl is your girlfriend?"

"Yeah. Billie is my girlfriend, Destiny."

There it was. I had a name and a title. Not just some biker chick holding his hand. That told her we had a relationship, that we were intimate, that we had a future as soon as she was left in his past.

Ominous storm clouds grew in Carmen's eyes. Saw the lightning behind her pupils.

Stunned and bewildered, their daughter said, "Didn't know you had a girlfriend, Daddy."

My lips went up into a loose, very uncomfortable smile. Wanted somebody to beam me up off this planet before I embarrassed myself. I told his daughter, "Your father told me so much about you."

Awkward silence invaded our spaces again.

Then they showed up. The older couple. He was dressed in Nike sweats, standing at the top of the escalator carrying a kazillion bags from Nordstrom Rack. The woman he was with held a tall Starbucks cup in her hand. She frowned down on us. Destiny saw them first, pointed up at them, and Keith looked that way, as did I.

I wondered what could be worse than running into Carmen.

Keith's woeful expression deepened, his voice a harsh whisper. "Your parents are here?"

Running into Carmen's entire family.

Carmen gritted her teeth, said, "Yes. First Saturday of the month."

"I know it's the first Saturday of the month, Carmen."

"It's Family Day, Keith."

"I know what day it is."

"Family Day hasn't changed. It's still the same."

"I know it didn't change, Carmen."

"Then why aren't you with your daughter?"

"I see Destiny. . . . Look, this is your family's thing, not mine."

"Is Destiny not your family anymore?"

"Don't even go there."

"Then why aren't you with your daughter today?"

"I'm right here, Mother." Destiny huffed. "Hate it when you talk about me like I'm not here."

I didn't know what to do, to say.

I said, "Keith, I'll . . . I'mma run get a manicure . . . right over there . . . manicure shop by the fountain."

"Don't leave, Billie."

"Keith . . ."

"Carmen, don't step in my face talking crazy."

His tone, so hard, so firm, a man who didn't take shit.

But at the same time I could see he was burned out from years of . . . of . . . Carmen.

I turned around and saw the rest of that familial crew coming right at me.

Carmen's mother, that stoic face, her tight lips and keen eyes were on all of us; she came down the escalator. She didn't like Keith, could tell that right off the bat. As she held her head high and came our way, chill bumps raised up on my arms. Low heels, jeans, salt-and-pepper hair, Gucci handbag, Rolex. She was an aged Stepford wife, like somebody whose address would be someplace like the heart of Wisteria Lane. Then Carmen's mother's eyes were dissecting me, dismembering Keith. She was Carmen with thirty more harsh years on her bones.

Her first words to me were, "You cut me off."

I said, "Excuse me?"

"One morning I was going down La Brea and you cut me off."

I shrugged. "Well, I'm a pretty conscious driver. More than likely you tried to cut me off."

She frowned.

Her name was Miss Ruth. Ruth. The first syllable in the word *ruthless*.

She said, "And who are you, *child*?"

Both her attitude and accent were thick and strong; most definitely from the islands. But her face, the way it remained rigid and damn near without expression, told me that Botox was her best friend.

I said, "Billie. I'm Billie."

Then we were enveloped by awkward silence.

Keith said, "Billie, I'd like you to meet Destiny's grandparents."

That gloaming moment, I'd never forget the smileless expression on that older woman's face.

Carmen. Her mother. Her daughter.

Not until that moment had I understood how Custer felt when he realized he was surrounded.

Carmen's father introduced himself, pleasant, almost smiling.

"I'm William."

Sounded like he'd had a childhood rooted in jerk chicken, pigeon peas, and rice, maybe salted fish and akee.

Her grandfather had a limp. A dignified limp that made me feel sorry for the man. Like it was an injury he had earned in combat, maybe he'd been out in the fields defending a country that would never defend his people. Thought it strange the way he carried all those bags without any help, the way his wife marched on with her Starbucks, not walking side by side with her husband.

But, hey. The slave master always walked in front of the slave.

Miss Ruth looked me up and down, asked, "And you are . . . ?"

I hesitated.

Destiny jumped in, said, "She's Daddy's girlfriend."

"*Girlfriend?*"

Miss Ruth readjusted her posture, looked at me like she was a magistrate sent to administer justice. She glowered at Keith. Eyed his tattoo. Shook her head.

I stood in front of three generations of either embarrassed or shock-filled eyes.

Miss Ruth shook her head, corrected her granddaughter, said, "Keith is married to mi daughter."

Mi daughter. Definitely from the islands.

Keith grunted, stepped up his game, did that in a way that showed he owned no love for his in-laws, at least none for Carmen's mother. "What's the problem, Miss Ruth?"

"What the problem?"

"That's what I said. What's the problem?"

Miss Ruth didn't back down. "What you think is the problem, *bwoy*?"

"Don't tell me your daughter didn't tell you that I moved out. That we are divorcing."

Carmen put her hand on her mother's arm. "Momma knows. Everyone knows, Keith."

Miss Ruth. "I notice that you're not wearing your wedding ring, Keith. Why is that?"

"Don't get loud, Miss Ruth." Keith stood firm. "Respect me and there will be no problem, okay?"

Miss Ruth snapped, "*Bwoy*, you walk out on your family and you *tink* dere is no problem?"

"I didn't walk out on my family."

"Last time me tell you. Don't raise your voice at me, *bwoy*."

"With all due respect, Miss Ruth, don't talk crazy to me. Don't act like you don't know."

Miss Ruth looked at her daughter, compassionate eyes, looked at Carmen like she was three years old and needed her protection, then switched gears and frowned at Keith. Parental love ran deep. So did the disdain of those who had wronged your child.

Miss Ruth said, "You tell Keith what his child did? How she has been acting out?"

Carmen. "No, Momma."

Keith asked, "What happened?"

Carmen shook her head. "It doesn't matter, Keith. You're not there for Destiny anymore."

"What happened, Carmen?"

Carmen's dad had already seen where this was going, gathered up all of his wife's shopping bags, and limped over and sat down in front of Johnny Rockets, all of those bags surrounding him like they were an impenetrable fort, checking his watch, frowning like he'd rather be anywhere but here.

Keith asked, "What did Destiny do?"

"I'm right here." That was Destiny, rolling her eyes. "You don't have to talk like I'm not here."

Carmen said, "Destiny got into trouble at school."

"I'm right here, Mother."

Carmen went on, "Keith, I needed you to talk to her."

Keith asked his child, "What happened, Destiny?"

"Almost got into a fight."

Miss Ruth jumped in. "White girl was messing with her."

Destiny said, "I didn't start it. We were having a discussion about intelligent design and I told her I wasn't feeling that intelligent design stuff because it has nothing to do with science and she called me a refugee. Told me I was going to hell. And I told her if people like her were going to be in heaven, then I would rather be in hell. Then she called me a refugee again. Then I hit her in her eye."

Her grandmother. "She straightened out the white child good. Just like mi only child used to do when she was growing up. The white girl start the ruckus, then the racist pigs, dey said they didn't want to accommodate me grandchild anymore, when mi grandchild was only defending herself."

"Miss Ruth, please." Keith said that, then turned to his daughter. "They expelled you?"

"They tried." Carmen. "I prevented it."

"How, Carmen? Did you file against the school?"

"No." She took a hard breath. "This incident required an eight-thousand-dollar donation."

Keith groaned. "Where did you get eight thousand?"

"Borrowed it from Daddy."

"Money doesn't solve everything, Carmen."

"Well, if you were home with your child, Keith . . . maybe we wouldn't have this problem."

"I'm right here. Mother. *Hello*. Don't talk about me like I'm on the moon."

Keith. "Eight thousand dollars?"

"It's tax-deductible. I'm not stupid."

Keith. "Money does not solve things, Carmen."

"Money doesn't solve things? Bullshit." The grandmother. "This is America."

"All due respect, I wasn't talking to you, Miss Ruth."

Keith hugged his child. Their child. Destiny. The pawn on their chessboard. She hugged her daddy back. An awkward hug. But a tight hug. They moved to the side, had a daddy-daughter conversation. Carmen and I faced each other, eyes as sharp as scalpels, dissecting each other.

Starbucks in hand, Miss Ruth adjusted her Gucci purse, went over and stood by her husband, those aging hips swaying like she was the bomb, Queen of the Wine when she was in her prime.

Carmen, she remained right there, next to me. Wanted to be up in my face.

For months I had wanted to meet her. Now I wished I hadn't. Not like this.

Carmen toyed with her wedding ring, said, "Girlfriend."

I nodded.

She said, "Have to admit, that was the most humiliating moment in my life so far."

I didn't say anything, glanced at Keith, hoped he'd hurry it up before I died.

Territorial. Her words, her stance, her every breath, territorial.

She evaluated me, nodded her head. I pretended she didn't faze me. I wanted to create peace in the valley, establish some sort of understanding while I gained clarity for myself.

I said, "I love that outfit you have on."

It was a thing women did. We always searched for something to compliment each other about—hair, clothes, shoes—even if we didn't mean it. But she wasn't in that frame of mind.

Carmen snapped, "Bitch, please."

That disarmed me. Something wasn't right about this woman. That same something was in Carmen's mother's eyes. The way Destiny had looked at first, that *ain't right* was in her eyes too.

I was standing in the middle of three generations of *ain't right*.

Carmen looked me up and down, asked, "How long have you . . . you and Keith are what, exactly?"

"If you're asking if we were together while he was still living with you—"

"Yes, that's exactly what I'm asking."

"I don't want to get into that with you. Just ask Keith."

"I'm asking you. How long have you been fucking my husband?"

That stalled me. Didn't stop me. Just stalled me. Abrupt evil had a tendency to do that.

I firmed up, shot her a nasty smile, became as petty as she was, said, "I'm sorry, but you are separated, right? He filed for divorce, right? I think that's what he just confirmed two minutes ago."

That hit her hard. More lightning in her eyes. "And you think you're his girlfriend?"

"Is there going to be a problem between us, Carmen?"

"Don't get too comfortable."

"Comfortable? Did you not see his new tattoo?"

"Tattoos can be *removed*."

"Is that a threat?"

"It's a *fact*."

"Well, *Carmen*. You heard him."

"Well, *Billie*, I don't give shit where he gets a tattoo. I'm still his wife."

"Uh-huh."

"That makes you his mistress."

"Is that right?"

"Suck mi out."

"Excuse me?"

"You're nothing more than his whore."

That island girl walked away, all finger pops and attitude, went and stood by her mother.

A wife scorned.

A grandmother with hate in her eyes.

Both of them talking, staring at me.

Carmen's daddy, shaking his head, staring at the ground.

Carmen's mother motioned, pushed her mortified daughter, directed her.

Carmen nodded, sashayed over, and stood with Keith and their daughter.

Carmen put her hand on Keith's shoulder. A light touch that disturbed me.

Carmen's father shook his head even harder, looked away.

Carmen's mother's smile was as crooked as San Francisco's Lombard Street.

Something inside me broke.

The part of me ruled by logic, it shattered into little pieces.

Snap. Snap. Snap.

And those little pieces broke into pieces so small they became microscopic dust.

I blinked away from that disturbing memory and stared at Keith.

Keith was as naked as my emotions. Still on the phone with Carmen. His come inside me. A million sperm on a useless journey.

I hated myself. Wanted to dig my nails into my flesh, then rip that flesh off until I saw bones.

Plain and simple, the heart wanted what it wanted. The heart wanted to win.

And it was all about how bad you wanted it, what you would do to get it.

I went to my dresser. Opened it up. They stared at me. My abandoned birth control pills. Pills I had stopped taking months ago. Stopped popping the baby stoppers a few days after I ran into Carmen and her family. Seemed like everything changed the evening Keith and I were coming out of that movie theater and we ran into his wife and kid. Became jealous. Insecure. Scared. Afraid I would lose him. Wanted him focused on me.

Somewhere down the line love stirred everything up and I lost my damn mind.

Love made you dumb. Made you pull desperate moves. Made smart women stupid. Something about possibly losing the man we love made us do really, really, really dumb shit.

I had lied to him. Told him I had been taking my birth control. I had stopped taking my pills because . . . because I was insecure . . . scared I would lose Keith. But I couldn't lose what I never had.

Put my hands over my belly, shook my head. Felt so ashamed of myself.

Sometimes it was best to withdraw from battle in order to end conflict. My daddy used to say that.

I wished I hadn't told Keith I was pregnant. Wished he had spoken first, had told me that he was going back to Carmen before I had opened my mouth and told him I was carrying our child.

Too late.

When I went back Keith was getting dressed. Shaking his head. Face tense with anger.

I said, "Whassup?"

"Have to leave."

My hormones . . . so out of control . . . felt so vulnerable . . . so damn needy right now.

I said, "She calls. You run."

"She's dropping Destiny off at my apartment."

"Can't your daughter stay with her grandparents for a little while?"

"She's my child, not theirs."

"I mean, she's already at her grandparents' house, right?"

"Billie . . ." He took a breath, frustrated. "Right now . . . after today . . . I need to be there for her. You have no idea how bad I felt. No idea at all. Standing up in front of the world, letting them know that I was . . . was . . . incompetent as a parent. Everybody calling, asking questions. You have no idea. Kept praying nothing bad had happened to her. Kept thinking that maybe if I had been there for her . . ."

I nodded like I understood. Or wanted to understand. But I knew I never would.

We didn't talk as he dressed. His come still draining out of me.

Dammit.

The tears came.

Something inside me broke, my voice cracked, said, "I can't handle this anymore."

"What did I do, Billie?"

"Don't make love to me . . . don't get inside me . . . stir me up . . . get me confused . . . don't make me feel beautiful, then . . . she calls and you . . . you . . . you run out of that door . . . don't. . . . I'll feel like shit if you do."

He took a hard breath. Lowered his head.

He said, "I have to be home when she drops off Destiny."

Over and over, I wiped my eyes. "I understand."

"Don't make me choose. Not today."

"Not trying to make you choose."

"Then what's the problem?"

"Just need to know where I fit in your world."

He hugged me a moment. "Billie, you are my world."

His damn cellular rang again.

"Guess you're not responding to the slave master's whip fast enough."

He groaned. I felt the frustration coursing through his veins, in the way his chest rose and fell.

He asked, "What can we do? What can I do to make it better? Tell me. If I can do it, I will."

I asked, "If I have this baby, if I call, I wonder if you will come running . . . or if I'll be alone. It's not about me. Guess I'm thinking about the baby. About what you said about your time . . . Never mind."

"I don't want to have to choose between Destiny and our unborn child. What if . . . heaven forbid . . . our child is ill . . . asthma . . . sickle-cell . . . lupus . . . has special needs . . . anything . . . and . . . I need to be there . . . then something happens to Destiny . . . she gets sick . . . needs me . . . with you and Carmen at odds . . . how do I split my heart in half and handle a crisis like that? Whoever I go to . . . that will make it look like I love the other child less. That would be a nightmare."

"Destiny . . . she's almost an adult."

"But she is still my little girl. No matter if she is fifteen or fifty, she'll be my little girl. She has feelings. A girl always needs her daddy. You saw that today. You saw a girl who needed her daddy."

My life had gotten complicated, but it wasn't as complicated as it was going to be.

Eyes closed, I wished my daddy were here. He'd make everything all right.

Keith said, "If I could cut myself in half, if I could stay here with you twenty-four/seven, I would."

"Not asking you to."

"Yes, you are. Every time you do this shit, that's what you're asking me to do."

"Just asking you to . . . was hoping . . . wishing you could stay a little longer."

"Soon as things slow down, when I get Destiny situated, I'll call you."

He let me go. Then I let him go. Keith was hurrying to the door. His choice had been made, that was clear. He stepped outside, looked back at me, his expression heavy, laced with confusion.

He took a step, then turned back, "You gonna be okay?"

He waited for my answer. And my answer was so hard to give.

Then his phone rang again.

That was our answer.

I said, "Don't call me. Don't come back."

"Billie . . ."

Before he could respond, I closed the door, locked the door, turned and walked away.

My throat tightened. My face turned hot. My legs, so weak I could barely stand.

I leaned against the wall, head down, hand on my stomach, and the tears wouldn't stop.

eleven

BILLIE

"DUCATI, EVERYBODY SAW YOU ON THE NEWS."

Hair down, makeup in full effect, I was pimping a T-shirt that read SLIGHTLY GHETTO. Other people had on T-shirts with Michael Jackson's new face and the phrase NOT GUILTY on it eleven times. My favorites were CLOSE GITMO and BUSH SHOULD HAVE PICKED JUDGE JUDY.

But I was getting all the attention.

"Ducati, you're a superstar."

That's how it was all evening. People who knew me as Ducati were giving me love. I was throwing down behind the bar; seemed like more people came to see me than they did to see the show.

Saturday became Sunday while I was dead on my feet. So damn tired, but had to keep moving. Hadn't had any sleep, not for the last two days. Doubt if any decent sleep would come my way tonight.

The room was packed, over two hundred hot bodies, most standing. Simfani Blue was on stage, playing her Takamine, strumming that acoustic guitar and blowing out the title track to "Love Addiction."

The room had bonded, held hands, and took a walk down Memory Lane.

Love was crack, we all knew that. Had us as strung out as David Chappelle's character, Tyrone.

Men were singing too. They knew the lyrics. A few of them were bona fide crackheads too.

Two customers got their drinks and moved away. That was when I saw her. She was here. Standing right in front of me. Had no idea how long she had been staring at me, stalking me.

Carmen.

I stumbled, almost dropped a shot glass.

Carmen had walked up in my job, posted up, and was staring me down.

She had on jeans. Expensive boots. Chandelier earrings. Colorful shawl. Makeup, flawless.

That cold expression she was giving me. Looking like twenty pounds of hate in a five-pound bag.

We stood there for a moment, engaged in a simple, wordless, expressionless exchange.

She eased up to the bar.

"Mimosa, please."

Her tone, patronizing and insulting. Just like that she attempted to turn me into a servant.

I said, "Sweetie, I ain't your house nigga."

"Excuse me?"

Hormones blazing, I walked away, went to other customers.

She watched me. That vulture waited. Still expressionless.

She came back over, asked, "Can we talk?"

"You're welcome."

She looked baffled. "I'm welcome?"

"The yellow motorcycle out front. The one you passed by on the way into my job. That was the motorcycle your daughter was on today. Maybe you didn't recognize me, but I found your daughter."

She pushed her lips up into an angry smile.

She raised her voice over the music. "There was a reward for finding our child."

I gave her an incredulous look, shook my head, said, "So hard for you to just say thank you."

She took an envelope out of her expensive purse and slid it across the counter.

"The reward."

I shook my head. "I don't want your reward money."

"Then consider it a tip."

She sashayed away, left an envelope stuffed with cash resting on the counter.

I picked up the envelope. A family of C-notes winked at me. I stuck it in my back pocket.

Five thousand dollars. Never had that much cash. So light and so heavy all at once.

Carmen motioned toward the front door, wanted to take this outside, away from the noise.

She wasn't going to leave. This job wasn't much, but it was my job. My feel-good place. And she had brought her negative energy up in here and was spreading it around like smoke from a brushfire.

I told the other bartenders I was going to take a break, that if I wasn't back in fifteen to notify the coroner and the paramedics; somebody was going to be dead and somebody was going to be hurt. I pulled my hair back, took off my jewelry, wished I had time to slather Vaseline on my face, just in case.

Then I stepped out on Wilshire Boulevard. The night had some chill.

Arms folded I walked with her, moved my wretched business around the corner.

Her three-inch heels clicked with her every step.

My four-inch heels did the same.

She stopped walking first. I chilled out a few feet away from her. Not close enough for her to attack me, but close enough for me to get to her if I gave in to my irresistible impulse to whoop her ass.

I reached in my back pocket, took out the envelope. Threw it, made it land at her feet.

She gave me a crooked smiled, squatted, picked it up, shaking her head like I was a fool.

Carmen said, "Keith is my husband. I am his wife. We are family. We have a child."

"Stop repeating yourself and get to the point."

She took a breath, cleared her throat.

She said, "That is the way I want it. No outside baby mommas, no other women I have to deal with on that level, on any level, no ancillary family, no visitation. I want it . . . to be as if . . ."

"I didn't exist."

She nodded. "Exactly."

"Well, you can get over that idea. I'm keeping the baby."

"In that case . . ." She raised a hand, licked her lips. "We are willing to compensate you."

"What do you mean by that?"

"Compensate you. For mental anguish. For your inconvenience."

"You're asking—" I stopped and cleared my throat. "What are you asking?"

"This is a pro-choice era, well beyond Roe versus Wade. Well, let's just say the ball is in your court. We are pretty much powerless. So the choice is all yours."

"Look, why don't you kill the damn polite act? Say what the hell you have to say and leave."

"You're right." She firmed her stance and voice. "Let's stop bullshitting each other, Billie."

"Sure, Carmen."

"You're pregnant either by choice or because you didn't do anything to prevent it."

"Keith knew the chances we were taking."

"He's a man, for Christ's sake."

"Meaning?"

"Meaning if you throw your legs open, you're attractive enough, still young . . . men are opportunistic creatures, so if you open your legs he's going to slip on a banana peel and fall in. You were the coconspirator. You betrayed me along with him the first time you were in bed together."

"Betrayed you? We ain't friends. Besides, you were separated."

"Separated ain't divorced."

I told her, "And keep it real. The only thing Keith fell in was love."

"Right, let's keep this shit real," she retorted, and had the nerve to do the neck a little. "Look, sweetie, when a man has his dick inside your pum-pum he says all types of things. Things that he doesn't mean. It's all about getting inside the pum-pum. Or if he is getting sex, how he keeps getting laid. Now that his dick is not inside you, what is he telling you? I don't want to get into pointing fingers—"

"Please don't."

"Keith and I had a rift. But we are working on putting things back on track. We are a family unit. We stood before God and we are honoring that commitment. Marriage. That's something I bet that he's never talked about or even considered doing with you. You are the woman he met on the rebound."

I chuckled. "Oh, so I'm rebound?"

"If that. Face the facts, honey. That's who you are. The rebound chick."

I chuckled again. "That's not the impression he gave me."

"You don't understand the hierarchy of situations such as this, do you?"

"Enlighten me, Yoda."

"Yoda. Cute. I'll take that as a compliment, a statement of my being the sage one."

I repeated, "Enlighten me."

"The best you can be is number three. At best."

"Number three. Is that right?"

"His daughter will always come first. And I will always be in the picture. Package deal. So you see, those first two slots are already taken. He wants his daughter happy, so he will keep me happy."

"The best I can get is the bronze."

"Don't kid yourself. Number three in this game is plastic."

"Cute."

"Truth."

"Try this truth. We were not a one-night stand. We've been together for almost a year."

"We've been together for *eighteen* years. But I won't get into the need to rebut everything you say. You've known about me and his child since you met him. You were his little secret."

"I guess you know it all, huh?"

"We grew up together. We've changed. *Eighteen* years later, we're different people. People change a lot in eighteen years. We're not the same. Didn't have bills responsibilities back then. But we've grown up. You ride a motorcycle. You're a free spirit. No real responsibilities. You haven't grown up. He's with you because you represent fun. You're stress-free. That's what number three is always about. Fucking and fun. The escape. You're single. No children. Probably have sex anywhere at the drop of a hat. I've been there. Was there when I met Keith. You're a work in progress."

"You don't know me."

"Don't have to know you. I know your type."

"Is that right?"

"You're unsettled, renting a room, zero investments, haven't quite decided what you want to do with your life, still act like you're all that, but deep down inside you're depressed because you know that you're not. I'm established. But you're thinking Keith *likes* you. Of course. They always *like* us better before we progress. When we're less polished, seemingly more inferior. The minute you retire your little motorcycle and move up to a car seat and a brand-new baby, when you start needing things, demanding things, expecting things, the moment your expectations start to grow, when you start demanding he live up to your needs, then your number is definitely going to be up. Right now you represent his escape from reality, that's all. A free fuck, that's all you are. What you were. He's lost his job. He's losing in court. If you're pregnant, you'll represent another problem. A headache. You'll lose all of your sexual allure."

Cold air blew between us as a few people walked by. I was thinking about slapping her down.

One of the brothers slowed, flirted. "Hey, was that you on the news today?"

It was TJ. This Eritrean brother that always tried to get with me.

I said, "TJ, let me holla at you when I get back inside. In the middle of something right now."

TJ gave me the thumbs-up and walked on by.

Carmen said, "As I was saying . . . we are willing to offer you a settlement."

"A settlement?"

"We are willing to draw up papers through an attorney. We recognize that it takes a lot of money to raise a child. We are willing to give you one hundred thousand dollars."

I paused. "Excuse me?"

"The moment the baby is born and the DNA tests show that my husband *is* indeed the father—"

"Keith is the father."

"So you say."

"So I know."

She swallowed, created an edgy smile. "If it's true, we are willing to offer you a cash settlement, providing you sign the necessary documents which will allow my husband to give up all parental rights and not be perpetually liable for this little faux pas. My husband's name is *not* to appear on—"

"So you're paying me to . . . what? Go away? Disappear?"

"Since you are not willing to terminate this madness, we are being considerate and making it easy on you. We are going to pay you what it costs to raise a child. The estimated costs. We will wash our hands of the situation and you will be financially capable of raising your child."

"*Our* child. Me and Keith's child."

"*Your* child. Keith doesn't want to be involved. Sweetie, was that not clear to you?"

"My name is *Billie*. Not Sweetie. Not Honey. *Billie*. Call me by my name."

"This is *your* choice. That's all we're saying. We don't want to have to suffer and be penalized a lifetime because of *your* choice. And it is *your* choice. Having a baby is a selfish act. I know. That's why we do that. For self. Not for the baby. We claim it's for the baby, but it's all about us. What *we* want, when *we* want it." She took a breath. "So this little fiasco will cost my family, then so be it. We want to reach a settlement, a fair settlement, something within reason, then we can all get on with our lives."

"So, you came to my damn job to insult me and throw money in my face."

"How long will it take you to accumulate that much money, Billie? One hundred thousand. Be honest. You're a bartender. Not a *real* teacher, just a *substitute*. A glorified baby-sitter. That means you're not getting any kind of salary. And, what, you teach people how to ride motorcycles on the side?"

"Don't insult me."

"Don't insult you, or don't remind you of the truth? If I have insulted you, it was unintentional and I apologize. If I have said anything untrue, please correct me and we both will live in the truth."

I paused, looked out at traffic, back at the Temple Bar, evil thoughts going through my head.

I said, "You hate me that much?"

"Yes. I hate you that much."

"It's immoral."

"Some may see it as immoral, but it is not against man's law. And I bet if you took a poll among church members, I bet they would advise you to take the money, tithe, and get on with your life."

I hated her so much. Hated Keith too. Hated all of them.

I asked, "How do I know you have that kind of money?"

She laughed. "I have a career. I have credit. I own a home. I have equity. Don't insult me."

"What kind of woman are you?"

"It might be shrewd, but it's not horrible. It's business. Right or wrong, you have any idea how many women would love to be able to do this, what I'm offering? You have any idea how many women wish they were on your side of the table being offered one hundred thousand?"

"Why are you doing this?"

"I've worked too *damn* hard to get where I am to lose it all. I want *my* family back together. I want *my* family to be okay. I want closure. That's all I want. Closure. My daughter's father, my husband, and no other strays knocking on our door for handouts, emotional or financial. No strays."

"Strays?"

"No goddamn strays."

"You're an evil bitch."

"I'm an honest *bitch*. I'm a smart *bitch*. I'm a bitch that would *never* get pregnant by another woman's husband. I'm the *bitch* you don't want to fuck with. Yes, and when I think about it, I am an evil *bitch*. Disrupting my family makes me an evil bitch. And you don't want to see how evil this bitch can be."

"Carmen . . . are you threatening me?"

"Attorneys don't make threats, Billie. I'm advising you, simply serving you notice."

"If you ever come to my job again, Carmen, you will get served. And that's a threat."

I stormed away, left her and her offer behind me, moved with an angry and confident stroll, taking my hair down, but with every step I was frightened. There would never be any closure for me, I felt that. This was getting uglier by the second. I wanted to scream. I wanted to cry. But I had to go back to work. And Carmen was right behind me, chasing me down Wilshire Boulevard, howling my name.

She said, "One hundred and fifty thousand."

"You just don't quit, do you?"

"I'll pay you fifty thousand now, another hundred when you deliver."

"Part now, part when I deliver. What is this, a book deal?"

"That's my final offer."

"I don't understand conniving women like you."

"Like me? You're pregnant by my husband, ruining my family, and *I'm* conniving?"

"I wanna know why the hell you would want to force a relationship with a man that clearly wants out, and you're willing to make everybody miserable in the process. You're making Keith miserable."

"And your pregnancy is not making Keith ecstatic; did you fail to notice that? I don't understand women who keep insisting on having children outside of the covenant of marriage. I do not understand selfish women who intentionally disrupt the family unit. I do not understand why women continue to get pregnant out of wedlock, then celebrate in the name of the Lord. You have no family, you have no family values, you know that? You are just a hussy taking what she can get when she can get it."

I snapped, "Now I see why your daughter ran away from your crazy ass."

That did it, pushed her buttons real good. Her fingernails grew like claws and her eyes went big. I mean she had crazy eyes like the infamous runaway bride. Looked like she was ready to tear into me.

I warned her, "We're not at Starbucks and I'm not sitting on a toilet seat this time."

She gritted her teeth, wanting to fight, knowing my can of whoop ass was more potent than hers.

"Okay, Billie. One-seventy-five. Fifty up front, the rest after you deliv— after the child is born, paternity test withstanding. Have the child or not, fifty thousand dollars is yours."

I swallowed. "One hundred and seventy-five thousand dollars."

"One hundred and seventy-five thousand dollars. Fifty up front, whether or not you have the child. You can take the fifty, count it, and think about it. Wipe your ass with it, for all I care."

That was a lot of money. Too much to not consider.

"Where is all this money coming from?"

"One hundred and seventy-five thousand. In cash."

"You're serious, aren't you?"

She nodded. "So that's the equivalent of making three hundred and fifty thousand, before taxes."

I paused again. "Why are you doing this?"

"Don't you get it? I love him." She stressed. "I love my family. I want us to have peace."

"And you hate me and my . . . my baby . . . you hate us that much?"

"*Eighteen years*. You're talking about a few months of fucking and fun, I'm talking about eighteen years of ups and downs, of blood, sweat, and tears, of doing what I had to do to become the kind of wife he wanted, of struggling through law school so my daughter would have a better life, eighteen years of building a family. I refuse to lose eighteen years of my life because of *you* or any other *bitch*."

She trembled, said that with so much conviction, a chill ran up to the base of my skull.

My words fractured. "You'll insult me, threaten me, bribe me, whatever it takes to get him back."

"Yes. I will do whatever it takes to have my family back, yes."

I felt sorry for Carmen. Pitied her desperation.

But I wondered how I would feel if Keith were my husband and she was the other woman. Wondered if after a few years I would be out in the cold, facing some woman, trying to protect my nest.

Carmen wore the ring and that ring wasn't coming off, not while she was breathing.

She was his wife. I was the rebound chick. Number three. Plastic at best.

Maria Gonzales came to mind and I mumbled, "*Code 46.*"

Carmen said, "What?"

I shook my head. "Nothing."

Keith. Heard his voice inside my head.

Don't pretend money won't be an issue. They never stop needing. Everything costs.

I didn't want Carmen's money.

Love don't pay the goddamn bills, Billie.

Keith was right. Right now expectations were low. It was cool, maybe even romantic being two broke-ass people in love, but if you throw in a baby, we were bound to be two broke-ass people in hate.

I told myself that it wasn't for me. Told myself that it was all about the baby.

I said, "Sure."

She cleared her throat, ran her fingers through her wild Afro, again in control of the world.

She asked, "Do you have an attorney on retainer?"

I chuckled. "Why would I? I'm a bartender and a glorified baby-sitter, or did you forget that?"

She raised a hand in apology. "Get one."

I said, "You will pay the legal costs. For every stamp."

"You're insane. With the amount of money I'm offering, be reasonable."

"No. If you want us gone, pay for us to leave. Every dime."

She shook her head.

I asked her, "How bad do *you* want this over?"

She gave me a shrewd smile, every breath cursing my existence.

I remained stone-faced.

I held my hand out.

She glared at my hand, at the flesh her husband touched so many nights.

She snapped, "This is unbelievable. You do the crime and I get the punishment. You're the one getting pregnant while you're not married, pregnant by a married man, at that. If you were a felon, that would be two strikes. You should be incarcerated for what you've done."

"One more insult, one more shot at assassinating my character, and the price of hate will go up another hundred thousand dollars. Maybe another whopping two hundred thousand."

She stared at me long and hard, then at my outstretched hand.

I nodded. "Like you said, one seventy-five. Fifty up front. The rest on delivery. *And* all of my attorney's fees."

Our stare continued, moved us deeper into the land of heated animosity. If the stare didn't end, one of us would kill the other.

I said, "Deal or no deal?"

She gave me the tips of her fingers. As soon we touched, we yanked our hands from each other. Then she threw the money-filled envelope, made it land at my feet.

I said, "I don't want your reward money."

"That's not reward money. It's earnest money. Five of the first fifty."

I picked it up, held it in my hands. Five thousand dollars. It felt heavy. Like a ton of guilt.

She said, "No victory comes without a terrible price."

Our glares lingered.

She hurried away, head shaking, yanking out her cellular phone, no doubt calling her husband.

I wanted to call Keith too. Wanted to call him every minute of the hour.

But I kept seeing Carmen on her knees, that Afro bobbing as she sucked the dick she married.

She wasn't giving him a blow job. Wasn't romantic. She was sucking the life out of him.

Now she had sucked the life out of me.

I wanted this to be over. Wanted to lobotomize Keith and Carmen from my mind.

I hated love. But not as much as I hated Carmen. Not as much as Carmen hated me.

Part of me wanted to chase Carmen and throw this ton of guilt back in her face.

I know your type . . . unsettled . . . zero investments . . . haven't quite decided what you want to do with your life . . . act like you're all that . . . depressed because you know that you're not.

No. I wanted to wrap this guilt around that brick then *slam* it in her face.

"Billie . . . two people in love, two broke people in love will eventually be two broke people in hate."

Envelope in my hand, I hurried in the opposite direction, every step heavier than the one before.

I walked away, *Code 46* burrowing inside my mind.

In the sci-fi movie *Code 46*, Maria Gonzales was impregnated by a man and their relationship violated the law, code number 46 of that society. She had an affair, was impregnated by a married man from a different caste system. She was *depregnated* and the memory cluster surrounding the man and the pregnancy was removed, left her with scar tissue but no mental scars, left her smiling, living in bliss.

I just wished that type of technology existed. The world would be a much better place.

Maybe I'd wake up tomorrow, depregnated.

Maybe my memory would be exfoliated and I wouldn't remember any of this, Keith included.

Viviane shouted, "She stalked you down to the Temple Bar and straight-up bribed you?"

I was on my cellular, in the bathroom. Called Viviane as soon as I got back inside. She was still at the hospital with her family. Q wasn't doing that good, her injury worse than they had realized.

Viviane kept the conversation on my plight. "That's . . . Keith's wife is way out there, Billie."

"She offered me money to release her from all parental obligations, henceforth and forevermore."

"God, wish I was there. As tense and stressed as I am . . . no telling what would've gone down."

"We could've beat her ig'nant ass all up and down Wilshire."

"The way I feel, we could've beat her ass to Bakersfield."

I said, "Carmen seems to be loaded. Throwing five thousand around like it's a bag of quarters."

"Maybe the lunatic jumped rich. Maybe that's why Keith had the sudden change of heart."

"I guess. I mean . . . it's all about money to men. At least it seems that way."

"You should've held out for more. If she can offer you that much without blinking . . ."

I asked, "Am I doing the right thing? My moral compass ain't working right now. Am I?"

"That's some serious cabbage. Take it. Better to be pissed off with money than pissed off standing in line at the welfare office. Take the fifty and decide what you want to do."

"What do you think I should do?"

"Well, if you have a kid, fifty ain't that much. You'll spend that on pampers. And keep it real. One-seventy-five ain't that much either, not when you're looking at eighteen years with a dependant."

"What if I bought a house?"

"If you bought property, first off, you'd have to pay off all of your bills to qualify for a loan. That means a chunk of that money would be gone. The rest of it tied up in property."

"But if . . . if I don't have a kid . . . if I just took the fifty . . . didn't move . . . kept my same lifestyle . . ."

"You could be on easy street for a minute. You could regroup. Follow your dream."

"Guess I could."

"You could even get back onstage. Cut your own demo. Give it another shot."

I didn't say anything. Viviane held the phone.

She said, "Saw you on the news. You were on right after the reporters talked to my family."

"Enough about me. What's going on with you?"

She told me that they had had media coverage. Some, not much. News was for the privileged.

Hand on my back pocket, fingers on that envelope, I deserted my problems, asked, "How is Q?"

First silence, then Viviane choked. Sounded like she was having a hard time breathing.

I asked, "You crying?"

"Yes. This is messed up, Billie."

"What happened?"

Viviane said, "This ain't adding up, not at all."

Again I asked, "What happened?"

"Everything took a turn after you left. Pulmonary shit. Doctor said blood drained to her lungs."

"Pneumonia?"

"Yeah."

"What? Why didn't you call me and tell me?"

"It's been crazy down here."

"That bad?"

Then she gave up her emotions, cried. "I could kill whoever did this to her."

"Any idea who . . . ?"

"Police are working on a sketch."

"To catch who did this?"

"In case this turns into a homicide."

"Damn."

"I'mma make a run. Kick up some shit. See if I can find the assholes Q was hanging out with, find her friends, see what I can find out. Where is your gun, Billie? You have it or is it at the house?"

"Viv . . . ?"

"Not letting them bastards get away with doing this to my sister."

"Don't do nothing stupid."

"They already did something stupid, Billie."

"What are you going to do?"

"What do you think? They hurt my sister. You don't mess with my family."

"Pointing a gun at somebody gets you ten."

She sounded barbaric. "I'll do more than point."

"And shooting somebody will get you twenty."

"They've almost killed my sister, Billie."

"Viviane . . ."

Before I said the second syllable in her name she had hung up.

He was at the bar waiting on me. Looked like he had just walked in.

That pissed me off. Everybody was threatening and aggravating me.

I went over to him, snapped, "Are you stalking me?"

"Nope."

"You come to get your helmet?"

"Nope."

"Why are you here, Raheem?"

Black jeans. Leather jacket. Brown T-shirt with a picture of Richard Pryor on the face.

I had come out of the bathroom and Raheem was in the club. Waiting for me at the bar.

Raheem asked, "You okay? You look . . ."

"Going through some personal thangs right now."

I tensed up, walked away, went to the other end of the bar. He followed. He stayed away until I finished mixing it up for a few borderline alcoholics, then took slow and easy steps toward my space.

I snapped, "What?"

He said, "Brought you a peace offering."

"A peace offering?"

A worn gift bag from Barnes & Noble was in his hand. He handed me the bag. Everybody was at my job offering me bribes tonight. First Carmen, now this brother. People were watching, so I took it.

I looked inside and saw a book.

He said, "The way I reacted . . . when you said you were . . ."

"Pregnant. Don't choke. Saying the word won't make the baby yours."

"You caught me off guard last night."

Raheem said, "It's *The Alchemist*."

"I can read."

"Cool. Especially since it doesn't have any pictures inside."

I read the cover. "This is that Brazilian Paulo Coelho's book."

"Yeah."

"Why?"

"Wanted to apologize for the way I . . . I . . . responded . . . to . . . when you told me . . ."

Silence. Awkwardness. So many thoughts were in my head, none solid, each one like fog.

I said, "Let me guess. French Connection?"

"What?"

"Your favorite poison."

"You're good."

I nodded. "Dark liquor, smooth, expensive, only takes a little bit to get you messed up."

"Like me."

I laughed. I actually laughed. "Watch out. Pregnant woman over here."

He smiled, then said, "Congratulations."

"Thanks. I think."

I made him a French Connection.

I asked, "What are you trying to do, besides get me to file a restraining order?"

"Trying to be your friend."

"I don't do friends with men. Or women, now that I think about it. Not too many women. Women are too . . . they're women . . . would have to be a woman to understand. Bottom line, I don't do friends."

"Why not?"

"Letting people in your world . . . you have to be careful who you open the door and invite in."

"Well, I put my card inside the book. Just in case."

"Just in case . . . what?"

"In case you read it. Serious, it's a damn good book. Best ever written, if you ask me. Read it. Then we can talk about it. Over the phone or via e-mail, or instant message, whatever, if you want to."

"I don't do book clubs either."

"Either way, the numbers are on the card."

I blew air, got serious. "What if I don't want to call you?"

"Then use my card for a bookmark. Or to pick something out of your teeth."

"I'm not teaching you how to ride."

"Did I ask you to? I just asked you to read a damn book."

"No, you didn't snap on me."

"Don't want you to do anything you don't want to do. I'm taking the class. Start next week."

I said, "You're mean, you know that?"

He laughed. "I'm *mean*? You jacked me for my helmet and I'm *mean*?"

"That was an intervention. Like it or not, I saved your life."

I went away, made drinks, five grand in my pocket, Carmen's abrasive words grating against my mind. In pain but pretending that I was okay. Raheem got my attention and I sighed, went back his way.

Raheem asked, "What's your favorite movie?"

"Why?"

"So I can watch it."

"Okay. And why would you do that?"

"Then if we ever happen to talk again, or run into each other, maybe we can talk about it."

I shrugged. "Only one movie is on my mind right now."

"Which one?"

I swallowed, said, "Look, thanks for the book, but don't harass me. Okay?"

I watched the show. Wished I was up there singing from the bottom of my soul, getting that kind of applause and love from a room filled with strangers. But I wasn't onstage, was living behind the bar.

I wanted to cry. Hormones kicked in, brought my wall down and took my emotions up. Had to get away and go to the bathroom again, pull it together. Sat there looking at the go-away money.

Shouldn't have slept with Keith tonight. Felt him inside me right now. Felt him moving deeper and deeper. Felt the sweet pain he had left behind. Knew I was going to regret it, just not this soon.

Damn love and its fangs, damn the way that vampire sucked the blood out of you, made you weak.

I'd been in love before. Many times before. I knew that drug would wear off.

Not long after that I looked around the room for Raheem, wanted to see if my stalker wanted another drink. Didn't like how he was pushing up on me, but I felt bad for the way I was treating the brother. That drink would be my peace offering. And I was going to give him his helmet back. Wasn't my place to take his lid. Think part of me did that to save him, another part so I would have to see him again.

He was gone.

For a moment I wished I hadn't been mean to him, wished he had stayed.

For a moment.

But I knew that being mean to him was to push him away, that it was for the best.

Maybe that was why Keith had been mean to me at Starbucks. Because it was for the best.

Last call came and went.

After we cleaned up and I said my goodbyes to the crew, I geared up, put on my backpack, and sped away from the Temple Bar, a million thoughts on my mind. Decided not to get on the freeway, to ride the streets, take the long route and think. Maybe not think.

Five thousand dollars were in my pocket. And Carmen was offering me more.

It took a lot of money to make money in the music business.

Lots to pay for: studio time, musicians, singers, packaging, promotions. With fifty thousand in my pocket, if I had a team behind me, the right people to get it all flowing . . .

Carmen had put five thousand on the table, Viviane had whispered in my ear, and just like that I had forgotten I was pregnant. Maybe fifty thousand dollars would be just as effective as *Code 46*.

I had watched the show, imagining that was me up there. Then blinked that vision away. Needed to let that superstar shit sit in the back of my mind where it belonged. Reminded myself what I already knew, that making it in this business, for me, was bullshit. That men were in control of the biz. Ninety percent of them want to fuck you to *help you out*. I'd been down that road. Went down that road around ten years ago, when I was twenty-four. Ended up pregnant for the first time. Was dumb enough to sleep with a so-called producer who said he was going to help me. Got educated on the game. They didn't want to help. No sex, no interest in your project. Or if you didn't hit the couch they wanted total control of your career. Without power over either your body or your music, they weren't interested in making it happen. Yeah. I knew the men in the business. After stringing you along, the guy who signed you ended up fired and the new guy wasn't feeling you. Then you became another name on their tax write-off shelf until your contract was up. You got older waiting for that contract to expire. And when it was all over, with zero promotion or marketing, which meant zero sales, at the end of the day you ended up getting a fat bill from the label instead of a check. They didn't do a damn thing for you and wanted every penny back. If you didn't sell the records they never promoted, *you* owed *them* money.

Then there was bankruptcy to make that bill go away.

When you weren't a potential cash cow anymore, nobody wanted to touch you.

Then you gave up and became a flight attendant.

Then 9/11 scared the crap out of you and you became a substitute teacher.

Then you found out that teachers were underpaid and you taught motorcycle training.

Then you spent six hundred on bartending school so you could become a bartender.

You learned about every kind of drinking glass ever made, mixed every kind of drink there was, smiled and stood in the background, singing along with the crowd, watching everybody else blow up.

You hustled, dreamed, looked for love. Love mattered more than money or material things.

Then you met a man who was struggling, a man you thought you understood. A man you were happy to be in a relationship with, even if it wasn't ideal. A man you could trust. A man who loved you.

A man who you thought understood you.

You trusted. You dropped your guard. You slipped. Love grew inside you like a tumor. You ended up pregnant again. Pregnant and zooming down Wilshire Boulevard at two in the morning, crisp air numbing your extremities, trying to slice through the chill and outrun Carmen's voice.

Couldn't shake her raspy voice out of my head. It was all around me, like it lived in the wind.

My left hand on my hip, cruising in a forty-five-mile-per-hour zone, thinking of a thousand things I should've said to her when she insulted me, mind spinning and coming up with so many snappy comebacks, imagined kicking her ass while my eyes remained focused on what was in front of me.

Had the nerve to throw the money at my feet. And my dumb ass picked it up.

Once again, sheer anger and tunnel vision had blinded me to what was behind me.

Didn't notice the headlights of the car trailing me, running lights, matching my speed.

Didn't notice that when traffic thinned out, the driver turned off the headlights and accelerated.

Tunnel vision made that charging bull invisible. Didn't notice that car until it was right up on me. Felt eyes and energy on me. Heat triple-timed.

I cursed, hoped that it wasn't the Santa Monica P.D., then relaxed enough to catch a glimpse of the sleek body and the emblem on the hood. A Benz. The car swerved, rammed my back tire. She wanted me to do more than eat asphalt; she wanted me dead.

Then I was trying to escape.

I rocked like I was in the AMA races. And they were speeding behind me. All I could think of doing was making a quick turn, losing her on the side streets, all I could think about was getting away from that crazy bitch. And as I did turn, I knew I was going too fast. Way too fast to knee-slide my way out of this one. Turned too wide. Hit the front brake too hard and knew this was going to be ugly.

I went down.

twelve

DESTINY

DESTINY HATED HER DADDY'S CHEAP APARTMENT. OLD CARPET. FADED walls. Always smelled stale. Plus it was right under the landlord. She thought about how, whenever she spent the night, she could hear Juanita and her lover rocking and moaning when somebody had the big O. Usually at the crack of dawn. Juanita was old, biracial, at least forty, but her latest live-in lover was a college student majoring in nursing, a skinny white girl who wore dreadlocks, tattoos, and had her lip pierced. A Jewish girl who was no more than twenty. They fought all the time, just like her parents. Only the women upstairs were physical. At least three times over the last month, always late at night, half the neighborhood could hear them having a lovers' quarrel. They were up there loving and fighting and trading licks in more ways than one. Fighting and then making love. Just like her parents used to do.

She called out, "Daddy."

"I'm packing."

"Don't snap at me."

"You're supposed to be helping me."

Destiny asked, "Where your grumpy landlord and the skinny white girl?"

"*Where your?*"

"*Where's your* landlord and her anorexic freak?"

"Atlanta. I think."

"At one of those parades?"

"Probably down there waving her rainbow flag."

Destiny listened. No orgasmic screams from above, not a sound from across the street.

Destiny said, "I don't hear that baby crying tonight neither."

Her father told her, "Thank God for small miracles."

Midnight.

She watched her father, packing like he was in no hurry to move. Boxes were in the living room. Boxes were in the bedroom. Not many boxes, because her father didn't have much. When he had left her mother, he didn't take anything other than his clothes. Didn't take a single fork or spoon.

The phone rang. Her daddy answered. Somebody else calling to ask about the drama that went down today. Destiny heard her Daddy, for the hundredth time, telling the story. She stepped outside. Had to get away. She looked down at her T-shirt, read the first line. BOYS ARE STUPID. Then the next line. THROW ROCKS AT THEM. She wanted to do more than throw rocks. She wanted to find the people who had abused and stolen from her. She wanted to find out how corrosive bleach really was. Find out how deep a blade could cut. Robbed. Raped. Abandoned. Revenge. She wanted revenge. She wanted to get away tonight, but knew she wouldn't be able to get away, not from her daddy.

A convertible Mustang pulled up across the street, top down, music bumping R. Kelly. "Trapped in the Closet, Chapter One." The brother parked, talking on his cellular phone, blew his horn over and over.

"Destiny, keep off the porch. Bullets don't use a *Thomas Guide.*"

That man across the street was angry. "*Davina! I know your ass hear me out here.*"

Her father came over, stood behind her.

He said, "That's his damn baby that cries all night."

"Language, Daddy. Sometimes you get so ghetto."

"Baby screams. Momma screams. He screams."

Her father walked away, stepped around boxes. The movie *5 Days to Midnight* was playing on his small television, but he clicked that movie off, turned on his portable radio/CD player.

Destiny asked, "Where did Momma go?"

He shrugged as if he didn't care. "Don't know."

"She was dressed up."

"Maybe she went to see her boyfriend."

Time went by. The brother kept blowing his horn. R. Kelly's "Chapter Three" blasted.

"DAVINA! I KNOW YOUR ASS HEARS ME! I SAW YOU PEEP OUT THE WINDOW!"

Destiny stepped outside. Sat on the steps. Sang along. So much on her mind.

"WHO YOU GOT UP IN THERE? BET NOT HAVE NOBODY UP IN THERE WITH MY BABY."

Across the street the brother started throwing rocks at the second-story window. He walked with a LL Cool J swagger. Dark baseball cap, oversized jeans, FUBU boots, and Kobe gear on.

"QUIT PLAYIN' AND BRING KESHAWN DOWN!"

He was old, had to be almost thirty. Dressed in jeans. Leather jacket. Hair in cornrows.

Destiny jumped when her daddy snapped, "Destiny."

"It's stuffy in there."

"Open a window and stay where I can see you."

"So I can have a nice view of the Section 8 sign across the street."

Her father barked, "Don't leave this house."

"This is not a house. And I wouldn't run away from you, Daddy."

"Then stay where you can see me."

"Why? You're thinking about running away again?"

Her father said, "I've never run away."

"Momma said that's how you ended up in this funky apartment. You ran away from home."

She reached in her pocket searching for gum, pulled her pants pocket too far out, dropped all of her change, watched the coins roll across the porch, some falling over the edge by the bushes.

Her father said, "Come back inside. Stay where I can see you from my beat-up apartment."

She picked up some of her change, not all, got tired of her daddy calling her name, and went back inside, put two pieces of Dubble Bubble in her mouth, blew a bubble, felt like she was under house arrest.

Destiny asked, "How are you moving this ugly stuff?"

"U-Haul across the street. Carmen rented it for me. Three days ago."

"Why didn't you tell me you were moving back home with us?"

He didn't answer.

"Unless you weren't sure about it. Unless you really don't want to move back home with us."

Again he didn't answer.

Outside, trees shaking with the beat from R. Kelly's "Chapter Four."

"DAVINA! BRING ME MY DAMN BABY!"

Destiny went to the kitchen to get a glass of water. On the counter was a book. Paperback. *Divorce and Money: How to Make the Best Financial Decisions During Divorce.* She opened the book and skimmed over paragraphs about anger and hurt and resentment and sadness and fear about the future. Think financially, act legally. Next to that book, software. *The Portable Lawyer.* Destiny read the box. Twelve discs. Sixteen hours of legal tips, advice for people on a tight budget. How to fix damage done in divorce proceedings. Division of assets. Alimony. Child support. Child custody. Visitation.

She asked, "Does anybody win in a divorce?"

"The lawyers."

"Momma's a lawyer."

"Don't you have some homework to do?"

"Why didn't you get a real lawyer like Momma did? You could've got the house."

"What was that?"

"And I could've stayed with you. I would've liked staying with you."

"Really?"

"I like who I am when I'm with you, Daddy. When I'm with Momma . . . it's crazy."

Her father paused. "I'd keep you with me if I could."

"You went on the Internet and bought software and tried to be your own lawyer? That's the best you could do?"

Her father took the box out of her hands, tossed it in the trash.

Destiny said, "That was rude."

"Get out of my space. Stop being nosy. Go in the other room."

She mocked him. *"Get out of my space. Stop being nosy. Go in the other room."*

"Stop that, will you?"

"As soon as you slap yourself twice for being so rude."

"Smart-ass."

"When you get old and need help walking, or need a diaper, you will regret this moment."

She looked over a stack of opened envelopes. One was a note from the landlord. THREE-DAY NOTICE. Another was from CHILD SUPPORT SERVICES. That heading in bold letters, like a threat. Southern California Edison. Pacific Bell. Visa. Wells Fargo. There were other bills on the table.

She asked, "What happened?"

"What happened about what?"

"Daddy, don't act like you don't know."

She watched her daddy become uncomfortable. The way boys did when girls pried.

Destiny said, "Daddy, answer me. Don't ignore me. You know I'm unignorable."

Her father took a breath. "Don't know. It's never about the big things, or one thing. Little things over time. The counselor said that maybe we didn't manage our conflict well. Some bullshit about we didn't agree to disagree. We've become disengaged."

"People get engaged, get married, then become disengaged."

"That's pretty much the way it goes."

"Is that why you and Mom ended up having sex with other people? You become disengaged with each other, then go and engage with other people."

"Destiny, slap yourself twice."

"Quit playing. I'm trying to understand. Everybody gets divorced. Why get married?"

Her father shut down, walked away. Destiny went back to the table. Browsed through a stack of job applications. Her father had filled out so many. The stack of rejection letters was off to the side. Another set of forms was on the other side of that pile. Application to file bankruptcy.

Destiny yelled, "You're applying for a job with the Geek Squad?"

"You sound like your mother."

"And you have an application to be a . . . flight attendant?"

"Will you put that back where you got it?"

"Daddy, that job is so gay."

"Put my application down."

"Anything but a flight attendant. People will think you're on the down low or something."

"It's a fucking job."

"It's a *bleep*ing job, it's a *bleep*ing job, it's a *bleep*ing job." She mocked him. "A flight attendant?"

Her father came up behind her. "Getting a top-shelf job's not as easy as it sounds."

"Then what's the point of going to college? I mean, if you're going to end up . . . like this."

"Excuse me?"

"You know what I mean. You were an electrical engineer."

Her father, very frustrated. "I'm over forty now. It's a young man's market."

"So what? You're old but you're smart."

"Geesh, thanks."

"You know what I mean. You know, like, you have two degrees."

"Sometimes . . . well . . . my education . . . what I used to make . . . right now that's working against me."

"I don't get it. How can having an education and a good-paying job work against you?"

He smiled. "Well, I ended up working at the same place too long. Worked on a specific product. When they went belly-up, nobody needed that product anymore. I became obsolete. So all of us have had to start over. Hard to do that at forty. Hard being a black man with a family and no . . . Life is expensive, Destiny. Take your time about growing up. Don't rush to get married. Don't rush to have children. Enjoy life. Because when you cross that street, there's no going back to Neverland."

"Neverland? How did Michael Jackson's house get in this conversation?"

Her father laughed at her joke. That made her happy.

"*DAVINA!*"

Her daddy said, "Just don't grow up too fast."

Between her legs, with almost every heartbeat, that ache, that humiliation came and went.

She fingered through the bills, picked up the one for child support. This was the one she had caused. Again she wondered what her father's life would be like if she had never been born.

Or if she found the courage to unborn herself.

"Is your girlfriend pregnant, Daddy?"

Her father bit his top lip. "Yeah. She says she is. So, yeah."

"Soooooooooo . . . you've been having unprotected sex with her?"

"*Destiny.*"

"Why would you do that?"

"Stop it."

"*Father.* Answer me. Why did you have unprotected sex with her?"

Her father rubbed his eyes. "Why are you asking me these questions, Destiny?"

"I'm asking you the same questions you would ask me."

"Stop it."

"Not gonna stop it. Why all the secrets from me?"

"Always have to have your way." He stared at her. "Just like your mother."

That shut her down.

"You have a few secrets of your own, Destiny."

He marched into the kitchen, yanked open the cabinets, took out some glasses.

Destiny asked, "Do you want to have a baby with the motorcycle girl?"

He didn't answer.

Destiny frowned, went back to the front window.

The brother who had been blowing his horn, his car was still there. Destiny saw the feeble security gate to the apartment building was open, looked like the brother had found a way to get inside.

Destiny called out, "Daddy, looks like the screaming man broke in the building across the street."

"Mind your business, Destiny."

"What if the screaming man beats her up or something?"

"Bring your butt inside."

"And I'm not just like my mother."

Destiny went inside, headed for the kitchen. Her daddy, sitting on the counter, drink in hand.

He asked, "Want to talk about it?"

"Talk about what?"

"Last night."

Destiny didn't respond, just moved near her father, started ripping up newspaper, stuffing glasses. The glasses were old, not many matched. The few plates he had were chipped.

Destiny asked, "Daddy, why are you packing all of that old Salvation Army stuff?"

"Because it's *mine*."

Her father opened a bottle of E & J, poured a shot in his glass.

She asked him, "Where are you putting all of those ugly dishes and stuff?"

"In storage."

"Why in storage?"

She watched her father down the E & J.

"Just in case."

"In case you and Momma . . . in case you have to run away from home again?"

He didn't answer. His eyes avoided hers. He was too busy rinsing out the shot glass.

Her father said, "I've never run away from you, Destiny. *Never.*"

"You stopped drinking. Don't start back. Makes your breath stink."

"Stressed. Need to get the edge off."

She remembered him drinking a lot when they were all together.

She remembered him stopping when he moved away.

She asked, "This isn't going to work out, is it?"

He created a thin smile. "Well, we'll see what happens."

Destiny looked inside another box, saw so many pictures. Destiny knew that pictures were more than images on Kodak paper; they were precious memories, indelible images from days gone by.

Her mother was thinner, stomach flat, various hairstyles, not much older than Destiny was now.

Her father was slimmer, more toned, stomach cut, arms firm, looked like he lived in the gym.

In the pictures her mother and father were so much younger, looked so happy.

Like other people. Happy people. Like people she'd never seen before.

She looked inside another box. Recent pictures of her father and Billie. So many new memories. He looked happy with her, but it was a different kind of happiness, looked spiritual, much deeper.

Then she found one folded up. Opened it. It was a poster. Her daddy's girlfriend on a yellow motorcycle. All she had on were three-inch-heel boots and a yellow thong. Smiling. Her booty in the air.

Her daddy took that picture from her. He snatched it from her. Put it away like it was a prized possession. Nothing was said. A picture like that . . . worth way more than a thousand words.

She wondered if the things her mother told her were true.

A new woman. A new baby. A new life.

Wondered if Billie had her father's baby, if she and her mother would both be forgotten.

She asked, "You still love Momma?"

"Time goes by, things change. We walk a long road. Along the way, people change. Love changes too. Sometimes it moves with you. Sometimes it moves away from you."

"Don't ignore me, Daddy."

"And what you think is love at fifteen won't be what you think love is at forty."

"Do you love Momma?"

"The definition of love . . . evolves . . . as you grow, it evolves."

"Daddy."

He shut down.

She softened her tone. "Do you love Momma?"

No answer.

Destiny said, "But not like the girl on the motorcycle, right?"

"No two loves are the same."

"I don't understand. Love should be love, nothing else."

"I don't know if I can live the second half of my life the same way I've lived the first half."

"What does that mean?"

"Means I want to be happy. Means I don't want to struggle with life until I'm inside my grave."

"That means you really love your friend, right?"

"It means I'm scared, Destiny. I love her. But I used to love your momma like that too. She changed on me. And love is a slippery beast. And . . . all the shit I'm thinking . . . it's hard to explain. I'm just . . . having a moment . . . wondering if I'm doing my life right . . . by you . . . by everybody. And I'm . . . failing."

In silence, they continued packing, those depressing blues playing in the background.

Her father said, "I love you more than both of them combined."

She smiled. "Love you to the moon and back."

"I know."

"Always will, Daddy."

"You've grown up so fast."

The brother was back again across the street, screaming at Davina, his voice far away, each word indecipherable.

Destiny went back to the front window.

She mumbled, "Bet he cold busted her with another man."

She stepped outside. Saw more change. She turned on the porch light, looked down at the bushes again. Found two dimes. Touched something else. She looked closer, wanted to see what that was. Her heart sped up. A gun. A real gun. It was in the bushes. Like it had come out of nowhere.

Like it had been sent to her by God.

Bobby Womack was on the CD player now. "If You Think You're Lonely Now."

Her father came back into the living room, singing off-key, small box in his hand.

He waved his hand, shouted, "That's right, Bobby. Preach man, *preach*."

Her father was in his own breath-stinking, off-key world. She picked up her backpack.

She looked at the gun. It was real.

Her daddy kept on talking. "They're like children. Understand a child, you understand a woman."

He left and came back with another box.

Destiny stared out into the darkness. Thinking. Her thoughts were all on getting away, running away again, finding the people she had been with last night. The ache wouldn't stop, sometimes soft, sometimes hard, but that pain was always there. A memory that refused to wane. Her eyes watered up.

"Daddy, if you and your girlfriend moved in together, if you didn't move back home, even if you married the girl on the motorcycle and you were happy, I wouldn't be mad. I mean, most of my friends' parents are divorced. It's cool, you know? Maybe, after you got settled, maybe I could live with you and her for a while. Or, you know, stay on the weekends or something. I could baby-sit or something."

"Do you mean that?"

"Yes."

"Then why are you crying?"

She shrugged. So many conflicting emotions running though her veins.

She wiped her eyes, asked, "Why can't everybody just be nice to each other and be happy?"

"Hardest thing to do in the world is be happy."

She closed her eyes. Saw flashes of last night, a night she wished she could undo.

She asked, "Why do people get married and then go out and have sex with other people?"

"I don't know."

"I mean, why does everybody have affairs?"

"Destiny . . . look . . . sweetheart, that's a question nobody can answer."

"Why do people get married if they're not gonna be happy?"

"Because you don't know what a marriage is gonna be like until you're in it."

"I don't ever want to get married."

"You'll meet some boy and change your mind when you get older."

"And I don't ever want to have children. *Never.* Would never want to do this to a child."

She wiped her eyes, but the tears wouldn't stop.

She ranted, "I'd *never* have a baby because of endometriosis, just to make my cramps go away."

"*Destiny.*"

She snapped, "What, Daddy?"

She felt him struggling with himself. She felt his strength. She felt his fear.

He asked her, "Are you . . . are you . . . active?"

She didn't answer, couldn't figure out how to lie with her daddy staring in her eyes.

"It's okay. I won't be mad, baby. Daddy just needs to know what you're . . . Are you?"

She struggled with herself. "I have had sex before."

Her father took a deep breath. Shivered. Swallowed. He asked, "Last night?"

Her lips trembled. Tears leaked. In the distance, sirens.

Her father put his arms around her. She held him back.

She asked, "If something really bad happened to me last night, would you still love me?"

She felt the fear in his body. She felt he didn't know what to do to make the world right.

She almost told him that she didn't run away because her mother had hit her. That she had been drinking. Had been drugged. Almost told him that she had been raped. Almost because those thoughts were acidic and she needed to tell somebody. But she was too busy holding him, too busy crying.

Her daddy held her tight.

Her father's voice cracked. "What happened last night, Destiny?"

Sirens were outside, flashing lights from police cars, neighbors were running outside to find out why the brother was in the middle of the street, flagging the police, screaming with tears in his eyes.

Screaming like his heart had been ripped out of his chest.

The front door opened hard and fast.

"Keith, Destiny."

Her mother's frantic voice, the timbre of trouble.

Her daddy let her go.

The front door closed.

Neighbors were in their doorways, in windows, others gathering by the curb, mumbling.

Destiny asked, "What's wrong, Momma?"

Her mother stood there shaking her head, wild hair moving like it was in a gentle breeze.

Her mother said, "She drowned her baby."

Destiny blinked. "What?"

"The baby . . . girl across the street . . . she killed her baby."

Destiny followed her mother out to the porch. Her father stepped out, stared at the scene.

The brother was leaning against his car, crying and screaming, police trying to calm him down.

The police were leading his girlfriend out in handcuffs. Destiny stared at the girl's wrinkled pajamas. Weave in disarray. Looked like she hadn't slept for days. She was barefoot, tall, thin, barely twenty, eyes blank, slumped, the life gone out of her. The young woman never raised her head or made a sound as they eased her inside the police car.

The brother ran toward the police car, but the police jumped in between his rage and the car.

"WHY YOU KILL MY SON, DAVINA?"

Destiny followed her mother to the curb. Destiny looked at the young girl. She was shackled, devoid of emotion, the shell of a woman, in a world of her own.

"WHY, DAVINA? WHY YOU KILL MY SON?"

The paramedics came out holding a small silent bundle, the baby covered up. Lifeless.

Her mother went across the street. Always investigating. Destiny waited.

One of the old neighbors was shaking his old head, talking to another young man, telling him, "Heard somebody say that girl was up in that apartment with that dead baby still in the bathtub."

The young man said, "For real?"

"Killed her little boy, killed their poor little baby this time last night. Baby was crying, then stopped crying all of a sudden. I told my wife something was wrong. Babies don't stop crying like that."

"Dag, that's messed up."

"And when her boyfriend broke in there a minute ago she was sitting in the dark, over in a corner mumbling, *Wouldn't stop crying . . . wouldn't stop . . . did all I could to get him to stop . . . wouldn't stop.*"

"Damn."

"Little boy wasn't even a year old. Face down in the bathtub."

"Are you serious?"

Destiny thought of how people were born again in water. That baby had been unborn the same way, in water. Her mind went off on a tangent, tried to find significance in what that woman had done.

Maybe that was a sign meant for her. Her prophecy. She watched that brother, how passionate he was about his little boy. If Billie had a baby, her daddy would love him more than he loved her.

The young man said, "Baby wasn't even a year old."

The old man said, "Some parents wear down faster than others. Maybe she didn't have parenting skills. But I suppose that ain't required to make a baby. Anybody can do it."

People shook their heads. Cried. Destiny stood next to her mother, listened to people talk.

Other people closed their eyes and prayed.

Destiny looked at two people who had gone insane.

Everyone forever changed.

"WHY YOU KILL MY SON?" The brother fell on his knees, a thousand times he yelled, *"WHY?"*

The brother screamed about his baby, about his son, asked God why He let this happen.

Then.

Destiny saw that the young brother who had been talking to the old man was staring at her. Staring hard. Almost smiling. As if he knew her from somewhere. He came over and stood next to her.

He said, "You look familiar. You kinda look like one of the girls in this DVD I just saw."

"What movie?"

"*Hoodrats.* I think that's what it's called."

"What's that?"

"Adult joint. Was hanging with these niggas down on Western lil' while ago."

Destiny swallowed, raised a hand up, smoothed out her ponytail.

He said, "Sad, ain't it?"

"Huh?" Her voice turned cold, defensive. "Sad . . . what?"

"Sister went ballistic and killed her shorty like that. Some sad shit. I mean, *damn*."

"Yeah." Destiny took a breath shook her head, told herself it couldn't be, repeated, "Sad."

The brother walked away, pants sagging, head down, like he was trying to understand.

Western Boulevard. Streetwalkers and motel. Same strip she was on last night.

That red light from that camera. They had taped her.

There was a DVD. They were selling DVDs.

That brother had said she looked like a girl on a DVD.

He had looked at her like she was the girl on the DVD.

Her mother came back across the street, shaking her head, her hand up to her mouth as she cried and cried and cried. So many tears ran down her face. A side of her mother not many saw.

Her mother stared at her, tears met tears. Her mother hugged her, hugged her tight.

Destiny folded her arms under her breasts, followed her mother, nervous, head down, scared to look back, feeling as if some of the people were watching her, whispering, wondering.

"WHY YOU GO AND KILL MY SON?"

That outburst came like an earthquake, jarred the area.

Loud and clear, as deafening as the screams, R. Kelly was still trapped in the closet.

The spirit of a dead baby seasoned the air.

Woman across the street gone insane.

Father of that lifeless baby not too far behind.

Two o'clock in the morning.

Police gone. Most of the neighbors gone back to tending to the business of the living.

Back to their own problems while they waited for the next round of entertainment.

Destiny sat on the porch, leg bouncing, and listened to her mother and father arguing.

"Dammit, I need you to go to the bank with me tomorrow and sign some loan papers."

"Why in the hell do you need to take out a loan?"

"Don't worry about it."

"You using the equity in the house I bought to buy property? Starting a business? What?"

"Look, dammit, I need one hundred and seventy-five thousand."

"I do too. Hell, if I had that much money, I wouldn't be in the situation I'm in now."

"Sign the papers, Keith. Please? Could you just sign the papers?"

"Your ass wouldn't come down forty dollars on child support and you asking me for a favor? You on crack, Carmen? That equity is for Destiny's college tuition, for her future. Not for you. Not for me."

Arguing. Always arguing.

"I'll do it without you, Keith. I'll get the goddamn papers signed without you."

"You're gonna forge my signature?"

"If I have to. I'm not like you. I do what I have to do to get it done."

"End up in jail."

"Would you let the mother of your child go to jail?"

"Hell, that would solve everything. I get my house. I get custody. No more child support. Go ahead, forge my signature. I'll have your ass locked up in Sybil Brand so fast your head will be spinning."

Her mother stormed out of her father's apartment, the door slamming behind her.

Her father screamed, "Don't slam my goddamn door."

"Destiny, get your stuff," her mother snapped at her. "We're going home."

Destiny went back inside, her father still in the kitchen, drink in hand.

She said, "Daddy, I'm out."

There was a long pause. So much disgust in his eyes. "Call me when you get home."

"No. Get some sleep. Cruella De Vil's in a funky mood, that means she's gonna talk my ear off. So let me deal with Momma and I'll call you in the morning. I'll come down and make you breakfast."

"Pancakes?"

"Whatever you like, Daddy. Whatever you like. Arf! Arf! Woof! Woof!"

Her daddy laughed. She liked that.

He said, "Stop acting silly."

"See, I'll even bounce up and down on one foot too. Arf! Arf! Woof! Woof!"

"We'll finish our conversation about last night."

Again, despite the laughter, she saw all the condoms. Felt the pain. They were still inside her.

She nodded. "Okay."

She went into the living room, picked up her backpack. Looked back at her father. He was turning the lights off. Staggering down the hallway toward his bedroom. Destiny stepped outside. Her mother was in her car, eyes ahead like a lot was on her mind, that damn John Legend CD playing.

If she got in the car with her mother she'd never get away.

This was her only chance.

She called back, "I'm locking the door. Get in bed, Daddy."

"Okay."

Destiny eased the front door closed until the lock clicked. Porch light now off, she walked out, dropped her backpack in the grass, hoped her mother didn't see her do that, took a quick glance back toward her father's apartment. He wasn't at the window. Her mother had left him damn angry. He wasn't watching, not waving goodbye tonight. Her eyes went back to her mother. She wasn't paying attention.

Destiny hurried to the passenger side, motioned for her mother to let the window down.

"Momma, Daddy's drunk."

Her mother turned down the volume, John Legend now whispering. "Where's your stuff?"

"Left it inside. He's not doing so well."

"None of us are."

"He's tore up. I'm going to stay over here, cook him breakfast, and make sure he's okay. You get some rest too. Then I'll come home and make you a big breakfast in the morning. Cool?"

"Destiny—"

"What, Momma?"

"If I let you stay here, I need you to do something for me."

"Whassup?"

"I'm not a bad person, Destiny. I'm not. Mommy loves. I hurt. I want the same thing everybody else wants. I want to be happy. Do you understand that, Destiny? All Momma wants to do is keep this family together and be happy. Black families have suffered enough. Too many of us give up so easily. When you get older you'll understand what a marriage is. You'll see why Momma takes her vows seriously. We come from a strong family, Destiny. Strong men and women who survived the Middle Passage, rose above Third World countries. We're the best of the best. Don't you ever forget that."

"What you need me to do, Momma?"

"If that blood clot calls him, hang up. Don't let her speak to your father. Not one word."

"Why not?"

"Friend or enemy, Destiny?"

Her mother glared at her.

"Momma, I could sneak and turn his phone off. He wouldn't be able to talk to her then."

Her mother bit her top lip, worried. "His cell phone? What if she calls his cell phone?"

"Could turn that one off too. Or put it on vibrate."

"She could leave a message."

"No problem. I know how to delete his messages."

Her mother was surprised. "Do you?"

"Yeah. I know his password."

Her mother stared at her, so much distrust in her eyes.

Her mother asked, "Do you know my password?"

"Of course not, Mommy." She lied. "I would never do that to you."

Her mother shook her head, frowned.

She said, "You're just like your father."

"No. I'm you looking back. Don't forget that."

Silence. So much animosity hidden behind her teenage mask.

"Momma, why you need that much money?"

"Your daddy's funky little girlfriend. . . ."

"It has something to do with the girl on the motorcycle?"

Her mother's face hardened.

Then her mother stared her in the eyes.

"Why are you being so nice, Destiny?"

"I have no idea what you're talking about, Mommy."

"Don't bullshit me."

"I just don't want to see you hurting anymore, Mommy."

Her mother rubbed her temples, nodded. "And I'm tired of hurting. Tired of restless nights and waking up with tears on my pillow. Can't take this shit anymore. I don't need you acting out right now."

Destiny said, "I'm just trying to help."

"Are you?"

"I don't want to lose my daddy."

"I don't want you to, baby. Momma wants us to remain a family unit, you know that."

"I don't want that girl on the motorcycle to have a baby by Daddy."

"I'm trying to fix it, baby. Doing my best."

"That has something to do with where you've been tonight?"

Her mother stared at her. "I don't trust you, Destiny. Not at all."

Destiny pulled her lips in. "The motorcycle girl, I threw a brick through her window last night."

Her mother's mouth dropped open, horrified.

"When I left last night I went up there and threw a brick through her bedroom window."

Then her mother shook her head, chuckled, almost smiled. That was better than a gold star.

Her mother said, "You're off punishment."

Destiny smiled.

Now there was trust.

Her mother whispered, "Destiny, I went and saw his little girlfriend tonight."

"What she . . . did she ask you for money? Is that why you need to get a loan?"

"One hundred and seventy-five thousand dollars and she'll leave us alone."

"That much money . . . because she's pregnant?"

"Just gave her the first five thousand."

"You just gave her . . . that's fucked up, Momma. Straight-up fucked up."

Her mother looked at her. "It is fucked up."

"I hope this isn't a Pyrrhic victory."

"Pyrrhic victory. What does that mean, Destiny?"

"Pyrrhic means . . . is it worth it? I mean . . . if you give her . . . will I still be able to go to college?"

"Not back East. Not Harvard. Not Yale. You'll have to attend Cal State."

"I can't go to Cal State." Destiny gritted her teeth. "What are we going to do?"

"You see how one bad decision affects everything? See what your father has created?"

"Let me talk to Daddy."

"Don't tell your father. Don't repeat a word of this to anybody."

Destiny thought about last night, about her bad decisions, about the people she met in that hotel.

She thought about the mean biracial girls, that fight on the 'Shaw. She wanted to fight right now.

Destiny asked, "What if I could find a way to fix it?"

"Daddy broke this family. Let your mommy fix it."

"But what if I could help?"

"No. Just do what I ask you to do when I ask you to do it."

Destiny snapped, "That's my college money that blood clot is trying to take."

College. Her only way to escape her mother. Her planned route to escape this world.

She stared at her mother as her mother stared at her.

Worry pinched at her mother's face, that same worry pinching. For a moment, in Destiny's eyes, her mother looked like a scared little girl. Her eyes so out of focus. Her life so out of focus.

She wanted to hug her mother. But the atmosphere between them was too muddy.

Her mother sat there, unmoving, like her heart had left her in a state of quadriplegia.

She said, "I love your father, Destiny. I do."

"I know, Momma. I know."

"He was the first man I ever loved. The only man."

"Daddy was the first man you had sex with?"

"That's not what I said." She took a breath. "He wasn't the first, but I wanted him to be the last."

Her mother's tone, ruined. Eyes heavy, stranded in the middle of an epicenter of her own grief. Live by the sword, die by the sword. In that moment Destiny came to the conclusion that a sword could be made of love. And love was the greatest self-inflicted wound of them all.

"Momma . . . you're gonna make me cry too."

"I'll be okay." Her voice cracked, became fragile, so small, sounded so old. "Just don't act out, Destiny. I know this hasn't been easy for you. But Momma can't handle anything else right now."

"Don't cry."

Her mother struggled, but the tears came. Her eyes shone, so much beauty inside her sadness. Her mother smiled like she was a goddess without power. "When you love, Destiny, don't love in vain."

"What does that mean, Momma?"

"Love should be like getting up at dawn and watching the sun rise while the rest of the world slumbers. Love should be peaceful, tranquil. Should fill you with enthusiasm. But it brings fear. Love is deeply buried in the soul. Love should be God's blessing. But it isn't. Not for everybody. Not for me."

Her mother had drifted away, was in her own zone, talking to herself, nodding in return.

Destiny wiped her eyes a thousand times, sighed twice as many. Watched her mother fall apart, each tear chiseling away at her marble exterior, watched her mother cry like she was still a little girl, then pull herself back together. Still Destiny felt outraged, caught in a web of cause and effect that she didn't understand. Wanted her mother to be happy. Wanted her daddy to be happy. She wanted to be happy. She'd make sure that she never fell in love. Would never become a casualty of that wretched emotion that crippled people and left them doing desperate things in the name of self-preservation.

Then her mother's voice shook with a force to be reckoned with: "Never love in vain."

Destiny looked back at her father's bedroom window. Saw darkness. Couldn't tell if he was watching them. Couldn't tell if his ears were tuned to their conspiracy. She kept her cool, blew a kiss to her mother, wiped her eyes, headed back toward the apartment, never looking back at her red-eyed mother. When Destiny got to the front door, she sat down on the porch, hidden in the darkness. Sat there until she heard her mother's car pull away. Kept sitting there waiting to see if her daddy would open the door calling her name. Sat there twenty minutes, long enough for her mother to get home, park the car, and go inside the house. Long enough for her mother to pour herself a glass of pinot noir and sit in front of the fireplace, one hand in her bushy Afro, a thousand tears streaming from her eyes. For ten more minutes after that Destiny sat outside in the cold, waiting to see if her mother would reach for the phone, wondering if her father's phone would ring, thinking about how to find the people who had wronged her last night, sat there without moving, soundless, like a soldier out on the battlefield, planning her own war. She got up, eased across the grass, got her backpack, and began walking in the direction of Casura Bay.

She was scared. But she was in pain. Throbbing. Her heart demanding justice for her injustice.

Behind her she heard something she had never heard on this side of town: silence.

So quiet that as Destiny's chest rose and fell, she heard every heated breath.

She frowned across the street at that darkness.

Nothing followed her but the spirit of a dead baby.

Unborn by water, that baby would never cry again.

thirteen

DESTINY

TACO SMELL PERMEATED THE AIR AS SHE PASSED AUDUBON MIDDLE School.

More signs in Spanish than in English as she headed across Leimert Boulevard.

Graffiti on walls like on MLK Boulevard was a ghettofied museum. Music blasting. People yelling obscenities so loud, people in Arizona could hear. Destiny moved down MLK Boulevard like she was maneuvering through the residue of a Third World country. She stopped at a Korean convenience store.

A brother outside, back against a wall, inhaled his cigarette and said, "Whass yo name?"

She ignored him, hid her nervousness, turned away from him.

"Bitch."

Destiny went inside, bought a thirty-two-ounce soda from the fountain. She bought a small bottle of bleach too. Paid for her goods with the loose change she had in her pockets. Hurried back outside, moving like she was racing against time.

"Bitch. Know you hear me talking to you. Hate you uppity L.A. bitches."

Destiny stopped walking, tucked the bottle of bleach underneath her arm, faced the rude man, pulled her jacket back.

He saw the handle on her gun. He saw her gangsta frown.

He raised his palms in apology, hurried away.

Martin Luther King, Jr., Boulevard. The strip where, during the King

Day Parade, there was a gang fight every year. Nobody would respect the black man if the black man didn't respect himself. Her daddy said that every year. That was the only time she ever heard her mother agree with him. The only time.

Destiny closed her jacket and kept going. Felt other men staring at her. Heard them whispering. Heard how afraid they were of her.

She lowered her head, hoping her ponytails made her look different, younger, as she moved down MLK. Was worried about the police stopping her, but then she saw at least three children under the age of ten walking the boulevard unsupervised, cursing and smoking like they were grown men and women.

Nobody cared.

Music blared and nobody cared.

What it is ho . . . whassup . . . gimme dat number . . . I'll call . . . I'll follow that ass in the mall.

Up over her head, lit up like the Vegas Strip, was a huge billboard. WHO MURDERED ME? A pretty black woman's picture smiling down over the city. Lisa Wolf. Destiny wondered who she was. Destiny wondered what a woman that rich and pretty could do to make somebody kill her.

Maybe everybody in the world wanted . . . needed to kill somebody.

Then she didn't care about the face of some dead brown-skinned woman on a billboard.

The ache between her legs kept her focused.

Bits and pieces of a memory came back, floated around inside her head.

My momma likes my daddy to hit it from back . . . they be all on the ottoman . . . Is that right, Baby Phat?

So vivid it scared her.

Drink up. How you feeling Baby Phat?

Feel so good right now.

She took a hard breath, sipped soda. Chewed some ice. Poured the rest of the too-sweet soda out as she rushed toward motel row, her mind on the time. When she was close to Western she stepped over the piss-stained and chipped asphalt, found a spot, and opened her backpack.

Can I touch you right here?

That feels good.

She poured the bleach into the empty cup.

Her family had been blackmailed for five thousand dollars.

Was being blackmailed for more money than she could imagine.

The girl on the motorcycle was pregnant.

The girl on the motorcycle was trying to trap her daddy and blackmail her momma.

No way could the bitch on the motorcycle have that baby.

Destiny knew how to fix it all.

Destiny made it to the parking lot of Casura Bay. Crowded. Busy night.

The Escalade she had been in last night was there.

She heard a scream, and then stopped rushing. Almost dropped her cup, but didn't.

Underneath a palm tree, as the night air blew a sweet and cool breeze across the city, a man was slapping the shit out of a woman while six of her coworkers smoked cigarettes and watched, some of them looking angry, some disgusted, a couple of them owning apathetic expressions. All the women had multiple tattoos, weaves that stood tall and cascaded down their backs, had on baby doll shirts and short-short skirts, a couple wearing fishnet stockings under jean shorts cut like thong underwear, their breasts standing tall as their butt cheeks hung out. Six-inch heels. The man was standing next to his ride, a new-jack convertible Cadillac pimped out with more chrome than should be allowed to be on one vehicle. On the back of the headrests and on the dash, even in the rearview mirrors, were television screens with better clarity than the ones she had seen at Best Buy. In the background, a bootleg copy of *Hustle and Flow* played on the pimp's system. The brother was iced to the bone. All bling. Iced with an iced attitude.

He hit a button on his remote and the trunk of the car went up.

The girl screamed, begged, said she would do better, that she would work harder.

He yelled for her to stop yelling because it was too late.

Destiny put her cup down long enough to move the gun she had found, put the gun in the front of her jeans, like she had seen them do in all the movies, covered it up with her jacket, like she had seen them do in the movies. Then she picked up her cup again. She was two miles from her father's apartment, four miles from her mother's home, back on the side of town where pimpology was a religion.

She looked back in time to see the pimp hit the girl one last time and then grab her by her weave, drag her to the back of the car, make her climb into the trunk. He let the trunk down easy, didn't slam it. Expensive car. Amazing how he was delicate with his ride and rough with the women. Amazing. Then he stood in front of the other girls, pointing his finger in their faces. The girls nodded like they had heard it all before. He drove away. Smoking. Frowning. On his cellular. Music blasting.

You know it's hard out here on a pimp . . .

Destiny looked at the other girls, the ones that Mr. Pimp had left behind. They went back to smoking their cigarettes as they strutted up Western Boulevard, spying at every car that passed.

The women laughed, but Destiny could tell it was nervous laughter. They were all terrified.

Hardened by her own life, Destiny moved on.

Destiny saw her. The other girl who had been in the van last night. The black-mixed-with-Mexican girl was passing by, her eyebrows tight, squinting, so busy yelling into her cellular phone that she never glanced her way.

The black-mixed-with-Mexican girl got in a car. Drove away, still talking on her phone.

While women of the night led their johns into rooms on the ground floor, a hip-hop crew was going in and out of at least three motel rooms on the top level. An underground crew. People not too much older than Destiny. She saw the golden-skinned girl come out of one of the rooms upstairs. Goldie. The music was the loudest up there. The windows were open, setting free lots of voices, lots of shouting. Everybody in this world was having lots of fun. As if nothing horrible had happened last night.

As if she were nobody to them, Destiny thought.

The golden-skinned girl came down the concrete stairs, joint in her hand, hitting it hard, Prada handbag dangling from her right wrist, walked toward Destiny as if she had never seen her before. Too busy finishing the joint to look Destiny in her eyes. Goldie. Tight low-rise jeans that showed off a stomach that owned a little flab. Tight top on saggy breasts. She even had on Baby Phat jeans tonight.

Goldie tossed the roach, walked toward Destiny singing, "Dis goes out to all—"

Goldie's heel twisted and she almost fell.

Destiny looked down at the girl's feet. Jimmy Choo. Stretch suede. Kelsey suede, at that. Braided strap. Three-inch heels. She looked at Goldie's ears. Goldie had her weave pulled back so her lobes could sparkle. Destiny saw diamond earrings that had been stolen from her last night. Looked at Goldie's thin lips. Lips painted with stolen lipstick. Face painted with stolen makeup. Destiny's lipstick. Destiny's makeup. Destiny's boots. Destiny saw material things that had been taken from her last night.

Standing three feet away, Goldie lit a cigarette like she was a baller, a ghetto-star smile on her face, threw the match away, blew smoke out of the side of her mouth, and asked, "What you need?"

"What?"

"Got antihistamines." She blew smoke. "Cold meds. Ecstasy. Viagra. What you need?"

"What ecstasy do?"

"Sets you free."

"Really?"

"But you have to be careful. Can cause brain damage, bad for the heart too."

"You do ecstasy?"

Goldie tossed her cigarette. "Not as much as I used to. Kept forgetting shit."

That ache, that indignity between her legs magnified.

Destiny told herself that she wasn't the girl she was yesterday. Goldie looked her in her eyes and didn't even recognize her. That girl was gone. She knew she would never would be that little girl again.

Destiny choked on her words, asked, "If I was . . . if I had sex last night . . . and I don't want to be pregnant . . ."

"RU-486. Those run twenty a pop."

"What if . . . say I was more than a little pregnant. Would one of those . . . get rid of the baby?"

"Should. But be careful. Heard that at least four women done died taking this shit."

"So . . . taking three or four of them at the same time . . ."

"You take three or four of these, shit, you'll end up a lot more than not pregnant."

"Last night . . . I need at least one for me. Have to make sure I'm not . . . you know how it goes."

"Unprotected sex, huh?"

"That's what I need. One for me. And . . . and . . . maybe eight . . . or ten . . . for . . . you have that many?"

"That's . . . let's see . . . ten times twenty . . . ten times ten is a hundred . . . so that's about . . . ."

"Two hundred dollars."

"You sure?"

"I'm sure. Ten times twenty equals two hundred."

The girl shook her head and laughed. "Stocking up?"

Destiny repeated, "You have that many?"

"And you might want to take some antibiotics. Ain't my business, but if you pregnant, then you rocking the joint unprotected. Just looking out. Men out there got all kinds of diseases and shit. I got the stuff to fix the stuff that's fixable. You have to have money like Magic Johnson to cure anything else."

Destiny said, "The RU-486 . . . if you're pregnant . . . problem solved just like that?"

Goldie snapped her fingers. "Just like that."

"Sell *niggas* the blue pill to keep their shit hard, then sell the *bitches* the Kill Pill to make the problem go away. Bet you pimp a lot of those Kill Pills over at Crenshaw High. And at Audubon Middle School. 'Cause all the young dumb-ass, hot-to-trot girls letting high school niggas get all up in the cut. Bet you sell so many of those fucking pills it's a damn shame. Teenage pregnancies off the chain. Slangin' and helping out the community. Keeping these young-ass girls from being young-ass mommas."

Destiny recited most of their conversation from last night. The parts she remembered.

Her IQ hovering at 130. Heart beating so fast, galloping with unbridled resentment.

Goldie had gone quiet. Through her glazed-over eyes she said, "Baby Phat? That you?"

Destiny's heart was in her throat. "It's me."

Goldie looked her up and down in stunned disbelief.

Silence rested between them as a police car zoomed by, siren blasting.

Destiny said, "Guess that ecstasy got you brain-damaged, had you forgetting about me already."

"What's up with the ponytails and shit? Weren't you taller yesterday?"

"I was taller before you jacked me for my Jimmy Choo boots."

"Ain't nobody *jacked* your crazy ass. You *gave* me these boots."

"I gave you a pair of nine-hundred-dollar boots."

"You better put your pen to the wind and rest your neck. You gave me these boots."

"Guess I *gave* you my mother's diamond earrings too."

"Don't step to me trippin'."

"Guess I gave you my damn purse and all my damn money too."

"Ain't nobody took nothing from you. Better quit bulldoggin'."

Destiny gritted her teeth. "Whatever *poison* them niggas gave me last night . . . they got from you."

"Take the motherfucking boots. You want these damn boots, take 'em off my damn feet."

"You let them give me . . . whatever they gave me. How could you do something like that?"

"What, you mad? Last night you was a snowblowing cum dumpster in that rabbit session."

"Rabbit session?"

"You're a legitimate porn star now, baby."

"Did they . . . what did they do to me last night?"

Goldie laughed.

Destiny didn't.

"You were up to your chin in nuts, imitating your freaky-ass momma and sucking the hell out of dick last night. And you frontin' me? Little Miss Bourgeois from Bel Air using all those complicated words and shit. Acting like you so damn smart. Nobody gives a shit about your damn momma and daddy getting a damn divorce. Whining like you got some real problems. Trying to act all hard and shit. You ain't legit. I'm a *skraight-up* hustler. You ain't got no street cred with me. Er'body was laughing at your corny ass all damn night. What? Punk ass all up in my face. What? What? What you gon' do?"

Splash.

There was a splash.

Destiny watched Goldie stop laughing, saw the girl drop her stolen handbag.

Destiny looked around. Cars passed by, but nobody saw. Or nobody gave a damn.

Goldie was coughing, choking, screaming, jumping around like she was on fire. Destiny stood there, jaw tight, watched Goldie fight with herself, corrosive liquids raining from her face, saturating her weave, listened to Goldie struggle to get enough air to scream.

"Oh, God, oh, God."

Destiny looked at her empty hand, that plastic cup on the ground, rolling around, now empty.

"Bitch, what you throw in my face?"

The stench of uncut bleach lit up the air as it saturated Goldie's weave.

"THIS SHIT BURNING MY EYES!"

Destiny watched Goldie, saw how she was freaking out, grabbing her face, eyes closed tight, face showing she was in serious agony, trying to get the bleach out of her eyes, staggering and stumbling across the chipped asphalt, coughing, wobbling on her stolen boots, coughing, running into parked cars, falling on the ground, legs moving like she was trying to run away from the pain, on the ground screaming.

"WHAT YOU THROW IN MY EYES."

Destiny picked up Goldie's purse, the purse that had been stolen from Destiny that she had stolen from her mother. The bag filled with pills. She looked inside. Tylenol bottles. Midol bottles. She remembered how Goldie had put the RU-486 in an Aleve bottle.

She opened the Aleve bottle. So many pills. Salvation, just add water. A regular boot-stealing street pharmaceutical. Saw plenty of what she needed to make the world right. Destiny took the bottles from Goldie's bag, stuffed them in her pocket, then threw the empty bag at Goldie's feet. Destiny didn't want the purse anymore. It had been tainted. Violated.

Goldie's eyes watered. Tears fell. She clenched her teeth.

Destiny whispered, "Yeah, what's really hood, *bitch*."

"Can't breathe . . . help me . . . why . . . why you do dat . . . what . . . why you do dat . . ."

Destiny took the straight-edge razor out, held it tight in her hand.

Left in a seedy motel. Clothes stolen. A dozen used condoms on the floor.

The echo from last night throbbing between her legs.

She thought about that billboard. Lisa Wolf. Wondered what Lisa Wolf did to get herself killed.

Destiny wondered how many people would end up on a billboard before the rising of the sun.

Goldie, now down on the asphalt, crawling, coughing, throwing up, eyes closed tight.

"Help me." Goldie sounded terrified. "Baby Phat . . . you're right . . . I'm sorry . . . help me. Please?"

"Stop screaming or I'll cut you."

Goldie whimpered, hands over her eyes, body twisting in pain.

Destiny, nervous, thinking.

"I'm about to leave," Destiny said. "With my boyfriend. He's the pimp. And don't call the police."

Straight-edge razor in hand, gun that she had found tucked in her pants, backpack on, ponytails moving with her restless pace, Destiny stepped over Goldie and headed for the stairs.

"WHAT YOU THROW IN MY FACE!"

Destiny didn't look back.

Goldie. Left on the ground between cars. Out of sight.

Destiny followed a crowd of people inside the motel room, mean-walked inside the heat of a full-blown celebration. Tonight, dressed in simpler jeans, a T-shirt that promoted throwing rocks at boys, not wearing three-inch heels that made her taller, not wearing heels that made her butt look high and tight, hair in pigtails and not styled, looking Plain Jane, nobody looked at her twice; nobody stopped crump-dancing or killed a conversation when she stepped inside that smoke-filled room. The hardcore beat evolved from Fat Joe dissing 50 Cent to Jadakiss dissing 50 Cent. Another battle zone was going on. Shirtless brothers, Tims unlaced, some sisters in bikini tops, other brothers wearing big leather jackets, wearing skullies, baseball caps, sweating profusely, a girl and two boys with clown makeup on, everybody was trying to outcrump or outclown each other, dancing with their bodies doing a lot of different moves, fast-paced, sharp moves, intense faces, pushing each other, bumping each other, challenging each other, like they were bona fide and certified dancing warriors, fighting it out on the dance floor.

Destiny's breathing thickened. She felt dizzy. Insides bubbled with a new kind of anger.

A corrosive anger.

Destiny wondered if any of these boys left used condoms on the floor last night.

If so, which ones.

The gun that had been delivered to her by God, it only had so many bullets. Not as many bullets as she had counted condoms. The brothers she had met at the music store, she wanted to find them.

They had earned the first two.

A tall girl pushed a muscle-bound brother out of the way, jumped in the mix, eyes glazed over, popping her booty, switching up her groove, and doing some cold C-walking, switching up again, and shaking her whole body like an epileptic on a doubly-charged latte, her breasts bouncing up and down.

A short and thick girl pushed the tall girl out of the way, took over the floor, her face made up like a smiling clown, her moves limber and doubly explosive and athletic, breasts flapping like a bird's wings.

So much sweat from elevated body temperatures. Increased heart rates, she could almost hear every accelerated pulse. So much energy, lots of touching, lots of sexual trysts in the making.

The door to the motel room opened up and an Asian woman wearing bright red motorcycle gear stormed inside, her face as tight as the grip her hand had on her helmet. She was too old for this crowd. Destiny wondered if she had a daughter up in here. Destiny watched the woman as she moved through the crowd, her long black braids swaying with her anxious movements, eyes going from person to person, focused, a killer hawk in search of one prey in particular.

The woman asked a brother a question and the brother said something, looked like he laughed. The Asian woman got all up in the brother's face, talking shit. She was cursing him, was about to hit him with her helmet. The brother was shaken, backed down, then he pointed toward another hotel room.

Face tight and angry, the Asian woman in the motorcycle gear left in a hurry.

Destiny looked down at the hand of a girl she was standing beside, saw she was holding a printout of a DVD movie and CD music list, duplicate of the ones the brothers had shown her last night.

Destiny asked the sister, "Where the brothers slangin' the bootleg DVDs?"

"Mo 'nem probably down in the other room." The girl fired up a joint then motioned in the same direction the stern-faced, mean-looking Asian woman had just gone. "Think they down there making copies and shit."

"Copies." Destiny's insides fell. "How many people down there?"

The girl hit the joint again, fire crackling. "Bunch of 'em down there looking at that DVD."

"Where the other room?"

"Three rooms down." She pointed. "Down at the end. That's they little VIP room."

The girl touched Destiny's hand, flirting. Destiny saw it in the girl's eyes; the E had taken control.

The scent of Courvoisier VSOP & XO Cognac was in the air. Grey Goose. Hennessy. Everybody so crunk. High on ecstasy. Twenty-four hours ago she would've joined them. She would have fired it up and wanted to be their queen. She would have wanted to fit in. To be normal.

The girl extended the burning joint to Destiny.

Destiny shook her head.

"Your face look familiar. Crenshaw High? You a stripper? Barbary Coast?"

She shook her head, wanted to say that she was a fifteen-year-old girl in high school.

The girl went on, "You got nice tits and ass. Need a hookup, I knows some peeps."

Destiny mumbled, "If college doesn't work out for me, I'll keep that in mind."

The girl looked around. "Wonder where Goldie took her ass to. Probably with some nigga."

Destiny pursed her lips. "You trying to get a hookup? Kill Pills or something?"

"Nah. That's my road dog. Supposed to take her to Palmdale to pick her baby up."

"She . . . Goldie . . . she has a baby?"

"Our babies been up in hot-ass Palmdale with Big Momma all week. We rolling out to let them visit they daddies tomorrow. Visiting day. My boo locked down on a fo'-fiddy-nine that went bad."

A song with T.I. and Nelly came on; the room went berserk, chanting, fists pumping, the girls dancing like they were in the sequel to the "Tip Drill" video. The girl Destiny was standing next to screamed like she was on fire, that fire coming from her soul, then ran out on the floor, pushed another dancer out of the way, started popping her booty like popping her booty was what she was born to do.

Let me see you get loose get loose get loose get loose . . .

Destiny thought about her reputation. Forever tarnished. And now it was on DVD. Her image could end up on the Internet. One click away from her mom and dad downloading it, one click away from her grand-parents downloading it, one click away from her peers back at private school downloading it.

One click away from the whole world downloading it.

One click away from total humiliation.

One click.

Click. Click. Click.

The sound a gun made when its clip was empty.

Destiny walked out with the crowd, smoke from the ganja floating over their heads like clouds, Destiny headed toward the other rooms. That straight-edge was still in her hand. That gun still at her waist. Her anger now a beast.

Down below, she saw a silhouette. Goldie on the ground between the cars.

People were just getting near her, just hearing her screams.

Somebody yelled, "Something done happened to Goldie!"

fourteen

BILLIE

DAMN. DAMN. DAMN.

Two in the morning and I was running away from that psychopath, turning too damn fast.

Skidding, skidding, skidding.

My breath caught in my chest, heart rate tripled, and I braced myself for impact. Tires lost traction, felt my Duke sliding away from under me. World shifted at an angle. Ground raced up at me ten degrees at a time. Then time stretched out. Moved in slow motion. Everything. Was. In. Slow. Motion.

Heart moved up in my throat.

Don't high-side. Lay the damn bike down. Don't grab the front brake. Don't kill yourself. Lay the bitch down. Don't fuckin' high-side. Ride it on your back, don't land on your face and nipple-surf.

I . . . hit . . . the pavement . . . hard . . . grunted . . . the wind knocked out of me.

I was down, first on my back, sliding, rolling, tumbling.

Reality shifted gears and everything went too fast.

In the back of my mind, in that single corner that fear hadn't invaded, I prayed I didn't get thrown into anything solid. Didn't want to get impaled. Or broken in half.

Didn't want to lose my baby.

I didn't want anybody's money.

Just wanted my baby.

* * *

A car screeched, crashed into something. She'd lost control too. Side-swiped somebody.

Then the sound of that car backing up, tires spinning at a desperate speed. I thought she'd be fleeing the scene of the accident, but the screech told me that she wasn't finished. Then the wail of that beast turning fast, zooming down the street I was on. She'd backed up, come back to finish me. Headlights covered me. Tires screeched, felt like heat from the car, heard the hum from its engine.

The engine revved. Revved hard and mean. Sounded like the growl of a at least two hundred horsepower threatening me to move. The car lurched forward. I was about to be trampled by that cage.

But.

The car stopped in front of me, high beams right in my eyes.

The car door opened. Heard the *ding ding ding* as footsteps ran toward me.

I tried to move, couldn't roll over, just closed my eyes tight.

Shouldn't have moved. Now she knew I wasn't dead.

Wished I had my gun. I'd blow her evil ass straight back to Hades.

Everything went dark. Numbness continued to crawl over me.

Heard that car door slam.

Heard that engine revving again.

Revving hard.

Sounded like close to three hundred horses were ready to stampede my body.

I braced for a brand-new pain.

The car sped by me.

Just like that the car was gone.

I groaned. Tried to breathe. Sweat covered my face. Swallowed a hundred times.

Heard my Lady Duke rumbling, choking, struggling to cut off.

My bike had missed the parked cars and slid into the mouth of an alley-way, didn't hit anybody or tear up any public property, missed all the other cars. Small miracles in a time of high auto insurance and personal chaos. I screamed. Already knew my motorcycle was suffering abrasion damage, scratches on the fairing, a broken turn signal, same for the hand lever.

Hoped the damage was minor enough that I could hop on my bike and try and chase that bitch down, run her into the bowels of hell.

But.

Gas.

Smelled gas. That toxic stench crept up into my nostrils, stole my breath.

I was laid out, in the streets, helmet scarred; backpack, leather pants, and jacket with road burn.

My bike kept rumbling, calling for help because it was in severe pain.

Couldn't breathe. Choking. Had to fight to get my face protector up so I could get some air.

Then the scent of gas came at me fast and strong, filled my lungs.

I coughed. Hated my gear because I felt trapped.

But my gear had saved my ass from having a busted head and road burn up and down the right side of my body. I was in pain, but that pain was hidden underneath disbelief and numbness.

Salty sweat blended with my eyes and left me in pain and sightless, took me a moment to realize I could move all of my limbs, that nothing was broken, that I was still alive.

That bitch Carmen had tried to kill me.

I struggled to get up.

The middle of the night and I was laid out on the streets in Santa Monica, laid out and cars filled with people who'd wake up with hangovers or strangers, some both, kept going by on Wilshire Boulevard, moving at an urgent pace. Cars finally came down the side street. Witnesses who hadn't witnessed anything. Drivers came up, headlights shining all over me, gave up being self-absorbed long enough to slow down and look, then cranked their music up a notch and whipped around me like I was in their way.

God bless the narcissistic.

Carmen had disrespected me at Starbucks and I had let her get away with that shit.

She had thrown a brick through my window.

She had run me off the road last night.

She had come to my damn job. Invaded my world like Bush did Iraq.

Now that terrorist had, once again, run me off the road, tried to kill me.

No. That terrorist tried to kill my baby.

Starbucks was about me. Everything since then had been about destroying my baby.

For the third time in two days, Keith's psychotic wife tried to kill my baby.

My world was spinning. Struggled to my feet. Dizzy. Then sat down where I was.

I reached for my cellular phone so I could dial 911, but my shoulder ached like it was dislocated. Had to fight the pain and regroup. Lot of good getting my phone out would do. Still had my helmet and gloves on. Couldn't think. Was panicking. Swimming in anger and treading in shock.

Death had passed me by. Alive. I was alive.

I had managed to tuck the front end of the bike, let it slide from under me and not drag me across the asphalt. Didn't grab my brakes and high-side, thank God. Not the best fall, but it was the safest way to crash. Looked like I'd had a bad day at the MotoGP races, had wiped out at the AMA races.

A driver in an SUV slowed down, asked, "You okay?"

I struggled up off the ground, took my banged-up helmet off, dropped it, leaned against a parked car for a moment, then limped toward my bike. Didn't have to see my motorcycle to know the clips were broken. That the pegs were messed up. That my bike was jacked. That it wasn't rideable.

That meant I couldn't chase her. Wanted to catch her, beat her into oblivion.

"You okay?"

I snapped, "Do I look like I'm okay?"

The concerned driver drove away. God bless Los Angeles and all her narcissism.

Stranded. I was stranded.

Alone.

Without a friend in the world.

My hands hurt, felt the pain in my right leg from impact, sweat ran from my forehead down into my face, it was a struggle, but I got my cellular out. Yanked my gloves off, flexed my fingers. None were broken. Some pain in my elbow from the fall. Limped around and did a body check as I made a call.

Hoped I had enough strength to get that four-hundred-pound machine upright.

The stench met me head-on. Escalated fear.

The deadly stench of gas permeated the crisp ocean air.

Oh, God.

My gas tank had been damaged. Gas cap had popped open. Gas was spilling out like water.

Then.

Fire.

Flames rose.

I screamed, begged for my Lady Duke to not catch on fire.

But my bike went up in flames, it spread so fast, a nightmare rising from the ground.

The sound and stink and sight of a blazing bike, watching the fairings melt . . .

I screamed.

My hands were holding my belly, I was shaking my head, rage in my face, tears rivering from my eyes.

I screamed.

She tried to kill me and my baby.

I screamed.

Hell rose in my eyes, my own internal flames.

Once again I was surrounded by police officers. The police officers thought I had crashed my bike, didn't believe me when I told them I had been run off the road. They were too busy trying to write a ticket to listen to me. Paramedics wanted to look me over. Wanted to strap me to a gurney and rush me to the emergency room, but I didn't let them touch me. They touched me and I would owe them a grip. Bartending substitute teachers didn't have that kind of insurance. And right now I didn't have that kind of time. No broken bones, but I would be plenty sore for a few days, traumatized for weeks. Police lights were flashing, diverting traffic up the alleyway. Lights from a fire truck added to the spectacle. The reek of melted fairing, the overall disgusting odor from my burning bike, were almost too much to bear.

Couldn't stop crying. Damn hormones were working me hard and strong.

Raheem came over to me and asked, "You okay?"

"Thanks for coming . . . to rescue me."

"No problem."

"Would've called a taxi . . ."

"Ever see a taxi in L.A.?"

"Outside of LAX, not really."

I had called Viviane, couldn't get her to answer her cellular. Left her an emotional message, that Carmen had come to my job, tried to run me over, that I had gone down, my bike totaled.

I had called Keith. No answer. So damn upset. Left him a scathing message.

Stuck on the streets, I'd run out of options. When I crashed, somehow *The Alchemist* had fallen out of my jacket. The book had landed wide open, Raheem's card on the pavement staring at me.

I called him. He came.

He said, "Need to get you to an emergency room."

"I'll have to buy you another helmet."

"Will you stop talking about the helmet?"

Hated that he knew I was pregnant. I didn't want to go to the hospital. Was too scared.

He said, "What if . . . you know."

"I don't want to know."

"Sure. I understand. But still . . . you need to get to the hospital."

"I need you to take me . . . take me home."

"Okay."

"If that's cool with you."

My bike was put on the back of a flatbed tow truck. Fairing melted. Gas tank ruptured. Wiring damn near liquefied. Just on the electrical damage alone I knew the Lady Duke was totaled. One hand over my belly, the other holding on to my anger, I stared at my bike, hurting somebody real bad in my mind. Shook my head as another kind of sadness overwhelmed me. Felt like I was standing over the dead body of a good friend. Of my only reliable friend. But me and my bike were closer than that.

Another driver ran around the corner, her friends with her, all of them hysterical. All of them had just come out of a bar around the corner. Her red BMW had been sideswiped. She screamed and jumped up and down, waved her Prada handbag like it was the end of the world. That explained the crash I had heard after I went down. That was a good thing. Now the police knew I wasn't lying.

I told her the same idiot that sideswiped her car had run me down.

Then another man ran around the corner. He'd just come out of the same bar. He'd been sideswiped too. He was in a green Mazda.

I followed them around and looked at their rides. Whoever hit them had been riding in a black car. Had swiped them hard. Broken glass and detached bumpers were decorating the boulevard.

A red car. A green car. That meant red paint and green paint were on a black car.

Looked like coolant was on the streets. Radiator fluid was a car's blood.

A policeman asked me if I saw what kind of car it was.

I told him the car looked black. Didn't say any more than that.

While some policemen tried to calm down the hysterical woman, another found a sideview mirror a few feet away. If that sideview mirror was off, the passenger side of the attack vehicle had some nice damage.

The officer put it on top of his car.

The sideview mirror had come off a black Mercedes-Benz. Bits of glass on the ground came from a broken headlight. So that Benz had become a one-eyed monster.

He asked if I saw anything else.

I hesitated, inhaled the scents from my burned Ducati, felt Carmen's name standing on the tip of my tongue, but I swallowed, shook my head, lied and told them that I didn't know anything.

The police didn't have the balls to handle this the way I would.

Inside Raheem's car. Heading down Wilshire. Raheem shifting gears like a pro.

I said, "Keith's wife ran me off the road."

"Carmen ran you off the road?"

"The bitch drives a black Benz."

"You sure?"

"She just came to the Temple Bar and confronted me."

"Tonight? Carmen came to the Temple Bar tonight?"

"Yes. And she drives a black Benz."

"Well, this is Santa Monica. Half the people who live down here drive a black Benz."

"You think I'm crazy? Think I'm making this up?"

"Not saying that. Why didn't you tell the police you thought it was Carmen?"

It slipped right by me. My anger had me spewing out my words, messed up my radar. Again I was living in the land of tunnel vision. I missed the fact that Raheem already knew Keith's wife's name.

"She threw a brick through my bedroom window last night. They laughed it off. She tried to run me down last night. They said I couldn't prove it. Had an alibi. Like she probably has one now. All they'd do now would be . . . nothing. I have to handle this my own way. Never should've let her take it this far."

"So," Raheem said, then took a breath. "Carmen wrecked her car trying to run you down."

I told him that Carmen had offered me money to not have the baby.

He said, "You're joking."

I reached inside my pocket to show him the five thousand she had tossed in my face tonight.

Then I realized how *The Alchemist* had been tossed from my pocket onto the streets.

Not from my fall.

My pocket was turned inside out.

I'd been robbed.

Raheem took me to his house, all the way trying to talk me into going to the hospital. Told him I needed to sit down, needed to think, needed to get my head right.

As soon as he let the garage door up, there it was.

His Ducati 749. The key was sitting in the ignition.

I put my backpack on. Did the same with my helmet.

Before Raheem could say a word, I was on his bike zooming away.

DESTINY

THE BROTHER WITH THE JAMIE FOXX SMILE, R. KELLY EYES. MO. TONIGHT
dressed in oversized Marithé François Girbaud jean outfit, black cap
turned to the back, black boots. Destiny saw Mo as soon as she stepped inside the other motel room. A crowd of hard-core party people with glazed-
over eyes were dancing her way, getting their groove on, being all
touchy-feely with each other, the love drug in full effect, that crowd slowing her down. Too many eyes on what she was intending to do. The
brother was moving through the crowd, gesturing like he was pissed, arguing with the Asian woman in the red motorcycle outfit.

Toothpick hanging from the side of his mouth, he said, "Last time, I
don't know nobody named Q."

Destiny watched the tanned Asian woman move her long black braids
from her face. Watched her rush and grab the brother's arm to stop him
from peacocking away, heard her stressing, "LaQuiesha Frierson."

"Back up, Yoko Ono."

"They call her Q."

"Better get your goddamn hand off me."

"And for the record, my name is *Viviane*—"

"Get your fucking hand off me—"

"—not Yoko Ono, asshole. Don't you ever disrespect me like that."

"You better back off me before I send your yellow ass to see John Lennon."

"Don't walk away from me." She moved her hand. "My sister's name is
LaQuiesha."

"Told your ass I don't know no Chinese girl named LaQuiesha." He waved her off and walked away. "Out my face. I got the munchies. Looking at you making me hungry for shrimp fried rice."

"*Korean*, you racist prick." The Asian woman followed. "I'm *Korean*, dammit."

"My bad. Don't know no *Korean* girl named LaQuinta Fry Me Some Chicken."

"LaQuiesha Frierson, asshole."

"LaQuinta Fry Me Some Chicken."

"Why do you have to be an asshole?"

"Ain't that what you said, Shrimp Fried Rice? You looking for Fry Me Some Chicken?"

"Look, asshole. My sister said she hooked up with you and your friends down here and some girl you picked up on Crenshaw hit her in the face and you left her crawling in the middle of the streets."

"Last time, Yoko Ono. Wasn't me."

"Look, my sister is laid up in Daniel Freeman, her face messed up, in critical condition, doing her best to stay alive. I just want to know who the girl was who did this. Point her out. That's all I want."

He turned around, left the Asian woman and her frustration, left her with her mouth tight as she banged her helmet against her right leg. Tears fell from her eyes as she took out her cellular phone. Color fingernails. Destiny thought the Asian woman's nails were the bomb.

Through her tears, she gritted her teeth, said, "Jacob, it's Viviane. Need your help on something. I'm down on Western. Casura Bay. Western and King, across from the Snooty Foxx. Think I found the assholes that left Q out in the streets. Some wanna-be-gangsta-assholes-from-da-hood. No, I don't want the police to handle this. I ain't letting them get away with this shit. Hurry."

She hung up.

Destiny stood next to the Asian woman.

The Asian woman stared her up and down, look of death in her eyes.

Destiny asked, "Whassup?"

"How old you? Twelve, thirteen?"

"Why?"

"Go home before it's too late. It's about to get ugly down here. Real ugly."

Then the Asian girl shook her head and headed down the stairs.

Head down, Destiny followed the boy with the Jamie Foxx smile, R. Kelly eyes.

Go home before it's too late.

It was already too late.

About fifty people were inside the cramped motel room when she walked inside, straight-edge down at her side. Tonight was the same as it was last night. Crowded. Music bumping. People dancing wherever. Kissing wherever. Girls half naked. Bottles of alcohol all over the place. Everybody blown to the bone.

A couple of the guys and one of the girls were freestyling.

Then everybody was whooping, bouncing, jumping up and down.

The girls rapped out, *"Put a jimmy on that boner, ain't looking for no donor."*

Destiny's words.

The boys followed up with, *"Your ass gets pregnant, you'll be all a-loner."*

They had stolen everything from her, including her rhymes.

A stack of bootleg DVDs was on a table. All were written on with black markers. At least fifty. From what she could see, they were not all the same. A DVD was playing in the background.

There she was, throwing a brick through Billie's window.

People in the room laughed and applauded the wickedness.

Then there she was, beating down the black-mixed-with-Asian girl.

People laughed and pumped their fists.

Then there she was . . . on the screen . . . in a motel room . . . surrounded . . .

"Say you saw your momma and her boyfriend getting it on?"

Her face, so clear. Everyone else, so vague.

"Her and this Spanish-looking dude . . . will never forget that shit."

"Getting their freak on?"

"Big-time. Momma was on her knees taking deposits like she was an oral sperm bank."

"Oral sperm bank?"

"Giving a blow job. It's a euphemism."

"Ephe-what?"

"Nickname for sucking dick."

"Yeah?"

"Yeah."

"Your momma was on her knees talking to the mike?"

"Talking to the mike?"

"It's a ephe-whatchamacllit for sucking dick."

"That's her specialty. Talking to the mike. Giving head. Sucking dick. Heard her and one of her girlfriends on the phone laughing, talking about how to give blow jobs the right way. All about technique. They think they like the girls on Sex and the City. *Be up all night drinking wine and reading books about how to get nasty. Buy strange-shaped vibrators and all kinds of crazy stuff."*

"Is that right?"

"Heard my momma say she got one made that looks like my daddy's dick."

"No shit?"

"Old women are so nasty."

In the background, brothers passing out condoms.

"What's your specialty, Baby Phat?"

"What's yours?"

"You wanna find out?"

"Maybe."

Drinking, giggling.

"Think you can give head and throw it down like your momma?"

"What do you think?"

"You're cute as hell. Smart too. I'm feeling you, Baby Phat."

"I feel so good."

"For real, Baby Phat. I like you."

"I like you too."

Hands touching her.

Close-up of her face.

On her mouth.

Her expression became the cringe of penetration.

Her body was being rocked, fast and steady.

Then she was moaning. Her voice so strange and distant, someone else.

"That feels so good."

Then the music was too loud to hear. A chest-thumping soundtrack had been added.

"That feels so good."

Her words remixed into a song.

"That feels so good . . . sucking dick . . . so good . . . so . . . so . . . so good . . . so good . . . so . . . so . . . so good . . ."

Over and over, as men touched her, her words sounded so poetic and inviting.

"That feels so good."

Destiny cringed at the sight of herself. On the screen, her hair was down in her face, she looked wild, unkempt, skin damp with sweat, no doubt from dancing, maybe the heat from the E her alcoholic drink had been spiced with, the buzz from the chronic manifested in her light brown eyes. She looked so different, so uninhibited, so vulgar, so surreal, but she knew her own face. Seeing that recording, the camera focused on her sins, the things she was doing and saying in a room filled with strangers, the things some of those brazen strangers were doing to her as she passed out, Destiny felt like going on a slaying spree. She wasn't the only girl on the tape, there were other girls behaving badly, some looked younger than her, but the other girls didn't matter. The other girls seemed aware. Willing. Eager to perform for the camera and the crowd. Exhibitionists with low self-esteem, young girls who needed that kind of attention to feel validated. The camera cut, showed others engaged in oral copulation, girls in the backseats of cars, young women on Crenshaw on their knees in between cars talking to the mike, then a group of girls making their booties dance, other girls swinging from a pole, and when it came back to Destiny, she looked so high, like she was floating in the sky, in need of affection, in need of love, being used, her shame magnified, seeing herself on that soiled bed inside the motel, her boots missing, her purse missing, her jewelry missing, her clothes half on, half off. In a room filled with strangers she was an unknowing part of that eclectic group of girls those boys had recorded. She'd walked in on her parents, on her mother and her boyfriend, had seen bits and pieces of her grandfather's XXX DVDs before, even had seen the uncensored hip-hip videos on late-night BET, but this was different. This was *her*. She was onscreen moaning. Being touched. She was having sex. No, she was being sexed. She told herself that that could not be her. That limp girl with the dreamy eyes wasn't her. She stood there in a crowd of dancing and cheering people, mortified and invisible, watching herself being *pornographized. Pornographized.* That word being created in her mind and given its own definition as she stared at the pornography these people were peddling. *Pornographized*. Her parents could see this. Her grandparents. Everyone at her private school in Bel Air. The people at Faithful Central. The radio station her parents listened to in the morning, KJLH. Oh, God. It would become the news on Cliff Winston's morning show, and Janine would talk about it in the afternoons on KJLH, she imagined people in the community calling in while Rodney Perry told jokes to make light of her shame.

Pornographized.

That throbbing between her legs set her on fire.

Pornographized.

Nothing could stop her from going on a kamikaze mission.

Pornographized.

Nothing.

Anger rose and tears flowed.

She put her hand on the gun, the weapon that had been delivered to her, began casing it out.

The door to the motel room burst open, hit the wall with a boom. The cheap door opened fast and hard. A man shouted like he was the law and the place was being raided by LAPD. From wall to wall, male and female, people were being shoved out of the way. Hand on the butt of the gun, Destiny looked up at him. He was an angry Goliath. Dressed in black leather. Broad shoulders. All muscles. Like a superhero. The Black Panther. Destiny had seen a Black Panther comic book at school last week. This man could've been that character, someone who had leaped straight from the pages of that kind of mythology. He was a huge, dark-skinned man. He was equipped with the largest hands Destiny had ever seen, hands big enough to palm a watermelon. He came in the room shouting, angry, pushing people out of the way. Destiny was shoved, lost her balance, the gun almost slipped, but she bumped into some of the people she wanted to cut and shoot so badly, regained her balance.

The Black Panther was incensed. But he was rude. Had disrespected her like everyone else. Destiny wanted to run behind him, wanted to shoot him first. At least take out the razor she had in her arsenal and cut him good. But he was so damn big and scary.

In a pissed-off tone that rude man barked, "Point him out, Viviane."

The Asian woman, the one who had been in an argument a few minutes ago, was right behind him. Dressed in leather, braids wild, motorcycle helmet in hand, she came in screaming, body moving like she was a storm. Just as angry. Just as incensed. Just as aggressive. Just like the man in front of her.

His tone was destructive. "Show me the punk that called you out your name."

Her lips turned down, her arm stiff, the Asian woman pointed.

There he was. The light-skinned boy with the freckles and R. Kelly smile. Mo.

The man stepped to him. "Hey, boy. You call my woman a bitch?"

"Naw, I ain't called her no bitch." Mo sneered, looked the man with the big hands up and down. "I called that slanted-eyed Yoko Ono–looking bitch a cunt. Now get me some shrimp fried rice."

His homies cracked up.

The Asian girl grabbed the big man's arm, that huge arm dragging her as he moved toward the boys. She struggled to slow him down and shouted, "I don't care about that, not right now. Jacob, look . . . I just want to find the girl that hurt my sister."

The man slowed down, then when the Asian woman let him go he stepped up to the epicenter of the crowd, to that one boy in particular, pointed in his face, said, "Apologize to my woman."

"Nigga, both you better raise up outta this private party."

Mo was surrounded by his boys. The safety of being in a gang, even if they had no gang affiliation. At least none that Destiny recognized. Mo stayed back. His boys stepped up. All of them loaded and sipping green drinks, no doubt the brew called an Incredible Hulk, a concoction made from H&H, Hennessy and Hypnotiq, named that because the liquids mixed and turned green . . . like the Incredible Hulk.

The Black Panther with huge hands.

Destiny didn't know what to do, which way to go.

The army of Incredible Hulks were cursing and drinking, throwing up signs, talking shit, sticking their chests out, and walking up on the man dressed in leather, making threats.

The huge hand of the dark-skinned man became a huge fist . . . a fist the size of a bowling ball . . . a large black bowling ball in biker gloves . . . and the sound it made when he hit the first boy . . . Destiny could only describe that thunderous reverberation as that of a wrecking ball demolishing a building.

Demolished. The way that boy screamed out in pain, the way he fell. *Demolished.*

Shrieks from the girls in the room, just as many shrills from the boys.

The angry man charged into the crowd. The Asian woman followed, swinging her helmet.

Fists were flying. Glasses of alcohol were being thrown.

More screams as people stampeded toward the door.

The boys drinking the Incredible Hulks were being beaten and thrown around like rag dolls.

People were pushing, trying to get out of the room. Shoving. Jumping over the wrought-iron rail outside in high heels and Tims, twisting ankles, breaking legs, sliding across parked cars. Then, because of the weight from the intoxicated people leaning against it, the unsteady wrought-iron rail collapsed. People fell. Shouting as they crashed on top of parked cars. Screaming as they hit the pavement. Johns and prostitutes running out of rooms, hands covering their faces like roaches afraid of the light. Boyfriends leaving their screaming girlfriends behind. Girlfriends leaving their screaming boyfriends behind.

Every man, every woman, for himself, for herself.

The LAPD would come and shut this down, Destiny knew that.

She knew she had to leave.

But she couldn't go.

On the DVD player, even as all the pandemonium took place, that movie kept on playing.

Eye swollen from the fight, the boy with the R. Kelly smile bolted across the room, started grabbing equipment. He grabbed the portable

DVD player, then grabbed a duffel bag and stepped over the injured, pushed his way through the crowd, ran down the stairs, stepped over injured and crying people, dodging people as he lugged that heavy duffel bag toward the parking lot of Casura Bay.

Destiny raced through the panic and followed him.

Yelling and screaming. Running in the streets. Mass exodus. Car wheels spinning.

People laid out on the ground, intoxicated and wounded.

Destiny watched the boy with the R. Kelly smile hurry and load the equipment into the back of the Escalade. By the time he ran around to the driver's side and opened his door, Destiny was at the passenger side, her hand on the handle. When the door unlocked, she pulled the door open, got inside.

He got in and looked at her. "Bitch, you better get out my motherfucking ride."

"So it's like that?"

He paused. "Baby Phat?"

She nodded.

His music blasted. *Beat the pussy up beat the pussy up.*

"What the . . . when you . . . where the hell you come from?"

She said, "LAPD gonna be here in no time. Substation just a block away."

Without questioning, he put his truck in gear, swerved past panicking people, refused to stop for anybody, jumped out in traffic and sped up, drove away from Casura Bay as fast as he could.

They zoomed by the pimp. The police had him handcuffed, trunk open, the young streetwalker being taken out of the trunk of his precious cadillac. Destiny no longer cared.

Destiny asked Mo, "Why, man?"

He chuckled like he knew, but still asked, "Why what?"

"Why did you and D'Andre . . . why did you do that to me?"

His chuckle gave birth to a laugh. "We didn't do shit."

Beat the pussy up.

She growled, reached over, and turned the music off.

He snapped, "Bitch, don't you know better than to touch a black man's radio?"

"What did I do to you?" she yelled. "Thought we were cool. Why you rape me . . . ?"

"Nobody raped your crazy ass."

"There were . . . I woke up . . . in a nasty room . . . condoms all over the floor . . ."

"You asked for it. It's all on the DVD. The original director's cut."

"What?"

"Said you wanted to be like your momma any-damn-way."

"My momma . . . ?"

"The ottoman. You forget? You started doing the damn thing, pretending like you were in *Baby Boy*, acting it out, moving all that ass, saying you wanted daddy dick, how much you loved daddy dick."

"Bidness man. You call yourself a bidness man?"

"Yep. That's me."

Ghetto birds were overhead, those helicopters heading in the direction they were leaving.

Destiny wanted to go home.

She said, "For money. You . . . you . . . you did this to me for some damn money?"

"Shit, you think this Escalade was free? You think they giving away Sprewells?"

"How could you do some shit like that?"

"You see them crazy-ass fucking gas prices? Cost almost a hunnert dollars to fill this bitch up. A hunnert dollars for a tank of gas and you think the government ain't fucking me?"

"How many times have you done this?"

"Everybody fucks somebody. Either you fucking somebody or you gettin' fucked."

"I tell you I've been raped and that's all you have to say?"

"Bidness is bidness. You get pimped, get over it."

"Get over it?"

"Get the fuck over it."

He made a few turns, ended up on Slauson, heading toward La Brea.

Destiny said, "What . . . you . . . you don't even care what you did to me?"

"Shut up."

"Don't you dare tell me to shut up."

"I didn't make you do shit. All I did was tape it and edit it."

"All you did was pimp me. And now you're out here selling it."

"Want a free copy?"

She pulled at her hair, shook her head.

"Since you the star, I'll give you one for free. On the house."

"I want all of them. Every last one."

"You crazy. One free. The rest at ten a pop, half price. Cool?"

That gun down at her waist.

It was inevitable. She thought about Goldie. Wondered if she had been blinded. Maybe she had been blinded so she could see the light.

Destiny asked, "You have a shorty out there somewhere?"

"Why you asking me if I got a shorty? You trying to give me one?"

"Because if you had kids . . . or a kid . . . because I love my daddy . . . need my daddy . . . would hate for a kid to not have a daddy . . . if you had a shorty . . . maybe I'd change my mind. . . ."

"Whoa! You strapped?"

"Maybe if you did have a shorty . . . you're a horrible person . . . you'd be a horrible daddy."

"Baby Phat . . . whoa . . . easy with the gat . . . let's talk this shit out. . . ."

"Pull over."

"Okay, Okay. Soon as I cross Crenshaw I'll pull over."

"Now pull over now dammit pull over."

"Relax. See . . . pulling over."

"Stop in the alley behind the post office."

"Dark back there. Crackheads and shit might be back there."

"I don't care. Pull over."

"Pulled over."

"In park. Put it in park."

"Okay, in park."

"Turn the engine off."

"Okay, engine off."

"Lights too."

"Lights off. Now what?"

She sat there in that dilapidated alley, terrified, trying to think, breathing in the rank smell of garbage, oil, and urine. The scent of this section of L.A. Behind them, the headlights from cars zooming up Slauson. In front of her, the backside of the post office and a strip of third-rate businesses.

"Why did you do this to me?"

"Now . . . chill out . . . don't point that gat at . . . please . . . put the gat—"

"Why?"

"Hold on, now. Don't trip on me. I ain't the motherfucker set you up."

"Set me up?"

"She the motherfucker set you up."

"*What she set me up*? Who is *she*?"

"Put the gun down and we can talk."

"You're not in charge. I'm in charge. *I'm in charge.*"

"Okay. Damn."

"Who set me up?"

"Hard to talk with a gun in my face."

"Think it'll be easier to talk with a bullet in your head?"

"You bluffing."

"Fuck this shit."

"Wait, wait. Ain't you suppose to count to three or something?"

"Is this a game to you? You think I'm playing with you?"

"Okay, it was the Mexican girl."

"What Mexican girl?"

"The girl that was rolling with me when we picked you up da 'Shaw. The one sitting next to the girl you beat down. She set you up big-time."

"Why . . . why?"

"Shit, they came down to jump on you."

"You knew they were gonna jump me?"

"Everybody knew they were going to whoop your ass. That's why we rolled to pick you up. They wanted to get a girl fight, gang-bang-style, on tape. That's why they was ganging up on you and shit."

"When you came and got me . . . that's why you had the camera already on?"

"Tape was rolling. That's why they started talking that shit as soon as we opened the door. They was about to come at you, but you whooped the shit out of Q's ass."

"They were gonna jump me while y'all watched and taped it?"

"The Mexican girl, she talk shit, but her punk ass wasn't gonna fight no way. She just gassed up Q, spit a lot of nonsense in that girl's ear, got her hyped and shit. She like Don King. A promoter."

"Why would you do something like that to somebody?"

"Like Jay-Z said, I'm a bidnessman."

"You set me up?"

"You played yourself. And besides, I ain't had nothing to do with that part. I'm just a director."

"What you saying?"

"Lupe, she in charge of the project. She picks out the girls. We roll down da 'Shaw, hit Slauson Swap Meet, Baldwin Hills Crenshaw Plaza, other hot spots, and she be like a casting director; she point at who she think would look good in the project, then we go mack on 'em, feel 'em out."

"Like you did when I was at the music store."

"Yeah. She saw you walking by yourself, had that right look, sent us to feel you out."

"That's why you came inside the music store? You were following me?"

"Was feelin' you out."

Destiny shook her head. Disbelief. "Why would a girl do this to another girl?"

"She a hater. That's the truth."

"Don't lie. A minute ago you were running thangs."

"A minute ago I didn't have a gun all up in my face."

"Nobody likes a snitch."

"Nobody likes a damn gun in their face."

"I don't believe you, you know that?"

"She always shopping for a new bitch to play with."

"What you do shit . . . shit like this? Why?"

"It's in my nature, baby, I can't help it. You know how it's cracking. Either you a player or getting played. You get played and that makes you stronger, so take that lesson and get the fuck on."

In disbelief she repeated, "Take this as a lesson and move on."

"Don't blame the shit on me."

"And don't blame it on you. You gave me your number. You picked me up."

"You called me to come get you. Nobody made your ass call me."

"So it's my fault."

"Ain't mine. That woulda been Q's fine ass would've been slammed in that video. But you beat her down. Messed her face up. She wasn't fine no mo'. Then er'thang flipped. Peep this. I didn't know that she was gonna take it to that level with you. The Mexican girl, she who you need to be after."

"If I hadn't called you . . . come to meet you . . . you telling me . . . in that DVD . . . that woulda been . . ."

"The girl you beat down. Lights, camera, action. Woulda been her last night."

"I don't believe you."

"What, you don't believe me? Push play."

"What?"

"There's a disc in my DVD player. Director's cut. Push play. Check it out."

Destiny recognized the voice. That accent. Its cadence and familiar tone from the night before. The owner of that voice, her face was either blurred or off camera, whispering, but her voice was strong.

"Young-ass heifer jacked my girl . . . this is how you have your homey's back . . . I'mma show this skank how we roll . . . get her ass another drink . . . Goldie . . . break me off summa that E. . . ."

"Pay me first."

"C'mon, now. You know I'm good for it."

"Pay me first."

"Here. Thought I was your girl."

"Money is my only friend. And it cost twenty, not ten."

"Damn. Give a sister a break."

"I want that bitch's boots. See that purse that bitch got? That shit real."

"That bitch ain't nobody. Jack her shit. I got your back."

Goldie and the black-mixed-with-Mexican girl laughed and laughed and laughed.

Lupe, the camera followed her, showing her body, her butt, her breasts, never her face. Showed her hand extending a drink to Destiny. Showed Destiny taking the drink with a smile, sipping and dancing.

Lupe walked away, dancing her ass off, the camera following her.

"*So you pimping these hos, Lupe?*" Masculine voice. The cameraman talking.

"*I'm a bidnesswoman. You wanna get in the bidness? Let me break this bidness down. There are four categories. Black men. Black women. White men. Women who ain't black. You have problems fucking a white man? Then don't get paid, because that Jungle Fever shit sells. Have I done it? I do what I have to do. Now peep this. I'm about to drop some knowledge. Black men can make more cheddar than black women. America loves them some Mandingo. But a black bitch can make more money than a white bitch because there are so many white hos out there already. Black bitches are what sell. They are in demand. You feel me? You ready for the real deal? Come see me.*"

"*What kinda hos you got?*"

"*White bitches, Asian bitches, Latina bitches, black bitches, interracial bitches. I got 'em all.*"

Destiny was horror-struck. More police sirens zooming down Slauson. Destiny had seen enough. She turned off the DVD player, darkness again hiding them in that rank alley.

"That DVD . . ." Destiny shook her head. "Why you do something like that?"

"Bidness. Adult entertainment."

"For money?"

"Bet. *Hoodrats Gone Wild*. That shit sells a gang of DVDs."

"You don't get it, do you?"

"Just stop pointing that gat at my face and tell me how much you want."

"I WAS RAPED."

"What you want from me? What? The DVDS? Look . . . look . . . take 'em . . . you can have 'em."

"I can't let people I know . . . my parents . . . my grandparents . . . they can't see this."

"Look, cool. I understand your program. The DVDs are packed up in the duffel bag."

"What?"

"All I got left, they packed up in my Nike bag. Now get the gun out my face. Take 'em."

"How many you sell?"

"Not that many."

"How many is not that many? *How many?*"

"Twenty. Maybe."

"*Twenty?*"

"Don't point that gun in my face like that."

"*Twenty is twenty too many.*"

"Whoa!"

"Raise your hands."

"What . . . you jacking me?"

"I said raise your damn hands up." Like in the movies. She said that the way they said that in the movies. But she was still scared of the boy. "No . . . sit on your hands. Sit on your hands."

"Okay. Okay."

"Close your eyes. Stop looking at me. I said close your damn eyes."

"Okay. Look . . . let me call my uncle . . . he rich . . . I can get you some money . . ."

"You feel that? Feel that between your legs?"

"Don't point that gat at my— Oh, God, your crazy ass is tripping."

"Don't you dare use God's name. Don't you dare."

"Okay . . . okay . . . I'm sorry . . . didn't know you were one of dem church people."

She made a wounded sound. "I need to know everybody who put their . . . who messed with me."

"You serious? I don't know who all was up in there."

"I need to know everybody who . . . I need to know."

"I don't know who was up in there. You know how dem parties roll. Half the fools up in there, don't know 'em. People go on the Internet, post up where the party gonna be, word of mouth, groupies just shows up and they crashes it. Half of 'em end up get loaded and end up being slamhogs."

A police car zoomed by, sirens blaring.

"Baby Phat? What's that noise you making? You crying? Whassup over there?"

She snapped, "You think I'm a slut? A hoodrat gone wild? A damn slamhog?"

She screamed, let out the sound of an impaled animal, tears running.

He said, "Chill out. I know how you feel."

"*You know how I feel?* If I shoot you right there, *right there*, then you'll know how I feel."

"Please don't mess around with a loaded gat like that, Baby Phat."

"*Close your eyes and sit on your hands dammit I said sit on your hands.*"

"Okay, okay. Eyes closed. Sitting on my hands. We cool?"

She caught her breath, wiped her eyes with her free hand, her vision so blurry.

Pornographized.

In her heart Mo had earned his own billboard. She wondered if his friends would drop flowers on his grave and stand around doing that herky-jerky dance, elbows moving like a choo choo train.

"Yo, Baby Phat . . . what's going on?"

"Hush. The Lord is talking to me now."

"I don't hear nothing."

"Shhh."

The streets were quiet now. No cars passing by. Something that rarely happened, even in the wee hours of a Sunday morning. She wondered how many women had been drugged. Raped. Pornographized. She wondered how many others bore her shame. She wondered how to fix this.

"Baby Phat?"

"Shhh. God is talking to *me*."

"Uh . . . uh . . . what God over there saying?"

Finger tight on the trigger, she pushed the gun deeper into his groin.

"God said," Destiny whispered, "this is just bidness."

She pulled the trigger.

sixteen

BILLIE

"STOP RINGING THE DOORBELL."

I rang it again and again.

Night covered me. The darkness inside me overwhelmed me.

Throbbing and pissed off, I held my damaged helmet in my left hand.

My right hand, a strong fist.

Made sure my gloves were on. Icon gloves that had been scratched up from eating asphalt. Icon gloves that had steel protection for the knuckles—now that steel protection would have the effect of brass knuckles. I was ready to go *Kill Bill* on Carmen as soon as she opened the door. If she didn't open the door, I still had a brick in my backpack. Would shatter a window. Or kick down a door if I had to. Would smash her in the center of her face with my helmet, then use my helmet like it was a hammer and bash her the way Sandra Oh beat the jerk in *Sideways*. And while Carmen tried to crawl away, while she yelled, I'd jump on her, grab her Afro, and pound her with my steel knuckles until I was exhausted.

Shoulder ached when I rang the doorbell. Rang it and rang it and rang it. Pain told me I was alive as I looked up at the two-story stucco home that Keith had bought. And was going to lose. I'd always wanted to see what he was giving up to live down at the bottom of the hill.

I heard her. Heard the uneven clip-clop of heels coming through the darkness. Sounded like she had hurt herself. She was bumbling like she was disoriented. The movement stopped.

I ignored the pain in my body, told myself that my baby was okay, and rang again.

"Just a damn minute." Her voice was sluggish. "I said stop ringing the doorbell."

I gritted my teeth and rang the doorbell a thousand times.

"I said stop ringing the damn doorbell."

I kept ringing.

She snapped, "I'm coming. Dammit, didn't you hear me say I'm coming?"

I drew my helmet back, ready to knock her on her ass.

Q's image flashed in my mind. How her face was jacked up.

The same thing was about to happen to Carmen.

The door opened.

What I saw messed up my momentum, caused me to lower my helmet.

There she stood. That Afro swaying side to side. Wearing a wedding dress. Not a regular wedding dress, but the kind that little girls dreamed of wearing on the day they married their prince.

Her cherry-red lips came unglued. She shook her head, said, "Oh, God. It's you."

Carmen was holding a glass of wine and a bouquet of roses, was wearing a luxurious wedding dress. That white wedding dress was stunning, elegant, luxurious, and sophisticated, had a six-foot train. She was haute couture in smeared lipstick. It was cold inside her house, air was blowing out like the air conditioner was on high, but she was crying and sweating. Mascara melting like a mudslide running over her neck, that blackness dripping down over her pearls. Hours of tears had flooded down into the valley of her breasts, had stained her cleavage. Her eyes were so dark they looked like two black never-ending holes. Carmen had become a sad and inebriated raccoon-demon in Vera Wang.

That slowed my momentum. But I didn't ask. I was on a mission. Tunnel vision.

She lowered the roses, snapped, "What do you want? You come for the rest of your money? Well, I don't have it. And I might as well tell you that I won't be able to get it. So the deal is off."

The stench from her wine hit me dead in the face. My stomach turned.

I snapped back, "Take me to your car."

"My car? For what?"

"You know why."

"If I knew why, I wouldn't be asking why."

"You wrecked it when you ran me off the road."

"Oh, God. Don't start with that nonsense again."

"And you stole five thousand dollars out of my pocket."

"What? You're insane, you know that?"

"I'm insane? You're wearing a wedding dress, looking like the Corpse Bride, and I'm insane?"

She coughed. Had a hard time breathing.

I didn't back down. Owned no empathy. Snapped, "Let's go to your car."

She cursed me out, growled like a bear, put her foot up to the bottom of the door, tried to be slick and kick the door shut in my face. I stuck the helmet in the way and the door bounced back at her, messed up her momentum. Then I put my shoulder into it, shoved the door as hard as I could.

She staggered backward, dropped her roses and her glass of wine, that glass shattering as she fell into the wall. She tried to run. I went after her.

She snapped, "That's *assault*. Breaking and entering. You have committed the criminal act of entering a residence by force. You are here without authorization. *Leave my house.*"

I threw my helmet at her; raised my lid over my head and threw it as hard as I could, hit that psycho in the back of her Afro. She made an *uuugh* sound before she tripped and went down again.

That hurt my shoulder. But I didn't give in to the pain, held my scream for another day.

"Guess you thought you could just come up to my job and front me like I was a punk, huh?"

She took a few thin breaths, tried to laugh. "Now I have you for aggravated assault."

"What?"

"Aggravated assault is a felony punishable by a term in state prison. Looks like you're going to have that bastard child of yours in jail. They'll take that child from you and make it a ward of the state."

"Am I supposed to be scared of you?"

"Leave my house immediately."

"After all the shit you've done to me?"

She held her head and yelled, "Sweetheart you just committed a criminal wrong and a civil wrong. I'm going to sue you for that funky motorcycle you ride. Your life is over. I'll take everything you own. Everygoddamn-thing. I will sue you for mental distress. You're going to jail for a long time."

"Not before I send you to hell."

She struggled, made it to her feet, held her lopsided Afro.

I warned her, "Keep away from the phone."

"This is my home. *My* home." She choked on her spit. "You don't tell me what to do."

"And don't go near the keypad for your house alarm."

"Wonderful. I'm being held hostage. False imprisonment. Depriving someone of freedom of movement by holding a person in a confined space . . . your baby will be an adult before you get out of jail."

I picked the helmet up again, raised it high, grimaced like I was about to beat her.

She made a scared sound, raised her hands to cover her face. "Don't. . . . Stop . . ."

"Your car. Take me to your car."

"I'm not getting in my car with you."

"*What?*"

"You're not driving me out into the desert and . . . lunatic . . . I'm calling the police . . ."

She staggered away. Headed for the phone. Again I threw my helmet. It hit her on her knees. *Uuugh.* She stumbled over that long train and went down hard, hit the carpet like a broken mannequin.

"For the last time." I stood over her, fists doubled, shouting. "Let's go to your car."

Voices. That was when I heard a voice coming from the back.

My heart stopped and fear stole both my rage and my haughtiness.

I'd forgotten about her daughter. Was so angry I forgot to check.

I looked up and thought I'd see Destiny looking at me, horrified.

Destiny. A thousand pictures of her were on the walls. Two thousand eyes on me.

But she wasn't there, only her pictures. Baby pictures. Pictures of her at every age, pictures that spanned over fifteen years. Their child. Their Destiny. It wasn't Carmen's daughter's voice I heard.

I stilled.

Listened.

Keith.

I heard Keith's voice.

Then I scowled back at Carmen.

She was having a hard time with her words, said, "Don't . . . please . . . just leave . . . leave."

"Keith's here?"

"Leave . . . get off my property."

I hurried toward the voice, sharp pain cruising up my left side, making me limp.

She shouted, "Don't . . . don't go in . . . there. Dammit . . . please . . . don't go in my bedroom."

Keith's laughter led the way. I kept grimacing and limping, Carmen staggering behind me.

"Get . . . get . . . out of my fucking . . . my fucking house, bitch."

She whistled a ragged song every time she inhaled.

When I got to the bedroom door, my helmet hit me hard in my back.

"Bitch . . . I said don't go . . . go . . . go . . . in my bedroom."

After she said that I turned and faced her. Her hand was clutching her chest. Her back bent. Face changing colors. Sweat dripping from her skin. Taking in gobs of air like she was drowning. She could barely stand. She picked up a remote control. Drew back like she was going to throw it at me.

I asked, "You sure you want to go there?"

She got her wind, made a harsh face, and threw it at me. It missed. But that pissed me off.

I limped as fast as I could, went back and got in her face. "Call me a bitch again."

"Don't go in my bedroom, dammit." She caught her breath, stumbled past me in those four-inch heels, knocked me out of the way like she wanted to get to the bedroom door before I did. Along the way she kept throwing things back at me. Flowers. Candles. Anything she passed as she staggered in front of me. *"Don't invade my privacy."*

"You threw a brick through my window. You ran me off the road two nights in a row."

"You're delusional."

"Delusional? You invaded my privacy first."

"And you just broke in my house, throwing things, assaulting me, turning things over."

All the insane things she was doing . . . tearing up her own home . . . she was setting me up.

With that I took my backpack off, opened it, took that brick out, held it in my hand.

I asked her, "Front of the head or back of the head?"

"What?"

"Since I'm throwing things, you want me to smash this brick in the front or the back of your head?"

"You're threatening me with a weapon? This is premeditated. With intent, malice aforethought, and with no legal excuse or goddamn authority. In those clear circumstances, this is first-degree murder."

"And running me off my motorcycle was very Scott Peterson of you."

She coughed, wheezed, wiped her mouth with the back of her hand, smearing her red lipstick.

We stared.

I asked, "Why in the hell do you have a wedding dress on?"

"None . . . none . . . none of your goddamn business."

"You look pathetic, you know that?"

Carmen had her back to the wall, was sliding down, coughing, eyes wide, pulling her hair, crying.

Brick in hand, I walked past her. She reached out to grab me, but she missed my leg.

She lost it. "I hate you. I hate you. I hate you and everything you represent."

"Likewise."

I put my hand on the doorknob, got ready to push the door open.

"Don't . . . please don't . . . don't . . . don't . . . I beg of you . . . don't . . . invade . . . my privacy . . ."

Keith.

I opened the door and Keith's beautiful eyes met mine.

The brick fell from my hand, hit the floor with a thud.

He laughed.

Surrounded by candles, dressed in a black tuxedo, Keith was smiling and laughing.

His face was on a forty-two-inch LCD television that was anchored to the wall. It was their wedding. Carmen had dressed up in her wedding dress and was sitting up watching them get married.

"Shit . . . God . . . no . . . Billie . . . wait . . . no . . . Billie . . ."

Then came that inebriated voice, that broken whistling sound with her every breath.

"Billie . . . can't breathe . . . help . . ."

A black tuxedo was on the bed, laid out like an invisible six-foot-tall man was inside. It was the same tuxedo Keith had on in the video. Wedding pictures were scattered all over the table and floor. Empty bottle of wine on the nightstand. The air-conditioning was up on high because the candles would've had the room feeling like the center of the sun. I went to the bed. The bed that Keith used to have sex with Carmen on. Stared at that bed. At the things they had shared. Then I saw the other things. Warming lubricants. Ben Wa balls. A rabbit to stimulate her clit. But what stalled me was the vibrator. One that was deep brown, thick, nice girth and length. And it had testicles. Veins ran up and down the side. It looked just like Keith's penis. She'd been craving that memory so bad she went out and bought a stunt double.

My eyes went back to the big-screen television. Watched her and Keith getting married. They were on a cliff overlooking the ocean. It was . . . beautiful. Simply beautiful.

They kissed. They kept on kissing. His tongue was inside her mouth.

She told him she loved him.

He smiled the greatest smile of all time and told her the same.

They held each other and kissed.

That ruptured my heart. Felt like I was standing on top of Mount Everest in the nude. But I was standing in the middle of their precious memories, eighteen years ago.

Back when Reagan was president and *Rain Man* and *Bull Durham* were the films to see.

Back when my parents were still alive. Back when I was fifteen. When I was still a virgin and secretly in love with Stephan Mitchell, a boy who never noticed me. Back when I still had a family.

Carmen sang to Keith. She sang off-key, but she sang with passion, from her heart and from deep within her soul. On the verge of tears, she looked Keith in his eyes and sang Gloria Estefan and Miami Sound Machine's "Anything for You." Keith looked in her eyes and sang Billy Ocean to her. "Caribbean Queen." Then they sang an off-key duet. "I Knew You Were Waiting For Me." She was Aretha Franklin and he was George Michael. That duet was horrible and beautiful all at once. Then the DJ put a Bobby McFerrin record on. The room filled with Jamaicans and they all danced. *Don't worry, Be happy.*

Carmen. Keith. So much heat between them. Sad what time did to us all.

Then the room came alive with Kingston's dancehall music. Keith and Carmen, so wild.

They didn't have a child back then. It showed. Both of them looked so different now. It was more than the years. Parents owned a different disposition. One rooted in responsibility, not selfishness.

Carmen had big hair back then. Looked so likable. So pure. So unlike the bitch that was laid out in the hallway. Keith was so much younger then. Always fine as hell. Looked so happy while he and Carmen cut that cake and fed each other. A different Keith. He could pass for his own younger brother.

He kissed Carmen the same way he kissed me. He kissed her like they would be together forever.

Hands in fists, not knowing where Carmen was, I went back out into the hallway. Behind me was the sound of a gleeful wedding and Chris De Burgh singing "Lady in Red." In front of me, Carmen was still down on the floor, one shoe off, her train tangled around her feet. An aging mannequin falling apart.

She panted, "In . . . haler . . ."

"You need your inhaler?"

"Help . . ."

I got closer. Got right up in her face. Whispered in her ear, "You're asking this *blood clot* to help you?"

She squeezed her eyes shut. Her chest had an abbreviated rise and fall. Mucus made her breathing rattle. A mild cough. I watched her. Listened to that snake inside her chest. Her wheezing was getting stronger, more violent every time she struggled to inhale. The ugly faces she made. Kept grimacing. Almost like she was having back-to-back orgasms. Only I knew this didn't feel good. So similar, the expressions of both pleasure and pain. She was hurting bad. Her face turning pale.

"You just called me a bitch and threatened to sue me for everything I own. Right, Carmen?"

I pulled my hair back and stared deep in her eyes. Tried to see what type of monster lived inside her. She was sweating so hard a river ran across her forehead. She didn't wipe any of that sweat away. She was in respiratory distress. She was so fragile.

I whispered, "And now I'm supposed to pity you? I know you don't expect *me* to save you."

She reached for me, her eyes begging me to help, those eyes saying she wasn't bullshitting.

Neither was I.

"Remember when we first met? How I was polite to you? You called me a whore. What was that Jamaican crap you said to me? *Suck mi out?* Well, Carmen, catch your breath and you can *suck mi out*."

She tried to get up, collapsed.

My bottom lip trembled, my anger poured out as I said, "This is karma, Carmen. This is karma."

She tried to talk. She couldn't.

She was afraid. The snake had shed its skin and I stared at the coward left behind.

I shook my head, letting her know that I wasn't going to help her, not in this lifetime.

I erupted, yelled, mocking her. "Aggravated assault. False imprisonment. Trespassing."

I snatched up my helmet, the only evidence that I'd been here, and headed for the garage.

"You did all of that first. *You did.* Then you tried to kill me. You tried to kill my baby."

I limped away, Carmen's wheezing and coughing worsening with my every step.

"Die, bitch."

* * *

That wheezing sound reverberated, followed me as I made my way through their kitchen, then the wheezing faded as I made my way though the laundry room. I wondered if she was dead. Imagined her tilted to the side, face as blue as the sky. Sharp pain. Hurting bad. I was hurting bad. I put my hand on my belly, massaged my fear, and stopped in the mudroom, stopped and faced the door to their garage.

Their garage. Not *her* garage. *Their* garage.

Their home.

Their world.

I had to be sure. Felt like I was going crazy, but I knew I wasn't.

I'd been chased, been run down and left for dead, treated like I was less than an animal.

I opened the door that led to the two-car garage. Was cold in there. Saw the silhouette of her car parked on the far side, backed in. Almost as if it were a strategic move. That way the damaged passenger side would be hidden against the far wall. That way nobody could see the dents and broken glass, the missing sideview mirror, the fender that was mutilated, red and green paint in the fiberglass.

That way nobody could see she tried to kill me.

Bitch tried to kill my baby.

She deserved to die a slow death.

I fumbled around the garage, clicked the light on.

Leg ached as I hobbled my fury and throbbing over to the other side of her car.

Mouth wide open, heart beating fast, I shook my head.

seventeen

BILLIE

I STOOD OVER CARMEN, HELMET IN HAND, HANDS TIGHT.

Face dank, that big Afro a mess, lipstick smeared, Carmen could barely raise her head to gaze at me. Her eyes were glazed over, legs trapped by a six-foot train, a prisoner in her own wedding dress.

I told Carmen, "I'm dialing nine-one-one."

"No." She wheezed. "The neighbors."

"You want me to go get your neighbor?"

"No. No more embarrassment. Please. No ambulance."

"What then?"

"Get my inhaler . . ."

"Where is it?"

She wheezed.

I yelled, "Where is it?"

"Kitchen . . . counter."

I ran to her kitchen. Looked on the table, in the refrigerator, then finally found the inhaler on the counter. I'd run right by it.

I raced back to Carmen, put the thing up to her mouth. She put her hand on mine, made the thing squirt. She inhaled the best she could. Then she made the thing squirt again.

I asked, "You okay? Say something, dammit."

She wheezed. "Take me to the emergency room."

"What?"

"Drive me."

I yelled, "I'm on a damn motorcycle, Carmen."

"Take . . ."

"Bitch, look, dammit, don't do this to me."

"My car . . ." Wheeze. "Then . . . take me in my car."

"Don't do this to me." I pulled at my hair. "Your parents . . . give me your parents' number."

"No, no, no."

"Yes, yes, yes. Give me their number."

"No. Don't want Keith . . . my parents . . . see me like this . . . please . . . Keith will come . . . and Destiny is with him . . . no . . . don't let them see me like this."

I looked down on her. On her wedding dress. Part of me wanted to take her up there just like that, in her wedding dress, video, vibrator, and all. But I'd never been good at being that type of person.

I ran to her closet. Stood in her cluttered space. Her aromas. Touched her things. Found a pair of sweats. Then I hurried back to Carmen. Undressed her like she was a child. That wasn't easy. My arm ached and that eighteen-year-old dress was four sizes too small. Took some doing, but I did it. Was like stripping the skin off a snake without a knife. On the floor, naked in front of me, her motherly breasts exposed, the sag in her stomach exposed, the coarse hairs over her vagina on display. I helped her maneuver, shifted her weight, straightened out her legs, and pulled on the red and gold collegiate sweats.

I said, "Don't die on me, Carmen."

"Candles . . . blow out the candles."

"I'll leave you just like this if you die on me."

"Candles . . . blow out . . . house could burn . . . burn . . ."

I ran and blew out all those friggin' candles, hurried back to her.

"Carmen . . . open your eyes . . . look at me . . . put your arm over my shoulder."

I lifted and grunted, got her upright, leaned her on the wall, then I looked down at her bare feet. Damn. I propped her up and ran back to her closet. Found her a pair of sandals.

When I made it back to her, she had slid down the wall, was back down on the floor. I cursed. Wiped the sweat from my eyes and picked her up again.

She said, "Wait. . . ."

"What now?"

"The dress . . . hide it in case . . . Destiny comes home . . . or my momma comes . . . please . . . please . . ."

I rolled up her wedding dress, stuffed it in her closet, a closet that had more clothes and shoes than one women should own in a lifetime, myself included. Her vibrator, well, used a towel to pick it up, threw it in the closet. Then I saw the brick I had left on her floor. I picked that up, put it in my backpack.

She was back down on the floor. Had to strain to get her to her feet.

Carmen whined, "Billie . . ."

"What, Carmen?" I lost it. *"What what what what what?"*

"Makeup. Get my purse . . . my makeup . . . a comb."

I screamed.

I was sweaty and out of breath, it was a struggle, but we bumbled through the house and made it to her car. A dark, shiny car that smelled like coconut and didn't have a single scratch or dent in the fiberglass.

It wasn't Carmen who had chased me down Wilshire Boulevard.

It hadn't been her standing over me while my Ducati burned.

Hadn't been Carmen who tried to kill me and my baby.

She had been home alone, drunk, playing here-cums-the-bride.

She would've been in the hallway waiting on her last rites if her car was damaged.

My mind was so frazzled, so messed up, polluted with resentment, paranoia, and apprehension.

A brick was thrown through my window. Then an SUV ran me down. After that it was a Benz.

I wondered if getting run down was my karma. If I had kicked so many doors. Wondered if, maybe, one of them had seen me in my neighborhood, had thrown a brick though my bedroom window, then tried to run me off the road, and then maybe another had seen me on the way home from the Temple Bar, had seen me cruising down Wilshire on my bright yellow Ducati, and run me down for revenge.

I wasn't sure about anything anymore.

Karma. Not Carmen. This was my own karma coming back at me.

Inevitably karma always came back like a hurricane.

I was in pain. So much pain. But I could handle it. I'd been hurt worse.

All I knew for sure was that Carmen's car didn't have a single scratch.

I'd rather wrestle a fire demon from the volcanic depths of hell than help her.

But I couldn't let her suffer and die for a crime she didn't commit.

Inside Carmen's Benz. Her car felt colder than the rest of the garage.

A worn paperback was on the front seat. *The Alchemist*. At first I thought it was mine, but mine was in my pocket. I moved her book, tossed it in the backseat, did that without a thought.

All I heard was my own hard breathing and her *wheeze wheeze wheeze*.

Carmen sucked on her inhaler, her breathing staccato. "I never wanted to be an attorney."

I turned on her car, adjusted the seat, the mirrors, snapped, "What?"

"I said . . ." Wheeze. "I never . . ." Wheeze. "Never wanted to be an attorney."

"How do I open the garage door? Or should I just gun it in reverse and tear it down?"

She leaned forward, hit a button under the rearview mirror. I backed out fast, then hit that button again. As the garage door was coming down, I was screeching away, cutting through the darkness.

"Never wanted to be a damn attorney. I was content when I was a waitress."

"Shut up."

"Happiest days of my life. Don't bring your work home with you. Don't have all the other worries. Hanging out on Sunset Boulevard. That was a wonderful life. Didn't know that then, not until now."

Wheeze.

"Law school, that jealous beast changed everything. Changed my marriage. Changed me. All of a sudden, I was too busy. Was too focused. Didn't have a lot of time to be with my daughter. Keith had her most of the time. Took her to school. Picked her up from day care. Cooked. Cleaned. Took her to the park while I was in a study group. Wanted to be there, but law school . . . I was always too busy or too impatient. Too stressed out. Now this chasm lies between me and my child. Between me and . . ."

She stopped with that next thought. That wheezing irritated and scared me all at once.

I calmed my shaking hands and asked, "You . . . you . . . hey . . . you okay over there?"

Nothing.

"Carmen, talk to me. Say something. You okay over there?"

She said, "My life . . . my world has become so . . . convoluted. Liked it better back then. When I lived in Hyde Park. It wasn't much, but I was so content in my funky little apartment."

I said, "I think you need to save your breath."

She coughed a rough cough. I heard the phlegm in her chest.

I asked, "Can you cough it up?"

She let her window down, tried to spit. What spit didn't hit the car door drooled down her face. She wiped her mouth with her hand, sat back, weak, with tears in her eyes.

I asked, "You okay?"

She made a sound like a crying little girl. Her voice cracked. "No."

"We're almost there. Five minutes."

"I hate being an attorney." Wheeze. "Hate family court. He tell you that I work in family court?"

"No . . . he . . ." I took a deep breath. "Keith . . . your husband just told me you were an attorney."

"He talk about me?"

"Nothing that you would want me to repeat."

"I work in family court." Wheeze. "The most despicable place on the planet. And now I'm ending up in family court. I've been one of those people. Ironic, huh? This home . . . my home has been built on the hate and animosity of others, built at a rate starting at three hundred dollars an hour."

"Why don't you shut up . . . work on that breathing until we get you to the emergency room?"

"That's the cost of hate at my firm. Three hundred an hour. Sometimes it's pro bono, but it runs about three hundred an hour. When I was a waitress I was more than happy to take home three hundred a week. Amazing, huh?"

I took another deep breath, sighed. Wished she'd stop wheezing and quit rambling.

She went on, "I live off other people's pain and anguish. Off cruelty. Off viciousness. Off vindictiveness. It's despicable. My job is to grind people into powder. It changes you, like it or not."

Her eyes were closed. Chest tight and a pained look on her face when she inhaled.

Three times I asked, "You okay over there?"

"No." She was in agony. "Ruby Dee and Ossie were married for fifty-six years. Almost six decades. They had arguments. They had other lovers. Even had an open marriage for a while."

"Where are you going with this?"

"I don't know. Don't know. Just . . . I don't know."

"Then shut up and breathe."

She wiped tears from her eyes. "Embarrassed myself at Starbucks Friday night."

"Breathe."

"Made an ass out of myself by coming to your job tonight."

"If this is your deathbed confession . . . should I be writing this down?"

"Doesn't matter. I'll deny it anyway."

She wheezed and cried. I didn't know if the crying came from her emotions or from the pain. She put her hand up to her mouth, bit at her nails like she was a child. Her foot was shaking. She was afraid.

Carmen said, "Keith is not the only one with problems."

"What do you mean by that?"

"I'm trapped inside that house. Held down by a mortgage. My child. Keith. All of those are my anchors. Anchored by mortgage . . . responsibility . . . and by my heart. So many anchors that I can't move."

I pulled my lips in, so much heat and hate in my heart for that woman.

Then she said something that almost made me crash her car.

In her raspy voice, in what sounded like her last breath, she whispered, "I envy you."

I pretended I hadn't heard her say that.

She said, "Can we find some way to work this out?"

"What do you mean?"

She said, "Keith was in love . . . with me . . . the moment he saw me.

Love at first sight . . . Moved in with him . . . two weeks . . . after I met him. He asked me . . . to marry him . . . six weeks after that. And he was . . . so happy . . . when I got pregnant. He was . . . with me . . . the entire time . . . I was pregnant. From the moment . . . we found out . . . we . . . were pregnant . . . was with me . . . at every Lamaze class . . . was right there . . . when Destiny was born. He held her . . . before I did. He held our child . . . and he cried . . . thanked me for giving him . . . Destiny. He said we . . . were . . . destined to meet. Soul mates. Our child . . . represented . . . our . . . destiny. We named . . . our child . . . after our love. Eighteen years. We have . . . grown . . . up together, went from . . . being children . . . in love . . . to parents . . . and I am . . . not . . . about to let . . . all of that . . . go."

"Shut up, Carmen. Please shut up."

"I need Keith because . . . I can't . . . I can't do this by myself. I can't do . . . this house. I can't do my child. I just can't . . . do all of . . . this by myself. I don't . . . want to be alone. It scares me. Terrifies me."

"Don't get yourself worked up again."

"I was thinking that maybe . . . maybe I could adjust . . . be like Ruby Dee . . . have an open marriage. For a while. As long as he came home at night . . . maybe I could find the strength to not question where he'd been. Maybe I could . . . endure . . . not question things . . . do that until I was strong enough to move on."

She had me ready to break down and cry. I hated that I felt sorry for her.

This time it was my voice cracking. I said, "We're almost at the hospital."

Wheeze. Wheeze. "Cedars-Sinai?"

It wasn't until then that I realized her eyes had been closed most of the way, if not the entire time. Had to be. And if her eyes were open, the tears and fear and struggle for air had left her sightless.

I said, "Daniel Freeman. We're in Inglewood."

"Oh, God, no. I wanted . . . to go . . . to Cedars-Sinai."

"Well, you're in the hood at Freeman. Welcome home."

"Across . . . across . . ." *Wheeze. Wheeze. Wheeze.* "Across the . . . street . . . from . . . a . . . cemetery."

"Shut up and breathe."

When I parked, she reached over, put her sweaty hand on mine. She touched me in a feeble way. My eyes went to where our hands met, then I looked at her. Wanted to frown at her, wanted to snatch my hand away. But I didn't do either of those things. So much sadness in her eyes.

She smiled a little, spoke right above a whisper, "Tonight . . . you smelled like Keith."

I didn't respond.

"He came to you."

Tears flowed from her eyes.

I said, "I'm his whore. That's what he's supposed to do, right?"

"You're . . . not his . . . whore."

"It was goodbye sex."

"Oh, God."

"We're done. I told him that. Happy? We were done before you showed up at my job. I told him that this baby . . . told him not to worry about it . . . that I would . . . would . . ." I stopped talking when I felt that ache. It hurt where my legs met. I was scared. Needed to cry. Not in front if her. Never in front of her.

"He . . . loves . . . you. I can tell."

"He's your husband."

"He loves you . . . so much . . . that . . . it scares me."

Again I didn't reply to her being so vulnerable. I liked her better the other way.

She wheezed.

"Horrible to love so deeply . . . and not be loved . . . that deeply in return."

Wheezed.

She said, "Get my insurance card . . . give them my inhaler. They will want to know what meds . . ."

I was so glad that she moved away from that former conversation, asked her, "Can you walk?"

She shook her head, then it looked like she passed out.

I called her name three times. No answer.

I reached over, put my hand on her chest. She was breathing.

I hurried into the emergency room and called for help. Something tragic had happened across town. Some teenagers had been brought in. Something about a party down on Western that got out of control. A rail broke and a bunch of them fell, crashed down from the second level. One look at the pandemonium and I could tell that the hospital was overworked and understaffed. I stole a wheelchair and ran back toward the car. Tried not to limp, but the pain I felt in my legs . . . between my legs. The way I grimaced, seemed like I should've been in that wheelchair myself. Then when I got back to the car, had to pick Carmen up. With my aches, picking up her dead weight was like lifting a Buick. Then I was sweating, panting, pushing my hair away from my face, pushing the rickety wheelchair as fast as I could, trying to get my own breath, calling for the doctors and nurses as I rushed her inside.

The bright lights made her close her eyes. She worked on staying alive, held my hand.

I said, "We're here. Hold on, we're here."

"Momma . . . Daddy . . . call my parents for me."

"What's the number?"

"In my purse . . . my cell phone . . . scroll down . . . to Big Momma 'Nem. . . ."

One look at Carmen and the nurse frowned at me like I was a fool, snapped at me, asked me why I hadn't called an ambulance. Before I could answer them, they had rushed her into the back.

I stood there, Carmen's car keys in one hand, her cellular in my other hand. I stepped outside, called her parents. Her mother answered. Miss Ruth was in a deep sleep, I could tell by the roughness of her voice. I didn't tell her who I was, just that Carmen had had a severe asthma attack, that she asked me to call them, that they needed to come to Daniel Freeman as soon as possible.

A thin nurse with butt-length red braids stepped out and interrupted me.

She asked, "Ain't you the sister that was on the news yesterday morning?"

I nodded, not in the mood for conversation.

She said, "Told them that was you. Can't believe I met you. I'mma have to get your autograph."

She walked away, adjusting her rainbow-colored uniform.

I paced, nervous.

I called Keith. Had to. Carmen was his wife. They had a child. He needed to know. Their child needed to know. They needed to be here. Had to dial his number six times before he answered.

"*What*, Carmen?"

Then I understood why he hadn't answered. I was calling from Carmen's cellular phone.

"It's not Carmen, Keith."

The wails of ambulances were deafening by the time Keith showed up. Keith came in a taxi. The scent of Easy Jesus perfuming his breath, his red eyes, all of that told me that he was a hangover waiting to happen. He made it here before Carmen's parents, got out of the taxi just as four more ambulances rushed to the emergency room. More banged-up kids from that party down on Western. Found out that it had happened at Casura Bay, a motel in the heart of the red-light district. That was what a nurse had told me a few minutes before Keith showed up. She told me that she thought the melee had started when a young girl was hit in the face with bleach. Nothing about the situation was too clear.

I met Keith and we stood outside the emergency room and talked as we headed to the cafeteria.

I asked, "You're not going up to her room?"

"Eventually. Tell me what happened to you. I came here to see if you were okay."

"I'm okay."

"You sure?"

"Doctor looked me over," I lied. "Outside of road rash all over my leather, everything is fine."

I told him about being chased by the psycho, gave him the scoop on that on the elevator.

Keith said, "Maybe whoever ran you down was just a random drunk driver."

"I don't think so."

"It was two in the morning. When all the bars close down in Santa Monica."

I told him that if a drunk driver had run me down and sideswiped two more cars, the last thing he would've done was wobble back to the scene of the crime, rob me, then leave me for dead.

He said, "Robbed you?"

"Stole five thousand dollars from me."

"Where would you get that kinda money?"

"Sure you don't already know?"

"Don't talk in riddles, Billie. Not in the mood for games."

"Does it look like I'm in the mood to play games? I was robbed."

"Maybe the money had come out when you fell, he saw it, took it, left."

It wasn't Keith who tried to kill me. He had no idea. Wasn't Carmen. I didn't know anymore.

He said, "Maybe the drunk driver ran you down, kept on going, somebody else stopped to see if you were okay, saw the money, grabbed it, got the hell out of there before anybody else came."

"Maybe a Martian came down, grabbed the earth money, and drove away in a Benz."

By the time we got off the elevator, my head was hurting so bad I had to give up trying to figure that out. Nothing made sense. All I knew with any certainty was that my bike was totaled. Crashed and burned in a case of attempted murder. I could be dead right now, cooling off in the morgue.

Keith needed a keg of caffeine. We sat at a table, rubbing our eyes, drinking black coffee from paper cups. I told him what had happened with Carmen. Explained while he listened, shaking his head the whole time.

"Carmen came to your job, Billie?"

I nodded. "Guess that was the errand she had to run."

After that I told him that whoever did this to me had tried to run me off the road right after Carmen had left, told him that my Ducati was totaled, that I was lucky to be alive. And so was Carmen.

He said, "You went up to the house?"

Keith said that, and the image of Carmen in that wedding dress took over my mind.

I said, "Keith . . . something else . . . when your wife came to the Temple Bar, she made me an offer."

"An offer? What kind?"

"The fifty-thousand-dollar kind."

That halted him. Eyebrows tight, the words fell out of his mouth: "Fifty thousand?"

"And she said that you and she would pay more after the baby was born."

"I hope you don't think I had anything to do with it."

"She said *we*. *We* are willing to offer a cash settlement. *We* are being considerate and making it easy on you. *We* are going to pay you what it costs to raise a child. *We* will wash our hands of the situation and *you* will be financially capable of raising *your* child. Over and over she said *we*."

"If there is a *we*, I'm not part of that *we*." He was stressed. "How much more did she offer?"

He didn't know anything about it, that truth showed in his eyes. There was no *we*. Just *she*.

She wanted Keith to come back home and it was worth a poor man's fortune to make it so.

After I sipped my brew, I told him about the deal for one hundred and seventy-five thousand.

I said, "That was the price of her hate. Well, all the hate she could afford."

"That's why she wanted to mortgage the house."

"What?"

"The equity in the house . . . Destiny's tuition money . . . she was going to give that to you?"

"I didn't ask where the money was coming from. Wasn't my business."

He shook his head. "And you were going to take it?"

"She came to my job and offered me five thousand as a down payment. Had cash money."

"You took it."

"What would you do? Well, you pointed out that kids cost a grip. That I was broke. And there was a chance that I would be by myself. Had to put my emotions to the side, be practical. That's what you did, right? You put your emotions to the side and became practical when it came to me and you and this pregnancy. All of your decisions were rooted in logic, right? See? I'm learning, thinking like a man."

He fell silent, shook his head.

I said, "When I was down, whoever went inside my pocket took the five thousand dollars."

"Where would Carmen get five thousand in cash?"

He didn't say anything. I don't think he believed any of this. It was too much for him to process.

I asked, "Where were you all evening, Keith?"

"You think I had something to do with it?"

"Where were you?"

"Packing at first. Then I was drinking, thinking, trying to figure out how to make this work for us."

"Don't, Keith. This can't work. You said that, you meant that, and you were right."

"So you're gonna bite me with my own damn dog."

"That dog bit me first."

He raised his paper cup, sipped his coffee. I did the same.

"I love you, Billie. And you were right. When people love each other, they can make it work."

I sucked my bottom lip. So many aches and pains covering my body.

"How does this work, Keith?"

He said, "Destiny goes away to college. I file for divorce. I won't have anything, but Carmen will, so everything will be flipped. If I don't work, she's the provider. Then I'll hit her for alimony. Child support won't be an issue. She'll have to pay me back for all those years of paying for her to go to law school."

"And like I said to you before, what do I do until then? Destiny is fifteen. What do I do for the next three years?"

"Sue me for child support. I'm not working, but they will look at household income. So they will garnish Carmen's check. Play the system the way she plays the system. It's win-win for both of us."

"So you want me to take Carmen's money?"

"To support my child, yes."

"Dirty pool."

"What goes around, Billie. What goes around. Every dime she has came from my pockets." Keith gritted his teeth, his hands turned into fists. "The money she tried to bribe you with, that was my money. She was going to use the equity in the house I bought to bribe you. So we need to flip it, beat Carmen at her own game. First we hit her for child support. Then, when Destiny's gone, I can divorce her, use that 'accustomed to lifestyle' bullshit and make her pay alimony through her nose. I'll bleed that bitch dry."

"Damn, Keith."

"And we can still be together. She can't stop that. I can be there for you. For my child."

That disturbed me.

I said, "You sound vindictive, just as calculating as Carmen."

"Guess I've learned from the best."

It was a shame when love had deteriorated and left that kind of scum behind.

I vented, "You don't see it, do you?"

"See what?"

"It will never end."

"What will never end?"

"You and Carmen. If I stick around, your slow-burning hell will become my slow burning hell."

He shook his head. "Won't."

I nodded. "Will."

"Destiny will be in college. Carmen will be gone. We can raise our baby and be happy."

"You think it will be that easy?"

He asked, "What are your concerns?"

"Fifteen years from now . . . if not sooner . . . I'll become Carmen. Not the same Carmen that you married, but this will wear me down, harden me, make me bitter. I can't do that. Can't live like that."

"You won't become Carmen, Billie. You are nothing like her."

"It makes you think, Keith. I'm watching you give up on somebody you had a child with, have so many memories with, just give up on them . . . all the time you've invested in a person . . . makes me wonder if you would give up on me. That's always a possibility. Will always be in the back of my mind."

"Eighteen years have gone by. I'm not giving up, it's just time to move on."

"That's cold."

"The truth is ugly. You want it sugar coated? I don't know how to sugar-coat. I don't sugarcoat."

"You're a man and I'm a woman, I guess."

"This is the bottom line. My bottom line. And don't think this is because of you. Billie, divorce or not, my marriage was over before we met."

Images of the way I found Carmen were messing with me. I asked, "Is it?"

"It will never be the same."

"Not supposed to be the same. Nothing stays the same. Everything evolves. It'll never be what it was when you first married, but it can be as good as you allow it to be now."

"She's not the girl I fell in love with."

"But she is the woman who has been by your side all this time."

"What, are you her advocate now?"

"No. I'm just . . . confused. Putting myself in her shoes. Imagining what it would feel like if after being married that long . . . if I was married . . . and loved my husband . . . had a child . . . shit. I'm afraid."

"You don't have to be afraid."

"When you married Carmen, did you know that your marriage had an expiration date on it?"

"You know I didn't. Nobody does."

"Exactly. If you and Carmen, if that's us five years from now, where would that leave me?"

Silence settled between us. His wife was upstairs, maybe on her last breath, and he was here with me. I was platinum, not plastic. Yesterday that would have felt like some sort of victory. Yesterday.

But it was no longer yesterday; it was today.

He said, "Billie, I'm doing my best to fix this mess I've made. I'm just trying to make sure you're going to be okay, can't you see that? If I have to go back there, if I have to live with Carmen in order to make sure you're okay, I'll do that."

Keith sat there, nodding, tears in his eyes.

"Keith." I took a nervous breath. "I stopped taking my birth control pills a few months ago."

"*What?*"

"You didn't make this mess." I swallowed. "Guess I . . . guess I got pregnant on purpose."

He took a breath. "Why?"

"Because . . . wanted to have your child . . . be a family . . . guess . . . love makes you do crazy things."

"Why would you do that, Billie? Children are not toys."

I couldn't look at him, and I couldn't answer.

I said, "I lied, Keith. Now you know the truth. I did something stupid, something horrible."

I almost told him about the first time I was pregnant, when I was young and didn't know any better. But now I was older and still didn't know any better. Had made the same mistake twice.

I didn't tell him; that part of my life was my cross to bear. I shook it off, said, "That's why my karma is so bad. Because of what I've done. I hate what I did because . . . I was insecure."

Tears were in my eyes too. So many innocent victims because of our crimes of passion. We never saw beyond our own desires. We only saw what we believed was possible, even when it was impossible.

I whispered, "The heart wants what it wants."

I told him the truth, eased my soul, expected him to go off on me, push me away, but he didn't.

I said, "This is my doing. You don't have to feel guilty anymore. It's all on me."

"So, Carmen meets you, she goes crazy, revokes the divorce. You meet her, you get pregnant."

A voice inside me whispered, told me that I wouldn't *become* Carmen. Because I'd already become the type of woman I loathed. I had to remember who I was, remember the child that my parents raised, had to find my way back to being Billie. Just didn't know how to get back to that peaceful road.

He said, "Having a baby is about what we need. Never about the baby, not until it gets here."

"I know. What I did . . . there are no excuses . . . this was selfish."

Tears were in his eyes, flowing like the River of Grace and Wisdom. My tears flowed the same.

He said, "The hate that lives between me and Carmen, it's settled between you and Carmen. I tried to keep you from that hate. That's been hard. Living two lives. One good, one filled with pain."

He reached over and patted my hand.

He said, "Accident or on purpose, it's still my child."

"Why now, Keith?" I wiped my eyes. "Why couldn't you have said that at Starbucks?"

"Things weren't so clear to me, not at that moment. Maybe . . . maybe I never used a condom because part of me wanted you to be pregnant. Part of me wanted you to have my child. Our child."

"Because you wanted a son."

"Before my knees go south and I can't throw a football."

"What if it's a girl?"

"Oh, God. Well, she better be a tomboy, have a good right arm, and be able to take a good hit."

He smiled. I smiled a little too.

He said, "So, Billie, now that we're being open, you've always wanted a baby."

"It's bigger than that, Keith. Deeper than that. My heart needs to feel connected to something. To have a purpose. And I might look twenty, but I'm not going to live forever. I have no one. Not even you. I've never had you. I have friends, but none of them really know me. I'm still a loner."

"Son or daughter, you'll never be alone, not as long as you allow me to be there for you."

"Thought you didn't have any more time."

"We make time for what matters the most. I grew up in South Central, baby. We know how to make the most out of having the least. We can make happen whatever we want to make happen."

In that moment I saw what I loved about him. I didn't care if he owned a Fortune 500 company or sold espressos at a kiosk. Wasn't about money. Or about sex. Well, the sex was devastating. But what I loved was plain and simple. He tried hard. He was a good guy. All good people had some bad in them, just like all bad people had some good in them. I'd seen the bad in him and I'd confessed the bad in me.

I said, "Carmen . . . your baby momma . . . she loves you . . . is obsessed with you, Keith."

I expected him to protest, but he agreed with a gentle nod.

I said, "Be kind to her. For your daughter."

"Sounds like you actually like her."

"Oh, hell, no. You told me she was an Aries. We're born to be enemies."

I wondered if there was any good in Carmen. She had some good in her. It wasn't on the surface. Sometimes I guess you had to dig deeper. Like to the other side of China.

I said, "Love . . . that drug makes us act crazy. Makes us fight. Makes us need to know things."

We were quiet for a moment. Listened to all the soda machines hum.

I said, "Your wife . . . I mean . . . Carmen . . . almost died."

"On that awkward note . . ." He wiped his eyes. "Guess I should go check on Carmen."

"Guess so." I was back to feeling like plastic. "Viviane and her family are in ICU with her sister."

"Some gangbangers jumped her?"

"Not clear on what happened." I took a breath. "They messed her face up real bad."

"Crazy world we're living in."

I shook my head. "It's not the world that's crazy. It's the people."

He stood up.

He said, "If anything like that happened to Destiny . . . God."

Head down, hands in his pocket, Keith headed toward the elevator, his pace anything but urgent.

Then he stopped, came back.

"Billie . . . got so caught up with everything . . . where is Destiny?"

"Uhhhh." I shrugged. "Haven't seen her since I dropped her off in front of the media circus."

"She left my apartment with Carmen. Wasn't she at home?"

"Carmen was . . ." I wondered if Carmen was alone. Then . . . the wedding dress . . . the video . . . the vibrator . . . those images answered my question. "Keith, I'm sure she said your daughter was with you."

"No, no, no." He shook his head, tried to become more sober. "She left with her mother."

"Carmen . . . trust me . . . she was alone." I shrugged. "Destiny . . . maybe . . . with her grandparents?"

"Carmen didn't trust her with her grandparents, not after all the shit we went through yesterday."

Back in panic mode, he took out his cellular. Dialed. Hung up.

He cursed. "They're not answering."

"Maybe everybody's already here, up in Carmen's room."

Keith left, this time his pace urgent.

I stood up, once again tense, once again wanting to fix this, wondering if he hated me.

Then wondering if God hated me. If He was on Carmen's side. If He was going to send down locusts and apocalyptic creatures, maybe shower a few biblical plagues on my Village of the Damned.

Lips tight, hormones blazing, I closed my eyes, shook my head.

I limped toward the elevator, ready to leave, then . . . damn . . . I didn't have a way home.

I had jacked Raheem's 749 and left it parked in front of Carmen's crib. Just hoped Raheem hadn't lost it and called the police. Shit. Whatever. Didn't really care if he called LAPD.

I stayed in the cafeteria, sipping cold coffee. Sat there hurting and crying and thinking and pissed off. Should've let the paramedics check me out after the accident. Should've limped up to the emergency room and taken a number. Was too scared to see a doctor. Didn't want to know. Denial was my friend. Wanted to go home. Lock my door. Turn the lights off and get into a fetal position. Cry. Scream.

Carmen's keys were in my pocket. Damn. Smelled her on my jacket, perfume had transferred when I carried her. Now she had invaded my world. Shit. Still had her cellular phone too. Both of those items were stuffed inside my scarred-up jacket. And my damaged helmet was locked inside her car.

Not that I could use it again, but I wanted to go get my helmet, then bring her keys and phone back, maybe leave them at the nurses' station. Didn't need to see her and Keith, not like that.

Just as I made my way out the door an SUV pulled up searching for a parking place. Any other day I wouldn't have noticed that gas guzzler. There were a thousand SUVs like that one on the streets.

The person behind the wheel was Carmen's mother. Miss *Ruthless*. Driving up in a white SUV. *White*. Just like the one that had stalked me from my home and tried to run me down the first time.

This felt surreal. Unreal.

I had been followed by a white SUV. Then run off the road by a black Benz.

In my mind I heard Carmen saying that one word.

We.

eighteen

BILLIE

FEAR ETCHED IN HER FACE, PURSE UNDER HER ARM, RUNNING LIKE SHE was at the last hundred yards of a 5K, Miss Ruthless sprinted into the hospital without noticing me. I never took my suspicion off her. She bolted past me, went to the security desk, panting, talking so fast her accent left the guard confused. She had to slow down her tongue. She got a badge. Sprinted for the elevators.

I left the hospital in severe pain. Had to look at that white SUV. My frown was so deep it hurt.

Went over and stopped in front of Carmen's car, leaned over in agony, her keys in my hand.

I had stolen a motorcycle. I'd already committed grand theft. Already had one strike.

I pointed the remote at Carmen's car. Lights flashed. Trunk unlocked. I cursed. Pushed another button. Lights flashed. Doors unlocked. I opened the door, stood there ready to earn what could be my second strike. If what I was thinking was true, would earn my third strike before sunrise.

Then somebody ran out of the hospital shouting at me.

That made me freeze up like I was a criminal.

It was the same nurse I had seen outside the emergency room earlier, the one with the back-length red braids. She was chasing me, pen and paper in hand. She still wanted my autograph, had been looking all over for me, happened to see me walking out, and ran to catch up with me.

She said, "Was crazy all last night."

"I bet."

"Soon as I got to work, some girl came in damn near blind. Somebody threw some corrosive fluids in her eyes. She didn't rinse it out in time. Plus she's so doped up it's ridiculous. She opened her purse and all these drugs fell out. Had to report her. The police will be all over her. We can't give her any meds until we get her blood work back. Then all those kids from Casura Bay came in here, messed up from when that rail collapsed. Kids who were broken up real bad. Now, few minutes ago, some young brother came in with his private parts . . . testicles blown off . . . penis damn near shot off. It was so mangled he'll be lucky if he can pee out what's left, much less get it to function. Medics said he got carjacked by some girl and she shot him in the genitals, left him in an alley down by Crenshaw and Slauson."

"Too bad."

"Good-looking brother, too." She scratched a colorful tattoo on her wrist. "What's too bad is he don't have any insurance."

Agony shot through my body and I grimaced.

She yawned. "You okay? Look like you pain."

"Don't matter." I shook my head. "No insurance."

She looked at the Benz, twisted her lips, and made a face like she thought I was full of shit.

I scribbled my club name on that wrinkled sheet of legal paper; she smiled, lit a Newport, the stench of cancer pluming around her head as she took her time about getting back inside to help the sick and wounded, at least those who could afford to be sick or wounded.

My eyes went toward the cemetery across the street. The one Carmen complained about.

Had to go. Morning would be lighting up graves soon.

I rocked that Benz from Prairie to Florence; L.A. was already congested with traffic. Hated being in a car. Couldn't white-line. Had to wait for drivers to speed up. I took out my cellular and tried to reach Viviane. Needed her right now because I was terrified, kept checking the rearview to see if the police were coming after me while I sped toward Crenshaw, let the windows down so I could breathe, called Viviane again as I made this four-wheel cage fly north to MLK. I drove by that house, turned right on Degnan, went back up to Crenshaw, then came back down MLK again.

Did that on purpose. I blended with traffic and went around the block, passed by that house twice before I got enough courage to stop.

Don't do this, Billie. I kept thinking, *Call the police. Or wait for Viviane to call you back. Don't do this alone.*

But I had to do it now. If I didn't ease my mind, after all I'd gone through, I'd go crazy.

Maybe I was crazy. Maybe I was.

I slowed down; pretty much stopped in the exact spot where I had dropped Destiny off, before I turned the headlights off and eased up in the driveway. The house Carmen grew up in. It was the darkest hour, right before dawn. Lights had been left on inside. I got out of the car, hurt for me to bend, but I did, I had to be sure. I got down on my haunches. Concrete driveway was damp. A thin trail of liquid heading toward the garage. I'd been riding for over two decades and even if I was blindfolded I knew the taste and smell of every automobile fluid the way I knew the difference between the scent and taste of an apple martini and a Tom Collins.

This was radiator fluid.

I stared at that house. Went back to Carmen's car. Got inside. Three buttons on the bottom of the rearview mirror. Those were programmable garage door openers. I pushed the first button. Nothing happened. Pushed the second one. Nothing. The third one. The garage door went up.

In the darkness the garage looked empty.

Yeah. I'd gone crazy. Nothing was here.

I put the car in reverse, had to leave before anybody saw me.

Then I smelled the tip of my finger. Tasted that diluted radiator fluid again.

I put the car back in park.

The lights inside that single-level home were on, but nobody should be there. Not with Carmen, their only child, hospitalized. As far as they knew, she was dying. They should be at the hospital in their pajamas.

My attention moved from the house to the concrete in front of me.

I followed the river of dampness on the ground.

That trail of radiator fluid led to the garage. I hit the bright lights, made them flash like lightning, used that flash to illuminate the darkness and reveal all silhouettes. There was a car in the garage. A car that was parked at an angle, one side lower than the other, like a dying elephant down on one knee, a car that had been covered up in a gray cover, and that gray cover had a black Mercedes-Benz logo.

Anything could be under that cover. An old Mustang. A broken-down-yet-classic Pinto.

But I didn't think a family that lived on Botox and Rolexes would keep a hoopty on standby.

A light in the back of the house came on. The back door opened. Then the gate.

He limped out in a hurry, raised his hands to cover his eyes, blinded by the headlights.

Carmen's father. Dressed in black pants, a sweater. Like he was about to leave.

If only I had waited ten more minutes.

He limped toward Carmen's car, toward me, grimaced, and called his daughter's name.

I swallowed.

"Carmen? You're here? Ruth . . . that you?" He had called out in a trembling voice. "What in the world is going on? Been calling the hospital over and over and the line in the room was . . ."

The crippled man saw it wasn't Carmen. Or Ruth. Bewilderment swooped down and covered his face. The grimace that had settled on my face, it floated through the crisp morning air, took up residence on his. Then fear changed into anger. Just like that his anger magnified, became unadulterated outrage.

Mouth wide open, eyebrows tense, he came closer. "You? Can't be you in mi child's car."

Inside a car. Behind doors and glass. Inside a cage. In pain. Unable to move the way I wanted to move. A trapped feeling came over me. I hurried, got out, left the lights on, engine purring.

Faced him.

"What on earth are you doing here in mi child's car?"

I kept my cool, said, "I need to see the car in your garage."

"Answer me. What are you doing in mi child's car?"

I moved. He hobbled my way, did his best to cut me off, his anger volcanic.

I said, "Call the hospital and ask her."

"What have you done to mi daughter?"

I moved. He moved again. Moved faster than I could move right now.

I said, "Look . . . just . . . just let me look in your garage and I'll be on my way."

"Keep away from mi wife's car. Get away now. Trespassing on mi private property."

The old man blocked me, fists doubled, chest out, letting me know he wouldn't back down.

I said, "You're right. I'm trespassing. Go in the house and call the police."

"Are you gone insane? Away from mi child's car. Get off mi property."

He wouldn't move. This was bigger than trespassing. Saw that in his indignant eyes. Behind all of that abrupt anger lived a well of trepidation. He was scared stiff. Protecting his nest at all costs.

My adrenaline was on high.

It was too late.

I'd been run down. Robbed. Left for dead. Didn't know if my baby was dead or alive. Then it hit me hard . . . reality that right now I could be walking around with a . . . that my unborn child . . . it might be dead.

That trail of radiator fluid that was in front of me.

That car covered up in that garage.

This old, crippled bastard standing between me and the truth.

I rushed toward the garage, growled, and rode my pain toward that car. He limped after me, moved so fast he got between me and the car, spun me around, then when I tried to get by him, he extended both of his hands, got in front of me, put his shoulder into me, and shoved me back. Pain had slowed me down. From my body through my heart, I ached so fucking bad. Wanted to fall to my knees, cry right then. Was so damn tired of crying. Worried about what I had done. While I struggled through that emotional moment, he grabbed at me, caught my jacket, and shoved me back toward the streets.

"Get your hands off me."

"Tired of hearing mi daughter cry because of you and your evil ways. Go now. Off mi property." He cursed me again. "You are the spawn of the devil's own strumpet, just like Keith has proven to be."

His face was clenched and stern as he pushed me. He pushed me harder than I'd ever been pushed before. I didn't back down. Bastard came back at me and shoved me so hard he lifted me off my feet and I flew toward the ground. The skies inside my mind turned light and dark as my hands went out to break my fall. I hit hard. Hands scraped the rough concrete. Got a bad case of road rash. Wrist might've been sprung. As hard as I hit the ground they could've been broken, just like my nails.

"Disgusting wretch. Home wrecker. *And fi dat mi bun a fire.* Last time . . . get off mi property."

I hurt too bad to scream. Felt stupid for not having my gloves on. He stood over me, his hands in fists; cursing me in an accent so thick I had no idea what he was shouting. Ears were ringing. That new agony created instant sweat, that sweat in my eyes. My hair had fallen free. I got it together, pulled my mane out of my face, looked up at him from the concrete, his expression just like mine, pure fire.

"Whore of Babylon. The Lord God Jehovah will guide mi hand in vengeance."

The day I met him, I had assumed he was a nice, peaceful man. Henpecked, maybe even cuckolded, but peaceful. He'd shed his sheep's clothing, glared down on me like he was a ravenous wolf.

That was when I saw it in his eyes.

We.

The way Keith felt about Destiny was the same way this man felt for his child.

We.

The same way my own father had felt about me.

He growled. "I should slit your throat, give you another mouth on your neck."

The bond between a father and daughter was strong; fathers would kill for their daughters.

We.

That crippled old man stood over me as I struggled to get up. Every time he moved, my body jerked, thinking he was about to kick me in my stomach. Hands hurt. Body hurt. Was too hard to get up, but when I did manage to stumble to my feet, that innate fight-or-flight part of my DNA kicked in strong and I hurried away from him. He followed, threatening to call the police.

My gloves were stuffed inside my helmet, left inside the trunk of Carmen's car. So was my backpack. That trunk was ajar, unlocked, never locked it when I drove away from the hospital.

He snapped, "Get away from mi child's automobile."

Before he could get to me, I yanked the trunk up. Inside my backpack was that brick.

I swung my backpack as hard as I could, that crippled bastard stumbling away from my rage.

I yelled, "Blood clot, *mi bun a fire* too. All you blood clots got *mi bun a fire*."

My hands throbbed, but I went after him, wild and swinging my backpack again, swung it until he stumbled back into the side of the house, kept swinging until he cowered and tripped, then hit him until he went down to the ground, kept swinging at him, not caring that he had raised his arm, kept hitting him.

Then a wicked spasm drop-kicked me, its epicenter right in my gut, made me bend in pain.

That agony and the throbbing in my scarred-up hands made me let go of my backpack.

Something shifted inside me. Or was swelling. Something bad was happening. I'd been running on adrenaline, and that adrenaline had been masking my hurting all evening, but now that adrenaline wasn't enough to keep me going. Couldn't breathe. Had become Carmen, struggling to stay alive.

That old bastard was cursing his way to his feet, more angry than before because he had been downed by a woman, threatening to come after me. Tried to move away, but another spasm stopped me where I stood. Couldn't stand the pain. The spasm was breaking me down, had become too much to bear. My own pain had shackled me. Crippled me. Had me panting against the trunk of Carmen's car.

Teeth were on the ground. False teeth that had a gold star in one of the eyeteeth.

That old man made it back to his feet, leaned against the house getting his wind. His mouth was bleeding pretty bad, looked deformed with his teeth on the ground. One of my wild swings had made contact and sent his dentures to the pavement. His face was bleeding too. He was an animal wounded.

And a wounded animal was a deadly thing. I knew because I was wounded too.

Horns blared out on MLK, right behind me. That disrupted my wrath. Road rage and the middle fingers of love flying early on a Sunday morning. An SUV made a hard left and sped up into the narrow driveway, bright lights zooming toward me, that SUV jerking like the driver wanted to get here as fast as she could. She wanted to run me down. Miss Ruthless had come back. I was frozen. Couldn't move. The SUV came to an abrupt, screeching halt. Not close to pinning me, but too close at the same time.

I felt the heat from that oversized cage, felt it breathing on me like a wild buffalo.

The door to the SUV opened. Was expecting to hear Miss Ruth's voice screech out. My eyes adjusted. That SUV was huge, wasn't white. Not the one I'd just seen Carmen's mother driving. This one was as dark as my mood. Bright lights were all over us. The door to the SUV closed.

A silhouette emerged. I closed and opened my eyes with the pain, looked again. Everything was blurry. Her ponytails became clearer. As did the Bambi eyes, same for the teeth that were a little too big for her young face.

Destiny.

A large, dark duffel bag was over Destiny's right shoulder, weighing that side of her body down.

Something about her was awkward, nonreactive to what she was witnessing: her grandfather with his teeth on the ground, me doubled over in pain, backpack at my feet. She was moving in slow motion, zigzagging steps. She staggered into the headlights. Her lips quivered as her eyes widened.

Her mouth opened, but not a sound was made as she stumbled by me like I wasn't there.

Her jacket and pants and T-shirt all looked like they were covered in a bucket of pig's blood.

She was Carrie at the end of the prom.

In her right hand, dangling from her fingers, was a razor, blood dripping from its blade.

nineteen

DESTINY

AN HOUR AGO THUNDER LIVED IN HER EARS.

Gun in her hand, that weapon pointed in the crotch of a boy who called himself Mo.

Destiny had pulled the trigger.

Mo screamed a scream that wouldn't end. He was so loud he scared the shadows out of the alleyway. She wanted him to stop screaming. Heart racing, her finger still on the trigger, tears in her eyes, desperation in her heart, Destiny stared at a fool who didn't deserve to live.

So many condoms had been on the floor.

Destiny clenched her teeth, pulled the trigger again. The gun bucked, but this time it was easier. She shot without hesitating. Hardly jumped when the bullet shattered the driver's-side window.

Destiny got out of the SUV, hurried to the driver's side. She opened the door. Mo had been leaning against the door, trying to get away from death. Now he fell fast and hard out of the SUV, landed face first on the uneven asphalt and broken glass, never letting go of the sacred place where he had been wounded. Blood. So much blood. Like he was on his period. Doubled over like he had cramps real bad. Endometriosis. She wondered if that's what women who had endometriosis looked like. If that was what they felt like. If that was how loud they yelled, like they were having a baby without medication.

Destiny said, "Shut up, Mo."

"Crazy bitch . . . you shot my dick . . . *shot my motherfucking dick* . . . oh God oh God."

"Stop using God's name, Mo, or I will shoot you again. I will. So shut up. Be quiet."

Head busted from falling out of the SUV, he bit his lip, muffled his sacrilegious and X-rated wails.

Now she had respect. Goldie would respect her. Mo would respect her.

If not respect, then fear would be okay. Either way, they would remember her.

The DVDs. The equipment. She needed all of that.

Destiny tried to step around Mo, around his grunts and tears, around piss and the river of blood, moved around all that to hurry to the trunk, to the DVDs, had to collect them, maybe dump them in a dumpster. No, she shook her head. She had to destroy them or else they would destroy her. She had to think, had to figure out how to dispose of them some other way. She had to dispose of them herself. And not here. Not in an alley. She had to go. She had to make it back home with that duffel bag.

That heavy duffel bag. A bag that Mo had lifted and carried away from Casura Bay with ease, but was too heavy for her to drag a hundred yards, let alone the two or three miles she was from . . . from . . .

She didn't know where she could go. Didn't have a key to her daddy's apartment. Couldn't slip inside her mother's home. Destiny felt trapped. Mad because she hadn't planned a damn thing.

One day she'd find the biracial girl. One day she'd look in the eyes of the girl who set her up.

A song came on. Startled Destiny. A Snoop Dogg ringtone: "Beautiful."

On the ground near Mo. His cellular was lighting up, vibrating, dancing. Destiny picked up the phone, flipped it open, saw the image of the black-mixed-with-Mexican girl on the screen, face looking beautiful and hard all at once, throwing up her middle finger, bottle of Hypnotiq in hand.

First God had delivered her a weapon. Now Verizon was giving her what she needed.

Her grandmother had said that all you had to do was ask. That was all you had to do.

Destiny answered the phone, but didn't say anything.

"Mo, where the hell you at with all my shit?"

Female voice. Spanish accent. Sirens in the background. Still in the hood.

Destiny wanted to be sure. She said, "Lupe?"

"Goldie?"

"Not Goldie."

"Who the hell this answering Mo phone?"

"Nobody. I ain't nobody."

"Well, Nobody, put Mo on the phone."

"Mo can't get to the phone now."

"Tell him I ain't got time to be playing."

"Mo want to know if you got out before the police showed up."

"Bitch, you think I'd be on the phone with you if I didn't?"

"Just asking a question."

"Give Mo the goddamn phone."

"He wants to know where he can meet you."

"He know where the spot is."

"He said to ask you so he can be sure."

"What?"

"*Where*, bitch? Mo said quit bullshitting and tell a nigga where the fuck you at."

Lupe told Destiny where she was. All it took was using their language.

Destiny said, "Mo said he's on the way."

"Tell that nigga to hurry his ass up."

Destiny hung up the cellular. Scowled down at Mo. Mouth moving but no sound. Pain had stolen his voice. So much blood. Like he was on his period. Cringing like he had endometriosis.

His faced begged her, asked for mercy, for help. Destiny walked away.

"Get over it," Destiny mumbled. "Get the fuck over it."

She climbed back into the SUV. Started the engine. Pushed buttons to find the headlights. Pushed the wrong buttons. The DVD came back on. Saw what she wanted to never see and hear ever again. Moans and groans and a hot soundtrack. Showed a girl with her eyes glazed over as she was being sexed doggie-style, on her hands and knees, looking back at the camera, the room filled with naked men, all of their faces blurred. The camera close on her face. Then the nasty shot. The come shot. All the young men chanted, *Skeet skeet motherfucker skeet skeet*. The dull-eyed girl became a smiling face glazed with protein. Frantic, Destiny hit the power button, turned that off. Took a minute, but she found the lights. Turned them on. Fumbled with the gears. Put it in drive. Gave it some gas. Went too fast. Scraped the dumpster in the alley. Heard a sharp scream. Slammed on the brakes. Looked out the shattered window. She had run over Mo's leg. It looked twisted, deformed. She cursed. Wished she had her permit. Or had taken driving lessons. But she was only fifteen. With a duffel bag of DVDs that she didn't want anybody to see. She tried again. Told herself she could do this. Hands at ten and two, the way her grandmother always drove. Easy on the gas. Maybe keep the other foot over the brake in case she needed to stop real fast. SUV seemed so huge. She told herself that she could drive. She had to.

She gave it some gas. Felt like she was going over a speed bump. Mo screamed again.

Destiny drove down Slauson, went east, then turned on Figueroa, went north.

At every light, every time she stopped, Destiny saw them all, creatures of the night.

Men stood in the shadows, waiting for someone to slow and buy their product.

Women stood in the shadows, waiting for someone to support their habits.

The street looked like bad news. Then Destiny saw the flashing lights. LAPD.

So many flashing lights. More flashing lights coming from both directions.

The gun was at her side. She wished she had thrown the gun away.

She slowed down. Shifted in her seat. Felt sticky. She touched the seat. Looked at her hand. Blood. Mo's blood was all over the seat. On her fingers. She wiped her hands on her clothes.

Now blood was all over her top. She was sitting in Mo's blood.

She swerved, wanted to scream, but got the SUV under control.

She raised her right foot off the accelerator, pushed her left foot down on the brake.

She stopped so fast, equipment, bags, other things in the back of the SUV flew to the front.

Blood was on her hands. On her clothes.

The police were behind her.

The flashing lights zoomed right by her. Stopped not too far ahead.

Destiny was terrified when she saw so many police cars up ahead.

Cars were behind her. She couldn't turn around. Didn't think she drove good enough to make a U-turn. Had only driven around the parking lot at the forum. In her daddy's SUV. Saturdays. Daytime. She knew she could drive straight, turn left when cars weren't coming, or turn right, then she was okay.

Flares were out on the street.

An ambulance was up there too.

And bikers. They were congregated on both sides of the streets. A few out in the street, acting like they were police officers, directing traffic. So many bikers. Men. Women. Most of them standing out in the streets crying. Some on cellular phones, some on Nextel, all shouting, pained looks on their faces.

"Biker down, biker down." The voice of agony. *"We're on Figueroa."*

Others were holding each other, consoling each other, and crying.

Destiny recognized a couple of the distraught faces. She had seen them at Starbucks last night.

The cool girls in the sexy clothes who did crazy stunts on their motorcycles.

One motorcycle was down. Middle of the street. Wrecked real bad. Not pretty anymore.

Feet away from the motorcycle was a BMW, the passenger side damaged.

Skid marks all over the street.

Somebody had hit somebody real abrupt and real hard.

Police were talking to a white woman, the driver of the BMW, Destiny assumed. That woman was frantic, pointing at the bikers in a very accusatory way, then at her BMW, hands moving all over the place.

Hysterical.

Paramedics on their knees, working on the injured biker. Destiny looked that way long enough to see the girl's long hair. Long enough to see that the motorcycle was beautiful, the color of indigo. Everything else on the motorcycle sparkled, was silver. The prettiest motorcycle she had ever seen. Destiny stared at the tragedy long enough to see the girl wasn't moving.

Hands shaking at ten and two, she kept going.

She had handled that situation. Proud of herself for driving this far by herself.

Destiny had seen all she needed to see.

The girl on the motorcycle was probably dead.

The girl on the motorcycle wasn't Billie.

She wished it had been.

People flashed their bright lights. Sped around her, flipping her off, cursing her, blew horns because she was driving the speed limit, going too slow. Or changing lanes too much, trying to get out of people's way. Mean people. L.A. was filled with so many mean people. And so many police. She never noticed that many police cars when she rode with her mother. Now they were everywhere. Zooming this way. Cruising that way. Her sojourn took forever. She drove slow, stayed in the right lane, got caught by every traffic light. Or maybe she slowed down before she got to the lights, scared of intersections.

Plotting how to get home. She couldn't go to her mother's house. No way she could pull this off.

Maybe she'd sit on her daddy's porch until sunrise. Then tell him that he had locked her out, that she had knocked awhile, that he didn't hear because he was drunk, that she fell asleep. She could take the DVDs and video equipment, dispose of all of that in the alley behind her father's apartment, back there by the parking garages that not many of the tenants used. Too dangerous to be in an alley in L.A.

People get robbed in alleys. Raped in alleys. Killed in alleys.

Raped for entertainment. Videotaped for profit.

That ache was still there. That reminder that she was not done.

She had done it. She had shot a man. A soulless boy who wanted to be a man, actually.

He had taken her dignity. She had taken his Escalade. A nice Escalade.

Too big for her taste, but nice. So many enemies. And her daddy's girl-friend. Destiny still had a pocket filled with pills.

The Kill Pill would kill Billie's dream of blackmailing her family. Would keep her family alive.

Her mother would understand. Her father would forgive her. Her grandparents would be happy.

All she had to do was figure out how to convince Billie to take the pills.

Destiny was coming up on USC. Her mother's alma mater. Hands locked at ten and two, hardly looking in the rearview mirror, she'd done real good. Had driven parallel to the 110 freeway and made it to the edges of downtown L.A. Had made it to a stone's throw from the East Side, where her daddy grew up. Where her uncle Jody was killed robbing a bank. An uncle she never knew. Her daddy would be proud of her. If he knew. If she could tell him. She wiped away a few tears. Turned left and went down Jefferson, one foot over the accelerator the other covering the brake, hands still locked at ten and two, scared to move her hands and wipe away her tears, and headed toward North University Park. Then made a right, headed toward that strip that housed fast-food places. Spudnuts. Star-bucks. Wendy's. Denny's was on the corner of Jefferson and Figueroa. Next door to Flagship Theaters.

The college town was dark. She couldn't tell if Denny's was open.

She almost panicked. Thought she had come to the wrong Denny's. Destiny slowed down in front of the Jewish Center, tried to spy across the street, tried to see if anyone was in that parking lot.

There she was. Lupe. Rushing out of Denny's, cellular to her face, smoking a cigarette, pacing and venting, too busy flipping her hair and yelling into her cellular to see her coming, probably too busy screaming about what had just happened at Casura Bay, telling them how hell had broken loose.

Too busy to notice her own personal hell had just arrived on twenty-twos, wheels spinning.

Lupe. The girl she hardly noticed Friday night. The girl who encouraged that other girl to jump on her. Lupe. So friendly and reserved after Destiny got inside the Escalade Friday night. The quiet one. The one in charge. So lean. Almost six feet tall in her three-inch heels. Hair long, hanging down over her shoulders. Take away a few pimples, she too could pass for a model. Wearing Apple Bottom jeans, tight, low-rise, posing like she hoped Nelly would pull up and drop her in his next video. Despite the chill of the night, she held her pink puff jacket at her side, did that like she wanted the attention her statuesque figure would garner, had on a tight wife-beater, cut to show off her stomach. Scissored right below her big breasts. Black wife-beater, silver letters across her huge breasts. KANYE WAS RIGHT.

Destiny felt like Lupe saw her. No. Windows were tinted. Like a limousine. She had seen the Escalade, its rims spinning. Lupe waved at the truck, waved for Mo, her hand saying to stop.

Part of Destiny told her to keep going, to find her way home.

She drove away, passed by the movie theater, headed toward the parking lot in the village that housed Spudnuts and Wendy's. Snoop Dogg's song about Brazil woke up Mo's cellular. Lupe's drunken face popped up on the screen. "Beautiful." Her ringtone. Mo must've thought she was beautiful.

Destiny pushed the green button, put the phone to her ear.

Lupe shouted, "Mo, why you drive by me like that?"

"Mo said the spot too hot. Five-O been behind us since we left Casura Bay."

"Who this?"

"Nobody. I ain't nobody."

"Look, tell Mo to turn around and bring me my equipment so I can get back to my dorm room."

"Mo said get your Mexican ass down here."

She snapped, "He said *what*?"

"Mo said walk your Mexican ass down here."

There was a pause. Destiny knew she had said the wrong thing.

Lupe snapped, "I ain't no wetback."

"My bad."

"Mo knows I ain't no goddamn Mexican." Now insulted to the max. "I'm from *Tegucigalpa*."

"That's not in Mexico?"

"Honduras, dumb-ass."

Not black-mixed-with-Mexican. From a Third World country Destiny knew nothing about.

Lupe ranted, "Why does everybody think everybody who speaks Spanish is a damn Mexican?"

It reminded Destiny of the fury her grandmother had when a woman asked if she was from Haiti. It reminded her of the Korean woman who was arguing with Mo at Casura Bay.

Lupe raged, "Don't let Mo end up getting your ass whooped."

"So . . . you're from Central America and now you go to USC? What, an exchange student?"

There was a pause that owned as much chill as the air.

Lupe snapped, "Who the hell is this all up in my bidness?"

Destiny didn't answer. Too busy aching and wiping the tears from her eyes.

Lupe. "Where the fuck Mo at?"

"Look, bitch, Mo said gas ain't free. Neither are his rims. Mo got all of your DVDs and equipment out before Five-O showed up, so the least you could do is walk your lazy ass down here where it's safe."

Destiny pressed the red button on the cellular.

Confused. Scared. Anger rising and falling in waves. Couldn't stop crying. Couldn't let go.

Part of her hoped Lupe ran the other way, that she sensed something was wrong and left.

But Lupe was sashaying her way, jacket in hand, back on her cellular, lighting a cigarette.

Her pace was so casual. So damn casual. As if nothing bad had happened to anybody tonight. As if nothing bad had happened to Destiny Friday night. As if nothing bad could ever happen to her.

College student. At USC. A university she wouldn't be able to attend because of Billie's greed.

That pissed Destiny off even more. Billie was blackmailing them. Billie's jealousy would change her life for the worse. Destiny wondered if there were any true friendships between girls.

Boys fucked you. Girls fucked you over.

Destiny told herself to leave. To get the hell out of their world. To be done with this madness.

She told herself that she wasn't like her mother. Her mother was unable to let go, even when she knew she should. Destiny told herself that this was different. That she was different.

Lupe was getting closer, hanging up her cellular, putting on her puff jacket.

Even the cold-blooded got cold. Strange seeing a reptile in a designer coat and Apple Bottoms.

Condoms left on the floor. Tossed. The way they had tossed her. The way they left her behind.

She had been nobody to them. *Nobody*.

That ache, the persistent throbbing between her legs.

Destiny saw her reflection in the rearview. Eyes swollen and red. Tears had rained down and soaked her T-shirt. THROW ROCKS AT BOYS. She wondered what needed to be thrown at girls.

So many mean girls in the world. So many manipulative, envious, resentful mean girls.

Closer. Lupe was getting closer. Destiny saw her as she crossed under a streetlight. Her skin dark and sexy. Highlights in her shoulder-length hair. With each step getting closer to her destiny.

The gun slept at Destiny's side. That gun's explosion had been so loud, like thunder. The gun had scared her, had left her heart pounding and hands trembling.

The razor. Destiny remembered the razor. She took the razor out of her backpack. Sliced it across the leather seat. The luxury seat split open with hardly any effort, without a moan or a sigh.

Destiny left the engine running. The sensor beeped as she slipped out. She closed the door, moved toward the rear of the Escalade. Hidden from the streets by that big black elephant with spinning rims. Now she was glad the oversized SUV owned the shade of midnight, matched the color of betrayal.

The evil people did to one another . . . Destiny just didn't understand why it was so hard to be nice.

She heard heels clicking toward her at an even pace, like the tick-tock of a clock.

Tears in her eyes, Destiny kept her face turned away, in the shadows, that razor tight in her hand.

Her hand was trembling. Shaking so bad she almost let the razor fall. Almost.

Goldie had done her wrong without remorse. She was a sociopath. So was Mo.

Now the girl from Tegucigalpa, the sociopath who called herself Lupe, was a few feet away.

She stopped walking, started dancing, arms bent, jerky movements, chanted Mo's theme song.

"Do the Mo, do the Mo, do the Mo . . ."

Destiny's eyes went to the silhouette of the razor.

That throbbing reminded her of what had been stolen from her, taken without second thoughts.

Goldie. Mo. What was done could not be undone.

No matter how deep the regret, nothing could be undone.

The heels stopped tick-tocking toward her. The clock had stopped. It was time to decide.

She felt Lupe's energy. Right behind her. Smoking a cigarette.

"Where Mo at?"

Lupe tapped her shoulder.

Destiny jerked. Lupe had owned the nerve to put her finger on her.

That touch reminded her of how people had violated her last night.

She felt their hands on her body. She felt the strangers inside her body. That simple contact. Fire to dynamite. Nitroglycerin mishandled.

Without a word, Destiny spun around, face filled with rage, her razor slicing through Lupe.

twenty

BILLIE

HEADLIGHTS WERE IN MY EYES. INSIDE THAT STUCCO HOUSE OF EVIL, THE phone started ringing.

Sweat covered my face, dripped down into my eyes.

Inside my pocket, my cellular phone started vibrating.

And Destiny was standing between her grandfather and me, holding a bloody razor.

She looked at her grandfather, at me, then back at him, at me again, all of that in slow motion.

Her eyes settled on that crazy old bastard.

Her grandfather was on his feet, stumbling and catching his balance against his house. I did the same, leaning against Carmen's car, managed to get my swollen fingers around the strap on my backpack.

He stared at me, ready to attack. I did the same, waiting to see which way this was going. I wouldn't fight him, not in front of Keith's daughter. But I wasn't going to let him push me around either.

We stared. Headlights covered us and we stared.

Destiny watched. Confused.

That old man hobbled toward his grandchild, his face swollen and bloodied from our battle. He wasn't thinking about me right now. Or his injuries. His concern had turned and gone somewhere else.

To a girl whose clothes were bloodied. To a fifteen-year-old girl who held a razor in her hand.

To family.

We.

"What happened to you, child?"

"Paw Paw . . . what . . . where are your teeth?"

That old bastard made it to his false teeth, picked them up, wiped them against his shirt.

"What are you doing driving that *ting*?"

"Daddy's girlfriend . . . she's here."

"Is that blood? Are you hurt, child?"

Hair in ponytails. Blood splattered and smeared on her clothes.

Destiny took a step toward me. That razor loose in her hand.

In the sweet voice of surprise she said, "Billie. You're here."

The sweet way she said my name terrified me more than her grandfather's rage. She saw my wounded and horrified expression, then looked at her own hand. Her eyes widened like she remembered.

She let the razor go, jerked like she had been hit with electricity and dropped the razor.

Again she looked at me, at her grandfather.

Destiny's grandfather hurried to her. He bent over, picked up what she had dropped, looked it over, then stood in her face. She wasn't there. When he touched her it was as if she came to life.

They spoke in mumbles as he took her hand, rushed back toward the house.

Destiny looked back at me as he dragged her, said, "Billie's here."

The gate squeaked open. The back door opened fast and closed hard.

Shouting. He was shouting in a tone that was beyond hysterical. His accent was too thick and his words were so fast that I didn't have the slightest idea what he was saying.

All I knew for sure was that the crazy old man wasn't happy.

I should've gotten away from there as fast as I could. I couldn't. My eyes were on the garage.

The back door opened and slammed so hard it sounded like a shotgun had gone off. That crazy old man ran back through the squeaky gate, hobbled out with a yellow bucket in his hand. He stumbled, dropped the bucket. A roll of paper towels and what looked like a liquid cleanser tumbled out of the container. When he bent over, I saw a pair of plastic gloves tucked in his back pocket. He gathered what he had dropped, then paused long enough to frown at me. He saw that I was watching him.

"Leave mi home now."

I shook my head. "Not while *mi bun a fire*."

He stood there, his face contorted like he was struggling to make a choice. He stepped toward me. Then the wail of sirens in the distance made him stop and look toward the streets.

Bucket in hand, he hobbled away from my glare. The Escalade was his focus. His tunnel vision. It didn't make sense. None of this registered. I was too busy trying to swim through my agony and figure out my own problems. My own tunnel vision had become the bright lights aimed directly at my eyes.

He struggled, climbed inside the Escalade, and cranked it up, revved the engine.

He turned the headlights off. An eerie move. That meant he was about to run me down, pin me between that truck and Carmen's car. The gears engaged. Then the SUV reversed at a bad angle, scraped the side of the house hard. He pulled forward, backed up again, barely made it out the driveway. I didn't know where he was rushing to, but I knew he wasn't going to the hospital to see about his sick daughter, not with a yellow bucket and cleanser. Not with the headlights off. Not without Destiny.

Not with me standing in the middle of his driveway.

Just like that he was gone.

The world was quiet again. Heard traffic on MLK. Smelled doughnuts at Krispy Kreme.

The garage. It was there, nothing between me and what I wanted to see.

I took a step. Pain took me down to my knees. Then I had to sit.

Whirrr. Crunch.

Wanted to lie down and ball up in a knot.

Whirrr. Crunch.

That mechanical sound followed by the echo of destruction kept repeating over and over.

One minute. Maybe two.

Whirrr. Crunch. Whirrr. Crunch. Whirrr. Crunch.

Seemed like forever went by before the pain in my gut eased up. Tried to stand, but I needed to lean on something to get all the way up.

Whirrr. Crunch.

When I did, I got my backpack.

Whirrr. Crunch.

Teeth clenched, sweat all over my face, I took a few short steps. The bulk of the hurting hadn't vacated the building. I didn't make it to the end of the driveway before I dropped my backpack. Struggled to pick it up. With the road rash on my hands, that took me an eternity.

Whirrr. Crunch.

Fingernails had been broken. Each finger felt like it was suffering from severe heartache.

Whirrr.

Crunch.

Crying. Sounded like I heard crying.

I kept hearing those sounds over and over.

That mechanical *whirr.*

That *crunch*ing sound.

More sobbing.

That endless cycle of destructive noises and sorrow came out of the back of the house.

The *whirr* startled me. Not at first. Its pace and frequency did something to my nerves.

Disrupted my journey to the truth.

The terrible *crunch*ing made me want to run.

But it was the mourning sound that made me stop my retreat.

In a pained voice I called out, "Destiny?"

Whirrr. That horrible *crunch*ing sound. More crying.

The crying rose and fell, the pitch of a child, then there was the gurgling, like Destiny was taking in gulps of air, drowning in her own tears.

Again I called out, "Destiny?"

Whirrr. That horrifying *crunch*ing echoed. The crying escalated.

I made my way toward the gate, opened it, then crept up to the back door.

Destiny was sitting at a chair in the kitchen, a kitchen painted in bright yellows and greens.

Whirrr. That *crunch*ing sound. More crying.

The duffel bag she had rested at her feet. I stood at the bottom of the porch, leaned against the door, watched her dig in that duffel bag and dump out a stack of DVDs, watched them scatter on the butcher-block table. She didn't notice me, moving inside her own world. A world that made no sense to me. She was rushing, anxious, snatching DVDs out of their jewel cases, the jewel cases crashing to the floor, frantically stuffing the DVDs inside an industrial-type document shredder. Had to be the kind with cutters made of solid, hardened steel. The shredder ate the DVDs without any complaint or hesitation.

More DVDs. More jewel cases crashing to the kitchen floor.

The *whirrs* ended.

That crunching stopped.

The sobbing continued.

I took a breath, said, "Destiny?"

She jumped up from the table, eyes wide, hands in fists. Saw me. Opened her hands. Looked down at herself. At the mess around her. Then she straightened her clothes, wiped her eyes.

I asked, "What's going on?"

"Nothing."

I turned around, headed toward the garage. Made it a few steps. Had a spasm.

Went down again.

Destiny rushed back outside. "Don't leave."

"I'm not leaving."

One of her braids was down. She had changed clothes. Had on a white skirt and flip-flops, a wrinkled T-shirt that said KATRINA WHO? She took measured steps toward me, almost smiling.

She said, "Let me help you."

I looked up at her, unsure. Then I saw in her childlike eyes what I'd seen in Keith's warm eyes. Love and kindness. The essence of a gentle spirit. I saw the twenty-plus chromosomes he'd given her.

The same chromosomes he'd blended with my egg and my own chromosomes.

She helped me to my feet. Fury resumed and I broke away from her. My eyes on that garage.

She wiped her eyes and asked, "Where are you going?"

Grunting, I went back to my original mission, the sound from her flip-flops following, her pace still measured and strange. She didn't try to stop me. I stood in front of that covered car, no one blocking my way. Heat was still rising from its engine. That trail of radiator fluid leading to that same engine, like following the trail of blood that led to a wounded animal. So many animals had been wounded tonight.

She moved, still using those measured steps. I saw her clench her teeth and grimace.

The steps weren't measured. She was in pain. Pain recognized pain.

My brain tried to sum up all I had seen. The total didn't make any sense.

I asked, "What happened to you?"

"Nothing."

"Are you injured?"

"Why would you ask me that?"

"You had blood on your clothes."

"No, I didn't."

"Then why did you run in the house and change clothes?"

"I always change clothes."

"When you got out of the SUV . . . thought I saw . . . was that a knife in your hand?"

"Fingernail file."

"Why were you in the kitchen crying?"

"I wasn't crying."

"I saw you. Look . . . I'm not crazy, dammit. I just saw you crying."

"I'm crying because . . ." Her voice trembled. "Paw Paw said that my mother's in the hospital."

That caught me off guard. Me and her mother in that hallway, that scene ran though my mind.

I said, "Your daddy was looking for you, did you know that? He thought you were with your mother and your mother thought—"

"She thought I was with my daddy. I know."

"Well, you should call him on his cellular, let him know you're okay, tell him where you are."

She didn't answer. A new kind of worry crawled across her face.

With swollen fingers, I tugged the car cover back. Had a hard time. Couldn't get it up over the tires without losing my grip. Was about to give up. Then Destiny helped. That surprised me.

Wanted to scream. Wanted to cry. But I just took a hard breath, chills running over my body.

Destiny said, "Your fingers are bleeding."

It was a Benz. Dark in color. I limped around the car. Saw it was wrecked on the right side, headlight destroyed, the sideview mirror gone, red and green paint all over the damaged fiberglass. Could still feel the heat, felt all of the hate rising from that one-eyed monster. The stench of leaking radiator fluid surrounded me, the fumes of envy.

I wasn't crazy. The truth overwhelmed me.

Destiny saw the damage and panic rose in her fragile voice. "What happened to the car?"

"Destiny . . . I need you to call nine-one-one for me."

"What happened? Just tell me what—"

"*Listen to me.* I need you to go inside the house and call the police. Do that right now."

She took off running, went back inside the house.

First a light came on, brightened up an opaque window on the side of the house.

Then the light went off.

I heard more *whirr*s. More *crunch*ing.

I stared at the end of the driveway, expecting that old man to show up.

The *whirr*s stopped. The *crunch*ing ceased.

Destiny came back out, wiping her eyes, those steps still measured, each step with the echo of pain. She had brought some things with her. A roll of paper towels and a bottle of peroxide.

She swallowed her emotions. "Hold your hands out."

"You call the police?"

"Yeah. Called 'em. They're coming."

"Thanks. Hate to get you in the middle of this shit."

"What's going on?"

"I have to go. Need to be out front when the police get here."

"Just hold your hands out. It could get infected."

I did what she told me to do. Wanted my hands to be okay. Had to be able to play my Takamine. Had to get onstage with Sy and Simfani and Chante Carmel and Inobe and Hope and all the sisters who were doing it. Had to. Destiny poured the peroxide over my scratched-up flesh, watched it sizzle over my bloodied fingers. She dabbed my hands with a paper towel. Each touch hurt like hell, but I didn't let it show. Just bit down real hard and tried to ride to the other side of that agony. I wouldn't be able to play anything decent on my Takamine, not for a while, not with my hands and fingers aching like this.

They had destroyed my Ducati. Now they were taking away my music. My baby.

When you lost something, you realized how bad you wanted it, how you had taken it for granted.

Destiny grabbed a small tin container. She had Band-Aids, gauze, other bandages too.

Abdominal pains came. I was scared. Didn't want to check for bleeding or spotting. Not here.

I said, "Listen to me, Destiny. The police will be here in a minute."

She shivered. "Uh-huh."

"Your grandfather jumped on me."

"He . . . Paw Paw . . . he said you attacked him."

"You see that car? It has red and green paint on the side. Paint that came from two other cars. And a broken sideview that will match the one left in Santa Monica."

"He said you came over here and jumped on him."

"Destiny . . . this car in your garage . . . it will tell the story."

"Be still."

She put the bottle of peroxide and paper towels to the side, helped me dress my wounds, wrapped both my hands with gauze. It was a sloppy job, but better than nothing. When she finished, she stuck her hand in her pocket, took out a plastic bottle of Aleve. She stared at it, shook it, made it rattle.

She said, "Billie . . . you . . . you . . . maybe should take one of these."

"What were you doing? Those DVDs."

"Nothing. Just some old movies. That's all."

"Your mother's in the hospital and you're sitting in the kitchen by yourself shredding old movies?"

"People do strange things when they're . . . when they're . . ."

"Stressed?"

"Yeah. When they are stressed out to the max. People do strange things."

"Your mother . . . she . . . she had an asthma attack. A real bad one."

She asked, "If your mother was in the hospital having an asthma attack, would you cry?"

"I . . . I . . . yeah. I would."

"Then its okay for me to cry."

Her logic, that kind of messed with me. I nodded. "I have to get away from here."

"When they get here . . . what are you going to tell the police?"

"The truth."

"I need to know what happened."

"When they see that wrecked car . . . this is bigger than you know."

She looked from the car to me, very confused, scared, so damn uneasy.

In her eyes I saw glimpses of Carmen. Of Miss Ruthless. Saw the edges of her that came from the Ain't Right crew. Then a chill ran over me, told met that that crazy old bastard had told Destiny to keep me here until he got back. That maybe he had zoomed away to get something to hurt me. Or a six-by-nine rug to roll my body inside. I was in the middle of a familial conspiracy.

Staying here was stupid, but I was running on endless pain, unbridled anger, and wild hormones.

Part of me wanted that old man to get back before the police showed up. Wanted to see his face when he saw his secret uncovered. Wanted to finish what we had started. Wanted to give him my pain.

But my pain was so great, I knew I'd lose that battle, then lose this war.

Had to get up. Had to get up and get to the end of the driveway, wanted to be out front so I could flag the LAPD down. Wanted to make sure I had my part of the story right, that I was only bringing Carmen's car to her parents' house and that old bastard attacked me. And I happened to see that wrecked Benz in the garage. Fuck that. He assaulted me. I came here in his daughter's car and that lunatic assaulted me. My mind told me that I needed to get away from this house, maybe see if I could get across MLK and wait. But the pain told me I'd be lucky to make it a house or two away.

Pain won that argument, rooted me where I sat, held me captive right here in the driveway of the man who had tried to kill me. Fingers hurt so bad.

Destiny shivered. "One of these . . . will . . . should . . . might . . . make things better."

I motioned at the Aleve. "Will take more than one of those to make me feel better."

She wiped her eyes.

I said, "Not sure if I should be taking any meds."

She nodded. "Daddy told me you're pregnant."

"Yeah."

I was being positive. Claiming what I wanted to be true, even if it was just a dream.

Destiny stared at the bottle of Aleve for a moment, thinking, then took two pills out. I wasn't really paying attention, my mind still stuck on the fact that I'd been run down, my bike totaled, and the motherfucker who tried to kill me had just run off in a big black SUV. Didn't make sense.

She mumbled, "More than one."

I asked, "What you say?"

"You were right. More than one. Should take more than one."

The Aleve, Destiny shook them in her hand, bit her bottom lip as she stared at her feet. Swallowed two pills dry. She shook two more pills out of the bottle. Handed them to me.

She smiled a pained smile. I gave her the same tight smile in return. Even smiling hurt.

Should've stayed at the hospital. Should've checked in, let them look me over after I crashed.

Destiny said, "Did you hear that she killed her baby?"

"What baby?"

"The girl who lives across the street from my daddy, the girl whose baby cried all the time. Her name was Davina. Davina had a little boy. She killed her baby. Drowned her little boy in the bathtub. It was crazy. Happened last night. The police handcuffed her. Took her away. Her baby daddy, he went crazy. He found the baby drowned in the bathtub."

"Last night?"

"Few hours ago." Her lips trembled. "Do you think that was a sign?"

"Postpartum depression. Had to be. Sister was stressed."

"What, you don't believe in God?"

"Personally, I would hate to think that a woman drowning a defenseless baby was a sign."

"Why?"

"Because every human life is . . . *sacred*. Life is . . . special. Shit. Her baby . . . dead? That's jacked."

I put my wounded hands on my belly, cradled whatever was inside me, alive or gone.

Destiny sat there shaking her head, confused.

Looked like a police car passed by. No lights on. No sirens. Cruising.

I wanted to get up and walk to the end of the driveway. Tried. Abdominal cramps hit me again.

I took the pills in my swollen hand. Held them with my fingers open. Didn't want to take any medication. But I had to do something to get the edge of this agony to dissipate. The misery and throbbing that went through my body came at me from all angles, screamed out for immediate relief. My puffed-up fingers needed something to take the edge off right now. I brought my hand up to my mouth.

I said, "Good looking out."

She was looking down at her feet. Shaking her head. Sounded like she was crying.

I swallowed, then asked, "You okay?"

She wiped her eyes. "Momma will understand. Daddy'll forgive me. Everybody will be happy."

Cold morning air moved across us, air almost as chilly as her tone had become. Her lips were trembling. Her young face so flushed. Eyes so damn red. Looked like she was floating in and out of a trance. I pulled away from my own angst and anger, focused on her right then. She rocked, shook her head, mumbled, tugged her hair. I mean she yanked her hair like she was trying to pull it all out.

Her voice cracked, "The world is . . . wrong."

"What do you mean?"

"Earthquakes. Hurricanes. That dead baby."

Destroying DVDs. Crying nonstop. Shivering. Breaking down. The kid was breaking down.

"And I just saw the other girl." She closed her eyes. "She was dead. That was a sign too."

"What dead girl?"

"She was in a car accident. Dead on the streets." She rocked and cried. "That was a sign too."

First Carmen almost went code blue on me, then her grandfather's bun caught fire, now this shit.

She went on rambling about dead babies and dead women. Had to get away from her.

I made it to my feet, the pain barely under control. I mean *barely*. Two steps later the book tumbled out of my pocket. *The Alchemist*. Tried to bend. Couldn't. Destiny picked up the book.

She asked, "You're jacking my mother's book?"

"That's mine. Her book is inside her car."

"Are you stealing, Billie?"

"Look inside her car. No matter what you think or heard, I don't take from people. I don't steal."

"My mother said that you were trying to steal our money."

Her dark tone shook me up. "What?"

"She said you were stealing my college money."

"What?"

"You're blackmailing us." She wiped her eyes. "Because you're pregnant."

"I don't want your mother's money. Your mother came to my job and offered me money."

She raised her voice. "Don't lie on my mother."

"She offered me money."

"Liar."

"She came to my job . . . offered me . . . Shit."

"Liar."

"This is crazy."

Destiny shivered again, like something inside her had gone cold. The poor child looked confused again. Like clouds were coming in on her mental landscape. That darkness moving away.

She emphasized, "Now you're stealing my mother's book."

"Do I look like I give a shit about that book? You want it? Take it."

"Somebody gave it to her for a birthday present and you're stealing it."

"The police should be here by now."

"Enough has been . . . taken. It's like . . . *rape*. I can't let anybody . . . rape us. You can't rape us."

"What is your problem?"

"That's my mother's book."

"Didn't I just tell you that your mother's book is in her car?"

"And you just happen to have the same book?"

Her measured steps took her to her mother's car. She looked in the window. Her expression changed when she saw that I wasn't a thief.

She said, "I'm sorry."

"I'm not a thief, little girl."

"Please forgive me. Let me help you."

Her words floated by me as she tucked the book inside my jacket. She did that with an apologetic face. I limped away from her.

She followed me. I wanted her to leave me the hell alone and she followed me.

She asked, "You having a boy or a girl? Will I have a brother or a sister?"

Her voice had become sincere. That slowed me down. My voice cracked. "Don't know. Too soon to tell."

I made it to the back end of her mother's car, remembered my helmet was still in the trunk, that trunk still unlocked. I raised the trunk, got the helmet out, closed the trunk, turned and faced Destiny.

We stared at each other. Carmen's daughter. That old man's grandchild.

I asked, "Did you call the police?"

She shook her head. "Sorry."

"It's cool."

"I called Big Momma. She knows you're over here."

"I see."

"I couldn't call the police. You don't understand."

"No, it's cool. I do understand. Don't know what I was thinking, asking you to do that. I wouldn't go against my family, no matter what they did. Just sorry everything has somehow come to this."

Getting away from here before her grandfather came back was all that mattered.

But it was too late for that. Her grandfather appeared at the end of the driveway, the sun rising on his anguished face. He hobbled up from the streets, his sleeves rolled up, panting, out of breath, that injured stride making an eerie sound like he was some kind of creature.

Good step, drag leg, good step, drag leg.

I gripped my helmet. That old man in front of me. Destiny behind me.

She had kept me here. Destiny had lied, talked to me, did all of that to keep me here.

That old man came toward me. Blood on the side of his head, his lip swollen. Hobbling down that driveway as fast as he could. I gripped my helmet, was ready to swing as hard as I could and send his teeth flying back to the pavement. He saw that in my eyes. He waved his hand in a movement of surrender, then went the long way, limped around me, no fight in his eyes, hurried to Destiny.

Good step, drag leg, good step, drag leg.

My eyes went to his crippled walk, to that unmatched sound that came from his labored stroll.

He asked, "What horrible ting happened, child?"

"What did you do, Paw Paw?"

"Don't you worry, child. I did mi best. Tell mi it all right now so we can fix the rest."

The tears came back. She shook her head. "I can't talk about it. I can't."

He moved past Destiny, went and stood in front of his garage.

He saw the car had been uncovered. Saw that I'd seen the truth.

"Mi brand-new car . . . ruined . . . good Lord."

I couldn't see his expression, had to read his worn body language, only heard his woeful voice. He stopped where he stood, pulling at his hair, shaking his head.

He turned to me. Terrified. Shaking. Hands opening and closing. Eyes watering. That old man looked completely overwhelmed.

He hobbled my way. *Good step, drag leg, good step, drag leg.*

He stopped short of me, stopped and pulled a folded envelope out of his back pocket. A thick envelope filled with five thousand dollars. He held that money out toward me.

I shook my head. There wasn't enough money in the world. He lowered the money, pulled at his hair.

"Woman, tell mi . . . ain't there some way we can . . . what can I do to make this better? Tell mi."

I said, "You tried to run me down in your wife's truck on Friday night, didn't you."

"I'm sorry . . . not in mi right mine . . . mi daughter . . . so unhappy . . . hurts mi to see her in such pain."

I almost felt bad for that old man.

Almost.

He said, "How much will it take to fix this? Tell mi. How much?"

I'd been ridiculed, bribed, run down, and robbed. Now the devil wanted to bargain with me.

I managed to get my cellular out. I had missed calls and had so many messages. Raheem had called at least ten times. Viviane had called just as many. Keith had called and sent text messages.

Had a text message from another biker friend. A biker had gone down on Figueroa a few hours ago. The message didn't say which member of our fraternity had gone down or how bad it was.

I wanted to call Keith, but I didn't want him to talk me out of doing what I had to do.

It was a hard call to make, physically and emotionally, but I dialed 911. I told them about the attempted murder, to get their asses over here right now.

The old man heard my call. Heard my anger. He hobbled back inside his home.

I limped toward the streets.

Destiny ran up behind me, grabbed my jacket sleeve.

Paranoia made me jerk away from her. Thought she was attacking me. Saw she wasn't.

"Billie . . . I can't do this. Can't do this to my little brother. Or my little sister."

"*Do what?*"

"I don't know how to . . . to . . . to be mean to people like they are mean to me."

"Get away from me, Destiny. *Get away from me.*"

"*Throw up, Billie.*"

"What are you talking—"

"Please . . . just . . . just . . . you . . . Billie . . . *throw the pills back up.*"

twenty-one

BILLIE

I FACED DESTINY, HER TEARS, HER PLEADING FOR ME TO THROW UP RE-sounding in the brisk morning breeze.

Destiny's hand was still on my jacket. We moved to the side of the house.

I got in her face, growled, "What did you give me?"

"I took the same thing. It's supposed to fix everything."

"Did you try to poison me?"

"Please. Throw yours up."

I pulled away from her. Headed toward the police.

"Wait, Billie. Wait. Please. Listen to me. I have to tell you this. I have to."

Destiny wouldn't let me go.

I told her, "Whatever you have to say, make it quick and make it good."

She said, "I was raped, Billie."

"What?"

"I was raped."

"Why would you say something like that, Destiny?"

"By these boys I met . . . this girl . . . they gave me pills. Did things to me."

"You are such an actress, you know that?"

"No, for real." She shivered. "I was raped."

I stared at her, wanted to strangle her until she said something that made sense.

She said, "The pills you took . . . I got them from somebody . . . please . . . throw up."

"You took them too."

"I know, I know. I took them too. Had to."

"Then why aren't you trying to throw up?"

"Because . . . *I don't want to be pregnant.* I don't want to be pregnant with a . . . rape baby."

"Save the drama." I pulled away from her. "What you gave me . . . are they Aleve?"

"No."

"What the fuck did you give me?"

"They're . . . RU-486."

"Abortion pill?"

"I'm . . . I'm . . . I'm so sorry."

"You're joking, right?"

"RU-486."

"Those pills . . . women are getting bacterial infections and dying from taking those pills, you know that? Those pills could kill me and my baby. Were you trying to kill me and my baby?"

"No, no, no," she cried. "Throw up, just throw up."

My hand that had been closed, I opened it. Her teary eyes widened.

Inside my wounded hand, stuck inside that gauze, were the pills she had given me. I never took them. Pretended to take them just to be polite. I had hopes, even the pain in my stomach told me they were unrealistic hopes, for my baby. Wouldn't take any medication, not unless it came from a doctor.

The anguished look on her face, it morphed into the expression of a fool who had said too much.

I asked, "How could you do some shit like that?"

She said, "I was raped."

"You can stop lying."

"*I was raped.*"

"You just tried to kill your little brother or sister."

"Listen to me, please listen to me. I was raped Friday night, Billie."

"And me. You tried to kill me."

"Momma said you were blackmailing us, taking all of our money, that we would be poor because you were greedy, that my daddy would be with you and forget about me when you had that baby."

"All of you have tried to kill me."

"I . . . I . . . wanted to fix it."

"You are some sick motherfuckers."

"We're not sick."

"You're sick."

"We're just . . . we love each other. We're a family."

She reached for my hand, for the pills.

I yanked my hand back, made it a fist.

"For real, Billie. I was raped. Even if you tell my daddy about the pills, just don't tell him I was raped. Please . . . don't tell my daddy. I'm scared. I'm embarrassed. He'll hate me if he finds out."

The look of paranoia and humiliation that lived in her eyes, that horror was indescribable.

"You're full of shit, little girl."

She backed away from me.

If my hands weren't injured, if I wasn't in pain, I would've choked her to death.

She looked like she wanted the ground to open up and swallow her whole.

"You don't know what I've been through, Billie."

"You?" I snapped. "You have no idea what the fuck I've been through."

Behind us, in front of the house, the flashing lights told me that, at last, they were here.

LAPD.

Nobody would jump on me now. No one would try to run me over. No one would attack me now.

For the first time in a long time, maybe the first time ever, I saw LAPD and felt safe.

They'd gotten here so fast. But then again, Krispy Kreme was right across the street.

Destiny ran away from my rage. Her sobs becoming the uncontrollable howl of an impaled creature. Her pace that of a terrified and injured girl. She moved like agony lived between her legs.

The gate squeaked open and slammed closed.

The back door opened and closed hard.

I didn't know what to believe. All I knew was I had to limp toward the police.

Two more police cars had shown up, joining the first. Five officers were out front, the sound of ten feet and at least half as many guns heading my way.

I stared at the poison in my hands. She had tried to kill me.

I closed my aching fingers again.

Death rested in my swollen hands.

That was the only thing I knew for sure.

By the time I got to the front of the house, three more police cars had showed up.

Traffic slowed. Lights came on at a few of the neighbors'. Others kept their homes dark and peeped out the windows. Everybody wanted to see, but no one wanted to be involved.

Miss Ruth's SUV pulled up right after that. She was driving fast, Keith was her passenger. Heard her raising her voice, first yelling at LAPD for blocking her driveway, screaming that they were standing on her grass, then asking a thousand questions before she turned her engine off.

By then I was out front talking to the officers, trying to explain what didn't make sense to me, pointing at that garage, at that one-eyed monster that had run me down.

Radios squawked while LAPD went to the garage and inspected that wrecked car.

Either Miss Ruth didn't know her husband had wrecked their Benz, or she was the best actress I'd ever seen. She howled, "William, what have you done? What have you done?"

The police report I'd gotten from Santa Monica P.D., it was in my backpack. I showed that to the lead officer. Told them that when I had come here the old crazy bastard had attacked me. My injuries were the evidence. That he had attempted murder hours before that.

I said, "I'm pregnant."

"Calm down, ma'am."

"He knows I'm pregnant."

"Ma'am, please."

"He tried to kill my baby."

My voice strained and emotionally I told the officer in charge how that old bastard's daughter had come to my job. I told him all about Carmen, about her threats, about her bribe. I told him how she had thrown money in my face. How I'd been run off the road by that SUV. About being robbed.

Destiny's grandfather, Carmen's father, that old man didn't say or mumble a word.

Miss Ruth screamed while they handcuffed him.

It was time for him to start counting cockroaches in an institution where men did awful things to other men. After what he had done to me, I hoped he'd die a slow and painful death.

Keith tried to come over and talk to me, but I lost it, screamed, told them to keep him away from me.

I didn't trust anybody.

Miss Ruth, yelling in an accent so thick I couldn't understand a word she said. Keith, off to the side, distancing himself from his in-laws, head down, in shock and disbelief. That old bastard, lip busted, his face swollen, handcuffed, in the back of a police car staring straight ahead, refusing to say one single word to the police, his wife, anybody who came over to him. And me, aching, hands wrapped in gauze, hair in total disarray, all cried out and trembling from all the violence I had been through. All of us were out on MLK, traffic slowing down like we the main attractions for the King Day Parade.

Carmen, they'd left her in the hospital. Raced from one emergency to another.

Only one person was missing. Destiny. Keith's daughter. The Bad Seed personified.

I looked around for that Antichrist dressed in angelic colors and pigtails. I didn't see her.

The distressed look I'd seen in her oversized eyes. Her telling me, *I was raped.*

That was a bloody razor I'd seen in her hand.

That was blood on her clothes.

Her walk had been the trudge of pain.

She wasn't old enough to drive and she'd driven up in a big black SUV.

Another chill ran over me, this one so deep it frosted my bone marrow.

When that brick came through my window last night, a black SUV had sped away.

A light-colored SUV like Miss Ruth's had tried to run me down after that.

And the one-eyed monster leaking radiator fluid in that garage . . . it spoke for itself.

I looked around for Destiny.

All of this was going on and she was nowhere to be seen. Wasn't out here trying to console or help or explain. She had run back inside that stucco house of evil, barricaded herself from this drama.

But in the distance, over and over, I heard crunches and whirrs.

Heard those crunches and whirrs as an ambulance pulled up.

The attendant said, "You a biker?"

"How'd you know?"

"Your jacket."

"Yeah. Totaled my bike earlier."

"You're lucky. We just transported a biker a few hours ago. Down on Figueroa. She crashed hard."

"She?"

"Yeah. She."

Those crunches and whirrs kept coming at a frantic pace.

I asked the attendant, "Who was it?"

"Beg your pardon?"

"The girl who crashed on Figueroa, who was she?"

"No idea."

"Was she Korean?"

"Black. Be still."

"I'm hurting too bad to be still."

"Let's get you stable."

Crunches. Whirrs.

Heard those crunches and whirrs echoing through the palm trees as they put me inside.

The attendant asked me, "What's that in your hand?"

I cringed and opened my fingers. The pills rolled into the attendant's hand. "I don't want these."

"What are these?"

"There is a girl inside that house . . . she said that . . . these are RU-486. . . ."

"Mifeprex? Did you take Mifeprex?"

"No. But . . . tell the police . . . a girl is inside the house . . . that's her dad over there . . . the girl . . . she's fifteen . . . I saw her take two of these. I saw her take them a few minutes ago. She has them in an Aleve bottle."

"We need to get you to the emergency room first."

"Now. Tell her father now. Tell the police. Listen to me. She might lie, say she didn't give me these, but she did. Tell them to please get her to the hospital. That's her father. I don't want her to die."

twenty-two

BILLIE

SIRENS BLARING ON MY BEHALF, RED LIGHTS ROTATING AND FLASHING TO announce my arrival, my agony and fears were delivered into the mouth of pandemonium. The emergency room at Daniel Freeman Hospital was packed.

If I never saw that hospital again, if I never inhaled the stench of the sick and wounded, it would be okay with me. Three times. I had been here three friggin' times in the last few hours. I'd been here once to visit Q, a beautiful young girl who had been attacked on Crenshaw for no damn reason; again when I had no choice but to drop off Keith's wife; and now I was back in this wretched place as a patient. This time I understood what Carmen meant about Inglewood Park cemetery being across the street. Catching a glimpse of the inevitable didn't do a lot for the way I was feeling right now. I wondered if my nameless baby had earned its grave. Wondered if they carved tombstones for nameless children.

Maybe I was delirious, but it seemed like I was in a bad surreal movie, everything slowed down, all words dark and sluggish, every light too bright, staring up at nonchalant faces, passing by people I had seen before, kept hearing both my name and my handle elongated over and over.

I closed my eyes for a moment. Saw that old bastard hobbling toward me.

Good step, drag leg, good step, drag leg.

A spasm hit me. Body jerked. I grunted, opened my eyes.

A few bikers were congregated in the hallways, so many heads being held low, most crying.

They were shocked to see me on my back. The usual Saturday night gunshot crowd and the incident that had left around thirty people injured at Casura Bay had the hospital working overtime.

I didn't care about any tragedies at Casura Bay or the Saturday night gunshot victims.

I turned my head toward the bikers, the look in my eyes asking who went down.

One of the riders in the all-girl motorcycle club came over. She told me.

Death had showed up ready to claim one of us.

I said, "Marcel?"

She nodded. Too emotional to say another word.

I said, "No way. Not Marcel. She was one of the best . . . if not the best . . . damn."

If I had had any more tears I would've cried. But the ocean inside of me had gone dry.

Not long after that the sun stole a peek through the window. I had an IV in my arm. Recycled hospital gown on. Eyes swollen. Bad taste in my mouth. Hair pulled back. Eyes burning from lack of sleep. Fingers throbbing. Shoulder ached. Some lower back pain. Could barely move. Needed help to get to the bathroom and back. Was in a room made for two, but at the moment I had the room to myself.

Outside that window, across Prairie Boulevard, I had a clear view of a bedroom for the dead. They could've at least put me in a room facing Sizzler or the Great Western Forum.

I heard their anxious voices first, heard them at the nurses' station asking for my room, asking if it was okay to come inside. The door opened and Viviane rushed toward me, her red leathers singing and boots clicking across the sterile tile. Helmet and backpack in hand, her long braids swaying, my girl was all geared up.

I spoke first, felt stupid. "I went down."

"Damn. Can't leave you alone for a minute."

I went down.

The three words a biker hated to say, an admission of carelessness, even if it wasn't our fault.

I went down. Just like saying, *I fucked up.*

A rite of passage that a lot of us didn't live to tell about.

Jacob was right behind Viviane, all black leather, his huge hand holding his backpack and helmet, black bandanna around his nappy head, those big feet of his making thunder with his every step.

Jacob said, "How is my favorite Made-in-Japan girl doing?"

"You have a big mouth, you know that?"

"What I do?"

"And I'm not Made in Japan."

"What I do?"

"Keep away from me, Jacob."

"What did I do?"

"If my fingers weren't hurting so damn bad, I'd flip you off in stereo."

Viviane took a seat at the foot of the bed, the thin mattress giving under her light weight. She looked at me with unadulterated concern and confusion. There was a lot to tell, but I did my best.

I told her about being chased down Wilshire Boulevard, about my crash.

I said, "I tucked, let the bike slide from under me."

Jacob said, "Like a pro."

Viviane looked at my hands. "Carmen's father?"

"Yes."

"Attempted murder?"

"Attempted murder. Felony hit-and-run. Few more felony charges."

Viviane asked, "How's the baby?"

Jacob turned around. "What baby?"

Big Mouth didn't know. Either that or he was a damn good actor.

Viviane said, "She's . . . uh . . . Billie?"

I said, "I'm pregnant."

Jacob's jaw hit the ground.

I'm pregnant. Never realized how powerful those two words were.

"Or I was. I have to wait and see." I was talking to Viviane. "I'm only six weeks. Not a lot that can do, from what I understand. It's so early, they said I have to wait, stay under observation."

"Don't let them X-ray you."

"They said X-rays are safe."

"Whatever. Let your baby end up with skin tags or an extra finger or toe. Tell them to do an ultrasound exam instead of an X-ray. No harm to an unborn baby has ever been reported from ultrasound. No MRI. Those are only safe after the first trimester."

"Viviane." Had to slow her down. "I already know all of that. It's under control."

She took a nervous breath. "How you feel?"

"Cramping."

"Bleeding?"

"Yeah, bleeding." My voice cracked. "Spotting."

We knew what that meant. That X-rays and sonograms were irrelevant. My favorite Korean girl started crying.

I patted her leg, pushed my lips up toward heaven. "It's okay. It's for the best."

"I'm so sorry, Billie."

"Not like I needed a baby, you know. Not with my income and lifestyle."

"Will they be able to charge that asshole with first-degree murder?"

I sat on that question, her tears blooming and creating misery in my eyes. I didn't want to be sad right now, didn't want to be mad, didn't want to cry another damn tear. I needed to change the subject.

I cleared my throat, but my voice still trembled. "How's Q doing?"

"Don't sit up, Billie."

I ignored her, made the bed go up to a sitting position. "She doing better?"

"She's stable. Wouldn't call it better."

"Police have any idea who attacked her?"

"Please. You think the police are looking?"

"She didn't die, so it's low priority."

"You say that like it's a bad thing."

"It's fucked up is what I'm saying. Bullshit. Straight bullshit."

Jacob said, "Language, Viviane."

Viviane waved Jacob away. "That's why I had to roll out and take the law in my own hands."

I asked, "What does that mean?"

Viviane and Jacob looked at each other, an uneasy conspiratorial stare. Jacob massaged his wrist, looked at his hand. Viviane's hand came up to her face, then she did nervous things with her braids. Redness had spread all over her cheek.

Viviane said, "Let me put it to you like this: If the police ask, I was with you all night."

Jacob jumped in. "Hello. You? Where the hell was I at?"

Viviane corrected herself, "*We* were with you all night."

Again I asked what happened. Again a conspiratorial stare was shared.

Viviane said, "This boy had called up here trying to get information on Q. Some boy named D'Andre. I took the call. He was worried about her. Said he was with her when she got jumped on."

"What he say?"

"He told me where the people went who jumped on her."

"People? More than one?"

"Not sure what happened. But he told us who was driving. Told us who left my sister in the streets bleeding. Motherfucker saw my sister get hurt and just drove his ass away and left her."

"Where were they?"

"Casura Bay. We went down there."

"No," Jacob interrupted. "You went down there. You couldn't wait for backup."

"Q is my sister." She was vexed. "That's all that mattered."

I said, "Family. She's your family."

"Yes," Viviane said, trying to calm herself down. "She's my family. I raised her."

"And you'd do whatever you had to do."

"By any means necessary."

The news was on, the morning anchors recapping all of the overnight violence. Typical news for people living in the freeway-crowded land of beautiful weather and palm trees.

This morning, even after all I'd gone through, I wasn't newsworthy.

I said, "A nurse told me that a lot of people got messed up real bad at Casura Bay last night."

Viviane's frown ran deep. "But none of them were hurt as bad as my sister. A lot of them might have been hurt, but none of them were fighting for their lives. None of them were disfigured. None of them were attacked because of ignorance and prejudice."

We shared wounded smiles for a moment. Became women communicating in silence.

I said, "You're scaring me, Viviane."

Viviane's angry face told me she was ready to change both the channel and the subject.

With a puzzled face she asked, "You sure Carmen's dad did this to you?"

"Found the Benz in their garage."

"In his garage?"

"Guess he didn't have time to hide it. Carmen's asthma attack probably messed up his timing."

Viviane had no idea what I was talking about. I told her about going to treat Carmen to a beat-down. Told her about the wedding dress, the vibrator, the video, about the asthmatic conversation in the car.

Viviane said, "*Envy?* The bitch actually used the word envy?"

I nodded. "Offered to let me have Keith in the daytime as long as he came home at night."

Jacob said, "Must be nice."

At the same time both of us said, "Shut up."

Jacob laughed, his voice husky and dehydrated.

"Damn." Viviane ran her hands though her hair, moved it from her face only to have it fall back in front of her eyes again. "Tell me everything that happened, Billie."

"The way you and Jacob look, as jittery as both of you are, I should ask you the same thing."

She had put her helmet on the foot of the bed when she sat next to me. My eyes were on her gear. Her helmet was cracked, the face shield off. Saw redness in her face, mild bruises.

I said, "Don't tell me you went down on your bike too."

"I didn't go down, but we did throw down."

Jacob, staring out the window, said, "Like Bonnie and Clyde. Punk-ass bitches."

Viviane shot him a look. "Language, Jacob."

"They got up in my face, like that was supposed to scare me."

She'd been in a fight, had taken a good hit to her jaw. Jacob was treating his right wrist tenderly.

"Long story," Viviane sighed. "For legal reasons, not sure if you need to know all that right now."

She winked at Jacob like he was her big-handed black knight in biker boots.

The way Jacob looked at her, that man would do anything for his woman. Anything.

Viviane said, "Saw a lot of bikers hanging around the emergency room when I came in."

She didn't know about Marcel. I told her what I had heard. More tears were in her eyes.

Viviane said, "Raheem's here too."

"Raheem? Hey, big-mouth, you called your irritating frat brother already?"

Jacob shook his head. "Somebody attacked his niece."

"No way."

"Way."

"Damn. What happened?"

"His sister was near her dorm down by USC." Jacob shrugged. "That's all I know."

twenty-three

BILLIE

THE DOCTOR CAME TO SEE ME. THE ROOM WAS GETTING A LITTLE CROWDED, so Viviane and Jacob left. My girl said she would go check on her sister, then run home and grab me some fresh clothes.

Jacob had to go and handle business with his son. With his family.

Across Prairie, men with brown skin were digging six-foot-deep holes in the ground.

I told the doctor I wanted to go home. He told me to take it easy, that he would see what he could do, depending on my condition and lab results. He left. I sat in my bed, television on the local news.

The police came. Talked to me again. Verifying what I told them about the accident. They left.

I walked the halls. Passed by hysterical grandparents going to see if their grandchild had been blinded, by women running to see about a friend who had been shot in his penis, by friends of a girl whose face and breasts had been slashed, by parents of kids who had fallen from the second floor of a motel, legs broken, hands crushed. IV at my side, I made my way past moans, tears, pandemonium, and drama that made it easy for me to slip by the nurses' station. My mind and heart took me on a journey, made me get on the elevator. The babies. I went to look through the windows at the babies. So many beautiful, sleeping babies. I stood at the window and looked at the babies. Waving.

A nurse passed by. "Which one is yours?"

I smiled. She kept on going.

A woman was groaning. Heard her laborious sounds echoing in the hallway. Nurses were walking back and forth, immune to the reverberation of agony. I followed those sounds, went and stood in the door to the room. Alone. No ring on her finger. No one at her side. In the throes of labor.

I didn't run away this time. Last time I had been afraid. Without asking, without fear, I went inside that room, sat next to her, took her hand, told her everything would be okay, that she would be fine.

I said, "Breathe."

I held her hand and we inhaled and exhaled together.

I sat there with her until the nurse came.

Then I kissed that stranger's hand, stood up, steadied my IV stand, and walked away.

Maybe one day somebody would do that for me.

When I made it back to my room, the doctor came to see me. This time with bad news. I already knew. I knew my body. Hearing him say it made it official.

He said, "I'm sorry."

I wiped my tears. "I'll be okay."

He squeezed my hand, held it a few moments, then he had to go. He had to see to his other patients.

I left my room, walked down the hallway, wiping tears away from my eyes.

I was angry.

So damn angry.

And sad.

I wasn't a mommy anymore.

twenty-four

BILLIE

KEITH WAS IN THE HALLWAY OUTSIDE MY ROOM. CLOTHES WRINKLED. EYES red. The signs of a tortured life. He saw me, hurried my way. So much awkwardness in his body. He didn't know how to greet me.

Something was wrong, I saw that in his face. I might not have been with him for eighteen years, but I knew that man pretty well.

He hesitated, so I spoke first. I created an angry smile and looked him in his eyes.

"I'm not pregnant anymore, Keith."

"How . . . ?"

"When I was run off the road. Hit the ground hard. Didn't let the doctors look at me when I came in with Carmen. Ironic, huh? I saved your wife. I saved your daughter. Lost the baby. I lost my baby."

"No."

"Tell your wife she can clap her hands. Tell her to tell her momma and daddy to do the same. We're not pregnant anymore, Keith. Baby gone to heaven. Poof. No child support. No worries about day care. No Chuck E. Cheese. But this isn't over. There will be a lawsuit. And this lawsuit will make child support look like a joke. Tell that old bastard and his wife to get ready to sell that house."

I moved past Keith, went toward my room. He followed, caught up, walked next to me in disturbed silence. He opened the door for me, then followed me inside my hospital room.

"How is she?" I asked. "How is Little Miss Destiny?"

"At Cedars-Sinai. Getting her stomach pumped."

"Better her than me."

"Not just because of those pills, but we don't know what's in her system."

Yesterday I would have cared. But it wasn't yesterday. There was a new sun in my life.

I went to the window, saw the brown-skinned men making more homes for the dead.

My hand went to my stomach. To what used to hold a miracle.

I had experienced death and there would be no funeral. No grave site to go to and mourn.

Keith tensed. "I'm still trying to understand everything that's going on . . . how it all got to this."

"Well, understand this: Your sweet little girl, she tried to poison me."

"But she didn't."

I froze and looked at him. I couldn't believe he had just said that.

"Keith, if I put a loaded gun to your head, but didn't pull the trigger, would you ever forget that?"

"Billie—"

"Would you?"

"Billie—"

I said, "She gave me the goddamn abortion pills. She tried to kill my baby. She told me that she wanted to kill my baby. So you can tell your precious daughter to start clapping her goddamn hands too."

"She told you to throw them up, didn't she? She told me she did. You didn't take the goddamn pills."

"Are you defending her? She could've killed me and you're in my hospital room defending her?"

"She didn't try to kill you, Billie."

"She tried to kill her unborn sibling. I'm all messed up, hospitalized, and you're defending her? Don't you dare come in my room, after all the shit I've been through, and fucking defend that monster."

Keith stood there, pulling his hair. Angered. If there was ever a moment that solidified that nothing good could happen between us, that this relationship, if what was left of this carcass could be called a relationship, needed to be taken across the boulevard and given to the ground, this was it.

I asked, "Why did you come here, Keith?"

"I can't explain why Destiny did what she did. All I can say is that it was wrong. Bad judgment."

"*You're* her father. *You* helped raise her. She tries to poison me and you write it off as bad judgment? Getting fish when you should've gotten chicken is bad judgment. Where is her moral code?"

"You're right. No, I can't defend Destiny for what she tried to do, but recognize this: She told you. She may have given you the pills, but she told you she had done wrong. She has a heart. She feels deeply. She has a conscience. She is not a monster. Her actions prove that. She's not a bad child."

"If I had died, would that monster still be a good kid?"

"She's not a monster."

"Monster, monster, monster."

"Blame the source of our grief. Blame Carmen. Blame Carmen's father."

"Your kid showed up. I saw the blood on her clothes. With a razor in her hand. I saw the razor. Your father-in-law vanished in the SUV she pulled up in, came back walking. What was that all about?"

"Billie . . . I need to talk to you about that. Need your help."

"Need my help?"

Keith paused, lowered his voice. "Did you say anything to the police about what you saw?"

"What?"

"What did you tell the police? I need to know what you told them."

There it was. The reason Keith was here. At least it felt that way to me. Not because of me. This was about his fifteen-year-old daughter. His angel. He was here to get information so he could protect his daughter from whatever evil she had done.

I asked, "You afraid I'll tell them about the pills, Keith? Is that what this is about?"

"No. That's not what this is about."

"I will tell the police what I saw, Keith. When they come to talk to me again, and they will, I will tell them what I saw. *The blood. The razor.* Your child inside that house destroying CDs or DVDs. I'll tell."

Keith was crying. Shuddering.

In a voice so weak, so fractured, he made a choking sound. He swallowed what he was trying to say and struggled with himself, his tongue moving back and forth like his mouth was filled with razor blades. Again he tried to regroup, his breathing becoming labored, like he was about to join Tom Cruise in his descent into madness. He fought with the words and lost that battle one syllable at a time.

He said, "Destiny. Was. Raped. Billie. She. Was. Raped."

It took me a moment to absorb all he said, his intensity, his unadulterated emotion, all of his pain, but I shook my head, the pain I felt reminding me that I had blood between my legs, gritted my teeth and spoke through all the anger that had blackened my heart. "Don't do this to me, Keith. Don't play me."

"She told me she told you."

"She's a liar and you know she's a liar. She ran away from home, got caught, and now her story, after she has to admit to the fact that she tried to poison me, is that she was raped? C'mon, man."

"I know she lies, I know she does bad things, but this is the truth."

"How do you know?"

"Because . . . I know she's not lying. I know. You have to help me."

"A family of psychopaths and liars, that's what you married into."

His voice turned strong. "My little girl was drugged and raped. The bastards put it on a DVD."

"All of that is on DVD?"

He nodded.

I heard that noise again.

Whirr. Crunch. Whirr. Crunch. Whirr. Crunch.

While Destiny's grandfather was being handcuffed.

While I was being put in an ambulance.

Whirr. Crunch. Whirr. Crunch. Whirr. Crunch.

Keith said, "They made God knows how many copies . . . of my daughter . . . and they were selling that shit on the streets. What they did to my daughter . . . she might lie, but I'd never lie to you. They were selling the DVDs. Those are the monsters, Billie. That's where she was coming from when you found her at the mall. She had just been raped. She was scared to come home. They raped her and tossed her away like she was nothing. That's why she went out last night. She went back to that . . . to find those people. To get those pills. To make sure she wasn't pregnant by those bastards."

I had been completely derailed. Left speechless.

"You think I'm lying? They're pumping her stomach. And they're checking her for diseases too."

"Damn."

"I know this is a bad time. But my daughter is not a monster. My daughter is a victim. Those are the monsters, Billie. I'm not asking you to lie. I'm not asking you to put your freedom on the line. Just don't bring it up. What happened to you, to our baby, tell the police everything you can think of. Tell them the truth. Tell them lies. I don't give a shit about the others. Carmen's family will pay for what they did. But my daughter . . . people did some horrific things to her . . . she was raped . . . I'm just asking you to not mention whatever you saw. I don't know what you saw, but just don't mention anything. I mean, they have the car that ran you down, they have William's confession. That's enough. You can sue them, sue Carmen, sue me, do whatever you want . . . but if you have any love for me left in your heart . . . I'm trying to get Destiny some help . . . I don't have time to keep trying to place blame . . . so . . . please, if you have any compassion—"

I snapped, "Compassion?"

"I'm not asking this for me. I'm trying to protect Destiny. That's all."

"I just lost my baby. Do you have any idea what I've been through? Even though your precious little girl told me to throw up, she gave me the goddamn pills. She changed her mind, but she wanted to kill my baby. I don't know what that monster did, but Destiny should be held accountable for her actions."

"I know. I agree. But consider the circumstances . . . Shit. Fuck. What the hell can I do, Billie?"

"To keep me from telling everything to the police? Ain't a damn thing you can do. I lost my baby, Keith. And you're in my face . . . I'm in a hospital gown and all you care about is Destiny? My baby died, and this is what you bring me? No flowers. No card. You walk in here carrying me some more bullshit? You're not even here out of concern for our child. Our child. Do you think I deserved what happened to me? Do you? You think I give a damn about Destiny or Carmen or any of those crazy mother—"

"Are you listening to what I'm telling you? *My. Child. Was. Raped.*"

"*My. Child. Was. Murdered.*"

Our words echoed.

Keith tried to regroup. "What Carmen's father did, I can't change that. If I could take it back, I would. All of this . . . this is hard on me, Billie."

"Destiny is alive."

"Don't you think I'm hurting too?"

"All I know is that Destiny is alive and my baby is dead."

"Our child is dead."

"*Our* child?" I exploded. "You know what? Don't you ever . . . ever . . . say this was your child. Don't you ever disrespect me and say that. If you dream this was your child, I'll wake you up and beat your ass. I'll kill you if you ever claim my child. I will kill you, and I swear to God I will . . . you're the goddamn monster. You know that? You are the goddamn monster, Keith. You come in my hospital room while I'm bleeding, you come in my room and ask me to help you? Nigga, I wouldn't even piss on your ass if it were on fire."

Someone knocked on the door, then the door flew open. It was one of the nurses. We were making too much noise. Keith apologized, then moved his red face and tears to the window while I avoided touching him and went to the nurse. She saw the fire in my eyes. She asked me if everything was under control. I told her it wasn't anything that I couldn't handle. She told me that the doctor was making his rounds, would probably be back to check on me within the hour. They might send me home, if I wanted to be discharged. I let her know that I wanted to get out of this place so bad.

She asked, "Sure you're okay?"

"Just tell the doctor to sign the papers and discharge me."

As soon as she left, I stood behind Keith. His reflection showed more pain that I felt right now. More physical pain. He'd never come close to feeling my emotional agony. He moved past me. Sat down.

He looked up at me. Those red-rimmed eyes still begging me for an answer.

Keith had been between more rocks and hard places than Ulysses was with Scylla and Charybdis. I had been willing to be in those horrific places with him. But not anymore.

Someone else tapped on the door. It was Viviane. She was alone this time. She had changed from her leathers and had on jeans and sandals. Her braids were down; now her long hair cascaded down her back. She had makeup on. Sunglasses. She'd come back for me in her four-wheel cage. She had a backpack filled with a change a clothes. As she walked in, she saw Keith and looked surprised.

Keith stood in silence, crying, begging clemency for his daughter.

"Forget you ever met me, Keith. Forget my name. If you ever see me, run the other way."

Without acknowledging Viviane, his head down, with labored steps, Keith walked out of my life.

He was right. At some point he would have to choose.

So would I.

twenty-five

BILLIE

THE SUN WAS SETTING ON MY ANGER. THAT SAME ANGER WOULD FIND ME up when the sun rose again. That anger was all I had. Viviane was driving me home. Inglewood Park Cemetery was at my side, then that final resting place moved to my rearview mirror for a while before it faded into the urban landscape.

She had been quiet since I exploded at the hospital. After that wretched moment, I had needed some space, to be alone, to grieve by myself. She had left for a while, and came back when I called her.

I wanted to talk. But not about my problems. I felt like a shark, had to keep moving or I'd die.

I asked, "Any more news on who attacked Q?"

"Those punks scattered like roaches. Cowards. Doubt if they go back to Casura Bay."

"You done looking?"

"Not until I find the girl who hit my sister. The brother we were looking for, the asshole they said was driving his friends around and left my sister out in the streets, he vanished after we . . . he vanished."

"Now what?"

She took a hard, unsettling breath. "Need to focus on Q. Getting her better."

"That poor girl."

"If I ever find out who did this—"

"Slow down."

"—it will be on like Donkey Kong. Oh, yeah. It will be on an pop-pop-popping."

L.A. was in full swing. Traffic was still as bad as Bae Bae kids. The middle finger of love was being extended as people cut us off. Then came the gridlock. A train was zooming by, running parallel to Florence. Nothing but brake lights up ahead. A few bikers zipped down the middle, left all of us sitting in our cages. In my mind I was with them, lane-splitting my way to the front. Never noticed how impassable traffic was when I rode my Ducati. When I was on my bike, the world became my obstacle course.

I asked, "How is your mom, Q's dad, how are they taking this?"

"Don't get me started. Her dad is her dad. What can I saying about that trifling—"

"Sounds pretty bad."

"Have no idea what my mother sees in him. 'Cause I sure don't."

"Your mother was a wreck. Make sure she's okay."

"I will. I always do. Not sure if my mother can handle the situation. That's her baby. She has so much guilt for not being able to relate to her own child. She thinks that whatever happens to Q is her fault. Plus Momma still needs to work. Same for Q's dad. So it looks like Q might come stay with us for a while."

"Cool. I'm here for her. She's my little sister too."

Viviane got emotional, and when her emotions ran high she couldn't hold the truth inside her. She broke and she told me everything. Told me all about how she got a phone call from a boy who called himself D'Andre, a miracle phone call from a boy who had sprouted a conscience, and how she ran downstairs and hopped on her bike and went to Casura Bay looking for the girl who had attacked her Q.

The insults. She told me how one of the boys down there insulted her.

She said, "I have never seen so many misguided and rude children in one spot ever in my life. Those boys . . . their idea of what a man is . . . looked like a bad hip-hop video. And the girls. They were all so high. Doing damn near everything right in front of everybody. Ecstasy all over the place."

"And those are the people Q was hanging out with."

"Jacob . . . I called the man . . . and he dropped everything . . . got a baby-sitter and came right down there . . . should've seen him . . . had no idea he would defend me like that . . . the man kicked ass. I mean, he had those punks running to get up out of there. He was hitting those fools like he was Mike Tyson."

"Mike Tyson?"

"The original Mike Tyson, not that I-give-up and let-me-put-some-ketchup-on-your-ear Mike Tyson. I'm talking the beat-Leon-Spinks-into-retirement-in-under-two-minutes Mike Tyson."

Hearing her say that made me realize how Keith had never dropped everything for me.

Keith told me he loved me, but in the end he never fought for me.

It didn't show on my face, but I was happy for Viviane. Despite what I had gone through, I was happy for her. Somebody needed to be happy. And my girl deserved it.

I said, "Sounds like it turned you on."

"You have no idea. He told me that I was his woman and he loved me and no man or woman would ever disrespect me and live to talk about it. I would've fucked him right then. Good thing we were on motor-cycles. I'd've been deep-throating his crazy ass all the way back to Daniel Freeman."

"TMI."

"I would've. I know it's a bad time to say that, but I swear to God I would've."

"Well, from what you've told me, that wouldn't be much of a challenge."

"Shit. I know you're going through some things, Billie, but I'm a lit-tle bit messed up over here. I'm talking about Jacob. He's so amazing. Never met a man who loves me like that. Never. But the sex part . . . I mean, damn. This is really messed up, you know? What do you think I should do?"

"Honestly?"

"Honestly."

"Talk to Jacob. He's a cool guy. Talk him into buying a couple of those penis pump things."

"You're joking, right?"

"Serious. It's a muscle."

"It's not cool to tell a man he's not tall enough to get on your ride, you know?"

"You don't have to tell him that. Hell, I'm sure he knows. Make it a game. A sex game. You have to exercise it for him. They have these erotic techniques. Kama Sutra stuff that can make it bigger."

"You're joking, right?"

"That's how a man makes his penis bigger and longer and all of that stuff."

"That crap work?"

"It's a trip. We do Kegels to tighten it up and they pump it up to make us keep doing Kegels."

"Does it work?"

"You saw Keith naked, right?"

"Damn."

"Yeah."

"Why didn't you tell me?"

"I thought you knew."

"Why would I know something like that? Because I'm Korean?"

"Because you're a freak. Pearl necklaces. Greek. Russian. Thought you knew everything."

"I hate you, Billie. I hate you so much right now."

"Oh, stop tripping. I can write down what he told me he did, if you're interested."

"Need a pen?"

We laughed a little. The train passed and traffic started moving.

She asked, "How long does something like that take?"

"About a year. I guess."

"Shit."

"Maybe less."

"Cool. He'll be right in time for the wedding."

"What wedding?"

"He asked me to marry him."

"When?"

"About an hour ago. Think he saw another side of me last night too. I'm not as demure as he thought I was. That turned him on. He told me he loved the way I swung my helmet."

"Stop. Hold up. He asked you to marry him an hour ago?"

"Yeah."

"What did you say?"

"I didn't answer him."

"Why not?"

"Was busy. Couldn't exactly talk."

"Doing what?"

"Don't think bad of me." She laughed. "I was . . . uh . . . giving him the best blow job he ever had."

"Wait. You were at Daniel Freeman an hour ago."

She smiled.

I asked, "What about Cottrell?"

"Who?"

"Kevin. Dude you met at Barnes & Noble. Two days ago. What about him?"

"Who?"

We laughed.

I said, "A man proposing to you—"

"Uh-huh."

"While you're on your knees, that doesn't count."

We laughed harder.

Viviane made a sharp right turn and headed up La Brea. The book that Raheem had given me, *The Alchemist*, fell off the dashboard and ended up in my lap, staring me in the face. Wasn't in the mood to read, but I read the jacket. It was a fable about following your dreams. I wondered if Raheem had given me that particular book for a reason. Hurt turning the pages, but I needed to occupy my mind. When I opened the book I saw the thick ink from a black marker on the title page. The paperback had already been signed. At first I thought that maybe Raheem had given me a valuable copy signed by the Brazilian author. Once again I was wrong. It was signed, but not by Paulo Coelho.

I said, "Viviane . . . look at this."

She read what I had already read.

To Carmen. From Raheem. With Love.

twenty-six

BILLIE

STARBUCKS. FIVE DAYS LATER. ME AND RAHEEM. BOTH OF US IN JEANS AND T-shirts.

I was outside at the same bistro table I had shared with Keith only a few days ago.

Four of my fingers were in Band-Aids. The road rash on the palms of my hands didn't bother me as much.

It was mid-afternoon, hours after Marcel's memorial service. Quite a few bikers were in the parking lot. No one was show boating.

The death of one rider made the others cautious, if only for a while.

Raheem and I sipped lattes and talked about that tragedy for a while. I gave Marcel her props, but reminded Raheem that even the best of the best could earn a tombstone in a heartbeat.

Part of me wished I had raced her. If I had raced her that night we were at Jerry's Deli, everything would have been different for both of us. That was the sci-fi part of my brain speculating.

We didn't talk about my miscarriage. That wound was too raw.

But we did talk about his niece. She was okay, but whoever attacked her had done some serious damage.

Raheem said, "Two hundred stitches."

"Any idea what that was all about?"

"She said she was leaving Denny's. Had been up all night studying." He shrugged. "Walked out to the parking lot to go to her car. She has no idea who attacked her."

"They rob her?"

"Nothing was taken."

"Was it a male or female who attacked her?"

"She thinks it was a female. But she didn't see a face."

"Cameras in the area?"

"Nothing. Not a single witness."

I said, "Too bad."

"Her face was cut."

"That's a crime of passion."

He frowned. "What difference would that make?"

"Makes all the difference in the world. That means it was personal."

"How do you know?"

"*Law and Order. CSI.* I TiVo 'em all. Crime of passion. Trust me."

"My sister, she has no enemies."

"We all have enemies."

"She has no enemies. Everyone likes her."

"We might not know who they are, might not be aware they exist, but we all have enemies."

The book he had given me was on the table. *The Alchemist.* I opened it to the title page.

I said, "Speaking of enemies. I think you gave me the wrong book."

He smiled at me. A soft and sincere smile. Then he sipped his latte and started talking.

Raheem. Exotic man. From South America. Born in Tegucigalpa.

Carmen. Beautiful woman. Descendant of the islands.

Lovers.

No.

Former lovers.

We sat at our bistro table. Starbucks coming alive. More bikers pulling up, some leaving. Outside in the gentle breeze, the strip mall decorated with palm trees. Poets in one area. Chess players were congregated on the side of building between the parking lot and TGIF. Ethiopians in their own little section, smiling and talking.

The Alchemist rested on the bistro table separating us.

To Carmen. From Raheem. With Love.

Raheem told me, "Until about six months ago. It ended abruptly."

"Is this how it ended? *With Love?*"

"Yeah, *With Love.*"

"You loved her?"

"I'm that kind of man, Billie. I am not afraid to love."

"If you could fall in love with a bitch like her, you have no morals and no line in the sand."

" 'Love does not begin and end the way we seem to think it does.' "

"Paulo Coelho?"

"James Baldwin. He wrote that a long time ago. It still holds true. You can't do love under your own terms. Love doesn't come like that. Baldwin said that love is a battle. That love is a war."

"How's your war going?"

"Just told you. My war ended over six months ago. Battlefields are clear."

It sounded like their relationship crashed and burned around the same time that I ran into Carmen and her family. No, not when I ran into Carmen's family. When I ran into Carmen and her mob. That day down in Manhattan Beach, that was one of those defining moments that changed life for everybody. I had been Keith's secret. Raheem had been Carmen's underground lover. Seeing me had ended that.

I asked, "When was the last time you saw her?"

"Hadn't seen Carmen for almost six months. Then I saw Carmen last Friday, the day I saw you up here arguing with her husband. Right after you spilled coffee on my suit. You had walked away from me. Then I was leaving. Made it to the door at the same moment she was walking inside. We made eye contact, then she walked by me like I never existed. I looked back, saw her following you toward the ladies' room."

I didn't need to hear any more. But I wanted to know more.

"How long were you seeing her?"

"Not long."

"What's not long?"

"Less than three months."

"Honeymoon phase."

"If that."

"And you tried to get with me?"

"I tried to befriend you."

"Bullshit. Why did you . . . why me? It takes a lot of balls to do what you've tried to do."

"Back it up. Carmen and I ended before I ever said a word to you."

"You were intimate with her."

"Yes. For a while."

"Where did you meet her?"

"Starbucks."

"Figures."

"Everyone in L.A. meets at Starbucks. Same for Atlanta."

"You came on to her?"

"It was mutual. We were in line. Think I was in front of her. We sat down, talked."

"Who ended it?"

"She told me her husband would not let go. That he would not give her a divorce."

I chuckled. "Well, that's a lie."

"I know that now. Didn't know it then."

"How did you . . . why did you try and talk to me?"

He told me that he went to confront Keith about six months ago, wanted to talk to him man-to-man, clear the air so everything would be above-level, in plain sight and understood. He found Keith. Sitting at Starbucks.

Keith was waiting on me.

Raheem said, "You pulled up on your motorcycle . . . you were right in front of me . . . you walked up a few seconds before I did. You had on heels. Leather. That yellow, hard not to look at a woman wearing yellow leather. You have a nice walk. Like a real woman. I couldn't take my eyes off you."

"That should be flattering."

"But it's not."

"Not when it's coming from a pervert."

"I'm being honest over here."

"No, Raheem. It's not flattering." I shook my head. "No. It's not."

"I told myself the same thing. I watched you for months. Asked about you. Saw you everywhere I went. Even when I stepped into a Ducati shop two thousand miles away, there you were, high up on the wall. So close to me and yet so far away. At first I felt bad for you because I knew Keith was still in love with Carmen. That you would be hurt in the end. The more I saw you . . . the more I admired you."

He told me that he wanted to, that he tried to tell me about his fling with Carmen. Said that after we had left Jerry's Deli, when I helped him get home he had wanted to tell me. But I was being so difficult that night. So mean. Then I had told him I was pregnant. Carrying Keith's baby. So he let it go. Dropped it.

I motioned at the book.

He said he had bought *The Alchemist* as a gift for Carmen, then misplaced it. He thought it was lost for good and bought her another one. Had found it and given it to me, forgetting that it was signed.

I said, "You hated Keith that much, huh?"

"What do you mean?"

"Hated him so much you had to come after me."

"Will you quit saying that? After the things Carmen had told me, I didn't care for him, no."

"What did Keith ever do to you?"

Raheem rocked. Couldn't answer.

I said, "Seems like he had everything you wanted."

"It's not about him."

"Or do you just want what he has?"

"However you want to see it. My words are no good, so why should I bother explaining?"

"Ha."

"How do you see me, Billie? Honest. What do you see when you look at me?"

"I see you as a very rich, very bored, very pathetic man."

He laughed. "My only crime is this: I fell for you, Billie."

"Oh, please. Save the melodrama."

"True."

"You fell for Carmen. She kicked you to the curb. You wanted to piss her off."

"By buying a fourteen-thousand-dollar motorcycle?"

"Told you that you were stupid. Damn checkbook biker."

"If being stupid means I liked you, yeah, I was stupid. I was interested in you. I expressed that. I admired you the way . . . the way kids admire Jordan. I bought a damn Ducati. Is that a crime?"

"I see it like this: You have two expensive cars and a top-of-the-line motorcycle. You can't decide what you like, so you buy everything. It's still not enough. Same probably goes for your women."

"Don't compare cars to women."

"Why?"

He said, "It's not fair to the car."

"Somebody got jokes."

"You know that was funny."

"Little bit."

We sipped and chuckled.

"I've been married twice, Billie. Divorced twice. I know that's not attractive to a woman who—"

He was about to say something, but his cellular phone starting singing a Spanish song.

He said, "Have to go to the airport, then back to the hospital."

"Your niece?"

"Yeah. My parents are flying here to see Lupe. I flew them in."

"From Tegucigalpa."

"You remembered."

"Your other brothers and sisters?"

"A few of them are coming. My older brother, her father, is already here from New York. Her mother came from Honduras. No one else is coming. The trip from South America isn't cheap. And not all of my relatives have visas. Only a few of us have made it here. In pursuit of the American Dream."

"Sorry about what happened to . . . her name is Lupe, right?"

"Yeah. Guadalupe. Patroness of the Americas."

"She was named after a saint."

"Lupe is a good girl. Film school. Top of her class. Never did a bad thing to anybody. Never."

We took our half-empty Starbucks cups to the trash cans that were stationed between Starbucks and Wherehouse. We tossed our cups. *The Alchemist* was in my left hand. I gave him back his book.

I said, "You can pass your gift on to your little girlfriend."

He tossed the book in the trash too.

I made an *Oh, please* sound. "What the hell was that?"

"A symbolic gesture."

"You could've just ripped that stupid page out."

"Accept my apology. Let me buy you a new one."

"You threw a brand-new book away? Don't you respect books? What kind of man are you? What's next? You're going to start throwing books in the front yard and going *Fahrenheit 451*?"

"I can afford another paperback book."

"You have too much money, you know that?"

"You don't have to talk to me ever again. But the book . . . it's a good book. I want you to read it. I'll get you another one. Brand-new. Jacob told me you have dreams that you never followed."

I reached in the trash, took the book back out, tore out that signature page.

"See how easy it was to fix that problem?"

"You ripped a page out of a book? Damn, Billie. What kind of woman are you?"

"Let Jacob tell it, guess I'm the kind of woman that has dreams she never followed. Don't believe Jacob said that about me. Big mouth. He called me a loser too?"

"No, he didn't call you a loser. Said you had unused talent."

"He called me a loser. I don't believe this shit."

"You're not a loser. Maybe the book will inspire you."

"Big-mouth Jacob. Geesh. I'm cursing him out big-time."

A group of boys were coming out of Wherehouse. They'd been floating around hawking bootleg CDs and DVDs. A couple of girls were with them, nice-looking exotic girls, all of them doing some stupid-looking dance that made the group look like they needed whatever medication people took for epilepsy.

"Do the Mo, do the Mo, do the Mo."

We walked away, headed toward the parking lot.

He asked, "Are you mad?"

"Books. Jokes. Women. What else are you recycling, lover boy?"

"You're mad."

"Actually, compared to everything else I've been through, this shit is kinda funny."

"You curse a lot, you know that?"

"Fuck you."

"See what I mean?"

The kids were getting buck-wild behind us.

"Do the Mo, do the Mo, do the Mo."

Raheem said, "My niece loves to do that same stupid dance."

We watched them.

I did the Mo a couple of times. It was an ugly dance, but fun, contagious.

I stopped and said, "All the dances the kids do look so damn stupid."

"Don't they, though?"

"The Cabbage Patch, now, that was a dance."

"No, the Electric Slide. That was my groove."

"Hell, no. The Prep."

"The Butterfly."

"Stop embarrassing me."

"Moonwalk, baby. Moonwalk."

"You're a fool, Raheem."

"Okay, the Running Man. Stop! Hammer time!"

"And stupid. I had no idea you were this silly. You're immature, you know that?"

"How many ways can you insult me?"

We laughed.

Halfway across the parking lot, Raheem started singing. Enrique Iglesias: *"Hero."*

He sang in good old español.

This time I sang along. In English.

It was nice. That moment was really nice.

He asked, "Think you could ever forgive me for being a fool and listening to my heart?"

"Never."

"Bad timing."

"Ha."

"Like you said. I wish I had met you first."

"But you didn't. Glad you didn't."

"Why?"

"Then we couldn't have been friends."

"Friends?"

"Yeah. Friends. Take it or leave it."

"The buddy plan."

"The good old buddy plan. They have that in South America, right?"

"Is that your final offer?"

"The best I can do today. For a while. Be happy or be gone."

He smiled.

I did too.

My cellular rang. It was my attorney. I had to go meet with him to talk about my lawsuit.

But whether the sun was high or rain fell, life went on. There was nothing equivalent to *Code 46* in my world. I had to deal with my choices. I had to accept my life. I had to embrace me.

Raheem asked, "Teach me to ride?"

"You're about to lose your status."

"Thought you didn't do friends with men."

"Fuck you."

"Potty mouth."

"Screw you."

"Better."

We laughed.

I said, "Your motorcycle is parked in front of Carmen's house. I'm sure you know where that is."

"Jacob told me. He got that information from Viviane."

"Uh-huh."

"That's why I drove Jacob over there. He drove it back to my house."

I paused.

Then I asked, "When you got to Carmen's . . . was there a U-Haul out front?"

Raheem nodded. "Yes."

A wave of relief and sadness ran through me. More relief than sadness.

He nodded. "I'm sorry about this, Billie. For not telling you about Carmen. I really am."

"Raheem . . . go take care of your niece."

He nodded.

I said, "Have Jacob tell Viviane to tell me when you've taken that MSF class."

"You're evil, you know that?"

"Don't call me evil. I like being called mean. That Spanish accent of yours makes it sound cool."

"Well, you're too mean to be evil."

"Whatever. Mr. Actuary. Whatever the hell kind of whacked job that is."

"And why in the world would I need to have Jacob call Viviane to call you?"

"Thought that maybe we could ride some trails up in the canyon together. All of us. Get you ready for that L.A.-to-Fresno run. Get your skills up so you can handle the curves on Dragon Trail."

He said, "Smoky Mountains. Three hundred and eighteen corners, eleven miles."

"You remembered that, huh?"

"So we're going to be friends long enough to fly out to Tennessee and ride it together one day?"

I looked at him. My face made of stone.

I said, "Stop smiling before I change my mind."

"Sure, Ducati."

"Remember whose name that is. I'm Ducati."

"Oh, hell, no. You don't own that name."

"Just because you have a 749, don't think—"

"Mean. Just plain old mean."

"Stupid. Just plain old stupid."

We said our goodbyes, smiling, then we went our separate ways.

I searched for the pains I had felt a few days before, I searched and I found them, not all of them, just most. The ones that were left, I felt each of those pains fading like a bad memory.

I whispered, "Love is a battle, love is a war."

My war was over.

A few minutes later I was behind the wheel of Viviane's four-wheel cage. Couldn't wait to get me a new bike. Raheem passed by in his SUV. He waved again. I waved back.

Cool guy. Kinda hard not to like him. His fine ass. And that damn accent. Geesh.

As I was driving away, I got caught at the light on La Cienega. I looked up and saw that billboard. WHO MURDERED ME? Lisa Wolf's picture looking down on the city, like a guardian angel.

The world had been an evil place for her.

My face could've ended up on a billboard just like that. Could've.

But I wasn't rich. My parents weren't powerful. There were no billboards for women like me.

Didn't matter. I'd survived.

This time next year I'd be back onstage. Still holding down my other gigs, but I'd be onstage, with my own band, under the spotlight, my Takamine in hand, opening the show at the Temple Bar.

A car pulled up next to me. Mustang convertible. Brand-new.

"Do the Mo, do the Mo, do the Mo."

It was filled with the kids I'd just seen hustling and loitering in front of Wherehouse. The boys were whooping it up. All of the pretty girls they were macking on were crammed inside. They were jamming big-time. Like they were young and all ready to hit the strip and have fun.

Sometimes I wished I could fall into a wormhole and go back in time.

Wished I could go back in time and do things over.

Not a lot of things, only a couple.

If I couldn't do things over, then I'd just warn myself . . .

No. I'd just spend some more time with my parents.

Sometimes I liked my life just the way it was. As fucked as it was, it was my life.

I told myself I'd call Sy Smith, ask her if she needed a background singer. Heard that Chante Carmel had moved to New York and was doing a play, *Rent;* maybe I could fill her spot for a while. Inobe was coming back to town, so I'd reach out to her too. I'd already looked up Hope.

Baby steps. I'd get off my ass and take baby steps. For my baby.

So all that I'd gone through wouldn't be in vain. So next time around I'd be ready.

I couldn't let bad experiences steal my voice. Or make me bitter. This was about earning wisdom.

I'd write some songs. Do some covers. Do it for the love of singing. Might even take my Takamine and get my hustle on like Hope used to do, squat on Venice Beach, do the same on Third Street Promenade in Santa Monica, sing my songs, build my own following.

My daydreaming was put on hold when I heard laughter and shouts of joy.

As those kids pulled forward, I saw a blinking red dot. One of the boys was holding a camera.

"Do the Mo, do the Mo, do the Mo."

The girls were laughing, doing that stupid-looking dance, bouncing around inside that car, all wanting to be the center of attention.

The boy driving said, "We saw you doing the Mo back there."

I smiled. "Yeah, I was trying."

"You was rocking, baby."

"Thanks."

"Lemme give you this."

"Whassup?"

He threw a CD through my open window.

I said, "What's that all about?"

"A lil' somethin'-somethin' for the honey. Some of our work. For you, baby."

"Free?"

"Merry Christmas. And it ain't even Christmas."

I gave him the thumbs-up as they sped away, music loud as hell, doing that crazy dance.

I popped open the CD and pushed it in the player. Got ready to hear something raw. Right now raw would match my mood. The player rejected the disc. I read the homemade label. *Hoodrats Gone Wild.* The kind of DVDs Raheem liked.

I put the porn back inside its plain jewel case, left it on the front seat.

Viviane liked those kind of movies too.

I'd be a lying hypocrite if I said I didn't watch a few myself.

But I'd give this one to my roommate. My present to her.

Something for her and Jacob to watch.

The cost of hate.

I would always remember those words spoken in that asthmatic whisper.

This time next year, Carmen's father would have died in prison. And Ruth would have gone back to Jamaica in shame. Keith would still be here, still in the area, working two, maybe three jobs. That divorce would never happen. He'd be back in that house he bought.

I would dream of how that marriage finally ended.

Or refused to end.

I could see Carmen stuffed inside that eighteen-year-old wedding dress, holding that huge vibrator in one hand, her Afro swaying, wheezing and cursing as she stalked Keith down the hallway, knocking over things as she passed by. Keith would march on, unaffected by her wheezing or her rage.

"Keith . . . two people who trust each other and are willing to go through life together, hell or high water. If you don't feel that for me . . . then . . . Keith . . . I married the wrong person. I just regret it took me this long to realize that. A woman can only be a wife if she has a man who is willing to be a husband. I admit I've made mistakes, erred in judgment, as have you, but I'm willing to do the work. I'm willing to sit with a counselor and do the work, but I can't do the work by myself. I can't make you stay where you don't want to be. It's killing me trying to do that. So, if it is what you want in your heart of hearts, I'll sign whatever papers you bring to me. Uncontested. And I will box up my memories and I will move on."

She'd say that, then wheeze and wipe away tears as she stumbled away, that six-foot train dragging behind her like a bad memory. Carmen would go back to her side of the house, to her bedroom, to her toys and memories, and sit in front of the television, watch her wedding tape over and over.

She would give him the same speech every day.

Keith would go to the other side of the house, to his side of the house, into his room, and sit in a chair.

He'd look up at his wall. His favorite wall. With a heavy heart, he would smile.

The image of me from that magazine, he'd get that erotic shot of me on that Ducati 749 blown up so large that it would cover the entire divider. In his room. On his side of the house. Me on that bike, smiling, wearing a yellow thong. That's where he would spend his evenings. For a while, his weekends would be spent going to see Destiny. Riding in silence with his wife as they went to the juvenile facility.

But every evening, as soon as he came home from work, that's where Keith would sit.

And for me, all of this, these last few days, it would echo like a dream gone bad.

Every day I'd cry less and less.

Anger would diminish.

I'd smile.

I'd love.

I'd ride again.

Acknowledgments

But first, I gotta tell you this. You. The person reading this. Stop looking around.

I'm talking to you.

Oh, quit smiling.

I came to NYC last minute on biz, ended up getting first draft on this novel, and finally took a break. I got a chance to sneak away and see *The Color Purple: A New Musical* last night at the Broadway Theater, Broadway and Fifty-third Street, right here in the heart of Times Square. It rocked! Man, if you get to good old NYC, you have to check it out. That, my friend, is real theater. I came up here to finish this book and . . . oh . . . right . . . I'm supposed to talk about this novel you're holding . . . oops . . . but I was just so excited about *The Color Purple . . . A New Musical* . . . well, it's a big deal to me because I've been under deadline and chained to my computer like that brother in the basement on *Desperate Housewives*.

I'm hyped. After I left the musical, still in awe over LaChanze's moving performance, still talking about how Felicia P. Fields and Kingsley Leggs and Elisabeth Withers-Mendes . . . Brandon Victor Dixon . . . Krisha Marcano . . . Renee Elise Goldsberry . . . dammit the whole cast ROCKED so hard, seemed like NYC should've had a 9.0 earthquake at curtain call. Awesome. The crowd gave them love and they gave the city enough energy to run the subways for the next six months. That, my friend, was a true musical production. After that, couldn't sleep, hit a diner on Fifty-seventh then was up until about four this morning looking at *Never 2 Big* on DVD. Now it's nine in the morning and I'm back up bumping Keyshia Cole like I'm running a club. Her CD, *The Way It Is*, is rocking this hotel. It's so hot that the snow is melting outside my room.

Anyway . . . let me hurry up so I can go downstairs to Gravity and work out. LOL.

This is a work of fiction.

Chasing Destiny actually got kicked off via a writing exercise when I was taking creative writing classes at UCLA, the Extension program. The IBWA/LA (International Black Writers of America, Los Angeles) had given me the opportunity to study the craft through a SEED Scholarship. Anyway, the exercise was simple: create five opening lines, something that (hopefully) would grab the reader's attention. The opening line, the first words from Keith's mouth, generated a great response from a pretty diverse class.

Color Purple *was off the friggin' chains. I mean the cast was off the chains. The writing . . . damn. The music . . . double damn. The layering of the stories . . . like the late great Esther Rolle said . . . damn damn damn! At the end, I ain't never seen so many smiling faces, so much laughter and so many tears, so many applauding people with handkerchiefs in their hands. And . . . oh . . . my book. Told you I was hyped. Nice to see an intelligent play that was well-written, respected the original work, and didn't get dumbed down with shucking and jiving. It was worth the price of the ticket.*

That class I took at UCLA, that was at least seven, maybe eight years ago. After that opening line I wrote about one hundred pages, wasn't feeling the way the story was going, thought it was too . . . too . . . nice . . . and nice can be boring . . . so I tossed at least seventy of those pages. I need grit and suspense and wretchedness to keep my butt in the chair. I have to challenge myself. That opening scene at Starbucks has always been a keeper. Billie changed over the years. Her tone changed, had to find the right temperature for that character. There were so many versions of Billie. That wonderful character went from being a nurse who worked with De-bra DuBois, to being a Ducati-riding singer/bartender/flight attendant/substitute teacher. She went from being part of a story that would have had multiple POVs and having two sisters named Frankie and Tommie. (If I remember it correctly, Billie was yanked out of that novel *Naughty or Nice* because her story was too complicated and too dark to be in a novel meant for the yuletide season. Livvy was created, took Billie's place and did a wonderful job.) At one point, Billie owned a small home, but that was changed, decided I liked her renting a room. In the original one hundred pages, there was a nice fifteen-year-old girl named Melanie who lived next door to Billie. That character evolved, became her lover's daughter, and eventually became a troubled teen now called Destiny.

Sang, Keyshia! Sang! Hold up . . . gotta jump up and Cabbage Patch a minute . . .

I took a little break while I was working on this novel. I wouldn't call it a break. I let this story simmer—Billie was about to crash and burn on her Ducati—while I changed hats and worked on a *marvel*ous project. I wrote six comics for Marvel Enterprises, a miniseries involving Storm (of the X-Men) and the Black Panther. That project dropped in February and (at least) the third issue should be on the stands as you read this.

I just plugged myself. Damn right. Proud of it. Now let me plug my crew.

To my agent since the beginning, Sara Camilli. Okay, in the last novel, *Genevieve*, I said eighty-nine more books to go, right? Well the Storm miniseries counts as six, and this is one. So that leaves . . . uh . . . damn . . . I hate word problems. (Imitating Bones from *Star Trek*) *I'm a writer, not a mathematician!* LOL. Thanks for being in my corner, especially this year. It was a rough, stressful one. I've never met so many attorneys in my life!

To my hardworking family at Dutton/NAL. You've taken me a long way.

My editor, Julie Doughty, you are the best. I'm serious when I say that. The last two novels have been a joy to work on due to your patience and understanding.

Lisa Johnson, Kathleen Schmidt (Congrats on the new gig. I'm gonna miss you!), and the rest of publicity, MUA! I'm rested and ready to hit the road! How's about a book tour in London . . . Philippines . . . Nice, France . . . The Islands . . . Brazil . . . Amsterdam . . . Australia . . . please?

You know I have a few frequent flyer miles . . . please . . . purty please? I'll bring my own sack lunch . . . please?

Brian Tart, once again, thanks! Got the leather-bound XMAS gift yesterday!

Everybody at Dutton/NAL, you are a wonderful group to work with. You help make this career a pleasure. We're up to twelve novels. Dickey's Dozen. ROFL. Corny I know, but I likes.

And I have to thank a few of the peeps who opened my e-mails and read this novel as it was being created, being patient and supportive as I made a thousand changes along the way.

Eloise Chambers, Andrea Hamilton, Jackie Barkley, Vanelle Smith, Jennifer Law, Hyacinth Colbert, Bridget Mason, Crystal Dexter, my always-on-the-front-row-at-Zhara's crew who are holding it down at Herbal Life, thanks for reading that early draft. The heart of the story remains the same, but the meat of the story is so different now. Hope you enjoy.

Lolita Files! Thanks for reading this one. We've been rocking this biz since the mid-nineties. You're the best, o ye Queen of the Blog. I can't wait to read your new book! *sex.lies.murder.fame* is hot! (Check Lolita out at www.thelozone.blogspot.com and www.lolitafiles.com.)

Yvette Hayward, my speed-reading Harlem gal, thanks for doing what you do!

Chante Carmel, super writer/singer/spin queen at Spectrum/Manhattan Beach sand-dunes walker and now appearing in the touring version of the musical stage production *Rent* as Joanne, thanks for all of your input on that world of music and looping. May your next "525,600 Minutes" take you to the top. . . .

I saw the musical Rent *too! That was the bomb! Mayumi, Matt, Frenchie, Ava, Keena, all of you and the rest of the cast helped restore my love for theater. Frenchie . . . you are the best.*

Simfani Blue, thanks! I rocked your debut CD endlessly while I was getting my write on! Sorry I missed your show at the Temple Bar. Hope to catch you on stage soon. Your info about the biz, priceless! Much love to you and your family.

To (some of) my friends, Audrey Cooper, Danny Fine, Grayland, Bobby Laird, Steve Jefferson, Dwayne Orange and the running crew, Scotty, John Marshall, Lady Evelyn Orange, thanks for the years of support!

In case I left out a few peeps . . .

I want to thank _____ for all of his/her help
while I was rocking this project. Without you . . . ☺ . . . no way I could've
done this.

Virginia, Lila & Vardaman . . . miss all of u!
NYC.
December 17, 2005.
9:27 A.M.
Le Parker Meridien. Room 1504.
Time to sign off and rock a spin class and lift a few weights at Gravity.

Eric Jerome Dickey

About the Author

Eric Jerome Dickey is the author of twelve novels, including the bestsellers *Genevieve, Drive Me Crazy, Naughty or Nice, The Other Woman*, and *Thieves' Paradise*. Dickey writes full time and has developed a six-issue miniseries of comic books for Marvel Enterprises featuring Storm (X-Men) and the Black Panther.